# HEART
*of* MINE

Center Point
Large Print

Also by Caroline Fyffe and available from Center Point Large Print:

*Heart of Eden*
*True Heart's Desire*

**This Large Print Book carries the Seal of Approval of N.A.V.H.**

# HEART
## *of* MINE

### A COLORADO HEARTS NOVEL

## Caroline Fyffe

CENTER POINT LARGE PRINT
THORNDIKE, MAINE

This Center Point Large Print edition
is published in the year 2019 by arrangement with
Amazon Publishing, www.apub.com.

The text of this Large Print edition is unabridged.
In other aspects, this book may vary
from the original edition.
Printed in the United States of America
on permanent paper.
Set in 16-point Times New Roman type.

ISBN: 978-1-64358-163-7

Library of Congress Cataloging-in-Publication Data

Names: Fyffe, Caroline, author.
Title: Heart of mine : a Colorado hearts novel / Caroline Fyffe.
Description: Large Print edition. | Thorndike, Maine :
    Center Point Large Print, 2019.
Identifiers: LCCN 2019000741 | ISBN 9781643581637 (hardcover :
    alk. paper)
Subjects: LCSH: Large type books. | GSAFD: Love stories.
Classification: LCC PS3606.Y44 H44 2019 | DDC 813/.6—dc23
LC record available at https://lccn.loc.gov/2019000741

Dedicated to our handsome grandson,
Hudson Bryce,
a boy who holds the moon and stars
in the palms of his hands.
We love you so much!

# CHAPTER ONE

*Santa Fe, New Mexico, Mid-July 1881*

Annoyed with the slight tremor in his hands, Beranger North stared at the twenty-two-year-old daguerreotype of his father, William Northcott, the Duke of Brightshire. Next to his father stood Beranger's eight-year-old half brother, Gavin, the heir to his father's dukedom back in Kent, and then Beranger himself, age seven, lurking half-hidden behind Gavin. On the duke's other side stood Beranger's stepmother, whose fear and treachery had been the catapult that had changed his life.

*Those eyes! Every time that boy looks my way I feel the whisper of death.*

Her words rang in his mind as clearly as when she'd first uttered them all those years ago.

Beranger took in his father's tall countenance, his wide, square shoulders, his vivid eyes—the color he remembered being the blue of the darkest sea, a deep cobalt that rendered most people speechless. Gavin's eyes were the same color—it was the trait of all the male heirs of the family Northcott.

*Except me, the illegitimate offspring of a commoner.*

7

Anger made his hand tremble harder, and the image shook. He was a grown man, and he felt that memories of long ago shouldn't have any hold on his emotions, but sometimes they did. Like today.

Except for the deep blue Northcott eyes, Gavin was the spitting image of Beranger's stepmother—winsome, to be sure, but fair-haired, rounder of shoulder and slighter of chest than the typical Northcott males. Beranger had grown up to resemble their father. He had the height and strength of his sire, the dark hair that became shaggy if left to grow, the strong chin and straight nose. Had he remained in Kent, Beranger could easily have been mistaken for the duke himself.

Beranger had always known he was different. Illegitimate. He was tolerated by some, possibly hated by others. But in the recesses of his boyhood heart, he'd wanted to believe he held the same status as Gavin. Loved and cherished. His mother and father had been lovers long before his father had wed the duchess—and for a short time after Gavin had been born. They belonged together, and Beranger with them. When his mother passed, his father brought him to live at the manor house without question.

Then, sixteen years ago today, the course of his life changed. He remembered every detail as clear as yesterday, but he refused to let himself dwell on it. "Does no good to look back," he murmured aloud as he slid the photo, his only memento of his former life, back into the burgundy velvet bag that had long ago lost its sheen.

"Happy birthday, Father," he said. He placed the keepsake in a small leather pouch and clipped the bag closed. The leather had grown supple over time, just like his ability to find the good in his new American life.

Beranger knew he had nothing to complain about. He'd made a fortune in the hills and rivers of this great country. Men considered him an expert in the field of mining. Eleven years ago, when Beranger was eighteen, an old-time prospector, in for a drink at some broken-down saloon, found him mopping floors to make enough money to eat. The grizzled fellow took him under his wing and taught him everything he needed to know to strike it rich. And Beranger had. Where to look, and then how to coax gold and silver out of the earth. How to read a man's eyes to see if he was bluffing at poker. By the time his mentor died, Beranger had a bank account bursting in a way that most men only dreamed about. Finished with mining, he'd packed up his tools and moved to town. But his reputation had spread. He was sought out for advice. Soon others were throwing money his way just for instruction, saying he had a nose for minerals.

*Yes, America has treated me well.*

He'd wanted to prove himself as a man, and

he had. The Northcott name meant nothing to him now—he'd abandoned it as soon as he ran away—nor did the lack of his family's acceptance. Faced with being illegitimate, he'd proven his legitimacy. Many times over. Ashbury Castle had no hold, and his home village of Brightshire was just a distant memory.

"And that's how I like it."

For the past year, he'd called Santa Fe home. It was the longest he'd stayed anywhere. Soon he knew the urge to pack up and move on would be upon him, just like always. As a matter of fact, he was planning to speak with a rancher about a new possibility that very night, at supper. If the draw was strong enough, he'd be headed for a town in Colorado called Eden.

As he placed the leather bag that held his father's picture back into the trunk for another year, he thought of his mother, his *real* mother, and wondered what kind of person she must have been. He hadn't known her, because he'd been too young when she'd died. But from his uncle he'd learned she'd been kindhearted and generous. A woman not impressed with riches, but with loyalty and love. A smile played around his lips.

Sobered, he closed the lid. It was time he headed to the saloon to scare up a game of poker. He needed something to pass the hours before his meeting tonight.

*Eden, Colorado,* he thought again.

Settling in one place sounded nice. If he found the right woman, would he be able to overcome his rambling ways? Or would that burning need to keep moving ignite once more?

# CHAPTER TWO

*Santa Fe! Why, the city is no more than a prairie dog town!*

Riding in the unmerciful Five Sisters Ranch buckboard, Emma Brinkman, repulsed by the billowing dust, pressed her handkerchief to her nose and narrowed her eyes. Warm early-morning sunshine produced a trickle of sweat between her breasts. Men called out to each other as their wagons passed at a quick trot.

*What's the hurry so early in the morn?*

She placed a comforting arm around Brenda's small shoulders, drawing the child closer. She was somewhere between four and five years old, and on her way to be adopted into a new home. The child had lived in Santa Fe before she was sent to Eden's orphanage, in hopes of finding a family there. But that had been almost a year ago. No one dreamed she'd have to make the long journey back.

*Is she frightened? Confused?*

She was usually quiet, so telling was difficult.

Belle turned from the front seat. Her older sister's thick blonde hair was plaited down her back, and a wide grin pulled at her lips. "Isn't this exiting, Emma? I'm so glad you came along." She glanced at Brenda and winked. "You too,

Brenda Blue Bird," she said, using their sister Lavinia's affectionate nickname for the child. "It's difficult to comprehend that only a year ago this used to be a sleepy little place reached only by mule-team traders." She waved her hand around, totally oblivious to Emma and Brenda's discomfort. "This is what'll happen if Eden ever gets a train. Imagine that!"

At the moment, Emma didn't want to imagine that. Horses, wagons, and cattle, all busily going somewhere, churned up the dust of the dry street and made breathing difficult. Her best dress—the one she'd saved especially for today's arrival— would be ruined.

Frustrated, she batted away a clod of dirt from her sleeve, a gift from a passing buggy going much too fast for such a crowded street. The action drew comical smiles from Moses Poor and Trevor Hill, the ranch hands riding alongside the wagon.

Swarms of people traveled the wider-than-normal main street of Santa Fe. Emma had pictured the town, whose name meant "Holy Faith" in Spanish, as a colorful place, meticulously clean, and prosperous. The first two it was absolutely not. But prosperous? Yes, Santa Fe was that. The town, which had received a spur line just the year before, was nothing like their beloved Eden—and for that she was grateful.

The whistle of the twelve o'clock train from

Topeka rent the air, startling Emma and causing Brenda to duck in fear. Horses spooked, and everyone turned to watch the arrival of the shiny black steam engine and its long snaking string of boxcars trailing behind.

"That's just the train's whistle," Emma whispered close to Brenda's ear. "Don't be frightened. I won't let anything hurt you."

Brenda moved closer. Emma smiled down into her upturned face and touched the tip of her nose. The child's soft brown eyes tugged at Emma's heart. Their trip from Eden had taken a week and a half in the slow-moving buckboard, and she had looked after the child's every need. The thought of handing her over to strangers made Emma's throat tighten.

Emma kissed the top of her dusty-smelling head. "Your new family is going to be wonderful."

*But I will miss you with all my heart. I pray that these people will cherish you always.*

Brenda nodded, and a sweet smile appeared on her face. "My new mama will make cookies and let me help."

"Of course she will, my darling." Fearful her eyes would fill, Emma cut her gaze back to the hubbub in the street. Brenda was calmer than she was at the prospect of going to her new home. Emma knew she needed to pull herself together. "I don't know about you," she said to change her wavering thoughts, "but I'm ready for a cool bath and a soft bed. Sleeping under the stars is romantic for only so long. First we'll clean up and have a nice lunch in the hotel restaurant. Then, after a nap, we'll go see what the town has to offer." After all, that was *her* reason for coming along. To see the latest styles the larger city had to offer. See how the shops stacked up against Eden's Toggery. Explore their stores, memorize their displays, size up their patrons. Stealing a few ideas wasn't against the law. Why reinvent the wheel when she could improve on it? "How does that sound?"

Brenda nodded shyly.

In the front seat, Belle and her husband, Blake, chatted about their own reasons for the journey— to meet the mining expert they hoped to hire for the never-prospected mine the five Brinkman sisters had inherited from their father ten months ago. Emma had to admit to her excitement about the venture. Imagine—a line of jewelry she could sell in her store, produced from her own mine! Silver or gold, it didn't matter. The thought was exhilarating. But as she watched Belle and Blake, their heads bent close together as their conversation segued to the ranch, which they ran together in a true partnership, a deep and abiding hurt struck her like a lance.

Three weeks ago, a letter had arrived. Mrs. Gamble, her old employer and dear friend in Philadelphia, had surprising news. Her son Tim had married, and Cooper, her other son, was engaged! For years, Emma had been besotted with both brothers, love-struck so deep she knew she'd never love again. As shameful as having feelings for both had been, she'd never told either, or acted on her desires—she'd just loved them from afar. She'd been young and shy, and so in love with the idea of being in love that sometimes it felt as if she were walking on air. She'd kiss her pillow at night, imagining their faces. If she lived to one hundred, she'd never forget the way Tim's dark-brown eyes made her feel when he gazed into hers as they went over the shop's orders. Or Cooper's silky-soft voice, patient and kind, as he asked for her input on the upcoming schedule.

And now *both* brothers had found other loves? *How cruel. How fickle love is!*

Whenever she imagined her wedding—as she often had—it was one of the two Gamble brothers beside her at the altar. She'd believed herself in love with them for so long. She'd been crushed by the news. And still was.

*That* was the true reason she'd decided to come along, although she'd not voiced her heartbreak to her sisters, who were all in the throes of love. Belle was married, Lavinia engaged, and Katie and Santiago had been inseparable until he left to visit his brother. Mavis was in love too, although she liked to pretend differently. Emma had needed to escape her surroundings for a time. To distract her thoughts and mend her broken heart in silence.

She huffed a deep sigh. When Brenda looked up to see if something was wrong, Emma patted her leg and smiled.

*Yes, I have things to do. Life will go on.*

At the moment, Santa Fe looked to be entirely devoid of women. All she saw were men, and stores catering to them. Saloons, hardware and dry goods, and a bank here and there.

*Where are the women? The millinery shops, the dressmakers?*

Emma desperately scanned the businesses that lined both sides of the street.

*I'll be hard-pressed to even find a tailor here.*

She noticed that there were not many tall buildings, not like in Philadelphia. These were Spanish mission style, and were constructed with wood, adobe, and brick. A few, which looked recently constructed, had European details—all brought about by the economic boom she'd heard so much about. Children stood on corners, waving flyers and calling out to anyone who would listen.

Emma reached down and found Brenda's hand. She wasn't sure she liked Santa Fe at all.

Trevor leaned in. "Don't worry, Miss Emma. A couple streets over, everything is much quieter—and the stores will be to your likin'. That's where they have the kinds of shops you're expectin'."

"Oh, and what would those be, Mr. Hill?" she teased amicably. He and Moses had been such a help, setting up camp each night, cooking over the fire, tending the horses. They made the chores look easy, when in fact she knew camping to be the opposite. Belle pitched in when needed, but Emma's job had been to look after Brenda. That part of the trip had been a joy. Trying to find privacy so she could take care of life's most indelicate operations amid the scant bushes and shrubs had not.

"You know . . . ," Trevor said, eyes twinkling, "tiny dollhouse buildings filled with frilly dresses, hats that would make Miss Lavinia's eyes go wide, and womanly gewgaws and whatnots."

Just as he predicted, a few blocks later the dust and clamor gave way to a more civilized street. Shops lined both sides of the way, all different and all catering to women—or men wanting to make their ladies happy. Still not many trees, like she was used to in Eden, but potted plants made the boardwalks attractive. A banner stretched the width of the road, welcoming all newcomers to Santa Fe.

Emma laughed with delight. "You were right. I couldn't have imagined this two minutes ago." Her gaze tracked down the street. "Four dress shops, two restaurants, several buildings I can't tell what they are, and not a saloon in sight. How refreshing."

"Better?" Moses asked, a knowing look in his eyes.

"Much." And she meant it. There wasn't time to dwell on heartache when all these riches awaited.

*Our first time away from the ranch since we've become heiresses,* Emma thought as the buckboard stopped in front of a medium-size hotel.

Blake set the brake and hopped down, stretched his back muscles, and gazed around. Then he helped Belle and Emma down. Tall and handsome with dark hair and intelligent blue eyes, her brother-in-law was a fine-looking man. He'd worked closely with their father until his death. He was funny and kind, but he also watched over all the sisters like a hawk. Blake was special.

While the ranch hands hefted their traveling trunks and started up the stairs to the hotel's front door, Emma reached for Brenda's hand.

Excited, she stepped into the foyer, Brenda tugging her hand the whole time. The little girl seemed to be as much in awe as she was, taking in the softness of the cream-colored curtains, the rich mahogany of the polished wood, the tasteful gold-leaf accents that drew the eye.

*We used to peek into the fine Philadelphia hotels, never dreaming we'd actually one day be able to afford staying in them.*

So much had changed for the five Brinkman sisters this past year. Sometimes life felt more a dream than reality.

*I shall take nothing for granted,* Emma vowed. *I'll remember everything I now have is a result of Father's blood, sweat, and tears. I'll be grateful with each breath I take, and live one day at a time.*

She hoped she could live up to that vow when the time came to hand Brenda over to the nuns. All the good feelings inside her turned to ice when she thought about the task ahead. She wasn't sure of that at all.

# CHAPTER THREE

You sure you won't come along with us, Belle?" Emma asked when Belle looked up from the pamphlet she was reading in the hotel lobby. Emma held on to Brenda with one hand. With the other, she grasped the rope handle of a large hatbox containing two hats Lavinia had made and sent along so that Emma could try to find a local merchant willing to sell them on consignment. Emma raised the oversize container, the excitement she'd felt before they'd begun the arduous trip returning.

"As much as I'd love to accompany you and Brenda Blue Bird"—Belle gently rubbed the child's head—"Blake and I have other plans. We need to talk with several establishments selling mining provisions before we meet tonight with the fellow we've come to interview. We'll have tomorrow to explore the shops."

*But not with Brenda. She'll be gone after tomorrow morning.*

"I hope you won't forget all your old interests," Emma said lightly. "Sometimes it feels like you never leave Blake's side. It's been over three months since Blake, Rhett, and all of us tricked the poaching lumbermen out of Eden. Seems I've seen very little of you since then."

Belle, dressed in a summer frock Emma remembered her sister had brought from Philadelphia—one Emma hadn't seen in a very long time—looked beautiful and feminine. The yellow taffeta made her golden hair glisten, and it flattered her creamy complexion that was now—after months spent outdoors—dotted with freckles.

"Really, Emma, what has gotten into you of late?" Belle placed her palm on Emma's forehead, a playful smile tugging her mouth. "I've never heard such strange things come out of you before." She lifted a brow. "I think the sun has affected you adversely. You'll be singing a different tune when you fall in love. Mark my words. Or better yet, ask Lavinia. Our little sister will tell you the same things I have." She gave a self-satisfied little laugh. "You'll probably fall the hardest of all."

Emma blinked. "Never."

"Never?" Belle replied. Her smile grew wider. "You sound pretty sure of yourself."

Brenda had moved to the window and was watching the street outside.

"Yes, I'm sure," Emma replied, making sure her tone was soft. She didn't want to alert Belle that she was suffering over the heartbreaking Gamble brothers. This trip was meant to be a holiday. "I like being my own keeper. My own boss. Love will never change my mind."

"Would you care to make a wager on that?" Belle's eyes glowed with challenge.

Emma glanced around the quiet lobby. Belle never wagered anything unless she was absolutely sure she was right. But Emma knew how she felt—at this moment, and how she would continue to feel into the future. She'd spent many hours thinking on the matter. She knew she'd never soften her stance. Not after *the letter*. And especially not after the pain their parents had suffered. Their history alone proved her point perfectly. Father had loved Mother with his whole heart, soul, and mind—but that hadn't made a difference when their mother had decided to leave him.

Emma wouldn't spell out her reasons to Belle, because doing so would be hurtful. Belle was a newlywed, still walking in the clouds, so she simply said, "Sure, I'll wager."

"Great. How about a month of foot rubs?" Belle laughed. "I'd love to win that, especially after all the hours you say I spend in the saddle."

Emma shook her head. "Let's make this a real bet. Something substantial, since I know I'll win—and so you'll see how serious I am."

"You must have something in mind."

Emma gulped. Rarely did she best Belle, but here was her chance. As girls, they'd competed in foot races, then over who could earn the best grades at school. There was once a cherry-eating contest, held behind the back of their guardian, Velma Crowdaire. Not only did Belle win, but Emma earned a stomachache that put her in bed for two days. It seemed Belle had also won the wager about who would first kiss a boy—Belle had been courted by the no-good Lesley Atkins back in Philadelphia. Embarrassed, Emma realized she was still waiting for her first "real" kiss—and a rare victory.

"How about our shares of the first haul from the mine?" Emma said boldly. "You think so highly of the man we're meeting tonight. Perhaps our wager will make the first profits even more exciting. I know we've been daydreaming about what we'll do with our profits, since most of our other inheritance is wrapped up in the ranch." The sisters stared at each other. "The haul could be a bust—or it might be worth a fortune. *If* we hit a vein at all. You decide if that's too big of a risk for you."

Belle laughed. "You're betting *against* your own happiness. You're betting you'll never fall in love. Love is the grandest thing on earth, Emma. When you meet the right man, you'll realize you'd give up all the silver and gold on earth for him." She shook her head and narrowed her eyes teasingly. "Someday you'll learn *not* to wager with me."

Emma gulped again, hoping she hadn't made an enormous mistake. Still, she shouldn't be nervous. She knew her mind, and how she'd felt about Tim and Cooper. True love hadn't prevailed, not then, not ever.

"I don't think so," she said. "One thing, though. I'd like to keep this between you and me. No one need know. Does the bet last forever?" That last question had just popped out. She knew she should be figuring out the terms on her own. "I mean, there should be *some* parameters. Don't you think?"

Belle tapped a toe on a braided rug made of colorful yarns. "You're right. Let's see . . . How about six months? That time span was good enough for Father's stipulation for us to inherit the whole ranch, so it's equally good for a bet of this importance. If you fall in love within six months, I win. If you don't, you win. And if the mine never makes a dime, we both can cry." She smiled the way she always did when softening a problem for Emma. Emma's heart warmed. "Does that sound fair? My wager needs a little time for the right man to come along and sweep you off your feet."

*Ha! Six months? There's as much of a chance of me flying to the moon as there is of me falling in love with anyone in six months' time. I have nothing to worry about.*

Emma spat into her hand and grasped Belle's as she'd seen the men do. "It's a deal! I can smell victory now."

# CHAPTER FOUR

Leaving Trevor, their escort, outside on the street, Emma and Brenda stepped through the front door of the women's apparel shop. Bells above announced their arrival. Emma immediately stopped to take in the feel of the store. One never got a second chance to make a first impression.

*Roomy and well stocked. The owner must be turning a profit.*

Sounds of teasing laughter floated back from the counter at the other end of the long, narrow establishment. She heard the murmur of a man's deep voice, but the words were indistinguishable. A woman's twittering giggle followed.

Ignoring the conversation, Emma turned to inspect several dresses displayed along the wall on her right. Setting the hatbox on the floor, she lifted a green woolen dress that looked detestably hot for the time of year, admiring its wooden hanger rather than the garment. The smooth pine was much lighter and narrower than the thick oak she used in the Toggery. The bowed shape supported the garment's shoulders nicely, and took up less room compared to the bulkier ones she owned. With something like this, she'd be able to display more garments than she did now. Excitement rippled through her. That insight alone had made the trip worthwhile.

She replaced the dress and began inspecting the next, an expensive-looking cobalt chintz with a light crinoline underneath.

*Oh, what a garment! To have supper in such a creation would be heavenly.*

Emma imagined herself descending the ranch's large staircase to everyone's admiration. She wondered how long this shop had been in business. The garments were truly enchanting.

"Look, Miss Emma. These little dresses are for girls."

Light danced in Brenda's eyes as she fingered a Spanish-style garment of colorful fabric. Emma looked at one in the prairie style, similar to what the children in Eden wore at the orphanage—and what Brenda wore today. The selection was quite astounding. Usually children's clothing had to be made at home or ordered through a catalog.

"Which do you like best, Brenda?" Emma took one of each style and crouched down so she was eye to eye with the girl. She'd need functional clothing, more than fancy, at her new home. Emma knew her adoptive family already had three children and subsisted on a modest income.

"Both are pretty," she whispered softly. Unable to contain her excitement, she bounced up and down on her toes, balancing herself with a hand on Emma's shoulder.

Emma laughed. "I think you're going to be a ballerina someday, sweetheart."

Gazing into Brenda's expectant eyes sparked a memory of being on a special outing with her mother. Emma had been six or seven years old, about three years after they left the ranch in Colorado and before Mother had taken ill.

*Why had Mother gotten sick?*

That question often beleaguered Emma. But speculating about the wickedness of Vernon and Velma Crowdaire, the couple who'd betrayed their mother and later become the sisters' guardians, would do no good now.

Her mother's hands had smoothed the yellow taffeta fabric on Emma's shoulders. "Now let's carefully slip the dress off so we don't damage the garment in any way. Then we'll go to the fabric store to get some cloth. I'll make one just like it for each of you. You'll all look like spring daffodils." She'd smiled into Emma's eyes with a look that always made Emma feel special.

"But can't I have *this* dress?" she'd asked, too young to know they didn't have the funds to splurge on a store-bought dress. If only they'd known the Crowdaires had been stealing the money Father was sending for their support, leaving only a pittance for them. How they'd scrimped and struggled to get by! And yet, what Emma remembered most was how her mother had kissed her cheek, turning her disappointment into a game. "What fun would that be, Emma?" she asked. "Of all your sisters, you're the one who gets to choose the fabric. After all, you're the one who knows what a princess might like."

"May I help you?"

Emma, lost in thought, hadn't heard anyone approach.

A woman in her forties was smiling down at them. A lace shawl draped her shoulders, and a delicate lace cap covered the back part of her hair—a style Emma hadn't seen in years.

"I'm Mrs. Sackett, proprietor of this shop. That's a pretty choice." She nodded toward the dress Emma held in front of Brenda. "If the length is too long for your little one, I can adjust the hem, if you have the time to spare."

Emma felt the words pierce her heart. It was an easy mistake to make—assuming Brenda was her child. At almost twenty-two, it was plausible she could already have a passel of children at home. Her bet with Belle slid through her mind.

*Have I doomed myself to never marrying, never becoming a mother?*

She longed to explain to Belle that it wasn't that she didn't want those things, just that after losing the brothers and losing Brenda, she couldn't bear the heartbreak if it didn't work out.

"Thank you, Mrs. Sackett," she said. "My name is Emma Brinkman." She looked at Brenda, who'd clasped her hands behind her back, again resembling a ballerina. "Brenda and I are just good friends out to do a little shopping. But we'd love your opinion on which dress to choose for a special occasion." She decided right then and there that she'd bring Brenda along to the supper that night to meet the mining expert they were considering hiring—after all, it might be the child's only opportunity for a fancy night out.

"I think the pink prairie dress is adorable with her coloring," Mrs. Sackett said. "What do you think?"

"Yes, that one suits her very well," Emma agreed.

"Would she like to try it on?"

"What do you say, sweetie?" Emma smoothed the fabric along Brenda's shoulders. "Do you like this dress? Would you like to try it on?"

"I love it, Miss Emma," she responded with a quavering voice. "Love it with all my heart." With her hands over her head and fingers touching, she did a fanciful twirl, swirling out the skirt she already wore into the shape of a teacup.

Both women laughed and clapped, bringing a deep blush to the child's cheeks.

"I guess that's our answer, then," Emma said. "And we'll try on these others as well."

Mrs. Sackett beamed. "Wonderful. Please follow me."

"If I may, before we try the dresses, I'd like to show you some samples a young milliner is producing in Eden, Colorado, where I'm from. She hopes to find a retailer in Santa Fe to do business with; I've brought them to you first." She quickly opened the box and lifted both hats out. "I own a dress shop myself."

Mrs. Sackett's eyes appraised the delicate stitching and ribbons on the hats. "They're lovely." She glanced up at Emma's hat. "And much like yours."

Emma did a slow turn so she could see it from all sides. "You have a keen eye, Mrs. Sackett. Mine is indeed made by the same artist. The small, flat style similar to a summer bonnet has caught on this season in Eden; it's a favorite with the women."

*The few women we have.*

"The flowers can be added in all different shades."

Mrs. Sackett nodded. "Quite attractive. I'll take this one and see how fast it sells." She plucked the smallest from Emma's hands, the one designed in lavender and green. "If the results are good, I'll order a few more."

"Thank you. Now to the dressing room. Do you have undergarments and other accessories in her size? I'd like socks, pantaloons, an apron, and the like . . ."

Carrying the hat, Mrs. Sackett led the way. As they approached the back of the store, Emma again heard the voices from earlier. A man stood

31

at the counter. A very nicely built man, she couldn't help noticing—exceptionally tall, with wide shoulders. He leaned nonchalantly against a post dividing the room. A young woman with curly brown hair that rimmed her pretty face was at work behind the counter. When the young woman giggled, clearly enjoying the man's attention, Mrs. Sackett stiffened abruptly.

"Here you are," she said tightly, her easygoing mood gone. She pulled aside a heavy drape and gestured for them to enter the fitting room. There was a chair, a tall standing mirror in the corner, and a lantern hanging from above. "Please let me know if you require any assis—"

Her sentence was cut off by a low murmur followed by feminine laughter.

Mrs. Sackett scowled.

"I'm sorry," Emma whispered, "but I must ask. Is everything all right? I couldn't help noticing your reaction to that gentleman up front. Is he bothering you?"

"Not bothering me, but perhaps bothering my daughter, Delphine."

*It doesn't sound that way to me. Just the opposite. I think Delphine is enjoying his company.*

"I see," Emma said, wondering if she really did.

Mrs. Sackett's hand fluttered to her throat, her smile nowhere to be found. "Mr. North is extremely wealthy and well known around Santa Fe as a rake. He's broken multiple hearts."

There was more to Mrs. Sackett's warning than just broken hearts, if Emma had to guess, especially since the woman was subconsciously rubbing her wedding band.

*Has the man been bold enough to break up marriages?*

"I just don't want any trouble for my daughter."

"No *man* should have that kind of power over *anyone*. Not his wife, not his daughter, and certainly not an acquaintance or friend. If you'd like, I'll tell him to leave straightaway. That way he can be angry with me and not you. Surely he'll understand. He seems much older than your daughter."

With all the newspaper stories that had been published about the Brinkman sisters, thankfully none had threatened their reputation or virtue, except for maybe the report of Lavinia's skinny-dipping escapade.

Emma stood as to walk past and do exactly as she'd said, but Mrs. Sackett blocked her way. "Oh no, please!" she urgently whispered. "Don't say anything. He's a very powerful man in Santa Fe. A well-placed word or two of reprisal could have a negative impact on my business. This shop is our whole existence. And to be honest, what I've heard may be rumors. I haven't any facts to back up my claims. I shouldn't have said anything to you at all."

The woman's crimson-stained cheeks amplified

the deep fear in her eyes. To speak out against a powerful man could mean ruin, something Mrs. Sackett was not willing to chance.

"All right, I won't. Even though I'd like to." Emma felt a burning urge to get the dresses tried on as quickly as possible—before *the rake* had a chance to leave the shop. She wanted a closer look. She'd never really known any rakes before. Tim and Cooper had been gentlemen in every sense of the word. She wondered if Blake could be considered a rake, or Rhett, or Clint. If yes, only in a good, handsome way, not the woman-ruining way. And Santiago? She pondered that longer than she should have needed to. They'd all worried about Katie. Yes, Santiago was a different matter altogether.

Emma helped Brenda try on the pretty dresses, each one making the child's eyes sparkle with excitement. When Emma lifted the last garment over her head, Brenda snuck her arms around Emma's neck for a warm, naked hug.

Emma's throat tightened, and she encircled her in an embrace. "Every single one looks adorable on you, sweetheart," she said, her eyes stinging unmercifully. "And just the right size for a pretty little ballerina like you. Not too short and not too long. We'll take all the dresses," she said, handing them to Mrs. Sackett. "And if you think the bloomers and such are all the right sizes, we'll take those too."

Feeling wonderfully lightheaded over all the items they'd found for the child, Emma stood. "Could you also add the cobalt blue chintz with the light crinoline to our purchases? The size looks as if it were made just for me. I hung the dress on the end of the rack and I can't seem to get the gorgeous prize out of my mind. If the fit is off, may I return it tomorrow? We're staying at the hotel on the corner."

Mrs. Sackett's eyes grew even wider at the mention of the expensive gown. "Of course you may, Miss Brinkman! I'll be right back. You will be gorgeous, just gorgeous, my dear. Stunning."

Emma hoped so. She smiled to herself, wondering what a rake would think of that gorgeous dress. Would he take her hand and insist on a dance, even though there wasn't any music, telling her they'd dance to the music in their hearts? Her gilded slippers would glide like ice across glass on the make-believe parquet floor, feeling weightless and free. With a devilish smile, he'd hold her much too close to be decent and then whisk her into his strong arms as if she weighed nothing at all, striding through the fifteen-foot doors into the night, where . . .

# CHAPTER FIVE

Beranger, his Stetson dangling from his finger-tips, glanced up as Mrs. Sackett approached the counter, followed by a customer and a young child. The proprietress's arms were full to overflowing, and she wore a smile befitting the queen. Once he caught her eye, he noticed that her smile seemed to dim. Rocking back on one heel, he nonchalantly set his hat down on the counter and crossed his arms over his chest, puzzled why his presence had seemingly caused her distress. The thought brought a momentary stab of culpability, but that didn't last long. The saucy smiles Delphine gave him whenever he passed their shop had tempted him, but before today he'd never had reason to enter.

The striking young customer's censorious expression was clear. But so was her interest. Her hair—fair with soft, almost pink highlights—was unique in Santa Fe. And her snapping green eyes were enchanting. He wondered what had dusted up her dander. Keeping the amusement from making his lips curl, he dipped his chin respectfully.

Delphine reached across the counter to receive the items from her mother, her cheeks now a burst of color as if she'd been caught with her hand in the cookie jar. Beranger groaned inwardly. She was too young and forward for her own good. She appeared to be so guilty, anyone would assume he had just tried some horrible transgression.

Indeed, the willowy beauty beside him raised her chin, seeming convinced he was up to no good. But when she looked into his eyes, she startled.

*My curse.*

She jerked her gaze away.

"Mrs. Sackett," Beranger began, "your daughter is recounting the mishap you had last week at the church picnic." He kept his voice light and his eyes respectfully on the shopkeeper's face, when he really wanted to stare at the gorgeous young woman by his side.

*Who is the little girl? Her daughter? Her niece?*

He noted how graceful she appeared even holding the child's hand. She drew him like a bee to honey, and he wasn't even ashamed to think it. "Seems you had a scare with an undetected good-size anthill." He chuckled and chanced a look at Delphine, who had indeed shared the telling—he omitted the part about the hidden place by the stream that all the young men knew, and how she'd invited Beranger to meet her there next week.

She actually batted her lashes at him and reached out to touch his arm. The action was not missed by the new arrival.

"Are your advances warranted?" the young woman asked, looking disapprovingly at him. "Should Mrs. Sackett be concerned about her daughter's reputation?"

Surprised by the question, he didn't have an immediate answer. This woman had spunk. Her tone was sweet, but the look in her eyes challenged him. He'd never had such a strong reaction to any woman—and he liked the feel. There was something about her that made him want to know more.

"I hope Mrs. Sackett is not distressed by my presence," he answered. "I mean no harm. But if you are indeed concerned, just say the word and I'll be on my way." He looked at Delphine's mother, whose face had gone scarlet. Her eyes apologetic.

"Miss Brinkman meant no offense," she squeaked out. "You're welcome in my shop anytime."

*Brinkman?*

*Miss Brinkman?*

His evening meeting about the mine job had unexpectedly become more interesting.

With a free hand, Miss Brinkman scooted the child behind her skirts. "Are you making a purhase of any kind, or just pestering this pretty girl?"

"I'm sorry to disappoint you, Miss Brinkman, but I *am* making a purchase—or at least trying to." He cut a fast glance to Delphine. "I'm soliciting Miss Sackett's opinion about a gift to bestow on a friend of mine. Not something so elaborate that the gift might be inappropriate, and not something so diminutive that it won't represent my great esteem. Have *you* any suggestions for me? I'd be most interested to hear."

Miss Brinkman exhaled like a puffin he'd seen in his travels, erect on an ocean rock amid the crashing waves, the white panel of her dress front resembling its white breast feathers. "I'm sorry, I do not."

The child peered around her skirts and regarded him with a thoughtful gaze. She didn't look frightened in the least. On the contrary. He smiled at her, and she smiled back.

He gave a small bow. "I regret if I've caused any discomfort to anyone." He glanced at each face, ending with Miss Brinkman, who, as he knew she would be, was staring at his unusual eyes.

One green, one blue.

*Send him away, Your Grace. He is cursed,* he heard his stepmother say.

"I'll take my leave and find my gift in another establishment. Good day to you all."

With an armful of boxes, Emma waited outside the store with Brenda by her side. She was distracted

39

from the smidgen of guilt she'd otherwise feel about her extravagant purchases by the memory of the rake's startling eyes. His eyes, one green and one blue, had set off a flood of fire within her veins. Were they some accident of nature? She'd seen a boy once in Philadelphia with a similar condition, only he'd been blind in one eye. Perhaps it was the same for this gentleman— although she didn't think that was the case. He didn't act blind—the exact opposite, in fact. She was quite certain he hadn't missed a thing in appraising her appearance.

Her hand brushed across Brenda's shoulder as Trevor came striding up the boardwalk and greeted them with his sleepy grin. "All done?" His brows drew down at the sight of the packages balanced in her arms. "It's a good thing I waited."

As he stepped forward to help, taking the packages one by one, Emma shook her head to clear it of Mr. North's striking image. There was still shopping to do, and then a fancy supper tonight. She'd not let Mr. North ruin her holiday here in Santa Fe. She glanced at Brenda, and was filled with melancholy at the thought of how much she'd miss the little girl. She nodded to the place next door. "I guess we'll continue right there, Trevor. If you don't mind."

"Mind? I expected as much. I'll watch you go in, then run these things back to the hotel. When you're finished, I'll be waiting."

"Thank you, Trevor."

With her arms empty, Emma took a calming breath and smiled at Brenda. "Our day is not finished yet, sweetheart. We have more shopping to do."

As she glanced up, she saw none other than Mr. North stepping out of a store down the street, a small package in his hands. She held her breath as his head turned in her direction. Spotting her, he flashed a broad smile, tipped his hat, then went on his way.

With an imaginary huff, Emma booted thoughts of him away and focused on all the extra jewelry she'd have commissioned after she bested Belle in their little competition. Now *that* would be a fun day to look forward to.

# CHAPTER SIX

*Eden, Colorado*

Clint Dawson entered his office, went straight to his coffeepot, and poured a cup of the cold brew. *Sludge, nothing more. I really should go to the café for fresh, but don't have time.* Henry was due any moment. The attorney was bringing by some new folks interested in Shawn's Café, the restaurant that had been called the Hungry Lizard until Rhett Laughlin came to town. Rhett'd reopened the place in honor of his deceased brother only to opt to go into the construction business instead. Clint hoped Henry's prospective buyers would jump at the chance to own a spot smack in the middle of town. Rhett had taken Clint into his confidence, told him that he didn't want to marry Lavinia with debt hanging over his head from the renovation of the restaurant plus his new office building.

Clint understood. Knowing the Brinkmans as he did, though, he was certain that if Lavinia knew how Rhett felt, she'd insist on paying off his bank note, being a wealthy woman in her own right. He respected Rhett for wanting to make it on his own.

At the sound of someone approaching, Clint

turned to the door. Expecting Henry and the prospective buyers, he was surprised to see Jeremy Gannon, Eden's recently arrived doctor. "Jeremy. What brings you by?"

Dressed in his usual brown corduroy pants and clean white shirt, Jeremy laughed and stepped inside. "Do I need a reason to be neighborly, Sheriff?"

Dallas, Rhett's dog that had adopted the whole town as family, trotted inside at Jeremy's heels. The half dingo had been one of the doctor's first patients when he'd gotten a mouth full of porcupine quills.

"Surely not. Come in, but be warned if you're looking for coffee your best bet would be to cross the street." Clint lifted his cup. "This will singe the hair right off your chest."

"That bad, huh?"

Clint took a sip and grimaced. "Worse."

"Then I'll pass. I've had my fill anyway."

"Good decision. You in for a social call, or you have something on your mind? You look a little cautious, if I had to guess."

Jeremy rubbed a hand across his face, expression uncertain.

"If you have something to say, you better spit it out. I'm expecting people."

Jeremy nodded. "You're right, I do have something on my mind. But it's not anything I'm sure of. That's what makes this difficult."

"Go on."

"You know my place is right across from the school. Well, the other day, ol' Mr. Lake was having a work day with some of the students, cleaning and painting the inside of the school. I heard more than a fair amount of yelling. When I went to see if he needed help, he cursed at me and told me to mind my own business. The boys helping looked pretty wide-eyed."

Clint nodded. "He's seventy-one and hard of hearing, which makes his regular speakin' voice louder than I can tolerate. Don't think he can help himself."

"At first, that's what I thought too. I'm afraid there's more. Out of concern for the children, I stayed around and eavesdropped. I'm not proud of my methods, but I felt them prudent. He was belittling the children, and more. If I spoke that way, my mother would have washed my mouth out with soap—no matter my age. By the boys' faces, they're frightened of him. I can't imagine much learning is getting done when school is in session."

Disturbed, Clint paced to the window and looked kitty-corner across an open lot to the small schoolhouse that now stood empty for the summer break. He'd heard Lake's voice ringing out more times than he'd like to admit, but assumed the volume was due to the man's impairment. If what Jeremy said was true, something should be done.

There weren't many families in Eden—*not yet*—but that wasn't an excuse for doing nothing.

"He won't be happy."

"With what?" Jeremy asked. "A talking-to, or something else?"

"If what you heard is a common occurrence, and I don't doubt you for a second, Lake should retire."

Jeremy nodded. "My thoughts too. I can go with you. I was the person to bring this to your attention."

"No. I think the observation will be better tolerated coming from me alone. I've known him . . . heck, he was my son's teacher. But I don't like the thought of the little ones sitting in a classroom with a tyrant." He put out his hand and took Jeremy's. "Thanks for speaking up. Being new to town, I know that took courage. Now we'll need to start looking for another teacher. That might prove difficult."

Jeremy reached down and scratched Dallas behind the ear, almost as though he didn't want Clint to see his face when he said, "What about Miss Brinkman? I've heard she has her teaching certificate. I haven't seen her around town much these last few days."

"Katie?" Clint said, pondering. "I'm not so sure. She's settled in with the mill and lumber office. Mavis has said before that she's lost her interest in teaching."

*Speak of an angel . . .*

Mavis—*Mayor Applebee,* Clint corrected himself with a private smile—breezed through the door looking as springlike as ever. To his eyes, she was more beautiful every day. As impossible as a woman being mayor seemed, no rule had been written into the town bylaws forbidding a woman to hold the office, because no man ever dreamed a woman would try. But they hadn't counted on Mavis.

Her chestnut hair, done half up and half down, bounced with each step, letting the few unconstrained locks dance at will around her face. She stopped just inside the doorway, her wide-set blue eyes more alluring than the most pristine lake. But it wasn't her eyes that had won her the mayor's office just last month. Mavis had run a convincing campaign against Donald Dodge, who'd been tainted by the scandals committed by his murderous brother.

Sure, she'd easily won the women's confidence with her commitment to better education for Eden's children with an investment in more books, since the school had been using the same five McGuffey readers for ten years. She'd also promised more community activities centered around families and to work toward securing women the right to vote. But the men hadn't just voted for her to appease their wives. She'd cannily brought in talk of her father, the proud John Brinkman, whenever possible and emphasized how much he'd loved this town. Who better than his eldest daughter to usher in the next phase of development for Eden?

Clint had heard more than one man in town say how impressed he was with Mavis's speech and ideas for encouraging town growth, such as pooling advertising dollars from individual shops to put to grander use than each little business could afford separately. Donald Dodge hadn't achieved one progressive thing while he'd been mayor. People were ready for a change. And the fact Mavis had been educated in Philadelphia and worked in the accounting department for a large furniture store gave her the credibility to pull it off.

"What're you smiling at, Clint?" she asked, bare hands holding tightly to a ledger she'd begun carrying around since replacing Dodge as mayor. "You look like you have a secret." She glanced at Jeremy and then back at him.

"Not a secret, exactly. I'm trying to memorize how pretty you look this morning." He glanced at Jeremy himself, a satisfied smile pulling at his lips. Mavis no longer wore gloves to hide the missing pinky finger on her left hand. The day he'd accidentally exposed her missing appendage without her approval, right here in this office, was imprinted on his mind for eternity. First shock, and then hurt, betrayal, and woundedness—

the parade of expressions across her face had frightened him. She'd forgiven him, thank the Lord, but he was glad for what happened. It had convinced her that what she saw as her handicap was to him just another way in which she was special.

Jeremy chuckled and leaned his hip on the edge of Clint's desk, crossing his arms. "Whatever you're eating, Mrs. Applebee, I'd like to feed to all my patients. You are the shining picture of health."

Mavis laughed, glowing in their praise. "What patients, Jeremy? I don't think you've had any in three months."

"And I'm not complaining about that at all. But you're wrong. I helped Sister Cecilia and Sister Agatha walk Sister Clover for three hours last night when that cow ate too many green apples. That bovine is as rascally as a goat."

Mavis came all the way into the room, patting Dallas on the head when the dog approached and sniffed at the hem of her dress. "So this Wednesday is our first town council meeting." She glanced between the men. "Is either of you gentlemen planning to attend?"

Clint nodded, wishing he could walk over and kiss her sweet lips. He'd been thinking about her much lately, and with the good, warm weather, dreaming about a summer wedding. Problem was, he hadn't admitted his feelings to her yet—let alone proposed. In eleven days, she'd be turning twenty-four. He was thirty-six. They were the best of friends, and at times the air fairly crackled with attraction between them, but there was a part of him that was reluctant to come out and say how he felt. She'd been a widow coming up on a year now. They never discussed Darvid, her first husband who'd died back in Philadelphia. Clint wondered if she missed him, if she was over what they'd shared.

*How long do women wait to remarry? What's a proper length of time?*

He wouldn't be able to bear her rejection if she said no. And there was the fact he himself was a widower too. How long had Ella been dead? Fifteen or sixteen years now? Hard to keep track with the years passing so quickly. Maybe Mavis wouldn't want him—or his almost-grown son, Cash.

"Now we know why you came in. I knew there had to be a reason."

"That's not true. I visit all the time. Why, I believe people have begun to talk."

*I hope they have.*

"And you haven't answered my question, Clint. Will you come and support me?"

"Wouldn't miss it for the world. On the contrary, I'm looking forward to watching you . . . uh . . . conduct yourself."

"Me too," Jeremy added. "I call anything besides staying home and eating my own cooking entertainment. Where's it going to be? In the back room of the mercantile, like usual?"

She nodded. "The space is cramped, but I don't want to make any changes right away. Some townsfolk still don't cotton to a woman mayor. They believe my place should be at home quilting a new bedcovering every other day. I swear. Don't they know the year is 1881?"

"I don't know about that," Clint replied, coming around his desk to get closer. Perhaps she had splashed on some of that tangy lemon verbena toilette water he was so fond of. "You beat Dodge by a landslide, ran him out of town. I felt kind of bad for him." He chuckled. "The huge signs you draped on your livery, Belle's tannery, the front window of Lavinia's café, Emma's Toggery, and both the sawmill and Katie's lumber office were pretty hard to beat. *I* wouldn't want to run against you."

"What?" she gasped playfully. "I won because of my vision for Eden, nothing else. Better school-books. More dances where the men and women can meet and get to know each other. And, as much as the men laugh and think I'm crazy, women's suffrage. Women have been able to vote in the Wyoming Territory since 1869, seven years before Colorado even achieved statehood, which was five years ago! Maybe we could be in the history books for being the first state to give women the vote."

Clint winked at Jeremy. "See what a head she has for numbers?"

Mavis shook her head, then tipped up the small watch pinned on her bodice and checked the time. "Getting back to ex-mayor Dodge . . . I guess his brother, after he tried to kill Belle and all the other horrible things he did to our family, was a millstone around his neck. Donald was guilty by association, even though he was cleared of any wrongdoing. I wonder where he went after he left town."

Clint shrugged. "Don't know. He and Ray had been a part of this community for as long as I have—longer, according to your father. Maybe they have relatives somewhere. They were both pretty closemouthed about their pasts."

"As are most people," Jeremy added.

Mavis beamed at the doctor. "I'm just so thankful Eden ended up with you, Jeremy. You're a perfect fit for our growing town. Young, newly graduated from medical school, and good-looking."

Clint straightened, a hint of jealousy making his brows drop. "Really? I hadn't noticed."

She shot him a playful look.

*Did she say that just to get my attention?*

"So Wednesday?" Clint asked in all seriousness.

"Yes. I may need you to whisper ideas in my ear if I get tongue-tied or forget something. Sit close by."

"I highly doubt you'll need any help," he said, liking the idea of sitting close. "You can talk your way around ninety-nine percent of the people in Eden. You won't have any trouble at all."

Her brow crinkled. "Who are the one percent that I can't?"

"The good doctor here and your favorite attorney, Henry Glass. I think they have you topped."

"And you too, Clint." She flushed, a sight he certainly didn't mind seeing. Then her tone turned thoughtful. "What should I talk about first?"

"Ahh, the real reason for this visit," Clint said. "How about this? Good-looking Jeremy here has reported that a few days ago he heard Mr. Lake cursing at a group of children helping him ready the schoolhouse for next term."

Mavis stood up taller, her smile fading away. "I see. I don't know the man well, but I have had a few conversations with him. I'll admit, some things he said made me want to scratch my head in wonder. We'll have to look into this."

Jeremy nodded. "That's all I ask. Now, I'm off. Good day to you both."

She watched through the window as he left, then, frowning, turned to Clint. "Have you seen Katie today? She's been miserable with Santiago out of town for so long. Every evening I think she's going to show up at the supper table with a wide smile, but that hasn't happened. Last night she didn't come over at all. She says she has a feeling like something bad has happened to him. She's a shell of her usual happy self."

"She shouldn't be so upset. The penitentiary where his brother is being held is in Utah. And who knows what he encountered along the way— or found when he got there. Maybe they wouldn't let him see Demetrio right away."

She gave him a look. "That's exactly the problem. Katie's worried that something bad has happened. Almost three months have passed. She fears he's hurt and lying in some ditch, waiting for her to find him, come to his rescue. Him leaving before her birthday was bad enough, but she understood. She's anxious to share her letter from Father. Says it proves something." She heaved a deep sigh. "Anyway, she's been on my mind all day. I thought I'd look her up. See if she wanted to go to the café and have a cup of tea. You know, have a sisterly talk."

Since the Brinkmans had arrived in Eden, he'd become very familiar with sisterly talks. Seemed they were the cure for just about anything.

*Should I make my move on Mavis's birthday? Is she expecting me to?*

He dared not speak with Blake for advice, knowing Belle would wheedle out the information and he'd lose the element of surprise.

Frustrated with his predicament, he smiled.

"Yes, I know. I'll let Katie know you're looking for her if she comes around."

"Thank you, Clint," she said with one of her devastating smiles, and then breezed out of his office the same way she'd breezed in.

# CHAPTER SEVEN

*Santa Fe, New Mexico*

Brenda was outfitted for the evening in her pink prairie dress, sitting primly in a chair and waiting patiently, decked out in all her soft underthings and shiny new shoes, content to gaze at her image in the mirror on the opposite wall. Emma hid a smile. What girl didn't love to feel pretty? Didn't matter the age.

Going to the door when she heard a knock, she opened it.

Belle swished inside, then stopped and stared. "You look stunning tonight, Emma. That new dress will turn every male head in Santa Fe. You might have trouble keeping our bet."

Emma, still riding high from the excitement of the day, ignored Belle's teasing wink and embraced her sister. "I can't tell you how much fun we had exploring. And Trevor was a jewel. Never complained once." She pointed to the chair in the corner of the room that was piled with a variety of boxes. "And look at what all he had to carry. I don't know how we would have fared without him."

Belle blinked her eyes, and they went wide. "I'm glad you didn't have to. Are those all things you want to feature in the Toggery?"

"Some. I envision making the northwest corner of my shop, where I have the two steer-hide-covered chairs and nothing of real value to display, into a space featuring garments I've collected from other places, beginning with Santa Fe. If they sell well, I can order more. I can't wait to get back and begin."

"Don't forget why we're here. To hire a manager for the mine we've neglected until now. Getting the operation up and running should be our first priority."

Emma smiled and lifted a noncommittal shoulder. The sisters wanted to do this on their own and be successful. They'd all agreed their individual businesses might suffer a little until the mine was running smoothly. That was all fine and good. She'd do her share, of course. And she had faithful Mr. Buns to run the Toggery while she was occupied with the mine, just as he'd done for their father until she'd taken over the reins.

"Are the men ready?"

"They are. Downstairs." Belle picked up Emma's shawl, holding it out. "Let's not keep them waiting any longer. Blake likes to arrive first so he can choose his seat. He's quite picky about that, you know."

Emma laughed. "Men are such strange creatures. I'm learning so many things in Colorado after growing up with four sisters."

Belle gave her a curious look.

"Nothing to do with love, mind you. Just that living in Eden is giving me a true education in independence."

Brenda hopped off her chair and moved to stand beside the women. A handkerchief Emma had given her to play with was folded nicely and tucked into the sash at her middle.

Emma crouched down—not an easy feat in her dress. "Are you hungry, my love?"

Brenda nodded seriously. "Yes, ma'am. My tummy hurts."

Emma's heart squeezed. Before this trip, she'd not had many maternal feelings. Not like Lavinia, who worked often at the orphanage. But now, after getting to know Brenda so well, Emma couldn't imagine not having a child to dote on.

*Will it be possible for me to have a family if I don't fall in love and marry?*

She glanced at Belle. From her expression of satisfaction, her sister had read her thoughts and was already counting on winning their bet.

But Emma had more determination than Belle gave her credit for. "Let's be off," she said, reaching for Brenda's hand. "Our table is waiting."

# CHAPTER EIGHT

From the restaurant's entryway, Beranger studied the group of people at the table in the far corner of the room. One of the men would be Blake Harding, the fellow Henry Glass had written to him about. Miss Brinkman was there, and the little girl.

He remembered Miss Brinkman's shock when she'd seen his eyes. At an early age, he'd learned to ignore the negative reactions to his unusual eye color. He'd had to, or else he'd have been fighting everyone who ever teased him about it, and many of the boys who'd insulted him were much older and stronger than he. Most times a curious question or even a sarcastic jab didn't bother him at all anymore. So why had Miss Brinkman's reaction today stung so?

*He scares me, Your Grace. I don't like him to look my way. What evil did his mother do to produce a child like him?*

As a baby only a few months old, Beranger was cared for by a wet nurse in a room a few doors down from his brother's. But as he grew, his stepmother had him moved farther and farther away from the family until he was practically in the servants' quarters. Left to himself to wander and explore, forgotten by his father, watched suspiciously by his stepmother, and looked down upon—and perhaps feared a little because of his eyes—by his half brother.

His uncle was the one who'd taught Beranger to disregard the looks and questions. Lord Harry had never explained why he understood his nephew so well, but Beranger figured that as youngest brother to the Duke of Brightshire, Lord Harry too had grown up in the shadow of the firstborn son. It was why he made sure Beranger was included when Gavin went for his pre-Eton boxing, fencing, and polo lessons, no matter how much his stepmother protested.

*Why does he have to partake? A gentleman's skills are not needed by a commoner. His time would be better spent learning the trade of a cooper or farrier, which he'll need when he comes of age. You coddle and spoil him, Your Grace.*

She'd been jealous of him, his uncle explained, because he was larger, better muscled, and a more natural athlete than Gavin was. If ever they competed, Beranger always came away the victor. When he was twelve, his stepmother forbade any more competitions between the half brothers, and Gavin was matched with someone smaller and less accomplished—and certain to give him the win.

Shaking off the memories, Beranger crossed the half-full dining room to join the others. Oil lamps with ruby-colored glass globes encased flickering wicks in the middle of each table. The heavy scents of garlic and onion made his stomach rumble with need. He walked with all the confidence his solitary life and success in the mines had given him. Here, he had no one to bow to, no one to fear.

He stopped in front of the table. "Mr. Harding?"

"Mr. North. It's a pleasure." Blake Harding stood, followed by the other men. He put out his hand, and they shook. "Thank you for making time for us in your busy schedule. You come highly recommended by others in the mining industry, from what our attorney says."

That was true enough. He could open and operate a prosperous mine blindfolded. Out of the corner of his eye, he caught Miss Brinkman's astounded, wide-eyed expression as she recognized him and heard this. Satisfaction slid through his veins.

"Thank you. And I've heard my fair share about the Five Sisters Ranch up in Eden in the last few months." He glanced around the table, his gaze stopping on Miss Brinkman. "And the arrival of John Brinkman's daughters as well. Are there only two here tonight?"

Blake smiled affectionately at the women at his side. "Yes, two only. But as you'll soon learn, two are plenty. Allow me to introduce you." He gestured to his right. "This is Belle Brinkman

Harding, sister number two, and my wife. Beside her is Emma Brinkman, sister number three."

*Emma Brinkman.*

Her pretty lips thinned out, and her nostrils flared in agitation just the tiniest bit. If he hadn't seen the exact same expression earlier today in Mrs. Sackett's shop, he would have missed it altogether. Beranger felt himself smile and nod as he scanned the faces. This was something new, something fresh. This endeavor might not only prove to be lucrative, but provide some fun as well.

Beranger nodded again as Blake introduced the men on his left as Moses Poor and Trevor Hill, foremen at their ranch. Moses would be helping out with the mine. "I'm pleased to make all your acquaintances," he said before training his attention on Emma. "And yours for a second time today, Miss Brinkman. I guess I better pull up a chair and hear what you all have to say."

"Oh?" Belle asked, her eyebrows rising so far they practically floated off her forehead. The sisters exchanged a loaded look, and he wondered if Emma had mentioned their meeting. Something was going on between the two women.

"Yes," Emma replied, her voice as cold as if she'd been hit in the face with a soggy snowball. "Mr. North was in a shop Brenda and I visited." She looked around at everyone but him as she spoke.

"I have to say, Miss Brinkman, the color of your new gown suits you well." He took the napkin from his plate and put the white cloth in his lap.

A wide smile spread over Mrs. Harding's face. "So astute of you, Mr. North. I agree, and I told Emma so just before we left our rooms."

He smiled amicably and poured on the charm, making a funny face at little Brenda, who smiled back.

"You have very striking eyes," Mrs. Harding went on. "Am I wrong, or are they two different colors? I don't think I've ever seen the like."

*Good. Get the obvious out in the open, right off.*

Blake and the hired help looked at him more closely, as if they hadn't noticed. That was the way of the world. Women were much more perceptive. "Some might say that, Mrs. Harding." He chuckled. "Others, not so much."

"Is the color difference a family trait?"

*Half. Just the blue.*

"No. I'm a rarity—in my family and elsewhere. There's no known name for my condition, but there are others, I'm told. The color discrepancy is infrequent and happens in animals as well."

"I think they're quite attractive." She glanced at her sister. "Emma?"

Emma stared at her, clearly unhappy to be put on the spot. Reluctantly, she shifted her gaze to him.

"Yes, of course," she responded flatly.

"Rarity or oddity?" A nagging desire to exact a tiny bit of revenge for how she'd treated him earlier raised its head.

Emma lifted her chin. "As my sister has said, they're striking. Being different is something to be proud of, Mr. North, not something to hide. I would think a man of your, uh, *character,* let's say, would know that."

Before any further arrows could be fired or business discussed, the waiter appeared with a bottle of red wine and filled their glasses. He took their orders and hurried away.

Blake lifted his glass. "To the Brinkman sisters' mine. May it prove a profitable endeavor."

"Hear, hear," Beranger echoed. Everyone touched their glasses with a soft tink, tink.

"I heard something interesting about you today in town," Trevor said. "I'm wondering if the chatter could be true."

"Oh? I think I know what that might be. With my unusual eye color, it's difficult for me to remain anonymous. In the twelve years since I stepped onto American soil, my reputation has dogged me like a hungry mutt."

Trevor nodded. "You're nobility—or whatever they call it."

"The son of a viscount or earl, or something like that?" Moses added, looking impressed.

Belle, who already appeared interested in the

conversation, brightened, but Emma watched him suspiciously.

"Wrong on both counts. I'm the second son of the Duke of Brightshire. My older brother inherits the title, the lands, the money, and so on. I'm not entitled to a thing. Everything I have, or will have, I've earned on my own."

*And I'm damn well proud of it.*

He'd gotten used to having to explain to Americans how the aristocracy worked. All the younger offspring got was the "privilege" of sharing the family name, which wasn't much help when you needed money to live on. Beranger left out the part about being illegitimate, because that was nobody's business but his own. Too many people automatically assumed the worst about his mother. He could take insults directed at himself, but he'd never put up with any slur against her memory.

"Well, it sure seems unfair to completely favor one son over another. Those laws make no difference to us," Blake said. "As long as you can evaluate the mine and tell us if you think the profit will outweigh the cost and effort of mining, that's all we care about."

Beranger nodded. "That I can do, to a certain extent. You know, there're no guarantees."

Belle nodded from behind her wineglass. "What should we call you? Lord Beranger North of Santa Fe?"

"Methinks our given names, if that's agreeable to you and your husband, will do fine."

"Only if you share with us some of the customs and things that make England unique," Belle added. "I'd like to travel to England someday."

Blake turned to her. "You would? That's news to me."

"We've only been married a little over four months, Blake. I hope there are things about me that still surprise you."

The waiter brought their food, and the talking quieted down for a few minutes.

The revelations of his heritage always had the same effect on the women Beranger met. There was something mysterious and romantic about all those lords and ladies across the sea. He didn't fight it, because he couldn't. The past had nothing to do with him now, yet everything still had to do with his history and roots. Almost everyone in America except the natives had migrated from somewhere in Europe; perhaps they imagined they might have some royal blood flowing in their veins as well.

Over dinner the girls, led by Belle, negotiated the sum they'd pay Beranger to come to Eden and assess the mine. At that point, if he deemed they should move forward, they would pay him a percentage of what was produced by the mine in the first three months, from any mineral. After that, they'd be on their own. If nothing had been found up to that point, it would be up to them whether they wanted to keep mining. For the first time in years, he felt challenged. They laughed over jokes and shared some family stories with him. Emma remained quieter than the others.

"Mr. North, I've been wondering about something," Emma said.

He put down his fork and gave her his full attention.

"How is a mine picked in the first place? My father was the second owner of this particular mine. I wonder how the person who owned it before him decided to file a claim there. What might have made him think there was gold or silver to be found?"

"A very good question, Miss Brinkman."

"The presence of a river," Trevor said quickly. "And the minerals washing down. And a gut feeling."

Emma nodded, but waited for Beranger to answer.

"That would be chancing a lot, Trevor," Beranger said. "There are several indications, Miss Brinkman, but I'd never rely on my gut alone. I'm much more scientific than that," he said with a slight nod.

The waiter cleared their dishes and brought dessert. Brenda's eyes grew as round as moons when she realized she had received her very own serving of cobbler, which made everyone laugh.

"Most likely," Beranger continued, "the person who chose this spot did a few simple tests, as I'll do myself before sinking a goodly amount of money into opening up a large-scale operation. I'm not sure why they state it's a silver mine, if silver hasn't yet been found. We could just as easily end up finding gold, or both. First, as Trevor said, for me, there has to be water close by. A river, stream, or inlet is critical. I'll prospect the stream for color, flakes, or small nuggets, and also do some digging around the banks and close hillsides, both above and below your spot."

She took a breath. "That's most exciting." When he spoke directly to her like this, she seemed to forget about how startled she was by his eyes.

"If that proves fruitful," he went on, "I move upstream and try to estimate the source. Find where the minerals originated. Another indicator is the rockiness of the ground and whether there is an abundance of quartz."

"The white rocks we've seen around Colorado?" Belle said, listening intently as well.

"That's correct. White is the most common color for the mineral, but quartz can also be black, purple, pink, or yellow."

He took a drink from his cup. "A mineral hot spring can be a good sign as well. Any sign of those kinds of things where you're located?"

"To tell you the truth, Beranger," Blake

responded, "I don't know much about the area. I'm a rancher. Not a miner. And I aim to stay that way. That's why the women opted to hire you. To weigh their possibilities so they don't waste time and money." He glanced at Belle and then Emma.

Beranger leaned one forearm on the table. "Absolutely. I want to hit pay dirt as much as you. If you make money, then so do I. I'll do some mining in the stream. Give the mine that's already started a fair chance. You say the former owner has a ten-foot tunnel begun. If possible, I'd like to use their tunnel. The beginning is difficult, as is digging deeper. Mining is soulless work. The process and heartache can break men without even trying."

"Moses is a hard worker, Beranger," Blake said. "They don't come any better than him."

"He saved my husband's life during the Civil War," Belle added, looking fondly at the serious man.

Beranger narrowed his eyes. "Just so you all know, it's dangerous work. Not fun and games. I'll have the final say about safety."

"We're counting on that," Blake answered.

"And what have you named the mine?" Beranger asked, taking a bite of sherry cake. "You've yet to say."

Emma sat straighter. "Named?"

"Yes, of course. Every mine should have a name

before it's properly christened. Could be bad luck, if not. That's something I won't chance."

The wine had mellowed her, and every now and again he'd catch a slight smile. She was a true beauty, something he hadn't seen in a long time. He'd like to get to know her better, but that wasn't happening now; once he got to Eden and the work started, he'd not get the chance. The mine was several hours out of town, so he'd be back in his camp tent.

Blake exchanged looks with the ranch hands.

"Do you know, Blake?" Belle asked. "Did Father name the place?"

"No," Blake responded, scooping up a large portion of apple pie.

"Not that I ever heard," Trevor chimed in. "He knew as much about mining as we do, and that's nothin'."

"That's why you've hired me," Beranger said. "But I was serious about naming the mine before work begins. A name is important. A fore-shadowing of sorts. You want the moniker to be something you'll be proud of if history is made."

Emma sipped her coffee, then placed her cup back in its saucer. "History? How do you mean?"

"When I take on a job, it's with a mind to finding the largest vein in the area. I think big—and want you all to do the same. Imagine in your mind how striking a lode as wide as a man's arm would feel." He rubbed his hands together as a shiver ran down his neck. He'd found enough veins to know what he was talking about. "When the lamplight hits that sparkle, a thrill runs up and down your body." He looked straight at Emma. "Nothing can compare."

*Except maybe kissing you.*

She flushed.

The women sucked in a breath and locked eyes. The men gazed off across the room, imagining.

"Have you made history before, Mr. North— *Beranger?*" Emma corrected when he arched a brow.

"No, but I've come close. I've matched several of the records for dollar amounts taken from a single mine. But it's not from the lack of trying. Perhaps the Brinkman mine will be the one." He tapped his chest. "Something that doesn't come from my family back in England. A history that begins with me alone."

*A mark that makes the name* North *mean as much in America as the name* Northcott *does in England.*

"I want a line in history all for myself."

# CHAPTER NINE

Last night, from the corner of her eye, Emma had watched Beranger carefully. His past mining experiences elicited a fluttery excitement in her belly. He handled his utensils differently than most. Stabbing a bit of beef or potato with the tines of his downward-facing fork, he'd either cut the morsel or put it directly into his mouth without switching the fork to his right hand. Other times, he'd use his knife to push rice or vegetables onto the back of the downward-facing tines, and again raise it to his mouth. He was smooth and accomplished and looked totally at ease. She could see how some inexperienced young woman might fall head over heels when in his company; as a matter of fact, an experienced young woman might as well.

She should have shared her worries about him and his behavior toward the Sacketts before the dinner. Then her sister would have better understood when she waged her complaint later on that night. As it was, Belle had been totally charmed.

Even Emma had to admit she'd forgotten her disapproval of him at times. More than once, she'd glanced up to find him watching her, a half smile on his moving lips as he chewed.

*He's still a rake. Just because he uses nice*

*manners and has a charming way of speech doesn't negate Mrs. Sackett's warning. He has a reputation for breaking hearts. He just knows how to hide it well. If I'd kept what I know to myself and then something happened, I'd be to blame. I had a duty to talk with Blake and Belle.*

Not that it had done much good. Now, setting the carpetbag filled with Brenda's new, neatly folded garments on a straight-backed chair, Emma forced a smile. Since the sun had risen, she'd been a bundle of nerves. Like a cat hiding in a wolf's den, she moved around the waiting room of the Santa Fe orphanage, which sat off Paseo de Peralta not far from the cathedral of Saint Francis of Assisi that was under construction. On the near wall, a small glass display case held mementos, old letters, religious items, and photographs. A desk sat kitty-corner between two windows on opposite walls, and the air was cool with the scent of jasmine. Outside, vines grew up the exterior walls, making the building seem relaxed and approachable.

*Then why do I feel so miserable?*

Emma's heart thumped painfully as she watched little Brenda take in her surroundings as if her life weren't about to change for all time. They'd arrived at nine, just as the large church bell of Saint Francis began to ring. Emma hadn't known today would be this difficult.

The young nun who'd greeted them upon their arrival had remembered Brenda. A quiet conversation ensued. Brenda seemed relaxed, and if she had any anxieties about meeting her new family, she didn't let them show. The nun offered her a cup of milk, but Brenda declined, although she'd hardly eaten a bite of her breakfast a half hour before.

The sound of children's laughter floated in from outside. As they'd approached, Emma had seen a garden, several trees—two with swings—and a gaggle of children at play in the sunshine. A few nuns watched, as did a nice-looking man and woman standing arm in arm. Were they leaving a child behind? Or hoping to adopt?

In a wave of emotion, Emma moved quietly across the cool flagstone floor until she stood behind Brenda, who was peering into the display case, her small hands resting on the glass. Emma placed her hand on Brenda's shoulder, and the child glanced up.

"What do you see in there that's so interesting?" Emma asked softly. "You haven't looked away in over five minutes."

Brenda smiled even though tears glistened in her eyes. Emma could pretend all she wanted, but Brenda knew why she was there.

"I like the pretty beads." Brenda pointed to several strands of colorful glass beads on the upper shelf.

"You're right, sweetheart. They're very pretty. You have a keen eye." Unable to stop herself, she lifted Brenda into her arms, hugging her to her chest. "I'm going to miss you." She kissed the side of her face. "More than the stars in the sky. But you're going to a wonderful new home with a mommy of your very own. And a daddy too. You'll be as happy as can be."

"And brothers?"

Her voice was so small and sweet, Emma could hardly discern what she'd said. "That's what I hear. Three of them. You'll be deliriously happy every single day. I promise you that." The feel of the child nestled in her arms was intoxicating. The tiny beat of her heart moved against Emma's.

*Dear Lord, how will I ever give her up? I thought I could, because the moment had yet to arrive. But n say if I bring her back to Eden? And what would I do with her while I work?*

Knowing that adopting her was impossible, Emma took a deep breath and rocked her back and forth. Her thoughts flew back to the intriguing, reputation-ruining Mr. Beranger North and the aftermath of last night's supper. Alone after dinner, Belle had countered Emma's every objection about the man, believing Emma was making too much of hearsay and rumor. When she'd protested too much, Belle had even accused her of *falling* for the handsome rake!

74

And then this morning, Belle had shared that she'd discussed Emma's concerns with Blake, and he'd sided with Belle. Regardless of his reputation, they wanted him, and him alone, to assess the mine.

On top of that failure, Emma now had to say goodbye to Brenda. The thought broke her heart in a million pieces.

She gave Brenda a tighter squeeze, trying to memorize the feel of her in her arms. Then the inner door opened, and the nun who had greeted them returned with an older nun who was introduced as Sister Theresa. Tall and straight, she reminded Emma of one of the lofty poplar trees growing on the edge of the meadow above Eden.

She smiled, and a beautiful light arose in her eyes. "Welcome back, Brenda. I don't know if you remember me, but I certainly remember you." She reached out and caressed Brenda's hair as Emma tightened her hold.

Sister Theresa's gaze moved up to meet Emma's. "Good day, Miss Brinkman. We've been antici-pating your safe arrival with our dear child." Emma was certain propriety would dictate that she should put the child down, but she just couldn't. Not yet. It felt as if they were going to wrench her from her embrace, and she'd never see Brenda again.

"Thank you," Emma replied respectfully.

"The trip was uneventful in the right kind of way, and we've had a nice time exploring Santa Fe." She turned a half step so she'd be able to see Brenda's face. "Since she's been staying with us, we've given Brenda another name. We call her Brenda Blue Bird because she's as happy and sweet as a little songbird." She rubbed Brenda's back. "And she's learning to be a ballerina."

"That's a beautiful name too, and fits you perfectly." Sister Theresa's eyes seemed to say everything was going to be fine. "God has provided a lovely home for you. A family of three boys, and a mother who dreams of a daughter to cherish, to teach to sew and cook. And a daddy. Would you like that, Brenda Blue Bird?"

Brenda nodded.

Emma didn't know what she would do without her sisters to confide in. She couldn't imagine a life with four brothers, and only her.

*Will this be a good place for Brenda?*

Emma felt a responsibility to speak her heart. "But is that best for Brenda? A house filled with boys? I do understand a mother yearning for a daughter, but I want what's best for Brenda. I can't worry about the woman's desires."

Sister Theresa moved her hand from Brenda to Emma's arm. "We all want the very best for the children, Miss Brinkman. I think you will feel differently after you meet Mr. and Mrs. Kenningston and their three charming sons."

"I'll get to meet them?"

"If you'd like. They're outside in the play yard waiting for Brenda now."

*Now?*

Emma's heart lurched. Things were moving so quickly.

"Yes," she said. "Why don't we go out and say hello?" She gazed at Brenda. "Are you ready to meet your new family?"

Brenda gave Emma a quick look and then nodded. "Yes, ma'am."

Sister Theresa clapped her hands. "Wonderful. We'll leave your things here for now. We can all have a cookie outside. Your new mommy made them just for you. Your brothers wanted some, but she said they had to wait."

Brenda's eyes went wide. "Cookies for *me?*"

Emma choked down a rock of emotion and, smiling, she set Brenda on her feet. The girl ran to the door and was gone.

Sister Theresa stopped Emma with a gentle hand. "She'll be just fine, I assure you. That family has wanted a daughter for years, and they'll pamper her and care for her kindly. I can promise you, this is harder on you than on Brenda. Thank you for loving her so much."

Emma could only nod.

"Now wipe those tears, and let's go out and say

hello. You'll see what I say is the truth and you won't worry. You've done your part, and now you have to let her go and trust in God. He knows what He's doing. Are you ready?"

Emma nodded.

Brenda and her new family stood in a small circle under the trees, talking as children played around them. The mother, beaming with joy, couldn't keep from petting Brenda the whole time they talked. Emma walked slowly forward with the nun and stopped.

Brenda basked in the attention, and everyone watched with admiration as she showed them her ballerina twirl. As much as it broke Emma's heart to lose her, it was clear that with the Kenningstons, Brenda would flourish.

"We'll be good to her," Alice Kenningston whispered, putting a hand behind Emma's back. "Please don't worry. This is a dream come true for us. Brenda Blue Bird will be cherished and loved."

Emma fought to keep her lips from wobbling. "That's all I can ask. Do you mind if I tell her goodbye?"

"Of course not."

Emma led Brenda a few feet away and sat on a bench. "It's time for me to say goodbye, my love. I'll write to you, and maybe I'll even come and see you someday." She nuzzled in, trying to remem-ber every tiny detail of the way Brenda felt in her arms. Oh, how she would miss her. "Be very good, as I know you will, and enjoy your new family."

Brenda nodded and kissed her cheek. Her small arms circled Emma's neck and stayed that way for a few moments. Finally, she pulled back. "Goodbye, Miss Emma."

Emma set her down, and the child ran off.

"Goodbye, Brenda," she whispered. "Farewell."

# CHAPTER TEN

With his hat in hand, Beranger knocked at the small house on the outskirts of Santa Fe, the birthday present he'd purchased yesterday wrapped and tucked under his arm. Breaking the news of his departure to Fran wouldn't be easy, unless he was able to cajole her into coming to Eden with him. As much as he tried, Fran never accepted any handouts. There was no doubt in his mind she'd consider the move charity, so he could look after her, keep an eye that she was eating, and had fresh water and clothes. He didn't want to leave her, but she was more stubborn than fifty mules put together. But something whispered to him not to let this opportunity slip through his fingers. If he did, he'd regret the decision for the rest of his life. The chance was a new lease on life—a life that had become lonely after achieving much of what he'd set out to do when he'd stepped onto the mighty shores of America twelve years ago.

When nothing happened, Beranger knocked again a little louder, making sure he'd be heard. Coming to the door was becoming more and more difficult for Fran.

Unbeknownst to Fran, Beranger paid her neighbor to check on her each day, to visit, and make sure Fran was doing well.

The door opened. "Beranger?" Fran blinked and glanced around. The frailty of her frame almost made him wince. "It's not Wednesday. Why have you come?"

He stepped through the door and kissed her cheek. "I think somebody has a birthday tomorrow."

Her face exploded in wrinkles as she beamed from ear to ear. "You cheeky boy, how did you know?"

"I have my ways. Don't tell me you're complaining."

She hugged his arm as he walked her into the living room. "Never."

After he settled her into her rocker, he held out the package. "How are you feeling? Do you have enough to eat?"

"You sound like an old grandma," she chortled. "I'm fine. How many times do I have to tell you?" Her hands shook as she painstakingly unwrapped the present. Reverently, she lifted the delicate white lace shawl from its box. "Oh. This is too fine for an old woman like me."

"I hope you like it." He helped her drape it across her shoulders.

"Do you even have to ask? This is the finest gift I've ever received. Thank you, my boy. I don't know why God blessed me so with finding you." Her eyes went wide. "I warmed some water. Let me get you a cup of tea."

"No, thank you. I ate before I came by. But . . ."

"Yes?"

"We need to talk. Are you feeling up to it?"

Her eyes flashed in her fragile face. "Oh? Something has come up? Did you meet a pretty girl who's finally caught your fancy?"

She was always after him to settle down, have children, be happy.

He shook his head. "You're my only girl."

"You scoundrel. Honeyed words roll off your tongue like candy, but I know better. Still, I always have time for my boy Beranger." She looked him up and down, a keen light in her eyes.

He'd found her one night, passed out from hunger on a park bench, unaware that the sun had gone down and night had fallen. After rousing her and getting her a hot meal, he'd learned her husband had died long ago and she was alone. Since then, he'd been watching out for her. He'd procured this cottage. Furnished it and bought her some new clothes. She reminded him of the mother he'd never known. Leaving her behind would not be easy.

"You're saying goodbye," she said unexpectedly.

She had a way of reading his mind.

"Not saying goodbye." He clasped her hands. "I want to bring you along."

She chuckled. "Where? When?"

"About three hundred miles north, to Eden, Colorado. On tomorrow's stage." He'd get an early start, settle in, get the lay of the town before the others returned and work on the mine began.

Fran tipped her head. "Not that far away. What takes you there?"

"Work."

"Another mine?" Her brow drew down. "Thought you were done."

"An offer came up. This could be the big one. A chance for my name to go down in the history books. But I want you to come along. Eden's a small town, but growing. The temperatures are much cooler in the higher elevation."

"And more snow."

"That's right. But the heat here is more than you can stand in the summer months."

"I won't leave Wilber. We've been through this before."

And they had. Several times. He'd never been able to sway her.

"You really mean you won't leave Wilber's grave? He'd want you to come with me, Fran, not stay here alone, mourning him forever."

She tut-tutted. "I'm not alone. What would my poor neighbor do without me? She never tires of sharing her troubles and drinking my tea. She visits twice a day, for gosh sakes. Why, the poor woman would probably fall apart without my sage words of advice. Besides"—Fran patted his hands—"I'm too old. I've been through too much here to start over someplace else. I'll die here, and I'm not fearful of that. I've told you that before. Death is just a new beginning. Sometimes I pray peace comes soon . . ."

Once Fran got talking, she could go on for many minutes without taking a breath. She'd shared the story many times of how she and Wilber had been two of the sole survivors on a wagon train. The journey from the east had been harrowing; between the Indians, pestilence, bad weather, and misfortune, more than one hundred people had been buried along the way, including her sister-in-law, two brothers, and many good friends. Wilber and the few others who'd endured and settled in Santa Fe were all long since dead from various causes.

Getting her to undertake the long trek to Colorado was a losing battle, and he knew it.

"I'd never let anything happen to you, Fran. It's only a matter of a few days in a stagecoach—"

"And sleeping in shacks where marauding Indians can lift my scalp."

"Shame what's happened to such a proud people. They aren't much of a problem anymore. Two young women and a little girl made the trip coming here in a buckboard, and they'll return the same way. The people hiring me—you'll like them. You'll see."

Her eyes lit up. "Did you say women? Who are they and how old?"

She was still on her never-ending search for his perfect mate.

"Go on, spill the beans."

"Young. Early twenties, I believe. One is married, and one is single. That's all I know except they're the owners of the mine, with three other sisters, and they need me to open it up." He couldn't stop his face from getting warm, and knew she'd pick that up like a hawk after a chick. She didn't miss a thing, especially if a romance might be in order.

"And fair of face?"

She knew him too well. "What do you think?"

She smiled. "You go. Find yourself a wife."

"I never said I want a wife."

"You don't have to. Every man wants a wife. And you, my boy, are the kind of man every woman wants. I'm staying here until my dying day, which isn't that far off, to be buried side by side with the love of my life. I'll not be a mound of dirt along a desolate road through some valley to eventually be blown away by the wind. My life in Santa Fe is fine enough. I'm not wanting anything more."

Leaving the chatter and fuss of the orphanage, Emma walked toward the hotel at a brisk pace, trying to keep her emotions in check. She passed a mercantile brimming with customers, a bank, a candy store, and other businesses she didn't particularly notice. She crossed streets and a small park. All the while, her arms felt empty.

She missed the feel of Brenda's small hand in her own. The world went on around her as if nothing had happened.

The thought of traveling all the way back to Eden in the slow-moving buckboard felt insufferable. She needed to get home, where the store would keep her busy. With all the new garments she'd procured, she had many hours of work ahead of her, re-creating, decorating, planning a sales campaign to highlight her new fashions. Yes, she had a lot to do.

Nearly back to the hotel, she rounded a corner deep in thought. She was almost upon Beranger before she saw him. He stood in the shadow of a building, a tall stack of feed bags partially obscuring the view. A young woman was at his side. Emma couldn't see her face, but from the back, she could see that her waist was tiny and the skin on the hand that held Beranger's was creamy and smooth. They spoke in soft whispers. Beranger hadn't spoken of a wife or intended, but with the way he was leaning forward and looking into her eyes, that was the association that sprang to Emma's mind. Would he kiss her in broad daylight?

With a swift sideward step, Emma darted through a dry goods shop's door, her heart beating rapidly. The last thing she wanted was to be caught spying on the man, but she had a duty to her family to see what was going on.

*Is our new mining expert embroiled in a scandal of the sort Mrs. Sackett hinted at?*

Wiping away the remnants of the tears she'd cried at her departure from Brenda, Emma took a deep breath, inhaling the scent of lavender soap, and leaned out the door, straining to hear.

"Beranger, I shall die if you go," the young woman lamented. Her dress, of the latest style, was adorable from the back. "Will I ever see you again? What about our . . ."

She whimpered, drew her hand away, and turned.

*Delphine!*

Shocked, Emma had barely finished her next thought—*The rake! He's scheming on Delphine when he knows it upsets her mother*—when a shout rent the air.

"North, I've a bone to pick with you! You dung-filled coyote!"

The ruffian who'd shouted flung down something he was eating and started across the street. He was large and burly and looked like he'd seen a fight or two.

Emma shivered.

Turning from Delphine, Beranger watched his approach. "Our business is over, Letherson. Just go home before you bite off more than you can chew. I'm in no mood for trouble."

"Don't lecture me! I'm broke, and you're liable." When he stuck his face in Beranger's,

Delphine yelped and backed away. "I deserve a chance to win back what I lost."

Beranger laughed. "That's why poker is called gambling. You better be prepared to lose—and you did."

*Not only a rake, but a gambler and possibly a cheat? Is he also a fighter?* Letherson's face was livid with rage. *Surely the two will come to blows.*

Letherson shook his fist. "It's common courtesy, you slimy charlatan."

*There! The proof!*

"I was in the saloon two nights ago, Letherson, intent on extending an olive branch, giving you a chance, but you were so drunk you couldn't even hold up your head. I'll wager you don't even remember. I'm not playing nursemaid anymore."

Letherson laughed. "North, you're nothing but a freak. Can you even see outta them eyes?"

Emma gasped inwardly. She waited for Beranger to punch Letherson silly. Beranger didn't seem like the kind to let an insult pass without some sort of retaliation.

But Beranger dismissed him with a wave of his hand. "Get lost. You're scaring this young lady."

Letherson looked at Delphine and smirked. "Young lady, eh?" He rudely let his eyes roam up and down her frame. "I'll agree on the young part, but not a lady if she's speaking with the likes of you. I'd say she's more a—"

Delphine inhaled sharply.

In a swift move, Beranger grasped Letherson by his shirtfront and yanked his face to within an inch of his own. People had gathered around and were staring and whispering behind their hands.

"Say whatever you want about me. But don't insult this woman again, or you'll regret knowing me till your dying day, which might come sooner than you anticipate." He shoved Letherson away.

Propelled backward, the man caught his heel and fell hard on his back, landing in a pile of fresh horse manure.

Everyone laughed.

Furious, Letherson climbed to his feet. His muscles bunched as if to throw in, but he must have seen something—a look of warning?—in Beranger's eyes. He let out a long breath and took a step farther back.

"I'll be in the saloon tonight," Letherson growled as he continued to back away.

Beranger smiled sardonically. "But I won't."

*My! Why can't Belle and Blake see Mr. North's troublesome ways? Nothing I say does any good, so why even try?*

Emma slipped out the back door and over one street, heading to the hotel. *The real question is, what in the world will he be like once we reach Eden?*

# CHAPTER ELEVEN

"Five minutes!" the Wells Fargo attendant called loudly from the ticket office as Beranger waited to board the morning stage out of Santa Fe. The sun had just topped the horizon, and the day would prove to be hot. Six horses were hitched to the front, and all looked fresh and had large, sturdy legs and well-muscled stifles, forearms, croups, and shoulders. The harness leather was clean and shone in the rays of golden light. The wood grain of the conveyance also stood out, making him think the coach had recently been oiled. He hoped the inside was as clean and cared for as the outside. He'd been in some stages that had ripped upholstery, missing seats, and were foul smelling—or bloodstained. Everything that made for a nasty journey. Eden was only three to four days of travel, depending on the horses and terrain, but in the wrong circumstances that could feel like an eternity.

He lifted a shoulder as he felt a half smile form on his lips. The conveyance wasn't a gold-trimmed carriage befitting a duke, like one of the sizeable collection of transports his father owned, but then, he'd not seen anything that could compare to those since arriving on American soil. Sixteen years may have passed since he'd left England, but he'd not forgotten one iota of his past life. In reality, he preferred a clean and comfortable coach here to all the glitz and glamour of England.

A large black gelding, harnessed in the lead on the right side, pawed the earth impatiently as if he knew his race was about to begin.

"Just hold your horses, Diablo, you ebony *devil!*" a burly youth going over the harnesses shouted to the front, not caring whether some people might still be abed on this early Sabbath morning. "You're well named, you beast," he added, checking each buckle and shaking each chain. "Never lets me rest. Never lets me relax one minute. I curse when I see you coming in the harness."

The animal's muscled chest and sleek black back were covered in scars caused by a whip. There was also what looked to be a healed rope burn around his throatlatch. No animal should be treated in such a manner.

*I understand your fury,* Beranger thought.

When the kid caught Beranger watching him, he pulled up his half-rolled sleeve to reveal an ugly black-and-brown bruise on his forearm. "He done it, just to be mean. Got another one right here." He grasped his shoulder. "Grabbed me as I walked by the corral fence and shook me like a doll made of yarn. Six months ago, he kicked a fella in thechest and burst his heart. If he weren't such a large brute, with the strength of ten, he'd be gone to the butcher to feed the dogs!" The end of the sentence was shouted in the gelding's direction, as if the horse would understand. "But he ain't. He's celebrated by the uppers since it's been rumored to have pulled for more than two twenty-mile legs. Still, I ain't seen it. Don't know if it's true."

*Forty to sixty miles? That's punishing. And cruel.*

"Management thinks he's the best thing since apple pie—but *they* don't have to handle him."

Snorting, the animal threw his head and pawed impatiently. His bushy black forelock landed over his eyes, and his ample mane draped both sides of his thick crest.

*Descendant of the warhorses in England, I suspect. I can see why you'd be celebrated.*

Intrigued, Beranger strode forward until he and the horse were eye to eye. The animal stilled at his nearness. As crazy as the notion sounded, the gelding seemed to be looking back into Beranger's eyes, and deeper.

*Into my soul.*

The feeling passed, and the champion tossed his head.

*"But the black gelding is mine, Father. I worked him from the start. He doesn't like anyone else but me, and we're friends."*

*His father looked at him with mock affection.*

*"Gavin has taken a shine to him, Beranger. Now be a good lad and pick another from my stable. A horse is a horse and not a friend. They don't know one boy from another."* He ruffled Beranger's hair, but Beranger didn't feel any love. *"Give it a day or two. You'll like another horse just the same."*

Beranger had stood there, all of nine years old, and watched his horse being led away by his brother, the heir to the dukedom and Ashbury Castle. A deep, dark anger had burned in his gut. Had his father ever taken his side against his brother? Had a discussion ever gone his way?

*Never!*

Not the time Beranger had found a small, tarnished dagger, fallen through the cracks of a wooden cupboard in the weapons room. Beranger had painstakingly buffed and cherished the forgotten thing until Gavin had noticed. That he already possessed many of his own, jewel-studded as well, made no difference to Gavin. When he stole the dagger from Beranger, their father backed him. And when an invitation to hunt with the gamekeeper at nearby Penshurst Castle was issued to Beranger, Gavin had wheedled it away.

"Stay back, mister!" the stable hand called out, now finished with the harnesses. "Diablo can't be trusted."

Another employee loading the rear boot shouted

to him, "Stop yer complaining, Gomer, or we'll be late. I don't want another tongue-lashing because of you."

The animal was a fighter because he'd been forced to be. The look in his eyes resonated with Beranger. So often growing up in England, he'd been forced to strike out, exact some revenge on whoever was making sport. Over the years, sometimes the desire had almost been his undoing.

*"Look at them eyes! I think he's a dog even though he ain't no bigger than a pup. Gimme the coins in your pocket, young mongrel."*

*Beranger stood his ground, taking on three or four at a time, only to end up on the street, bloody and bruised, as the urchins ran off with the little money he'd saved.*

Beranger strode back to the waiting area. Two trunks were loaded into the rear boot that must belong to the two women on his left. They stood closely together, whispering, one behind her handkerchief next to the other's ear, checking him and the other travelers over as if they carried some horri-ble disease. He nodded politely when they looked toward him, wanting to put them at ease, but when they noticed his eyes, they jerked their gazes away.

Still, he smiled, used to the reaction. Sitting beside or directly across from him—or with their knees wedged uncomfortably together if Wells Fargo took on a full load—they'd get comfortable

with him soon enough. They appeared to be somewhere in their forties, and he pegged them as
schoolteachers or seamstresses.

One male traveler, who looked to be not yet
twenty, waited with a jutted hip, his saddlebag
draped over one shoulder, and a smirk on his lips.

*He'll be trouble. Or just a plain pain in the
backside. I'll keep an eye on him.*

An old man clutching the handle of a carpetbag
ignored everyone.

"You want that in the boot?" the fellow loading
the coach asked. He reached to take the bag.

The man drew back. "It'll get crushed back
there. I'm keeping my belongings with me."

"Space is limited. Your fellow travelers might
not like that so much."

The old man frowned. "I said I'm keeping my
bag!"

The worker shook his head. "Suit yourself.
If you change your mind, do so at a stage stop.
Happens all the time." He chuckled and wiped
his gritty brow with a handkerchief. "Two
minutes, ladies and gentlemen, until this bucket
of splinters departs." He gave a hearty laugh
when the women twittered apprehensively. "First
come, first served for the window seats."

The ticket agent, enjoying the show, looked
at the women, then at Beranger. He winked.
Walking forward, he placed a stepstool below the
door. Climbing in, he rolled up the leather shades

on the far side of the coach that had kept out the rising sun.

Beranger ran a finger around his collar, thinking that with the warmth of the morning they'd all soon look like the employee's brown, wilted handkerchief. He hoped his trip to Eden turned out to be worth the days in the stage. Time would tell.

A bag of mail was stuffed none too prudently into the rear boot. With all the cargo loaded, the whole stage was buckled up tight.

"Load up!"

As much as Beranger would have liked a forward-facing seat next to a window, he would let the two women take their pick. But as the attendant gestured to the open door, the cocky-looking lad moved forward. Beranger grasped his shoulder before he could climb inside. He nodded to the women. "Ladies first."

The kid scowled.

The women climbed inside with the help of the ticket agent's hand and the stepstool, making the leather braces of the coach softly creak. When they were settled in two of the three front-facing seats, the older of the two by the window and her friend in the middle, the boy Beranger believed fancied himself a gunfighter made another move to step up, but Beranger shook his head.

The old man tottered forward, refused help from the attendant, and climbed inside with some difficulty. He settled beside the women and stuck his elbow out the window, placing the carpetbag in his lap.

Even if Beranger had to sit backward, at least there would only be the two of them on the bench. Elbow room was a good thing, and maybe it even outweighed the front-facing bench as an advantage for the long journey. The kid wasn't wide or tall. Things could be worse.

Beranger waited, giving the youth the okay to climb in, thinking he'd made an enemy before they'd even pulled out. Beranger followed and found himself opposite the old man. *Not so bad.* He had a book in his saddlebags in back. He'd loosened his gun belt so that wasn't digging in his middle. He thought of Letherson and wondered if the man presented any real threat he'd need to watch out for. Surely he didn't have funds to come to Eden for revenge, especially after losing so much to him. But one never knew about a wild hare like him . . .

With everyone loaded, the ticket agent slammed the door closed. The coach dipped as the driver and shotgun messenger climbed aboard.

"Wait! Please, hold up!"

*I know that voice.*

Glancing out, he saw Emma Brinkman, garbed in a dress much too fine for travel, hurrying forward as if she intended to board the stage. Blake and Belle Harding were at her side, and Trevor

Hill carried a carpetbag close behind. Blake ducked inside the stage office.

"What's goin' on?" the kid beside him asked, leaning toward Beranger's window.

One of the ladies glanced over at the man. "Looks like we're getting another traveler. A woman. Nicely dressed. Young. Pretty."

Beranger stifled his smile.

The kid eyed the empty seat between them, thinking the same thing Beranger had a few seconds before: the empty seat and all the extra elbow room was about to vanish.

The youth shook his head. "No. We're settled and past time to depart. No last-minute deals."

"It's not up to us, young man," the woman replied curtly. "They'll take on more if they can make more money—and there *is* an empty seat. The term for this phenomenon is *capitalism*. Has to do with profit and loss. You'd do well to go back to school and study your books." She eyed the revolver strapped to his thigh. "Gunslinging only gets people killed and makes mothers cry."

*For sure, a teacher.*

"And you'd do well by mindin' your own business, *lady*," the kid responded. "Being a busybody gets people killed too."

The woman didn't seem to mind the comment, but Beranger sent a look of warning.

The door opened, and Emma Brinkman smiled brightly into the coach. "Good day, everyone!"

Her smile instantly vanished when she saw Beranger. "You!"

"Good day to you as well, Miss Brinkman. Are you joining us?"

Her long lashes batted several times. "Ah . . . No, actually. I'm not. I'm waiting . . ."

"Of course she is," Belle said, giving him a winsome smile, her eyes sparkling with mischief if he'd ever seen any. "She's decided she'd much prefer to get home quickly than take the longer route with us. We're picking up livestock on our return journey." She put her arm around Emma and gave her a strong hug. "Now climb inside, sister. You're holding up the coach. The next one does not depart for five whole days. Or would you rather wait? I'd *wager* no."

She'd said the word *wager* so boldly even Beranger couldn't help but wonder if something was up between the two.

"Beranger!" Blake chortled happily. "I'm relieved to see you. All of a sudden Emma decided she'd had enough of Santa Fe and wanted to get home. Having you on board, I feel much better about letting her go."

Emma hadn't said a thing. She just stared at the seat between the two men. Finally she looked up into Beranger's eyes. "Fancy meeting you here."

"Indeed. Would you like the window, Miss Brinkman?" he asked. "I'm more than happy to let you have it."

"If you're going, get in," the edgy stage-office director said with a scowl. "We're already late."

Beranger began to scoot to the middle, but Emma stopped him. "The middle is fine with me, thank you very much." She gathered her billowing skirt and stepped up, gingerly accepting his hand of help. She gave everyone an apologetic smile when the hat she was wearing bumped the top of the coach.

Blake appeared beside his window. "I really appreciate you watching out for her, Beranger."

"Not a problem."

Belle peeked over his shoulder. "She has a tendency to find trouble, and sometimes she has difficulty sleeping, and—"

"Belle, really!"

Belle pushed in front of her husband, the sassy smile gone.

Emma lunged across Beranger's lap and pressed her cheek to her sister's. A lightly fragranced toilet water drifted into Beranger's nose. "I love you, Belle. Don't worry about me. And you be careful as well—driving the wagon and moving the cattle."

When the girls had separated, Blake stuck his hand through the window. Beranger grasped it, sealing his fate.

"Thank you, Beranger. Safe travels. We'll see you in Eden. Now we both have more at stake than just the mine." His gaze cut to Emma, and he smiled.

*Famous last words.*

The driver slapped his lines and called out to the team, making the box of splinters jump forward. In all his travels, a stagecoach had never felt so loose in the springs. Santa Fe rolled away, and Beranger wondered what he'd gotten himself into.

# CHAPTER TWELVE

The stagecoach had sounded like the answer to her prayers when Emma had first thought of it. Spending more days in town, and then another week, give or take a few days, on the hard buckboard seat and moving at a snail's pace to get back to Eden hadn't been an option any longer. Thoughts of Brenda, even though she knew the child was happy, hurt. That was all she could think about. She was no good to anyone moping around, so she'd just as soon go home early.

The stagecoach lurched. Now she wasn't so sure. The coach's suspension wobbled like a poached egg taken too soon from the water. Every bump, every divot made her stomach roil unsteadily. She pressed her hanky to her lips.

The sisters across the way watched her closely.

*Hadn't they ever been told staring was impolite?*

Once the stage had departed town, Ester Nunes, the older of the two women, had asked everyone to introduce themselves. She and her sister, Peggy, were traveling to assist an elderly aunt in Denver. Ester pulled a very large ball of blue yarn from her large reticule and began knitting, all the while engaging her fellow travelers and asking them to divulge their life's stories.

The young man who might be a gunslinger was

called Jimbo Lance. He was, he said, on his way west, trying to outrun a string of bad luck. Emma suspected he'd made the story up to frighten them, for he appeared too gentle-faced and soft-voiced to be anything more than an ex-schoolboy looking for adventure.

Old Frank Tug had been in the Union army. He was much too feeble to be making this trip alone—but that was all the personal history they could glean from him. He called the sisters busybodies and told them to mind their own business when Ester asked him to elaborate.

Mr. North similarly divulged little about himself. Just that he was interested in mining in Colorado.

Ester looked at Emma. "And you, Miss Brinkman?"

Following Beranger's lead, Emma didn't mention their plans for the mine. "I own a clothing shop in Eden. I've been in Santa Fe acquiring a few new garments," she eked out through shallow breaths as the stage hit another bump. The Five Sisters buckboard was starting to seem like a luxury carriage in comparison. At least Blake drove at a reasonable speed. "I have four sisters, who all reside in Eden as well since our father's passing . . ."

Beranger gently nudged her leg.

She smiled and closed her mouth, all too grateful not to have to go on.

"Your father has passed?" Ester asked. "That must be difficult for you."

"Y-yes." She'd barely gotten the word out when the coach swayed on a bend in the road, first one way and then the other. A small moan escaped her lips.

Beranger glanced over. "Feeling all right, Miss Brinkman?"

Emma pressed her handkerchief more firmly to her lips. "I don't think so."

"Motion sickness?"

She nodded. Setting her hanky in her lap, she hastily untied the ribbon under her chin, removed her hat, and began fanning her face. "I believe so."

The faces before her swooshed back and forth. Her insides squeezed. She'd been on ferries in the harbor with no problem. Katie was the one who generally suffered from motion sickness; Emma had never had a tender stomach in her life.

*Why now? Was my breakfast of chipped beef on toast tainted? To force the stage to stop now would be humiliating. Especially in front of Beranger.*

"Do you need to stop?"

She couldn't answer.

"Miss Brinkman?" Beranger asked more forcefully.

She nodded.

He reached overhead and pounded on the ceiling.

A moment later, one of the men on top appeared at the window of the moving coach, a long rifle still in his grip. "What's the problem?"

"Stop the coach. Miss Brinkman needs some air."

"What do you think these windows are for? We'll stop when we change horses."

Emma blinked, her hanky still pressed to her lips. "How far might that be?" At that moment the coach lurched again. Her mind and stomach swished in tandem, causing her to emit a loud groan.

"We just left, ma'am. Stage stops are twenty miles apart. We got a hundred miles ta go today, before nightfall. We can't be stopping for just anything."

Moisture slicked her mouth. The contents in her stomach pushed upward. "I won't make nineteen more miles—or one, for that matter. I'm going to be sick in my lap before a fly can blink."

"Stop the coach!" Ester pleaded. "Traveling will be insufferable if she gets sick."

"Throwing up only takes a moment," Peggy added. "The delay will be minimal—the reward plenty."

Emma supposed she should feel grateful to the sisters, though they were more concerned with their own comfort on the trip than they were with her health. She couldn't blame them much. She'd not like to see and smell vomit for the next three days either.

"Pull up!" Beranger commanded. "Better a few minutes off schedule than the alternative."

*So much for Mr. North. The rake is only worried about himself as well.*

The guard climbed away, and a second later Emma felt the coach's momentum decline. She counted to ten, praying she'd get outside in time. The wheels finally rolled to a stop. The last jerk, and then the sway . . .

Bile rose in her throat, and she began to gag. "Huurrr . . ."

Beranger scooped her into his arms and vaulted out the door Mr. Tug had thrown open.

The moment her feet touched dirt, she snapped forward and emptied the contents of her stomach. Beranger's large hands anchored on her waist kept her on her feet.

She heaved again and again. At some point, the rake had reached forward to draw back a lock of her hair so it wouldn't be soiled.

Her heart slowed. A buzzing sound of some insect reached her ears. Lifting her gaze, she noted the horizon and the way the trail meandered over the desolate landscape until it finally disappeared over the distant hills.

"Better?"

She nodded. How would she ever live this down? "Yes. Thank you."

Back at the stage, Ester handed her a cup of water, and Emma washed out her mouth.

Taking her elbow, Beranger supported her as she stepped inside. He placed her by his window. With a jerk, the stagecoach started off as if the whole incident hadn't happened at all.

Feeling a thousand times better, Emma leaned her head back and closed her eyes. The other occupants were quiet, and her thoughts drifted to the man beside her. He'd helped her without complaint. She wondered if he and Delphine were already much more involved than Mrs. Sackett thought. And what did she think of a man who took another man's livelihood, even if it were in a game of poker? Letherson had looked down on his luck, or worse. Did the rake have a conscience at all? She couldn't imagine that sort of behavior from Tim or Cooper—not in the least.

She glanced out the window at the landscape passing by.

*I'll be so happy to be home. To be back on the ranch. Sleep in my own bed. See my sisters and have a calm day in the Toggery.*

"Feeling better?" Mr. Tug asked in a scratchy voice.

From directly across, she could see that he had no eyelashes left. Scaly dark patches marred his face. His craggy hands clutched the handle of his bag as if he'd never put it down.

"I am, thank you. Nothing left inside to slosh around, I guess."

"Let's hope not," Jimbo stated flatly. "This rig wouldn't stop for me, if I was sick." He snorted. "Women and their privileges."

Emma glanced up to find Beranger pinning Jimbo with a steely stare that would frighten the skin right off a snake's back. Instead of being intimidated, Jimbo pulled a flask out of his pants pocket, unscrewed the cap, took a swig, wiped the back of his hand across his moist lips, and then held the container out in invitation. "Anyone?"

All the women shook their heads.

"My mama taught me to share," Jimbo said. "It's the polite thing to do."

"And one of Wells Fargo's rules." Mr. Tug reached forward and partook of the libation. "Much obliged," he mumbled, handing the flask back. "That's good whiskey."

The coach bounced in a rut. Jimbo let go a loud belch, then wiped his mouth on his shirt-sleeve.

Emma buried her face in Beranger's shoulder, not caring if the action was improper, and not caring if he minded. She needed a buffer. His shoulder was not only available, but actually smelled very nice—a fact she'd discovered when he'd carried her from the stagecoach. After a moment, she stuck her face out the window and took a long breath into her lungs.

"Miscreant," Beranger mumbled beneath his breath.

This was the second stop of the day, and the temperature had grown hot. Shouting sounded from the front of the stage. Beranger hurried forward to see the problem with the men switching out the team. The scarred black gelding—the one named Diablo, who'd started in Santa Fe—still stood in his traces, dripping with sweat. His sides heaved in and out, and his eyes were dull. That didn't stop him from lunging with pinned ears each time a man leaned in to unhitch him.

*Those sons of perdition ran Diablo an extra twenty miles! Just like the kid alluded to in Santa Fe. Who knows how often the reprobates abused this horse?*

Beranger couldn't abide such cruelty. It wasn't right.

Beranger stepped forward. "I'll buy that animal, here and now."

All activity stopped. "What? You want to buy that horse?" a red-faced employee asked incredulously and pointed at Diablo. "He's a mean cuss. He'd just as soon kick your head off as take you for a ride."

A man leading two other horses toward the stage

shouted, "Hell, I'll give *you* ten dollars to take him away."

Red-face shot the man a dirty look. "Shut up. How much you willin' to pay, mister?"

"Three dollars each." There were four men. They might enjoy making extra money.

The spokesmen's eyes narrowed. "Not enough. Now get lost."

Beranger tossed each man a five-dollar gold coin, and one on the ground to the man still working. "You can say he got away and ran off."

That was about a week's pay for getting rid of an animal they hated.

"Three minutes," the driver called.

"Sold," the spokesman said.

"What are ya gonna do with him?" a younger man asked, scratching his head. "Put him in the coach?"

The men laughed.

Trusting his instincts but staying on guard, Beranger strode forward. He grasped the lead rope clipped to Diablo's halter and, as quickly as he could, unbuckled the harness, remembering his days of working in his father's stable. Then, keeping him an arm's length away, he led Diablo ten feet beyond the corral. "If any of you men try to catch him up, I'll find out, come back for my money, and then beat you to a bloody pulp. Is that understood?"

They nodded, happy with their pay.

"We won't. No, sir. Never. We hate that horse and are glad to see him gone for good."

Being cautious, Beranger ran his hand up and down Diablo's moist neck, talking quietly. The horse's black sides still heaved in and out as he sucked in lungsful of air. "You're free now, boy. No more running the Wells Fargo line. Or tasting the sharp end of the whip. Stay away from stage stops. Stay away from *all* men. Find yourself a herd to run with. Be smart and stay free."

*There you are, Beranger, boy. Wave goodbye to good ol' England. Don't worry, you'll find your sea legs soon enough, young chap. You're free now. Free! There's no feeling like it anywhere else in the world.*

"Mr. North!" the driver called angrily. "We're all loaded up. Move it."

Reaching up, Beranger unbuckled the halter, stepped back, and shouted. When the horse didn't take off directly but surprisingly reached out his muzzle, Beranger raised his arm, swinging the rope.

Diablo flung his head and galloped off in a cloud of dust.

Beranger's heart squeezed. "Run fast, Diablo. Run free . . ."

Carrying the halter and lead, he returned to the waiting stage. He rolled up the equipment and brought the leather items inside as Emma watched.

*What is she thinking?*

She'd insisted he take the window seat back some time ago, but other than that, she hadn't said more than a frightened yes and thank you when he'd offered to remove the spider he'd spotted crawling up her arm. He'd thought they'd made progress during dinner the other night, but was she still so disapproving of his presence in Mrs. Sackett's store?

Try as he might, he couldn't get the feel of her small waist out of his mind. She may have been throwing up, but he *was* a man. A fool who found himself attracted to her, which wasn't all that wise because of her obstinate nature. Even now, after all day in the stuffy coach and her bout of motion sickness, a light, airy lavender scent reached his nose whenever a slight breeze made it through the window. And it wasn't coming from anyone else but her. A nice distraction in a never-ending day. If she didn't seem to despise him so much, he'd try to draw her out. But he knew that was no good.

Distracting his thoughts from the third-eldest Brinkman daughter—who would soon fall asleep and nestle against his side—seemed wise. He glanced down at Diablo's rolled-up lead and halter, taking comfort from them. At least he'd done right by the gelding. Who knew? Perhaps someday he'd hear a song about a legendary horse that had once pulled a Wells Fargo stagecoach for forty or more miles a day and was now running free.

He smiled to himself, liking the thought. At least one of them would get something out of this journey.

# CHAPTER THIRTEEN

Every bone in Beranger's body ached as he followed the group of scraggly travelers into the Wells Fargo stage stop, hoping for a good supper. The rustic wooden furniture scattered about was well used. Red gingham curtains hung to the sides of the two small windows by a rod made from a tree branch. A cast-iron pot holder above the stove held a multitude of cooking utensils, pots, and frypans. The place was rather homey.

Riding a stagecoach for more than one hundred miles was not romantic. Only fools believed that. Unbeknownst to her, Emma had fallen asleep on Beranger's shoulder as the miles passed. He suspected she'd be angry, if she knew.

"Welcome! Welcome! Come in and get comfortable. My name's Cricket, and I'm glad to meet y'all."

*A woman!*

Although she was dressed like a man and looked as strong, two features gave her gender away: her voice and her eyes. Dark hair was shorn to just below her ears and was slicked back with some kind of oil. She wore men's boots and clothes.

"Hope you washed at the pump and bowl you passed on your way in. If you didn't bother, makes no never mind to me." She glanced at the table. "This all of you?"

"We got a sleeper in the coach," the driver said, stepping inside and closing the door. "Most likely he'll be in when the aroma floats his way."

She nodded and stirred the contents of the large kettle.

"May I help you with anything, ma'am?" Emma asked, her eyes at half-mast. She took a biscuit when the cook passed around the platter.

"No, you can't, honey. Just sit there and rest. As soon as you're eatin', I'm going to share with you how I became boss of this station."

Once everyone was served and more biscuits were cooking, Cricket, perched on a tall stool, began to spin a yarn.

Emma couldn't be happier. The food was delicious, and Cricket's storytelling abilities were razor sharp. She chanced a quick glance at Beranger across the table, taking note again of the different way he held his utensils.

Emma didn't know much about different cultures; her only exposure to a foreigner had been a Muslim man who used to sell papers on the corner back in Philadelphia. Each morning she'd run down for Vernon Crowdaire and give the man a nickel. He'd give her a paper, but only after he'd placed his hand on his heart and gave a little nod in greeting. The gentleman had always been kind, and she'd loved his accent. He was called Haji Baba, he had explained on a slow day, because he'd made the pilgrimage to Mecca several years before. But she'd never had a chance to share a meal with Haji Baba.

Had she and Beranger come to an unspoken truce? He'd stopped asking questions when she began responding monosyllabically. He glanced up from his plate and looked at her at that moment, as if he'd read her thoughts. She had to return a small smile or she'd be seen as rude, didn't she? She didn't want to do that. He was still a rake, but perhaps a nice rake, after what he'd done for that poor horse. Everyone in the coach had been impressed. She'd felt herself warming toward him. He'd seemed a little sad and introspective after letting the beast go. But she had to remember her wager, and *why* she'd made the bet with Belle. She had her own life and work to focus on. She didn't want to be beholden to a man, but rather independent, like Cricket.

Cricket cleared her throat, gaining everyone's attention as she began her next story. "It may surprise some of you to know that I was a mail-order bride. Not the typical kind, mind you. My destiny was arranged by an evil matron in the orphanage where I lived.

"Being all of fifteen years old, and a comely lass, I was bundled up and sent off to southern Nevada Territory, without any notion of what to expect.

116

When the driver called out the name of my town, I got off in the middle of nowhere. I stood on the side of the dirt road dumbfounded, for more minutes than I like to remember. The sign beside the rickety bench read PURGATORY, NEVADA. HOME OF HARD WORK AND SUNSHINE. I took that as a warning."

Cricket stood, set her coffee aside, and took a sheet of perfectly browned biscuits out of the oven. She set them on the counter to cool. "I'm not too proud to say I shed a fair number of tears that day. From fear. From anger. From feeling sorry for myself in the worst way. When my groom-to-be finally showed up three hours late, I was hungry and desperate. It took me all of one second to determine I wasn't getting hitched to that foul-smelling ol' billy goat. He smiled nice and friendly, but evilness peered at me hungrily from his beady black eyes. I tried to talk myself out of my instincts and blame my edginess on the magazine I'd found in the basement of the orphanage about ghouls and goblins, but he pretty much fit the description of everything that frightened me. He was old enough to be my grandfather, and as I learned on the ride to his broken-down farm, he'd paid fifty dollars for me with five gold eagle coins."

Emma stopped chewing. The story had turned to heartbreak. She thought of Brenda, and her new home with the Kenningstons.

*What if . . . ?*

She glanced up to find Beranger watching her.

He shook his head, seeming to read her thoughts. As if he wanted to reassure her. He'd been taken by Brenda at the dinner—they all had—and Belle had explained the reasons for her presence on the trip.

*Could a man who went out of his way to care about horses and children be as bad as she'd made him out to be?*

She lowered her gaze and reached for her water. "What happened next?" she asked softly, terrified to learn the answer.

"Did you and the old goat marry up?" Ester asked.

Cricket's eyes opened wide. "Look at me! Do I look stupid to you? As soon as he parked that buggy in front of what was a rat hole more than a house and ran his filthy hand along my thigh, his fingernails packed with so much dirt they could grow a patch of potatoes, I knew he wasn't waiting on nothin'. Not the preacher, not getting to know me, not letting me use the outhouse. When he climbed out of the wagon and came around to help me to the ground, I jammed my finger so far down my throat a tidal wave of sour-smelling bile gushed out. I didn't even try to get out of the way. I let the mess coat my dress, shoes, and his wagon."

Cricket burst into laughter and slapped her leg.

"You . . . you . . ." Grasping a napkin, she blotted away tears as her laughter continued. "You should have *seen* him. His ugly face screwed up in disgust as he jumped back, cussing every foul word under the sun. Although terrified by him, I gathered my courage and told him I'd been sick for several days and needed to lie down. That several girls at the orphanage had passed, and my fever was growing worse. As soon as he shut the bedroom door, I jumped up, grabbed my carpetbag, and jimmied open the rotting window casing."

"That was in Nevada," Ester said. "How did you come to be here? And your own boss as well?"

"I stayed hidden until it was safe for me to walk the road. I hitched rides by offering to do chores and cooking."

"Did you know how?"

"I'm a fast learner. Turnover at stage stops is frequent. Once I found one, I worked hard, kept my nose outta other people's business, and kept at it. After six months, and after I turned sixteen, a Wells Fargo boss gave me a promotion from helper to stage-stop boss. Imagine that. I was at that stop fourteen years, and was just offered this station last year, with a bonus in pay. I guess I'm moving up in the world." She beamed with pride. "For a woman, I ain't done too bad."

*No,* Emma thought, *not bad at all.*

Her gaze strayed once more to Beranger, who'd

pushed back from his place at the table and crossed his arms over his chest. Perhaps she shouldn't be so prickly toward him. He hadn't done anything directly to her to complain about— quite the opposite. He'd been a gentleman in every sense. That was worth remembering.

# CHAPTER FOURTEEN

After supper, Emma relaxed in a chair in the front of the stage stop, quietly looking at the stars. A campfire burned a few feet away, scenting the air with alder and smoke. The delicious fare tonight had revived her body and spirit. Tranquility settled all around. Everyone except Cricket and Beranger had gone in to bed. She thought of Brenda, and the many nights they'd snuggled together on the wagon trip out, feeling a tight smile curl her lips.

Emma pulled her shawl tighter and then tied the ends. She'd changed her dress after supper and rolled the soiled one into her carpetbag. She was wrinkled but clean. She would sleep in this garment—and wear it the rest of the journey home.

Quiet and peacefulness returned. The dark sky, alight with sparkling stars, seemed to stretch on forever. A chorus of coyotes began in the distance, yipping and singing so enthusiastically Emma smiled. She wondered where Beranger had taken himself off to.

"Are you ever lonely out here, Cricket? Or do you ever long for another kind of life?"

"Me? I had that other kind of life in the orphanage. I can tell you what, I didn't like it. And then I almost became a slave to a dirty old man. I like being my own boss, so to speak. No one around here tells me what to do."

*Mmm . . .*

"Besides, who could be lonely with all the people I meet?" Cricket asked. "I've spoken with the lowliest as well as the loftiest. My life is rich and fulfilled. I love cooking. That's all that I really want to do. What more could I want?"

*Indeed. What more?*

A thought struck Emma. "If you *do* ever long for something different, we have a bunkhouse of seven men, and we've been looking to hire a cook. The ranch hands have been handling it so far, but we've promised them a cook of their own. Plus, in the future, we're going to open a guest ranch, and we'll need a fine cook for that as well. The place is beautiful, and we have lots of women there—me and my four sisters. And our good friend Lara Marsh, who came up with the idea for the guest ranch. It's the Five Sisters Ranch, in Colorado."

When Cricket didn't respond, Emma turned in her direction to find her staring at her in the darkness.

*Is she considering saying yes?*

"Eden, Colorado?"

"That's right."

"I've heard that name before. And the Five Sisters Ranch."

"You have?"

"Maybe three or four months back. Like I said last night, before I got this station, I was working out of Los Angeles, out California way. A fella came through, not sure where he was from or where he was headed. Didn't talk much about himself, only about five young women who'd inherited a big spread in Colorado. Whenever he mentioned Eden, his face lit up like Christmas. He seemed to know a lot about your family—or more exactly, you girls. That fact struck me odd at the time, but I didn't want to pry. Didn't put two and two together about him and you until now."

Emma bolted straight in her chair, all the fatigue she'd thought she'd felt gone.

*Could this be the man who was responsible for all the articles?*

The mystery had haunted her and her sisters for months. "Really? What was his name? Someone ran a series of articles in a San Francisco newspaper about my family. How our father, who had built up this great ranch and holdings, had died and left the inheritance to us. How we were unmarried and looking for husbands, which wasn't the truth at all. We want to find who's responsible, but with little to go on, it has been like looking for a grain of salt on a beach. Please, Cricket, can you remember his name?"

Cricket stubbed out her cigar and put the remainder into her front shirt pocket.

123

"I feed so many people, see so many faces. From one day to the next, I can't rightly remember."

Excited and disappointed at the same time, Emma nodded. This was the closest any of them had been to discovering the person behind the articles. They knew the information had come from Lara Marsh's private diary. Suspicion had fallen on Lara's older brother, who had been home at the time for a visit. He'd sworn that it wasn't true.

"Does the name Harlow Lennington ring any bells?" Emma asked. It was the name the article's author had used.

The cook sat quietly. "That's a strange name. You'd think I'd remember that if I heard it." She shook her head dismally.

Emma laid a hand on Cricket's arm, feeling rife with urgency. "What about Vernon Crowdaire?"

She shook her head again. "I can't rightly say yes or no, Emma. I'm sorry."

"Then maybe what he looked like? How old was he? Maybe he's living in Eden right now under a different name. Maybe he's writing more articles at this very moment."

Cricket stared at the night sky for a long time. "Not yet middle age—or maybe in his late twenties. Brown hair, I think, possibly brown eyes." She shook her head. "It's hard to remember. Keep in mind, this could all be wrong. I'm not helping at all."

Disappointment pushed on Emma. "Maybe by morning you'll remember the name. My mind does that sometimes. But, regardless, you've given me hope that someday the mystery will be solved. Please consider my offer. Our men would appreciate you taking over."

A shadow of uncertainty crossed the woman's face. Perhaps Cricket really did like living out in the boondocks, away from any pretext of people or civilization, except for the few travelers she cooked for. Or was she in hiding? Was there someone out there looking for her?

Emma stood, knowing she best not push the subject too far. "Is it safe for me to stretch my legs a little? Just out to the corrals and back."

In the firelight, Cricket's face softened. "Sure is, sweetie. Just don't go no farther."

# CHAPTER FIFTEEN

Beranger, finished with his walk, started back toward the stage station. Emma had been so cool to him all day he wondered if he should avoid any and all contact between them from here on out. If she could speak in one-word sentences, then so could he—and enjoy doing it. She'd tried and convicted him with no basis at all. That had singed his pride. Made him think of his stepmother, something he tried never to do.

He spotted Emma by the corral fence. The light breeze played with her tresses, and the moonlight made them shine. It angered him to admit she looked gorgeous.

"Miss Brinkman? I'm surprised to find you out here alone." He expected a terse "women like to stretch their legs too," but instead her lips wobbled, and then she straightened.

"I lay down on my cot with good intentions of falling asleep, but my mind wandered. I miss Brenda. And I wonder how she's doing with her new family. And if . . ."

She pivoted away.

"If she misses you?"

Slowly, Emma turned back and looked up at him with the most tortured expression.

He knew the feeling, having run away at

thirteen, assuming he'd never see his father, his uncle, or even his half brother again. Perhaps his stepmother had been correct about his curse, and after he left finally was able to conceive another child. Did he have other half siblings? The fact that he didn't know bothered him more than he expected.

*Does anyone miss me?*

"She's settled in by now. Children are resilient," he said, speaking from experience. Time was a healer, as they say, and the pain of losing Brenda would lessen eventually for Emma as losing his family had for him. "Her brothers are keeping her busy with teasing and games, and her new mother is showering her with love—a love she's not had for years, if ever. As much as you miss her, you'd not want her to miss you. You want her to be so happy she doesn't give you a passing thought. In your heart, you know I'm right."

"You sound so sure of yourself."

On this topic, he was. "The family asked for her. The nuns made sure the household was kind and their intentions honorable. You have nothing to fear."

"Look, Beranger! Your horse!" Emma cried, her eyes now shining with excitement.

He jerked his gaze to the corral that had been empty when he'd started out, the gate swung open wide. He scanned the darkness, then spotted a black horse on the far side of the corral.

*Is Emma wrong? Or has Diablo actually fol-
lowed the stagecoach?*

The horse was surely Diablo. He smiled. "Well,
I'll be," he said, slowly circling the enclosure
to close the gate. As soon as he dropped the
latch, Diablo bolted down the fence, kicking and
bucking.

"Beranger," Emma gasped. "He followed you?
I can't believe it."

Beranger chuckled. "Looks that way. He must
have tracked the stagecoach these past sixty
miles. I'm amazed. Much better to run behind the
stage than pull it."

"Are you going to keep him now?"

"No. I'll set him free again in the morning.
But for now, I don't want him out getting into
trouble."

Diablo rushed the fence, then stopped by
Beranger's side. He slammed his front hooves
into the dirt, pawing madly. With a jerk of his
head, he bolted off and cantered the perimeter of
the corral, putting on a show for him and Emma.

*Me and Emma? That is a dangerous thought.*

"Why're you out here by yourself?" Beranger
asked, finding some irritation to chase away his
attraction. "I promised your sister and Blake I'd
watch out for you. It would be an inauspicious
start to my employment if you were bitten by a
rattler or trampled by a horse."

Her smile surprised him.

"Women like to stretch their legs too."

*Ha!* He almost let out a laugh.

"Cricket assured me I'd be safe if I went no farther than the corrals."

"The next time you want to walk, tell me."

"Why did you buy the horse and set him free, Beranger?"

*I saw something in him that we share—I don't know what. Just something . . .*

"Beranger?"

"It was the right thing to do. I overheard talk. The men were tired of his aggressiveness, and of having to be so watchful." Anger at what they'd planned roiled inside him. "They were going to kill him and claim he'd broken a leg."

She drew back in shock. "That's horrible."

"I agree."

She slowly approached the fence again, as if she were going to try to see inside the dark enclosure, but with a hand to her shoulder, he held her back.

"Stay away from the fence, Emma. He's fast. I don't want you to get hurt."

"Why did you let him go?"

"Wasn't much else I could do. I'd bring him to Eden if I could, but a horse can't run as far as a stage travels in one day without long rests. That's why they change horses every twenty miles."

"But won't someone catch him?"

"There's always that possibility. I can only hope he's smarter than that. I suspect he came in for water, after finding none along the way."

Diablo came to the fence, his muzzle wet.

Beranger laughed. "See?" He didn't need the problems this animal would bring, but he'd been compelled to act. He couldn't in good conscience close his eyes to his plight, as his father had done to Beranger's. "I'd like to put him out to pasture somewhere and let him be a horse. But with no way to get him to Eden . . ."

The gelding cantered the fence again, the signs of his mistreatment hidden by the darkness. But Beranger knew they were there, and what the horse had suffered.

"They say he never tires, and that's why Wells Fargo valued him. But I don't believe that. He tires, just like the rest of the team, but he keeps going anyway, keeps pushing through until he's given all he has to give. Someday, that toughness in him might kill him." Beranger had enough similar wounds on his soul to see them in others, even a horse. His own strength had kept him alive this long—working, moving, making his mark. Would there ever come a time in his life when he'd be able to settle in one place and feel he'd done enough?

Moved by Beranger's empathy for the horse, Emma patted his arm, and then let her hand slip away. He'd been nothing but kind to her, yet she'd rebuffed his every attempt. She'd never met anyone like him. He seemed like such a strong, fierce, and sometimes frightening man. Still, he was able to see the potential in a damaged horse. The dichotomy was quite amazing.

"How kind of you, Beranger," she said sincerely. "You've given the horse a second chance, something a lot of people never get." She strolled to a nearby log and sat down, not ready to enter the hot cabin and try to fall asleep.

He stared at her. "Shouldn't you go inside? It's late, and morning will be here sooner than you think. We still have two more days of travel."

"I will. Soon. I won't sleep even if I do go to bed now. Besides, the cool breeze is so nice. And the stars. We have the horse to entertain us, and we're plainly visible to anyone who might wonder." In a bold move, Emma patted the log next to her. "You have to admit this is much more pleasant than being inside. Most everyone needs a good bath, to be sure."

He chuckled but remained standing.

"Beranger, won't you sit for a minute? I'll sleep in the coach tomorrow." When she realized that was exactly what she'd done today, on his nice-smelling shoulder, and perhaps that was the reason why she was not able to sleep tonight, her face heated up.

Was he being shy because he was now an employee of the Brinkmans'? Or maybe English manners forbade such an action. She'd heard that the English were very proper. Exciting to think he'd sailed all the way across the ocean. More than anything, he was most likely missing his love.

He made a noncommittal sound, but finally sat.

"He's a beautiful black color," she said, changing the subject as the horse galloped by. "I think you should call him Charger. Diablo only reinforces his bad behavior in people's minds, and dictates how they'll treat him. He's magnificent. Charges everywhere he goes. Even loose in the corral. I think the new title fits him perfectly."

He gave her the queerest expression. She almost laughed.

"All right," he said, his voice melding with the crickets in the dry shrubbery, filling the night with their song. "Per your request, and from this moment on, Diablo's name shall be changed to Charger. But *not* for the reasons you've just stated. Rather because *charger* is another name for destrier, and that is exactly what the animal reminded me of when I first laid eyes on him in his harness in Santa Fe. Tall, strong, magnificent— possessing a heart filled with courage."

Wonder filled Emma. This *was* new. Exciting. "Destrier?" she pronounced slowly, trying to get the difficult word correct. "What is that?"

"A warhorse of the medieval era. In my father's home, there are many tapestries that have been

132

handed down through the generations. They go back hundreds of years. Very old, very beautiful. They depict times and events long past. One, in the dining room, takes up a whole wall. It tells a story from five hundred years ago, when certain men were trying to overthrow their duke, call him my great-great-great-great-grandfather. Knights in full body armor, bristling with weapons, ride into battle aboard their massive warhorses. Those destriers were as much warriors as their riders, tough enough not to run from the noise and the danger, and strong enough to carry steel-plated men-at-arms on their backs. Seasoned warhorses wore scars like badges of honor on their thick legs and broad chests, just like the gelding in this corral. If Charger were still a stallion . . . I have no illusions. We'd not be able to handle him at all."

Fascinating. The knowledge made her wonder what had changed his course and brought him to America. "I'm not sure what man-at-arms means, except for how it sounds."

"You're correct. A knight."

She breathed out. Was Beranger descended from a knight? That sounded even more exciting than a duke. The clashing of massive blades, drinking rich bitter ale from silver goblets, and marching off to war without a care in the world . . .

A small smile played around his lips. "The terms *knight* and *man-at-arms* can be used interchangeably only to a certain extent, for every knight was a man-at-arms, but not every man-at-arms could be called a knight. Some were plain old soldiers or mercenaries. Are you an experienced horsewoman, Emma?"

"Not like my sister Belle. But I do have my own mount at the ranch. Dusty's a long-legged chestnut gelding that Trevor says was never very good at cutting. He has a small white star, and I'm truly taken with him." She looked up into the stars, missing the ranch. From the corner of her eye she studied Beranger. "You must have a good deal of experience to be able to handle Charger the way you do, with how difficult and dangerous he is. The other men keep far away from him."

"They're smart to. He has a reputation."

"Beranger, won't you share with me how you've come to know so much about horses and how to handle them? Did you learn that here in America, or back home in England?" She thought she saw him tense up. "But only if you want to."

He stared up at the moon for so long she didn't think he was going to go on. Then he turned and looked into her eyes.

"I have to tell you my big, dark secret if I do. Can I trust you?"

Her eyes grew round. She nodded.

"Something I failed to say the other night at supper was that while I'm the second son of a duke, I'm an *illegitimate* son. It's not uncommon in England. Most aristocrats have a few unclaimed children dotting the countryside. Their wives look the other way for the most part and pretend the other women or their husband's bastard children don't exist. I was luckier."

Shocked and humbled that he was sharing such an intimate detail with her, she remained silent, hoping he'd go on.

"When I was only a baby, my mother passed. As soon as my father learned that, he brought me to live in his castle. My father and mother had been in love before he married the duchess. My stepmother was an arranged marriage he was unable to avoid. I was fortunate, I guess, that I lived at Ashbury at all. Most children born out of lineage are usually put to work in some commoner's job and left to fend for themselves. As I grew older, my stepmother suggested I should work with the horses. At four or five, I was feeding them treats and mucking out the stalls. When a bit older, I was grooming, feeding, and polishing tack. By the time I was ten, I could gallop over hill and dale, hunting and jumping fences."

A whisper of a smile actually crossed his face. That was clearly a good memory for him. She wondered about the rest. She thought of the Crowdaires, and how they'd treated her and her sisters as if they were pint-size servants. Her face heated with shame. She'd even seen Velma accidentally-on-purpose knock her cup to the floor just to have Lavinia jump to her feet and wipe up the mess. For some reason, she'd not like him to know that shameful part of her life. But then she wondered if, despite his more illustrious upbringing, that was how he felt as well.

"I see. Well, your father must have been proud of you for that."

"If he was, he never said so. But my uncle made up for that. Uncle Harry gave me what my father couldn't—or wouldn't. I continued to watch our trainer, working the young stock and stallions. He treated them with respect but was firm. The horses understood him. He was killed in a pub, and the new stable manager they brought in from one of my father's country estates only knew how to be cruel. The stallions that had once been manageable turned vicious, retaliatory. By the time my father believed what I was telling him, many of the horses were ruined. The sneakiness couldn't be trained out of them. And they had to be replaced."

"That's dreadful, Beranger. What happened to them?"

"The studs were worth a great deal of money, so they were sent to another of my father's estates to be used for breeding. The geldings and mares were sold to tradesmen to be used in front of a cart or wagon—to be put to real work, I'd guess you'd say."

She sensed his sadness at the memory, and now she felt she knew why he'd taken to Charger.

He turned and drilled her with a look. "I have a question for you, now that we're becoming so friendly. Why is it you dislike me so much? I'm traveling quite a long ways to take this job for your family. If you intend to make things difficult for me, I'd rather know why now."

She bolted to her feet, wanting to protest, but she could hardly deny his claims. She'd spent most of the day making sure he knew where he stood.

He stood as well. "Don't deny it."

"All right, I won't. As long as you don't deny that I saw you yesterday with Delphine—standing in a lovers' embrace. From what Mrs. Sackett shared about your character, I don't think your intentions toward Delphine are honorable. That's all."

"That's all?"

She didn't know if he was angry, or if she'd shocked all speech from the man.

He threw back his head and laughed at the moon.

Irritation streaked up her spine. She liked to be laughed at as much as anyone else. "What's so funny?"

"You!"

"I'm only looking out for Delphine and Mrs. Sackett."

"You have no idea what you saw. Or what you're talking about."

Charger had moved to the corral fence and was watching them over the top rail.

"You're a rake, Beranger North. Plain and simple. You have no qualms about ruining a girl's reputation and leaving her in tears—just look at Delphine. And besides that, you're a gambler, and who knows what else? I question if you're the right man for our mine."

"So you not only spied on me with Delphine, but with Letherson as well? I'm impressed."

The little minx had a lesson coming. With her angry, flashing eyes, it was all he could do to hold back from kissing that look right off her face. She heated his blood more than any woman he'd ever met—but she also made him angrier than any woman he'd ever met. Perhaps he should run the other way, but he'd never been a quitter. Nothing he loved more than a good challenge.

"And what do you believe you saw when you were eavesdropping on me, pray tell?"

She lifted her chin. "You were consoling her after breaking her heart. You must have been scared off after Mrs. Sackett asked about your intentions and hinted for you to leave her shop."

"She didn't ask me to leave—you did."

"She wanted to."

"For your information, Delphine has been

138

flirting with me for weeks. That day was the first time I'd entered her shop, only because she grabbed my arm as I passed and dragged me inside. When you came to the counter, *she* was inviting *me* to a place young lovers go to steal a few kisses. Now say you're sorry."

She stared at him.

"I mean it, Emma. Do you believe me?"

She hesitated, defiant, but then a look of chagrin came over her face. "I do. What about her tearful goodbye?"

"Again, I was going about my business, having just visited an old friend, and I ran into her. When she again asked about seeing me in secret, I informed her that I could not. That I was leaving town."

"And the embrace?"

"I was consoling her."

"I see."

He wondered about her spirited reaction to his involvement with Delphine.

*Is she giving me the cold shoulder to hide her own attraction? That's an intriguing thought.*

Charger tossed his head. When Beranger looked his way, the horse snorted and ran off.

"He needs to settle down and get some rest."

She didn't respond.

"We're bothering him, Emma. He pulled the stage for forty miles today, with only a few breathers in between, and then followed us miles more. That's unheard of. It couldn't have been easy."

She just stood there.

"Emma, we're keeping him up."

"Oh! You should have spelled it out sooner." She took a small step away, searching the corral. "Good night, Charger," she whispered. "I'll see you in the morning."

Beranger watched her go, enjoying the defiance she showed by saying goodnight to the horse but not to him. She wasn't ready to concede that she'd been wrong about him just yet. But he was going to enjoy it when she did.

# CHAPTER SIXTEEN

Emma groaned when someone shook her shoulder. When she didn't move, the hand gripped more tightly and pushed back and forth more briskly. "Miss Brinkman. Wake up! Everyone has eaten."

*Ester.*

Emma's eyes flew open. Sleep had eluded her after last night's disturbing conversation. Thoughts of Beranger filled her head. And his claims about Delphine. Had she really been so wrong about him? If she had, she'd done him a grave injustice. Still, the fact that he had not been dallying with Delphine's affections, as he claimed, did not take away the reputation he had otherwise gained around Santa Fe for being a rake.

Worrying about Beranger last night had not been the only thing that had robbed her of sleep. A flimsy sheet was the only barrier separating the women from the men. Loud snores, which sounded much like they came from Mr. Tug, had resonated all night. Putting her pillow over her head didn't help at all.

*How on earth will I survive another two nights?*

"I can't get up," she groaned. "I'm exhausted. I don't think I've slept more than five minutes."

"You have to if you want to eat," Ester said, her blue gaze troubled. "Cricket said this is last call, and the stage will be leaving soon. There's warm water at the wash stand for you to use."

Emma, still dressed, gathered her carpetbag and hurried outside. She ignored Beranger, who was standing by the corral fence. Charger, she thought with a smile, stood close by.

Finished, she ran into the building. "I'm sorry I'm late."

Cricket set a full plate before her.

Emma shoveled in two large bites of the leftover stew, followed by a mouthful of biscuit. She chewed and swallowed quickly, bringing to mind the stray dogs Lavinia sometimes fed behind the restaurant that seemed to chew and swallow at the same time, wolfing down any tidbit she threw out. Finished with her stew, she wiped the leftover gravy with the second half of her biscuit, and down the hatch that went as well. She found herself enjoying eating fast without Mavis around to scold her. With a smile on her face and the grace of a lumberjack, she cut her fried egg with the side of her fork and stabbed up the wobbly white drenched with the dark-orange egg yolk.

"Load up!" came the shout from outside.

She stood and snatched up a lonely strip of bacon from the center platter. "Goodbye, Cricket. Thank you for everything—the food, the information. And I meant what I said about you coming to Eden. Please consider my offer. We *need* you at the Five Sisters!"

# CHAPTER SEVENTEEN

*Eden, Colorado*

*This is one part of the new mayor's job I'm* not *going to enjoy,* Mavis thought, *but I did promise to see to the education of the children, and that means making sure they have a good and fair teacher, nothing less.*

Walking at Clint's side toward the schoolhouse, a multitude of butterflies exploded in Mavis's stomach. The cause wasn't Clint's charming good looks, even though he was exceptionally handsome today. Mr. Lake, the schoolteacher, was an early riser even when school was out. He'd be in the vacant schoolhouse as he usually was, doing whatever he did all day long. Speaking with him before the town council meeting on Wednesday was crucial. She'd consulted with several mothers, who'd confirmed what Jeremy had reported. Mr. Lake needed to have his chance of rebuttal, and after that . . .

Eden needed a spirited teacher. One who filled the children with curiosity and a desire to learn. With the right instructor, school could be fun. She didn't have anything against Mr. Lake's age, but his temperament was another story. They had to think of the children above all else.

The crunch of their boots on the dry road mingled with the call of several mourning doves. She dropped her gaze to her bare hands, which held the ledger she now carried around with her most of the time. She had Clint to thank for the absence of gloves as well. Once he had seen her secret and not judged her for it, her missing finger had lost its shame. She breathed deeply of the crisp morning air, feeling content and happy.

Clint's hand touched hers. "Look who's coming."

Mavis drew her gaze from the glorious San Juan Mountains. A man approached. He was towing a wagon with tall, wobbly wheels.

"Who's that?" Her steps slowed as she took in the sight. A cape hung from the man's shoulders and was fastened with a buckle at his neck. The garment fell all the way to his feet, and a wide-brimmed hat that had netting bunched on the brim was held under an arm. His shoulder-length, light-colored hair was shaggy. His feet were bare. His whole appearance brought to mind John the Baptist coming in from the desert.

"You don't know?"

She shook her head.

"Eden's beekeeper. Jack Sprat."

She gaped at him.

"That's right," Clint said with a chuckle. "Now wipe that look off your face so you don't hurt his feelings."

"I've heard tell of a beekeeper, but we've never met."

"He's a nice fellow, though we see little of him." When the man was within hearing distance Clint called out, "Good to see ya, Jack. The thought of making a welfare trip up to your place has beleaguered me. I'm glad you've saved me the trip."

A wide grin stretched Jack's face. As he got closer, Mavis realized he was much younger than she'd originally thought.

"I don't have much reason to come to town." He glanced toward the mercantile and then hitched a thumb toward the hotel. "But I've brought some early honey." He gave Mavis a tip of his hat.

"This is John Brinkman's eldest daughter, Mavis Applebee."

The pride in Clint's voice warmed her. She resisted the urge to hide her hand from the new fellow. Her life had changed so much, and all for the better.

"Mrs. Applebee's the new mayor," Clint continued. "Mavis, this is Jack Sprat. Took up his pa's passion for bees a handful of years ago. He supplies the café and mercantile with the sweetest honey you've ever tasted."

Jack pushed aside his cape to reveal lightweight tan pants and a ragged white shirt. "I'd heard about you, Mrs. Applebee, but haven't had the pleasure of making your acquaintance yet. I'm delighted to remedy that today. I do deal with your sister Lavinia at the café."

Now the long cape and the netting fastened to his hat brim made perfect sense. "I'm fascinated," she said. "May I ask a silly question?"

"It's not silly at all. I rarely get stung," he said before she was able to voice her question. "Only if I make fast, unexpected movements. My bees know me well. If I startle them, they let me know with a buzz around my head, or even a sting."

Mavis thought she detected him holding his body in a strange way. "I see." She glanced up at Clint to find him smiling at her.

"That was my first question too, when we met," he said. "And most likely why Jack has a ready answer. What's kept you from coming down the mountain for so long? You're usually in twice a year."

He pulled up the lower portion of his sleeve. Mavis gasped.

Long, angry-looking red lines ran down his left arm. Some of the wound had crusted over, but not all. He had a salve of some sort covering most of it.

Clint scowled. "What happened? Those look bad."

"Had a disagreement with a young bear sniffing around my honeycomb. I wasn't in the mood to share."

Mavis shuddered at the sight. She couldn't tell if the wounds were infected, but they were severe enough that she knew he was lucky to be alive.

"Now that he's had a taste, he'll be back at some point. Every bear I've ever known has a sweet tooth he can't resist. When he decides to try again, I'll be ready. Next time, he won't take me by surprise."

"You need me to organize a bear hunt?"

Jack shook his head. "I'll deal with him as my pa used to, and his pa before him—one on one. The bear's family was in those mountains before we were. He's got the right to be there. There's a chance something else will distract him, and that's the last I've seen of him. I'm hoping, anyway."

"Be sure to see Eden's new doctor before you leave. Dr. Gannon took over for Dr. Dodge, and is in the same building," Mavis ordered.

Jack nodded, and a ghost of a smile pulled at his lips. "I'll do that, ma'am. I'm no dummy." He gently rubbed his hand over the sleeve covering his arm. "This gets to aching sometimes. I don't want blood poisoning."

"Be sure to stop in after you see the doctor and before you hike back up that mountain," Clint said. "I'd like a chance to talk."

As Jack nodded, a bee appeared, circled his head once, and then whizzed out of sight. He lifted a shoulder at Mavis's widened eyes.

"A friend?" she asked.

He nodded and started away. "I can't go anywhere without being followed."

"You be sure and come by," Clint called to his back as Jack continued toward the mercantile, and she and Clint proceeded toward the schoolhouse and the unpleasant task ahead. The man waved his good arm in salute.

"How scary," Mavis said. "I haven't heard much about bears, and now we have to deal with a different kind of bear. What if Mr. Lake refutes Jeremy's claims? What do we do then?" she asked, hoping Clint had answers. He'd been dealing with Eden's citizens for years. That thought gave her some peace in her moment of panic. "Can the town council force his retirement? I really don't know, and I'm not looking forward to finding out."

Confrontation wasn't her greatest strength, and neither was hurting someone's feelings. But there were issues that needed to be addressed. What if Mr. Lake got so angry he had an attack of some kind and died right there on the spot? She'd not like to have that on her conscience at all.

Clint nudged her with his arm as they walked along. "Don't look so glum. Everything's going to work out, Mavis. People get old. He'll most likely feel relieved."

"But how will he survive?"

"He's been the teacher for years and has never gone anywhere or bought anything lavish. I'm sure he has a pile of savings under his bed. We'll cross that bridge if we have to. Look, here comes your little sister. Is she feeling better? I'm not used to seeing any Brinkmans without a smile."

Katie waved. Jackie, from the orphanage, walked beside her, looking glum. Two red braids hung to the eight-year-old's shoulders and were tied off with blue bows. As they got closer, Mavis noticed Katie's puffy eyes and her sallow skin. She appeared thinner than normal and listless. Mavis didn't know what Katie would do if Santiago didn't return soon.

"Good morning," Katie said when they reached Mavis and Clint's side. She put her arm over Jackie's shoulders. Her usually sparkling blonde hair was a little dull and wound into a bun on the back of her head. "Jackie and I are on our way to see the dentist. She's finally getting her false tooth fitted."

Jackie's lips trembled. Self-conscious of her missing front tooth, she smiled with her lips closed and twisted a short length of twine in her fingers. And Katie's smile didn't reach her eyes, confirming Mavis's suspicions that she hadn't slept much again. Her sister was worrying herself sick. She wanted the happy Katie back. Everyone missed her.

"Isn't this usually Lavinia's job? Seeing to her little friends, I mean?" Mavis asked, and winked at Jackie. Lavinia loved helping out at the orphanage and spent almost all her free time there. On any given fair-weather day, you'd see her and a gaggle of orphans headed up the path to the upper meadow for a picnic. "I hope Dr. McGrath is in his office."

Since Russell McGrath had arrived in town, the dentist, in his midtwenties, had been making friends faster than he'd been fixing teeth. Wherever Mavis went, she'd find him chatting up whomever. He seemed almost too friendly for his own good. But, one by one, people were beginning to remember to go see him instead of the town barber—so he must be doing something right. Eden owed the young dentist a large dose of gratitude. Not only had he brought modern dentistry to town, but looking to make investments, he had purchased several of the small buildings around his office in the cobblestone area that were now empty.

Katie smiled and lifted her brows. "No worries on that count; we have an appointment. And I offered to fill in for Lavinia today because she wasn't feeling too well. I hope Jackie doesn't mind too much."

The child shook her head, looking positively terrified. "Oh no, Miss Brinkman"—the word *miss* whistling slightly—"I like seeing you." More whistles, and she looked at Mavis's feet.

Mavis's face warmed at the child's plight. "You must be excited to finally get your tooth fixed."

"No, Mrs. Applebee." Her face reddened this time on the whistle. "I'd rather not go. But

Miss"—another whistle—"Lavinia and Sister Cecelia"—several more—"say"—more again—"I have to. That I'll be glad when I'm older."

Mavis and Katie exchanged a look.

"But the hard part is over," Katie interjected softly. "The poking around and forming of the mold. Today will be as easy as pie. And I'll stay and hold your hand." She rubbed Jackie's back comfortingly as she gazed into her eyes. "We'll get through this together."

Katie would make a wonderful mother someday. Helping others was a good way to forget one's owns problems. Jackie was good medicine for her.

Everyone nodded. Mavis picked up Jackie's hand and patted the top. "You'll do fine. I hear Dr. McGrath is very gentle, so you have nothing to fear." She winked. "And you'll have Katie by your side watching his every move. She's a fierce protector, better than Joan of Arc."

Katie laughed. "Or maybe she'll get some laughing gas. We've heard all about it. That might be fun."

"Speaking of doctors," Clint said. "Dr. Gannon was asking about you today, Katie. He hadn't seen you around on his daily walks." He lifted a suggestive eyebrow.

*Oh, Clint. That's not the way to raise Katie's spirits. Speaking about one man is not as good as speaking about another. They are not*

151

*interchangeable,* Mavis thought. *Men can be so naïve sometimes, even if they mean well.*

Katie's smile faded, and she scanned the street.

*She's looking for Santiago again. It's as if she's lost a part of herself.*

"I can't imagine why," Katie finally said, agitated. "Anyway, we'd better go, Jackie. We don't want to keep Dr. McGrath waiting."

Mavis watched them walk away and then turned to Clint.

His expressive brows shot to the clouds. "What?"

# CHAPTER EIGHTEEN

For Beranger, the miles rolled by more quickly with the passage of each hour. Conversation in the stagecoach waxed and waned. Mr. Tug sat silently with his hands clutched to the handle of the cloth carpetbag, which had begun to exude an obnoxious odor, detectable infrequently, thank God, and yet still unpleasant. Jimbo, still feeling the sharp edges of all the whiskey he'd consumed the day before, sat stone-faced and grumpy. Ester knitted while her sister slept on her shoulder. Emma said very little. She only spoke to the sisters, and seemed lost in thought.

The rocking coach lulled his mind, and the feel of Emma by his side made him dream of a life that wasn't his. His eyes drooped to half-mast. Noon had come and gone. They had one more stop before the last twenty miles.

Beranger stretched taller and stuck the telescope to his eye. There she was! America. And his fresh start, his new life. They'd be docking in Virginia as soon as this storm would let them.

The ship rocked up, smashing into an enormous wave that seemed to push them back. Beranger grabbed a nearby rope and

153

quickly tied the line around his waist.

"Oh no you don't!" he shouted into the wind. "I've served my time. Four years, to be exact." He was seventeen now. He lowered the captain's spyglass and collapsed it in his palm, placing the tool back into a cherrywood case.

"I'm gonna miss ya, lad," Nelson Wadlly said sadly, his legs spread wide to keep his balance. The boatswain eyed Beranger's safety rope and shook his head. The old salt would never have bothered to tie himself down.

"I'll miss you as well, Wadlly, but I've served faithfully. Now I'm off to make my name."

"And ya will, lad. With eyes like yours, you'll make your mark. Others may scoff, but I say they's darn good luck. After ya came aboard, we really flourished. Till then, we was barely chugging along. Won't you reconsider yer decision? Cap'n won't say so, but he's gonna miss ya as well."

"Ha! Why should I? A man can't sail the seas forever. Why, I've been—"

A mighty wave crested over the tall masts, then they were hit with another, and another. America became smaller and smaller on the tilting horizon. The wind screamed in Beranger's ears. The thick rope he clutched to keep from being pitched over the rail dug into his flesh. In an agonizing moment, he watched as the boatswain, his protector on the ship since Beranger was a thirteen-year-old boy, was swept overboard. The man clung to the side of the ship, clawing and scratching to make purchase.

Beranger yelled and lunged forward, trying to save his friend. With one arm wrapped around a railing post, he leaned down to extend his arm as far as he could. Wadlly looked up, frantic, fear etched on his face. Then Wadlly's eyes changed, melding from a dark brown to a deep green rimmed with gold. Emma Brinkman's eyes, Beranger realized as Wadlly disappeared under the crashing waves, his flailing arms the last part of him to go down.

"No!" Beranger lunged forward, clutching vainly for an arm, a handful of material, anything. When his grasp finally loosened, he slumped back into his seat, heartbroken. Wadlly was gone. And now Emma Brinkman too.

"Mr. North, wake up!"

Beranger jerked open his eyes. The air, weighty like a wool blanket that had been left out in the rain, made him cough. The smell from Mr. Tug's carpetbag was almost insufferable. He must have food inside—cheese, or something that had begun to rot. The three across from him sat wide-eyed as if he'd just doused them with a bucket of water. From the look on Peggy's face, and the way she held her hand to her cheek, he realized he must have struck her with his right hand while he was dreaming. Now, to his relief, he remembered Mr. Wadlly had not gone overboard after all. That had just been a nightmare.

"You were dreaming," Emma said.

"I'm sorry, Miss Nunes," he said gruffly. "Did I hurt you?"

"Not too much," Peggy said, bringing her hand back down to her lap. "I'll live to see another day."

"We'll be stopping soon," Emma said. "You should have some water and take a walk. You were mumbling something about a storm and a wave, and perhaps something terrible that happened. Do you remember?"

He shook his head.

"That bag reeks." Jimbo's eyes narrowed and his mouth screwed up in a nasty scowl.

Ester stopped knitting.

Peggy's brow creased.

So soon after his outburst, everyone's nerves were agitated.

"What's in there, anyway?" Jimbo asked. "Open up and let me see."

"Go to hell," Mr. Tug replied in a scratchy voice. He kept his gaze forward, staring straight into Beranger's face without seeming to see him.

Jimbo leaned forward. "I've a right to know. Show me. Show us all. I think you have a rotting carcass in there—nothing else could smell so much in this heat. I'm gonna pitch that thing out the window in one second."

Beside Beranger, Emma tensed and pressed closer to his side. She was clearly frightened. If Mr. Tug had a gun in that bag as well as whatever was stinking to high heaven . . . by the look on his face he was about ready to pull it out and blow Jimbo's head off.

Peggy reached for her sister's hand.

Ester dropped her stilled needles to reciprocate.

Suddenly and with lightning speed, much faster than Beranger would have thought possible in the kid's hungover state, Jimbo pulled his revolver from his low-slung holster and shot three rounds out the window.

The women screamed.

The coach jerked, then veered off the road for a moment or two, rumbling and bumping through the dirt, rocks, and ruts. The women screamed again as their heads slammed against the front and back panels. Dust billowed. Everyone clung to whatever was handy that would keep them in their seats.

The coach regained the road.

Emma had thrown her arms around Beranger's

neck and buried her face in his chest. Her body was soft and warm, and he clutched her instinctively as the stagecoach tumbled them about.

Mr. Tug must have feared this was an attack on him to get his bag, because he doubled over his lap to hug his belongings. Tug's face was red as he roared curse words at Jimbo.

Jimbo lifted the weapon again.

Beranger lunged across Emma and grabbed the gun, smoke burning his eyes. A moment passed before the troublemaker realized what had transpired.

"You fool!" Beranger barked. "What do you think you're doing?" The acrid bite of gunpowder hung in air already heavy with the stink of the carpetbag. "This coach could have tipped over or landed in a ditch. Speak up before I toss you out the door."

"Settle down, big man," Jimbo replied angrily, staring at his gun, which was still warm in Beranger's palm. "I had to let off some steam before I did worse." He glared at Tug. "That ain't against the law." He held out his hand. "Now give me back my Colt!"

The guard appeared in Mr. Tug's window. "Who's shooting?"

"Him!" Both sisters pointed.

The guard narrowed his eyes. "The next time that happens, Mr. Lance, you'll be in the dirt watching us roll away. Understand?" The guard stared at him until Jimbo nodded.

Beranger handed him back his gun.

"Beranger, you aware that crazy horse has been galloping behind the stage?" the guard said. "The gunshots spooked him, and he's gone, but he's been appearing on and off since the last stop."

Shocked, Beranger stuck his head out his window. He looked around but didn't see Charger. He sank back inside amid a warm rush of sentimentality.

Emma actually rubbed his arm.

"I had no idea," Beranger said. "My intention was to set him free."

"I'll give you double what you paid for him." The story of the horse's endurance had clearly gotten around to the driver and guard. "Just his size alone is intimidating. But stamina like that is unheard of."

Emma leaned forward. "He's not for sale."

"She's right," Beranger agreed.

"Everything's for sale for the right price. How about triple? You'll never do better than that, or turn him over so quickly. That's a lot of money." The coach jolted over some rocky ground, and the guard had to scramble to stay aboard.

"Have a care out there," Beranger said. "Like Miss Brinkman said, Charger's not for sale today or ever. Looks like he may be coming with me to Eden after all." He chanced a quick look at Emma to find her smiling warmly. Then her knee nudged his.

*Perhaps rakes aren't so deplorable to her after all.*

The guard disappeared, and Beranger glanced out the window. He watched the dry, sandy landscape give way, here and there, to scenery of trees, some rolling hills, and a blessed coolness that lightened his spirit. At any time, Charger might meet a herd of wild horses and be distracted, but something inside him hoped that wouldn't happen.

*Charger. Eden. A new start.*

# CHAPTER NINETEEN

*Eden, Colorado*

Santiago rode into Eden weary of heart, gritty, and hot. The three-hundred-mile ride through Utah had him anxious to clean up and find Katie, his ray of sunshine, and feel her lips against his. As soon as he was presentable, he'd go in search of her and let her know just how much he'd missed her.

"Santiago, my boy!" Miguel Alvarado chortled when Santiago trudged through the back door of the Spanish Trail Cantina, sweaty and grimy from the hard push of his final day on the trail. His father pressed away from the table and stood, embracing his son. They stayed that way for several seconds. When Miguel finally stepped back, he searched Santiago's face. "Welcome home. I did not wish to lose another son. Did you see Demetrio? How is he? How does he look?"

*How honest should I be? Hearing the truth may be too hard on Father.*

In reality, he'd been shocked by Demetrio's appearance. His brother had appeared in leg irons and handcuffs, thirty pounds thinner, and with dark circles under his eyes. The spirit was gone from his eyes, his head was shaved, and his back bowed. If Santiago hadn't been expecting him to look altered, he would not have recognized him.

"Sí. I saw him. He sends you his love. He lives so someday he can return."

"You didn't answer my question. How is he? How does he look? I am his father. Please don't keep anything back."

"He's painfully thin, and downcast, but swears he'll live to come home. He will see his papa again before he dies."

With the back of his hand, Miguel wiped tears from his eyes and then paced the length of the kitchen. When he stopped, fire burned in his gaze. "I want to go see him myself. I feel he has given up."

"You cannot. The trip is long. The men won't let you in. We have to wait until his sentence is served."

"Ten more years! I may not live that long. I had hoped for a miracle. I have comfort that he knows we have not forgotten him." He rounded the table and placed his hands on the spot that belonged to Demetrio. "My son lives. And he will return. But what a price he's paid for falling in with the wrong group. For holding the horses while they robbed another."

"A man was murdered, Father."

"*Patrón!*" the bartender called from the cantina on the other side of the door. "*Patrón*, please come."

Miguel Alvarado turned, and Santiago followed. Both men stood straighter when they saw the vision standing in the light of the open front door.

"Larsala Zelinga," Santiago whispered, wondering if he was seeing things, or if Demetrio's love actually stood in the cantina looking like the angel he remembered. He blushed at the sound of awe in his voice, embarrassed. He was a man now, no longer a heartsick boy. She had been Demetrio's sweetheart since they were small children, and they had planned to wed as soon as she turned sixteen. But unbeknownst to her, her father had promised her to a man in Arizona, a lucrative arrangement. When she turned fifteen, the family had packed and moved.

The Alvarados never saw Larsala again. Until today.

Now here she was, home in Eden, dressed in mourning but as beautiful as ever.

"Larsala Zelinga *Salazar,*" his father corrected, using the full name he'd learned from Larsala's aunt, Maria Gonzales, who maintained a fire where she sold tortillas and beans. Miguel rushed forward to take the woman's hands. "You return. You are more beautiful than anything this old man has seen! Welcome home."

And she was. Even more beautiful than the day her father had taken her away, her face covered in tears, crying and grasping at air as the cart she was riding in bumped down the trail. She'd

163

screamed her outrage only once, and then tasted the back of her father's hand.

The years had been good to her, though, and by the quality of her dress—and the two tall armed guards by her side—her husband had provided well for her in the land of the sun. Santiago hadn't thought that he'd ever see Larsala again, and certainly not here in Eden.

His father kissed both of Larsala's cheeks and then stepped away for Santiago to do the same.

Santiago took her hands in his own, noting how cold, small, and soft they were. "Beautiful," he breathed out, still dazed at her appearance.

All the old memories rushed back with a vengeance. Demetrio, Larsala, and him, running through the upper meadow, emerald green and filled with flowers. The three of them carefully crossing the river, where there were stepping-stones aplenty. The three of them climbing trees, playing tag, and swinging on the walking bridge by the mill.

And then as they grew older, three turned into two, Demetrio and Larsala sneaking behind the church after Mass to kiss and hold hands, unaware that Santiago had followed and watched with a broken heart. The two of them watching the sunset over the mountains, asking Santiago to run home to fetch something so they could be alone.

"I see you're still the flatterer, my Santiago. So

many times, I've thought of you over the years. I see you are as handsome as Demetrio now—no, more so, I think." She gazed up into his eyes, the top of her head barely reaching his shoulders. "And so tall. When did you sprout up? You were not this tall when you were sixteen and one year my senior. That makes twenty-four."

*She remembers my age when she'd left! What else does she remember? Has she had any feelings for me at all? Is she still married? Or are her widow's weeds for the husband, who was fifteen years older?*

"I grew my nineteenth year, to my great relief," he said. "I didn't want to always be eye to eye with the *chicas.*"

She laughed, and every man in the room smiled, Santiago as well.

"Demetrio?" she asked again.

"We will talk in the kitchen," his father said, never speaking about Demetrio's business in front of others.

"Of course." She turned to her men. "Stay here. I'm in no danger in the Alvarado home."

*Danger? What does that mean?*

Santiago said nothing but strode forward to open the door for her. Once they were inside their personal quarters and alone, his father said, "I'm sorry to be the one to tell you, Larsala, but Demetrio found trouble five years ago. He's now in prison."

She sucked in a breath. "Where? For how long?"

"He has served five of his fifteen years. Santiago has just returned minutes ago from seeing him, in fact."

Her gaze darted to Santiago. "How is he?"

"He's alive. And desires to be home. Once you left town, Demetrio changed."

When she paled, Santiago pulled out a chair. She crumpled down like a limp rag, burying her face in her hands.

"I was unable to write, to send him anything. I was closely watched. I did not know he took my leaving so hard."

She withdrew a handkerchief from the small, black reticule attached to her gloved wrist and dabbed at the corner of her eyes.

"I'm so sorry, Miguel," she said softly, calling his father by his given name. She was no longer a young girl but a woman of high standing, if her clothing and escorts meant anything. "Maybe if I had not gone away, if I had stood up to my father, my family, this would not have happened. Poor Demetrio. My heart breaks to think of him penned up like an animal."

"It is in God's hands now," Miguel said, as he did often. "All we can do is pray. Demetrio knows of our love since Santiago made the long trip to see him. We must be patient. We must not despair."

She nodded, but her eyes filled with tears.

Miguel laid a calming hand on her arm. "Tell us about you, Señora Salazar, your life since you left us. Why are you wearing black?"

Santiago looked at the door that separated them from the men in the cantina, waiting for their mistress to return. Was she staying in Eden? Or was this just a short trip to see her lost love? Santiago felt a sudden urge to make sure that she stayed.

"My life has been good. I cannot complain. My hacienda is one of the nicest in the area. But I never adapted to the heat and dust in Arizona, and I longed for the San Juan Mountains many, many times."

"And your husband?" Santiago asked, unable to wait for her to get to the subject.

"As you must have guessed, my husband, Mr. Salazar, has passed away. Three months ago."

*Does she have any children? By now she could have many.*

"I'm sorry," he said, and was echoed by his father. "If there is anything I can do to help, let me know. What are your plans, Larsala?" he asked softly, using her first name as he had a thousand times when they were children. Time couldn't erase some things—past knowledge, past friendship, past love. "Are you here for a visit, or are you staying longer?"

"I have not decided. I didn't know what I would

167

find on my arrival. I've had no contact with anyone in Eden since leaving. My father and my husband both thought that best. I did not, but that made no difference to them." She took a calming breath. "But until I do decide, I shall reside with my aunt. She will not allow me to take a room at the hotel, although that is what I'd prefer. My expenses will be a burden, and she will not let me pay."

When she smiled, the well-remembered dimple appeared in her cheek and her eyes tipped up at the corners, making her appear very pleased.

"I've retained my hacienda down south, and I have several good men making sure things run smoothly, as well as my father and father-in-law, for the time I'm away." Her gaze lingered on Santiago's. "I hope you are happy I'm home."

His heart slammed against his ribs, and he wasn't sure if it was with happiness or fear. Before he could answer, a knock sounded on the back door. One he recognized and had been pining to hear.

# CHAPTER TWENTY

With excitement thrumming through her veins, Katie sailed up the back steps of the Spanish Trail Cantina as if they didn't exist. Shaking with anticipation, she made herself stop, take a few cleansing breaths, and slow down so Santiago wouldn't think a herd of buffalo had descended on his home.

She'd known his return would be a surprise. She'd just come back from the orphanage, where Jackie had proudly shown everyone her new smile. Dr. McGrath had successfully bridged the gap with a new porcelain tooth; the fit wasn't perfect, but the effect was much better than before. He promised to keep working until he was satisfied with the look. New and innovative adhesives were being created all the time, he said. Back in town, Katie had been enjoying the sunshine for the first time in days, her spirits lifted by her time with the frightened girl, when she spotted Santiago's horse tied in back of the cantina. She'd run all the way from the livery, joy making her feet fly as if they had wings. Had he just arrived? Would he be tired and hungry from such a long ride? So many feelings tumbled inside, every single one making her happy.

*Oh, Santiago, my love.*

Everything about him was perfect. He was

handsome and kind and thoughtful. He had a way of looking at her that made her insides warm and turn to mush. Together, they'd weathered the suspicion and objections from her family upon learning of their relationship. With each passing month, her feelings for Santiago had grown stronger, and his for her. She was sure he was on the verge of asking her to become his wife. That day would be the best in her life.

Finally breathing normally, she knocked.

Murmured voices sounded from within. She shivered impatiently at the thought of their sweet reunion. After a brief greeting, Santiago's father, the kind and knowing man that he was, would no doubt excuse himself for a few minutes and go into the cantina, allowing them time alone in the kitchen so they could say a proper hello. After that, she'd share the birthday letter she'd received from her father while Santiago had been away. The revelation inside would cement every notion that she had that they'd been destined to be together from the very day she'd been born.

The door opened.

She flew into Santiago's arms. A moment passed before she realized they weren't alone. Pulling back, she saw his father and an unknown woman.

"Miss Brinkman," Santiago said, barely above a whisper.

*Miss Brinkman? Why is he being so formal?*

Katie stepped out of Santiago's arms thinking

his welcome was less than warm. Less than loving. Although he gazed into her eyes, something was missing. Fear streaked through her. Was this woman, standing here in her widow's any man's heart, responsible? Had Katie ever seen more beauty on one person? Not in her nineteen years. The newcomer was small. Her neck would put a swan's to shame. Her heart-shaped face and olive skin made her stand out. And her brows, eyes, and delicately sloped nose made her face unforgettable.

Katie swallowed and tried to force a smile. "I—I didn't mean to interrupt," she stammered. "Forgive me, Santiago. You have company." She snuck a gaze into his face but found no answers there. "Should I return later?"

Blessedly, Miguel stepped forward and took her hands. "Señorita Brinkman, I told you Santiago was all right and that he would be home when the winds sent him here."

He grinned widely, but now, in his eyes, Katie thought she saw something different. Trouble was brewing.

*Or am I being silly?*

"He walked through that door only moments before you. See, he still wears his traveling clothes. He was saying he had to clean up so he could search you out."

*There. A seed of normalcy.*

She tried to let that seep into her soul, to calm

her racing heart, but something told her life would never be the same.

"Let me introduce an old friend, Katie," Santiago said, his voice sounding strange, a bit strangled. "This is Larsala Zelinga Salazar, from Arizona. She is the niece of Mrs. Gonzales."

Katie nodded, hanging on to each of Santiago's words. "Yes, the woman who makes the wonderful pastries. How could I forget? We have them every Tuesday morning."

Mrs. Salazar's gaze cut to Santiago, and one finely shaped brown eyebrow lifted.

"She and Demetrio were sweethearts for many years."

*Demetrio!* Santiago's imprisoned brother? Her racing heart slowed.

"She left Eden when she was fifteen to wed Señor Salazar in Arizona. Larsala," Santiago continued in his deep voice, its normalcy making Katie gaze up into his face with relief, "this is Miss Katie Brinkman, youngest daughter of John—"

"Brinkman," Larsala filled in. "I remember our beloved John. And all the talk of his daughters who would return someday. Am I to assume someday has actually arrived, and they have all come back to Eden? All five of them?"

"That is correct," Miguel responded. "Back from Philadelphia last September. They have inherited the Five Sisters Ranch and the rest of John's properties. Katie may be a slip of a girl, but don't let that fool you. She runs the lumber mill on Aspen Creek, right across the way. And she has recently built a lumber office in town. In the cobblestone area. She shares it with Eden's new contractor, Rhett Laughlin."

Katie was hit with the full force of Larsala's smile.

"How wonderful. It is with great pleasure that we meet, Miss Brinkman," Larsala said. "Your father was kind to me. I liked him. I'm glad he was reunited with his family, and I am sorry to hear of his death. How blessed you are to have spent time with him before his passing."

A great hurt welled up inside Katie. If only that were true. Even for a month, a day, or an hour. Fate hadn't been that kind. But she did have her father's letter, which was the next best thing. She'd be able to share it with Santiago soon, when they could get a private moment.

"We did not return before he died," Katie said. "We were summoned to Eden for the reading of his will." Guilt and heat rushed into her face. "You see—"

"The truth that he wanted to reunite was kept from them, for all these years," Santiago spoke up, helping her get through the painful story.

Larsala stepped forward and took both of Katie's hands in her own. "That is horrible. My heart breaks for you all. I hope we can become friends, Miss Brinkman. I think your father, our dear John, would like that." She tipped a knowing look up into Santiago's eyes, her gaze brimming with tenderness and bringing more heat to Katie's face. "And also, our dear Santiago too. No?"

What could Katie say? Perhaps she was jealous over nothing, and this beautiful, black-clothed swan would turn out to be a true friend. She'd been taught never to judge another, no matter how she felt about their appearance. Briefly, she remembered the unfortunate falling-out she and her sisters had had with their dear friend from home. They'd tried and convicted Lara Marsh of writing those horrible articles, based on much more evidence than she had here and now—but they'd been wrong. "I'm sorry for your loss as well, Mrs. Salazar. If there is anything I can do . . ."

"There is. Call me Larsala. I'm not that much older than you, and I've never felt much like a 'missus.'" She glanced at Santiago. "Right, Santiago? Being scallywags suited us well back then, and that might even hold true for today, now that I'm back. Eden has revived me. As if I've been in a deep sleep and have awakened to Christmas morning."

Enchanted, Katie smiled and waited for Santiago to look her way. Agree with the nice things her new friend had said. But he didn't. His gaze was anchored on Mrs. Larsala Zelinga Salazar's beautiful face as if there were nobody else in the room.

# CHAPTER TWENTY-ONE

Emma let a long sigh escape her lips when she felt the coach finally beginning to slow down. It was the second-to-last stop of the day; they'd switch the team and be on their way for one more twenty-mile leg. The day's end couldn't come soon enough.

The stage jerked to a halt.

Everyone except Beranger piled out of the torture trap, bent over, mumbling in pain, and rubbing their backsides. Beranger never seemed to be any the worse for wear.

Emma took a deep breath of cool evening air, thankful to be away from the others. Lifting her arms, she stretched them over her head and twisted her spine, loving the space and absence of the smelly coach. The sun had gone down, but darkness had yet to fall. Stillness and warmth wrapped around her. The wonderful aroma of horse sweat and prickly grass made brittle by the sun reminded her of the ranch. Two handlers came out to help the driver. The shotgun messenger went about unloading something from the back.

Looking to the front of the coach, she cried out in horror.

Four of the horses, in the process of being unhitched, were covered in small oblong cacti.

Spiny needles stuck to their faces, others to their legs and flanks. The horses bucked and kicked out, agitated with fear from the pain. One jerked away and ran off bucking until he was out of sight.

Beranger, watching, stood there perplexed.

"What happened?" She ran to his side.

"When we swerved off the road, we must have gone through a patch of cholla."

"Cholla?"

"Jumping cactus."

"Why aren't the men attempting to rid the poor horses of them? It looks painful."

"It's not that easy. Even with a docile horse, getting rid of them can be tricky."

The travelers had gathered around but kept a respectable distance.

"Don't try anything until morning," the driver called to the men. "Some'll rub 'em out themselves. You're less likely to get kicked after they have time to settle."

Peggy looked incensed. "All night? That's cruel."

The driver glared. "It'll be crueler, and maybe even deadly, to whoever is foolish enough to attempt the deed now. Them animals are crazy with instinct. They think a cougar has 'em in his claws." The driver spat tobacco juice into the dirt, and a dribble ran down his chin. "Let 'em be once you get 'em turned out. That's the only way."

Beranger still stood there, watching.

*What is he thinking?* Emma wondered.

He appeared taller than any man could, and his rugged handsomeness had grown on her. All day long, she'd had to check herself to stop from glancing up at his strong chin and expressive eyes too often. Even the dark stubble that covered his jaw looked intriguing.

She scoffed, thinking about the bet she'd made with her sister. Admiring a man's strength and beauty had nothing to do with falling in love.

"Where's Jimbo?" Beranger bit out.

Emma and the sisters gaped at his hard tone.

"He and Mr. Tug have gone inside," Emma said.

Hearing his name, Jimbo appeared. "What's all the fuss?"

Beranger pointed to one stocky mare, trembling in her harness. "Your little stunt caused this. Now get over there and get that cholla off her bottom lip, then try for the one on her shoulder. I warn you—be fast and prepared to jump back."

Jimbo sneered. "I ain't afraid." He stepped over to the horse and plucked at the cholla on her lip, but the ball of spindles failed to come loose. Instead, the mare's foreleg struck with lightning speed, hitting Jimbo on the shoulder.

Shrieking in pain, he fell to the ground, scrambling to get away from her hooves.

The driver laughed, as did several of the other handlers.

"I told ya so, you dimwit!" the driver hollered. "Ain't worth your life."

"Get up," Beranger commanded. "We have work to do."

Trembling, Jimbo stood, brushing off his clothes.

Emma ran to Beranger's side. "What are you going to do? Can I help? Perhaps I can distract them for you while you do whatever it is you're going to."

The light that came into his eyes brought a tingle inside. She wanted to help the poor, frightened horses, but she found his reaction to her willingness to help almost intoxicating.

*That's just admiration,* she told herself. *And it has* nothing *to do with falling in love either. Nothing at all.*

# CHAPTER TWENTY-TWO

Remembering he'd seen a sword being loaded to the top of the stage in Santa Fe, Beranger climbed the side of the coach and rustled around the luggage and boxes. He was soon back on the ground with a long saber sheathed in a brown leather scabbard.

"Hey, that's mine," Mr. Tug cried.

"I hope you'll let me borrow it for a few minutes. We don't have much time to help these horses before the driver will want to pull out to stay on schedule. But I'd like to try."

"You know how to use one of them?"

*Hold the sword straight, Beranger. Now aim, step, and thrust. I know the weight is a bit much for an eight-year-old, but I have confidence you can handle even more. Won't be long before you grow into it anyway. That's right. Good boy. Pull the weapon to you when you spin, now another step, aim, thrust.*

Beranger banished the memory of Uncle Harry, concentrating instead on the weight of the weapon in his hand, studying the length, gauging the weight. Years had passed since Beranger had held a sword, but one never forgot.

"I do," he replied in answer to Mr. Tug's question. He glanced at Emma watching, waiting for his command, and hid his smile. "All will be fine, Miss Brinkman. You needn't worry. I won't hurt any of the animals. And you'll not lose your mining expert." It felt rather good to have someone, especially someone as beautiful as she looked now, even in her rumpled dress, worrying about him. Then his gaze slid to Jimbo. "But I'm not sure about him."

Ten feet away, Jimbo still cradled his shoulder, looking dazed and despondent.

"Get over here, Lance. Stand by me. You're going to help."

Jimbo eyed Beranger with a scowl. "You think I'm gonna get near that beast again? You got another think coming. She's faster than a rattle-snake with those hooves."

The other men had taken notice and stopped their work to watch. Three horses covered in cholla still bucked and snorted in their harnesses; one had run off, and the other four, unaffected by the spines, were already in the corral. A handler stood close, with three lead lines of fresh animals to swap out.

"I'm not asking, I'm telling. You're the reason the mare and the others went through the jumping cactus, and you'll help me or you'll find yourself dumped in the middle of some cholla yourself. Just take a look out there." He pointed past the corrals to the open prairie, where plenty of the hazardous shrubbery could be seen. "You have any grain?" Beranger asked a handler.

The man shook his head.

Emma turned and ran toward the station shack, calling over her shoulder, "I'll get some, Mr. North. I'm sure they must have some rolled oats. I'll be back directly."

"I need a lariat too," Beranger said, looking around while he waited for Emma.

The mare trembled in her traces.

Beranger handed the sword to Jimbo while he received a lariat from a handler. He shook out a loop and practiced swinging the lasso over his head. It had been years since he'd done any ranching—work he'd done to survive before the old miner had taken him under his wing.

Emma returned with a bucket. A short, chubby fellow followed behind.

"I'll go in front, close enough to get her attention. But I'll stay out of range of her hooves." She mouthed the words "be careful" for his eyes only. The other affected horses still snorted and, every now and again, kicked out or reared, striking the air with their front hooves, struggling to get away. He needed to act soon.

With no words between them, Emma lifted the bucket and shook the contents.

The mare danced nervously in the harness but pricked her ears at the enticing treat.

Ready with his lariat, Beranger easily caught

her hind feet and tugged the noose tight. He handed the rope to Jimbo, taking the sword from his grasp.

"I can't hold her!"

"Keep the rope snug so she can't go anywhere and is unsteady on her feet. I only need a few seconds."

With the trembling mare trying to keep her balance and not sure whether to look at the bucket of oats or the men, Beranger plucked the six cholla from her flanks and legs with a swing of the sword, and then went for the one on her lip. The deed was done without a drop of blood being spilled.

"Take her away, and let's get the others cared for. We can't do anything for the horse that's run off."

A few minutes later, with new horses harnessed and the afflicted animals now free in the corral, Beranger sheathed the sword. Everyone except Emma and Jimbo had boarded the stage, but the sisters and Mr. Tug leaned out the windows and began to clap. With a swift lift of his arm, Beranger tossed the sword to the shotgun messenger on top of the coach.

He smiled at Emma, feeling satisfied—and maybe a little of something else as well. "Miss Brinkman," he said, taking her hand, "I believe the time has come to board." He handed her up as if they'd just finished up a routine stop. An undeniable warmth moved around his heart.

She'd been watching him, and he'd enjoyed the sensations she'd caused. Beranger had been alone for a long time. Twelve years since he'd come to America, and four on board the *Destiny* before that. Had fate brought him and Emma Brinkman together for a reason other than the mine?

She smiled, causing his heartbeat to quicken. "Thank you, Mr. North," she replied. "I don't think I've ever seen a display quite like that. You handled that sword with such precision. It took my breath away."

"I was happy to help, Miss Brinkman."

They settled in beside each other as if doing so were the most natural thing in the world. He reflected back on their days of travel. Emma had a keen mind and possessed countless qualities he admired—especially the way she argued. But maybe he enjoyed that because he was always imagining what making up would be like.

The miles rolled away.

*We'd better reach Eden soon, or I might lose more than a few hours of sleep to Miss Brinkman—I just might lose my heart.*

Breathing in the cool evening air, Beranger walked slowly in no direction at all. The Wells Fargo horses were illuminated by the full moon in the pasture. The travelers, including Emma, had turned in directly after supper had finished. He'd intended to go to bed as well, get a good night's sleep this last night before reaching Eden, but instead opted to stay outside. He didn't know how the ladies' side of the sleeping quarters smelled, but Jimbo, Mr. Tug, and Mr. Tug's bag had about done him in. He planned to pass the night sitting in one of the chairs out front.

"Beranger?"

Emma, moving toward him in the moonlight, looked like an angel. Her hair, free of any bond, flowed around her shoulders like a cape spun of glass. She reminded him of everything good. Of being a man. His heart thumped against his breastbone almost painfully. The sight of her chased away all his haunted memories and replaced them with unbidden anticipation.

He smiled. "What're you doing up? I thought you'd gone to sleep an hour ago."

She glanced away, a look of melancholy on her face. "What're *you* doing out here?" She scanned the rolling land illuminated by the moonlight. "Looking for Charger? Has he shown up?"

Beranger shook his head. That was exactly what he'd been doing. To his disappointment, the horse hadn't followed. He must have found some wild horses and stayed behind. "No. I'm sure he's settled somewhere with a herd."

She came closer and then glanced up at the stars. A light breeze stirred her hair, enticing him to touch. "You seem quiet," he said. He had an obligation to watch out for her, after all.

*When did looking after her welfare cease being a duty and become a gift?*

He devoured the sight of her face. "Is something bothering you? Are you anxious to get home to Eden? See your sisters?"

A smile returned to her face. "I am. Very much so. Mavis, Lavinia, and Katie all have so much going on in their lives—it's exciting. Mavis was just elected mayor of Eden, as I've told you before, and I'm looking forward to returning in time to attend her first official meeting tomorrow evening. Lavinia will be delighted I've sold one of her hats. And Katie! Her business has taken off. The mill is busier than ever before with all the new people flooding into Eden. She's hired several more workers, and now runs the mill in shifts, something she never had to do before—"

He laughed. "Before the Brinkman sisters returned."

She bashfully glanced away. "Well, that's true. As much as I feel a mite embarrassed to admit it, those are the facts."

"That's a big job for your little sister. Is she up to the task?"

"Yes, so far the challenge has given her wings. And, as you'll learn as soon as you reach town, she fancies herself in love with Santiago Alvarado, a young man you'll meet. I believe she's hoping for a proposal soon. Maybe she and Lavinia will have a double ceremony."

"That *is* news! Then almost all of the Brinkmans will be spoken for? Only you and your older sister, Mrs. Applebee?"

"Her too." Emma's mouth set into a hard line. It seemed so unlike her.

"I'd think you would be happy for her. For them."

She lifted a shoulder and nodded, looking beguiling in the moonlight.

"I am. Mavis has feelings for our sheriff, Clint Dawson. Even if she denies it. He's a very likable man, handsome too. It's just . . ." Her voice faded off, and she didn't finish her sentence. "Anyway, they haven't made a declaration as of yet, but the writing has been on the wall for some time."

"I'm confused. You seem to be giving conflicting signals about your sisters. Don't you want them to fall in love, marry, and have families?" Maybe he was presumptuous to ask, but she'd started on the subject. "Is that how you feel about Blake and Belle? And your other sister, the hatmaker and her beau?"

Emma's shoulders straightened. Seemed she didn't like him asking so many questions, prying into her head and heart. "That's not what I meant at all. I'm happy for them, I am. When the time comes, every single one will be a wonderful mother. It's just . . ."

"Oh, I understand. You've been hurt, and are worried they will be too."

She turned and studied his face. It was as if she worried he might think less of her because of it.

"I never want them to go through anything like I have. And I never intend to go through it again either. I'll not allow myself to fall in love again, Beranger. Not ever. I've made a pact with myself."

*Ah, the crux of the problem. I should have guessed it sooner.*

Now her innocent coyness made perfect sense. She'd set upon a path impossible to follow. And it also explained why she was so upset about him and Delphine in the shop. She wanted to spare the world of women her pain. Well, he didn't have a happily-ever-after story to change her mind—far from that. But if he were honest with himself, he'd already fallen for Emma, with her quirky ways and pretty smile. She was in his thoughts night and day. Could he bear to simply let her slip away?

He lifted a shoulder. "I have to disagree with you, Emma. I *do* think love is worth the price. Someday, God willing, I intend to find the woman who will be the perfect partner."

He held her gaze and didn't let go.

Emma shivered, but whether it was from the cool night air or the intensity of Beranger's stare, she wasn't sure. *Beranger believes in love? That seems farfetched.* With the sad story of his life, she was skeptical.

Confused by the intensity of his gaze, she took

a step away. He was exasperating. *Is he trying to mix me up?* She needed to redirect the conversation. He seemed talkative tonight. It was now or never if she was going to ask . . .

She straightened a bit and glanced at the moon. "I've been thinking about the sword, and how you deftly dealt with the cholla. You're interesting. Your history, I mean," she hurried on. "Why did you leave your home and come to America? Without your family? Won't you tell me, Beranger?"

"I've already told you. I'm an illegitimate son of—"

"I know all that, but *why* did you leave England? You never said. And you must have been very young to accomplish all you have and become so successful. I'm feeling sad for you, but perhaps I shouldn't. Maybe your story is a happy one."

"Yes, it's roses and apple pie. Better? Now, it's getting late. You should go in."

She shook her head. "I'm not sleepy."

"There's not much to tell."

"Of course there is. It's your *life*. You're English. You crossed the sea. I think your story fascinating just by knowing those few details."

He chuckled. "At least you find me fascinating. For a woman set against love, you are a bit forward."

Happiness filled her, and she laughed. "We've

become friends, I think. We've been stuck together, side by side, for days. Familiarity breeds fondness, and fondness breeds, well . . ."

*Love?* She'd talked herself into a corner. *Unquestionably not love.*

"Fascination?" he asked sardonically.

"Yes, that's it. Thank you."

"Fine. If you really must know the truth, I was a hooligan," he said, continuing the story. "Cursed by being born with eyes that didn't match. When I was thirteen, I stole a horse from my father's stable and ran away. I boarded a ship as an indentured servant and ended up here. End of story."

"But *why* did you run away? There's more to it, I know."

"You're imagining a pretty fairy tale."

The bet she'd made with her sister entered her thoughts. Her easy friendship with Beranger, and how happy she was when they were together like this, talking, sharing, had nothing to do with Belle. Nothing in the least. He understood how much she missed Brenda. He respected, even if he disagreed with, her decision not to fall in love. He'd shared so much of his background, she felt privileged. She remembered the way her sisters had looked when they'd first realized they were in love, and she wasn't acting even remotely the same. She could relax. Beranger was making this journey livable by revealing parts of his interesting background—nothing more.

He made a show of stretching his arms and then twisting his back.

"The day has finally caught up with me. I'm going to get some sleep. Come on, I'll walk you in."

When he placed his hand on her back, a flutter of warm feelings ensued. She thought of his hands spanning her middle when she'd been sick.

As hard as she tried to push the thoughts of him away, she wasn't at all surprised that she didn't sleep a wink that night.

# CHAPTER TWENTY-THREE

Arriving at the stage depot in Durango the next morning, Beranger helped Emma to the ground, followed by the sisters. He circled around to the back, where the shotgun messenger had already opened the back boot of the coach to extract the sisters' trunks. This was where they would part ways. The women disappeared to the back of the building in search of the outhouse. Mr. Tug, carrying his belongings, tottered toward the front door of the depot. The stench from his bag had become unendurable. Emma had kept her face turned into Beranger's shoulder for most of the day. Ester and Penny kept their handkerchiefs to their face. Beranger vowed to make sure the putrid thing was stored in the boot from here on out. The man should be grateful he didn't pitch it over a cliff—something he should have done from the start. To his knowledge, Tug had never opened the bag, so the contents couldn't be anything he needed on a daily basis. He was just being stubborn.

Knowing he didn't have much time for coffee, Beranger headed for the depot in search of a quick cup and whatever else they might have to fill his stomach. He passed Mr. Tug as the man tottered out. Beranger took a cup of brew and a couple of biscuits from plates stacked three rows high in the center of the table and headed straight for the old fellow, planning to catch him before the shotgun messenger had a chance of buttoning up the boot.

He ambled over to the side of the carriage where Mr. Tug waited for the others. "Another biscuit?" He held out the food in hope of softening him up.

The man eyed the offering and shook his head.

The driver was working the last buckle.

"Hold up with that," Beranger called. He looked down at the carpetbag as the women appeared with coffee of their own. Everyone was eating or drinking something.

Mr. Tug started to move away, but Beranger stopped him. "Let's stow that in back now that there's room. With the sisters' two trunks gone, there isn't a chance anything inside will be crushed." He reached out and smiled. "I'll handle your belongings with loving care."

The man frowned and snapped back, "What you say?" His gaze cut around the faces. "I don't take orders from you, you doctorial ass!"

Beranger hadn't thought he'd sounded bossy, just firm. The man was defensive—but why? He had to know whatever was inside stunk to high heaven.

"Now that you mention it, you *do* have to. Hand that over. The driver will pack it in the back or on top, wherever you prefer. The aroma is offensive to the ladies, and to me as well."

Jimbo stepped out of the stage office behind the man. "You mean the *stink* is offensive!"

Beranger reached once more for the bag, hoping to avoid a confrontation. Wrestling an old man wasn't in his constitution. He wasn't a bully.

Mr. Tug bared his few teeth, and the women gasped.

The man was deranged. The thought had previously crossed Beranger's mind.

Mr. Tug began backing up, his eyes glittering with malice. He must have already forgotten that Jimbo was directly behind him, with a mischievous slant to his mouth.

Beranger shook his head at Jimbo and narrowed his eyes. He didn't intend to traumatize the old fellow. He just wanted a peaceful, agreeable end to the problem. The solution was easy: put the bag in back. Beranger could talk his way through this, and everyone would be fine.

But by his expression, Jimbo had other ideas. He couldn't care less what happened as long as he got a laugh. Once again Beranger shook his head in warning, thinking he was going to tip Mr. Tug off, but that didn't happen.

"You ain't gettin' my bag. You ain't gettin' it," he mumbled over and over.

Beranger had to act. "Hold up, Jimbo. I've got this."

Hurrying so Beranger couldn't spoil his fun, Jimbo snatched the handle.

Mr. Tug held on.

A scuffle ensued.

With a sickening rip the thing split open, and a lump of what looked like three limp chicken carcasses fell to the earth. In the twist of rotting feathers, it was difficult to tell.

The women screamed and dropped their cups.

Jimbo shouted and jumped back as the glob landed on his boot. "My gawd, Mr. Tug! Wh-what is *that?*" He took a few steps back, his eyes huge.

Peggy turned into her sister's arms and buried her face in Ester's shoulder.

Emma stood transfixed, her eyes bulging.

The stage driver and shotgun messenger, who'd gathered around as well, stood in shocked silence at the sight before them.

The depot manager came forward with a shovel, but Mr. Tug shouted his disapproval and opened the ripped bag as if he was going to reclaim his property and shove it back inside.

"The man is stark raving mad," Jimbo uttered shakily. His face was white as the women's.

Beranger stepped forward, trying to catch Mr. Tug's gaze. "What is that?"

Mr. Tug glared. "My darlings."

The man with the shovel scooped up the rotting carcasses and strode away.

"I won't go without 'em," the lunatic shouted. He began to follow after them, but the shotgun messenger caught his arm.

"You're not bringing 'em, you crazy fool!"

"I am. I have my rights."

"Then I'm throwing you off the stage."

The depot manager called back, "Don't leave that nut with me."

The driver looked around and rubbed his whiskered chin. "Load up! We don't have time for this tomfoolery. We still have a schedule to keep."

Emma made her way toward the coach, looking reluctantly at the inside. "I don't think I can get back in."

Beranger didn't enjoy the thought of breathing the foul air either. Grasping the door, he opened and closed it a few times in an effort to rid the conveyance of the lingering stench.

Ester and Peggy appeared at Emma's side. "We hate to let you go after such a fright, honey," Ester said. "Maybe the driver'll let the coach stay on a while."

"Nothin' doing," the driver yelled. "We're pulling out in exactly three minutes, regardless who's on."

"How long will you remain here?" Emma asked.

"Just until tomorrow, then we'll be back on our way," Peggy answered. "You'll be home by then, washed up, and having had a good night's sleep in your own linen."

Emma sighed deeply and gave a little shiver. "That sounds too good to be true. But you two be careful with you-know-who until you depart tomorrow. I'm worried about you."

"We'll be fine. I doubt he'll leave that hastily dug grave."

"Emma, say your goodbyes." Beranger gave a gentle nudge. "The driver is ready to pull out."

She looked up at Beranger and then quickly hugged each woman. "I'm so happy to have met you both. You made the trip so much nicer. I hope you'll write and let me know how you're faring."

"Of course we'll write. We want to know how the adventure ends. Only you can tell us that."

They smiled at Beranger.

Ester winked and said, "It's been our privilege to ride with you, Mr. North. We're grateful for how you looked after us." Her gaze surreptitiously slid over to Emma, who was watching Mr. Tug stand morosely by the newly mounded dirt. "We hope you keep up the good work," she said to Beranger while wagging her brows at Emma. "Some jobs are more difficult than others."

He chuckled, and Emma glanced up. "Did I miss something?" she said.

"No, dearie. You just rest until you get to Eden. That family of yours will be glad to have you home."

# CHAPTER TWENTY-FOUR

*Eden, Colorado*

In the late-afternoon sun, Mavis and Clint sat on the porch of the hotel waiting for Emma's arrival. When Mavis had received the telegram, she'd been shocked at Belle and Blake actually allowing Emma to go off on her own. She was accompanied by their new employee, Mr. North, but what did they know of him? Really know? She was touched that Emma had been adamant about returning in time to make her first town council meeting that night, as Belle had said in her telegram, but knew there must be other reasons as well. Ones Belle hadn't relayed in the short message. A few nervous butterflies fluttered in her stomach. Running and participating in meetings for the Five Sisters Ranch was one thing, but standing in front of a full house as the town's first woman mayor was quite another.

Clint leaned back and took a sip of his coffee. "I'm thankful things turned out the way they did with Mr. Lake. Being nearly deaf, he didn't realize how he sounded much of the time. Got frustrated often. I hope the collapsing-trumpet hearing aid Jeremy prescribed works well for him. He seemed to like it very much."

"The handy implement certainly cured him from asking 'what' after every word we said," Mavis replied with a little laugh. "I was pleased he took our interfering so well. And he has apologized to each family already. It's only been a couple of days." She laid her hand on Clint's warm arm. "Thank you so much for standing with me. I'm sure it's because of you the intervention went so well."

Clint grunted his agreement. "Thank you." His eyes sparkled. "But don't sell yourself so short, Mavis. You did all the fancy talking. I was very impressed. Seems like he'd been contemplating retirement before we approached him, and then our concerns were the kick in the pants he needed."

Contentment rolled through Mavis. One problem averted. "Now all we have to do is find a suitable replacement before school begins. Then this issue can be wrapped up with a bow and set aside."

She glanced at her handsome lawman, admiring his profile. They'd been spending more and more time together, but she wished she knew how he felt about her—*really* felt. She'd never be the one to speak first; it wasn't in her to do so. "How does Cash like working for Rhett?" she asked. "The hotel they're building for Mr. Wells is quite complicated but seems to be moving along nicely."

A glow came over Clint's face. "I'm so proud of that boy. He's making something fine of himself.

He loves the work. It's much more challenging than his job at the livery, no disrespect meant to you and Maverick. I'm indebted to Rhett for taking him on."

"Don't be silly. You're not indebted to Rhett. Rhett counts on him. Says he's bright, a diligent worker, and brings a great attitude to work each and every day. You can't ask for more than that—and all those aspects came from you, Clint. Your teaching, your example. You're not giving *yourself* any credit. You've done an exemplary job raising Cash. You're a wonderful father."

A boyish smile appeared, looking out of place on the tall, rugged lawman. "I hope you're right, Mavis. That boy's as important to me as my life. I love my son."

The smile was suddenly gone, replaced with a look of wondrous longing. She reached over and stroked his arm with her left hand, not minding the damaged appearance anymore. "Of course you do. And he loves you. Where is this look coming from?"

Clint shrugged. "He's growing up. Someday he'll move on."

The moment was heavy with meaning. He turned his attention from the street and looked at her. "It's always been me and Cash. I'll miss him when he goes."

"Clint, he's only fifteen years old. He's not going anywhere soon."

"Almost fifteen. Not until the end of this month."

Maybe Clint was feeling his age. Now that Cash was nearly grown, how would he feel about raising another child, having a baby in the house—or maybe two? Mavis had raised her little sisters, but that didn't stop her from pining for a few of her own. Would children be a stumbling block for Clint? She'd never considered that before. Was the potential responsibility of new fatherhood stopping him from taking their relationship to the next level? That was too sad to contemplate.

Not knowing how to make him feel better or calm her own agitated thoughts, she looked up the road in the direction the stage would appear. "Emma should be here anytime." Mavis sat straighter. "Oh my gosh, Clint. Don't look now, but Santiago and that Mrs. Salazar are across the street."

The night before, Katie had been inconsolable, saying Santiago was in love with someone else. That the woman was gorgeous, and he'd known her from before.

"I thought Katie was exaggerating about how pretty she is, but now I see she's correct. Poor Katie. I heard her sobbing all night, and she didn't come out of her room this morning. I thought she might pull herself together to welcome Emma home, but now I hope she doesn't. I wouldn't want her to run into them here. Look how closely they're walking, and how they gaze into each other's eyes."

When Clint didn't respond immediately, Mavis looked over. Yes, Clint had spotted the happy twosome as well. He seemed to have a light of recognition in his eyes. The couple, in front of the empty café across the street, looked over toward the hotel. Santiago waved when he noticed Mavis and Clint. He started their way.

"Clint . . ."

He jerked his gaze back to Mavis. "What?"

She widened her eyes.

"They're old friends, Mavis, and he's showing her around. What else can he do?"

"And I suppose you and she are dear old friends too?"

"Well, yes, now that you mention it. Not *dear* old friends, but friends. She grew up in Eden." He stood and offered Mavis his hand, helping her to stand. "Now hush, or they'll hear you. You wouldn't want to make Santiago feel bad on his long-awaited return, would you?"

*Maybe! After hearing Katie sob all night long, maybe I would indeed.*

They came up the steps, and the men shook hands.

"Great to have you back, Santiago," Clint said. "Everyone was getting worried." He smiled at Mrs. Salazar. "Larsala, it's wonderful to see you again. Welcome back to Eden."

The way she fluttered her lashes looked so natural. Mavis would feel silly doing that.

"Sheriff Dawson—Clint—I hoped you were still the lawman in town," Larsala Salazar said in a low, refined voice.

The whole way through introductions, Mavis couldn't take her eyes off the woman's striking face, her confidence, the air of authority she held over the men. She was a force to be reckoned with.

"I'm so happy to meet you, Mrs. Applebee. I met your younger sister Katie yesterday. You know, since you and I are the same age, I have a slight recollection of you and another sister, when we were children. Before you were taken away by your mother, of course."

She smiled prettily, waiting for a response.

Mavis had no recollection of *her* at all. And the fact she'd mention such an emotional moment in Mavis's life was a bit off-putting.

"I can see you don't remember. Why would you? I was just another Spanish *niña* playing barefoot in the dusty streets, and you were the beloved daughter of John Brinkman. Oh, don't look like that. I mean no offense, just stating an observation."

The fact that Mavis indeed had no memory galled her further. She was struggling for a polite response even though she felt the woman had intended to put her in her place, wherever she thought that place might be. Mavis couldn't stop her ingrained response—to clutch her right-hand fingers over her left, and in doing so hide her missing finger from sight. Heat rose to her cheeks when she noticed Clint's displeased response.

"You're correct. I don't recall much of those times," she said. "I was only five years old."

"I know you saw Demetrio," Clint said to Santiago, his smile now gone. "I ran into your father earlier this morning. He said you had to bribe your way in to see him. Sugar House is known for being a hard and strict prison. How was Demetrio? What did he say when he saw you?"

Santiago shifted his weight from one leg to the other. The pain in his eyes brought a surge of empathy that Mavis wasn't able to ignore. He and his brother were close, like she and her sisters. The situation was hard on everyone involved.

"He was surprised and moved that I had made the long trip. He wants to come home." He glanced at Larsala. "Wants his old life back."

"I'm sure," Clint responded.

A long silence stretched between them.

"He's not as well as I told my father. Miguel is getting old, and counts the moments until Demetrio's release. I didn't have the heart to break his with more bad news."

Larsala withdrew a small fan from her reticule and held it in front of her face. Her eyes filled with tears. "I knew nothing of Demetrio's incarceration before I came," she whispered. "I thought he'd be here and I'd be able to see him after all these years. I thought perhaps he'd married and had children. I wanted to see that he was happy, that his life had gone on after I left." She blinked away the moisture. "What I found was devastating. I'm still coming to grips with the news."

Mavis wished she had the nerve to ask Santiago about Katie, but everything she thought of saying sounded contrived. She and her sisters had to remember this woman, Larsala, was—or had been—in love with Demetrio, not Santiago. She and Santiago were just friends. Katie shouldn't feel so threatened. Maybe she should have given him a few days to settle back in before she'd panicked.

Townsfolk at the corner cleared the street, and Mavis heard the telltale rumbling of wagon wheels that announced the stagecoach. Excited, she reached over and touched Clint's arm. He nodded.

"What is it?" Santiago asked.

"Emma should be arriving on today's stage. She's been in Santa Fe with Blake and Belle, but decided to come back ahead of them."

That was all she had time to say before the coach appeared. The driver pulled back on the long lines, slowing the horses. Mavis stuck her head inside the café and called for Lavinia. They descended the steps together.

When the coach was a few feet away, she saw Emma poke her head through the window like a girl, waving crazily with a wide smile on her face.

*Thank heavens my sister is home safe and sound.*

Mavis had envisioned every horrible thing that could happen on a three-day journey. Emma turned and positively beamed at someone in the coach.

*Who else could that be but the new Mr. North? Has something romantic happened between the two?*

That was exciting to think about, since Belle had sung his praises. Emma had been lovesick for the brothers in Philadelphia for so long, barely looking at anyone else.

Was this a romance for Emma? Yes, Mavis liked *that* idea very much!

# CHAPTER TWENTY-FIVE

*I'm home! Finally home!* Emma inwardly sang as the stagecoach passed the Spanish Trail Cantina on the left. She knew they would soon turn onto Main Street to arrive at the stage office next to the hotel. She searched out the window in hopes of seeing someone she knew. A delectable warmth spread through her chest at having completed the harrowing three-day journey.

Unable to stop herself, Emma smiled brightly at Beranger, though she knew she must look a sight. He'd not said a thing, but she was gritty and dirty and itchy—and had been even before the whole debacle this morning with Mr. Tug and the horrible carcasses. Every moment since they'd left him standing by the mound of dirt in Durango, she'd counted their blessings at being alive. He was crazy. Who knew when that madman could've snapped again? They'd all slept in the same room, separated by nothing more than a flimsy sheet. Her spine prickled. He could have chopped off their heads with his sword, for heaven's sake. Carrying dead chickens in your carpetbag for days? The man had to be out of his mind. And he'd seemed so normal—grumpy, yes, but ordinary for the most part.

"So this is Eden," Jimbo mumbled.

Emma nodded with excitement. "It is. My beloved Eden. The most beautiful place in the whole wide world."

On the last few legs of the journey, Jimbo had been quiet, staring out the window at the passing scenery. He must have felt embarrassed by his reaction to the dead chickens. His high-pitched scream when they'd fallen on his foot had rent the air as he'd leaped away in fear. Emma smiled to herself. It had been quite funny, now that she thought about it.

"There's the livery my sister owns," she said, pointing and then looking across at Beranger at her side. "And if you look quickly, right there, before we pass this road . . . there's my shop!" She bounced up and down, liking the ample room. "The Toggery. Down there on the right, directly across from the Hole in the Floor saloon."

She felt a huge swell of love for Eden. Not to mention satisfaction, thinking of all the new things she'd purchased in Santa Fe that would make her women's section shine. Before she'd inherited the store, the Toggery had mostly supplied men.

Beranger chuckled. "Hole in the Floor?"

She liked his teasing tone. "Don't ask. The name says it all."

Jimbo stretched his neck out the window. "Sounds like a place I'd like to see."

She beamed. "My shop?"

"No, the saloon."

She huffed. "Jimbo, you would . . ." As glad as she was to be home, she'd be a liar if she said she wasn't going to miss the closeness she'd enjoyed with Beranger the last three days. She'd gotten to know him, and felt they shared a special bond.

She sat straighter. "Look, there's the gun shop and the butcher shop. Across over there and down the cobblestone streets are an array of smaller shops, one of which is my sister Katie's lumber office. Rhett Laughlin's construction business is there too."

Beranger nodded patiently, having heard most of her sisters' history already. She'd shared just about everything about her family along the way to fill the long, boring hours.

"There's where you can send a telegram, if you need." She pointed to the right at the tall building that sold drugs and medical supplies, and was in competition with the town's mercantile. Unable to stop herself, Emma leaned out the window and scanned ahead to the hotel, hoping to spot her sisters. Seeing a group waiting, she waved her arm vigorously, impatient to hug them all.

"They're here! They're waving. Welcoming me home—*us* home!" she amended quickly as she smiled into Beranger's face. She hadn't known there could be a feeling so sweet.

The moment the stage had rolled to a complete stop, Emma sprang out of her seat. But before she could plunge out the door, Beranger extended his hand. "You'd not want to fall and break your ankle, Miss Brinkman. Not on your return."

The guard had jumped down, but had yet to place the stool.

"Phooey on the stool," Emma said, flying out of the stage.

She ran up the steps to Mavis and Lavinia as soon as her feet touched the earth. Clean, fresh air infused her lungs. The cool evening had chased away the warm July heat. This was Eden. She never wanted to leave again.

Mavis and Lavinia enveloped her, and the chattering began.

Karen Forrester, the motherly woman who worked for Lavinia in the café, looked on behind them, waiting for her turn.

It took all of ten minutes for Emma to rattle off the tales about the smelly chickens, Charger the beautiful wild horse, the near-crash and the cholla, her getting sick, and the fact that Cricket might have met the furtive Harlow Lennington who'd written the articles about them. Her sisters—and a beautiful woman she didn't know but who seemed to be a friend of Santiago's—stood in stunned silence. Clint and Santiago wore wide grins of surprise. As did Beranger, who she felt standing only a few feet away.

Lavinia sucked in a breath when Emma stepped back, giving her sisters a good look at her and the condition of her dress.

"Now we understand," Mavis said, looking her up and down. "Why you look so . . . well . . ."

Everyone laughed.

"I'm sorry to be so rude," Emma stammered, very unladylike. "And *this* is Mr. North, the mining expert who has been so kind as to come all the way to Eden to evaluate our mine. If he likes what he sees, he'll get the mining carts rolling." She ran over and tugged Beranger closer to the group. He came forward, his normal regal self. Now that she knew him so well, she could tell he was waiting for their reaction to his eyes. For someone to innocently ask about them, or to shy away in fear. Empathy filled her. He'd had to feel conspicuous his whole life. What would that be like?

Thankfully, at the moment no one noticed—or if they did, they weren't saying a thing.

Another thought entered her mind. That she'd become used to his eyes, had even argued with herself about which color she thought most attractive. Standing to his right, she decided that his blue, matching the clear sky above, was her favorite. Then she blushed and hoped fervently that her sisters wouldn't notice. Lavinia wouldn't hesitate to tease her, and word would certainly get back to Belle. Emma was determined to win their bet.

"We are delighted to welcome you to town, Mr. North," Mavis said. "We've been dreaming of this day for quite some time."

"Yes, Mr. North," Lavinia added excitedly. "Hopefully something fantastic will come of your efforts."

"That's what we're aiming for," Beranger said, his deep voice making Emma think of warm butter.

The rest of the group responded with welcomes and handshakes all around. Beranger was as tall as Clint, and Emma noted how the two stood straight, wide shoulders back as they silently sized each other up—something all men seemed to do. She wondered if Mavis and Lavinia noticed Beranger's voice, his subtle accent, the way his clothes seemed to fit his powerful build. They were just ordinary Western clothes, but the way he wore them like a second skin fascinated her.

Surprised to see that Jimbo had followed Beranger out of the coach, she called him over. She felt generous and even a bit sentimental toward the young man, though he'd caused more than a little strife along the way. "And this is Jimbo Lance, another traveler who's come all the way from Santa Fe with us—and the fella who exposed Frank Tug's stinky property."

Groans of disgust swept the group.

"I feel like I've been traveling with a mis-behaving younger brother," she said with a smile. "I was tempted to box his ears a couple of times." She smiled to soften her words.

Everyone laughed, and Jimbo's Adam's apple bobbed a couple of times as he glanced around and then nodded. "Howdy."

"You described Eden perfectly, Miss Brinkman," Beranger said. "It's as exactly as charming as you painted it." He glanced at the hotel. "And will the hotel have a room available?"

Mavis tipped her head. "You must stay at the ranch with us, Mr. North. We have plenty of room. And we've been planning on hosting you."

The driver opened the boot to extract Beranger's and Emma's few belongings. The shotgun messenger crossed the street and headed for Poor Fred's Saloon.

"Thank you for the offer," Beranger said. "For a few days at least, I'd like to stay in town. To get to know the place."

Mavis and Lavinia glanced at each other. "We're so sorry," Mavis said. "We didn't know you'd prefer to stay in town, so we didn't reserve a room. Rooms are a rare commodity around here of late. In fact, that's why a new investor, Mr. Wells, and his sons, Warren and Brody, are building a fancy hotel just outside of town. But that won't be finished for months."

"New people interested in our growing town have kept the old place booked," Clint said. "Sebastian may have a bed at the boardinghouse, but your best bet may be the ranch."

"I'll work something out. Don't worry about me.

And if I can't, I'll take you up on your kind offer."

Emma felt a little hurt that he seemed determined to avoid the ranch. *Is he sick of me after traveling side by side for three days? Just because I enjoyed his company so much doesn't mean he enjoyed mine. We are friends, nothing more,* she reminded herself, aware of his presence very near to her.

A memory of their moonlight walk warmed her cheeks. She didn't dare look at him for fear he'd read her mind.

"But you'll come to dinner tonight," Mavis said. "For Emma's welcome home, and yours. We insist. We all want to meet you properly, and I'm sure there will be questions about the mine. Our cook has already made preparations."

"How could I say no to that? Thank you."

Emma glanced at Jimbo, who still stood only a few feet away, listening to the conversation. "And what do you think of the town, Jimbo? You've certainly had an earful about it since we left Santa Fe."

Jimbo nodded, some of the confidence he'd shown before returning to his eyes. "Nice. I've been pondering the possibility of staying on here after all your talk of opportunity—for work, not a wife," he added quickly. "Thought I might apply at the mine, if it ever opens."

Emma almost laughed when Beranger's gaze narrowed.

"I don't allow guns on the job," Beranger said. "How will that suit you?"

"You won't have to worry about this," Jimbo replied, patting the revolver slung low on his hip. "I pretty much have learned my lesson."

Suddenly, something occurred to Emma. She glanced around in disappointment when she realized someone was missing. "Where's Katie?"

Mavis's and Lavinia's gazes briefly touched again.

"I believe she's at work," Mavis replied, a cheery note to her voice. "She wasn't certain she'd get a chance to greet you, but she will see you tonight."

*Santiago looks uncomfortable. But why should he?*

"When did you get back, Santiago?" she asked, unable to keep the question inside now that the subject of Katie's absence wouldn't leave her. "Katie's missed you horribly. Before I left for Santa Fe, she was walking around without her smile. Has she shared her birthday letter from our father with you?"

More surprise and unease crossed his face. *Don't tell me you forgot her birthday,* Emma thought. *Has something happened in my absence?*

"I returned yesterday," he said rather stiffly. "We only spoke for a few moments."

Emma didn't care for the way his gaze cut to the newcomer by his side. The woman's bold eyes took in everything. They were confident, especially when the topic of Katie came up.

*What aren't they telling me about Mrs. Larsala Zelinga Salazar?*

"Katie is beautiful," Larsala said with an upward tilt to her perfectly molded lips. "Just like the rest of you. I met her at the cantina, but she ran off quickly. So busy for such a young woman. She should learn to slow down, enjoy the beauty around her." She glanced at Santiago and then back at Emma.

*Is that a challenge? Would anyone be so bold?*

Pain for Katie sliced through Emma. Santiago's return had been all Katie could think about for weeks. And then this woman appeared, and he hadn't seen her since? The way Katie and Santiago had been progressing, Emma was shocked.

*What could have happened so quickly?* Actually, that was easy to piece together. *Larsala Zelinga Salazar had happened.*

Emma had no doubt that Katie was headed for heartbreak. In fact, she was probably already there. Love was fickle, not to be trusted. She knew she really should wait to find out all the facts before coming to any conclusions, even if the evidence was clear. Now her bet with Belle made more sense than ever.

At that moment, a clatter of hooves burst onto the scene. *Charger!* The horse galloped down the street and stopped with a flourish just feet before slamming into the back of the stage. He lifted his head and snorted, blowing out a huge gulp of breath.

Larsala sucked in a deep breath. "*¡Dios mío!* Look at that animal! He's magnificent!" She glanced around excitedly, then looked up at Santiago. "He reminds me of the horses they use to fight the bulls. I've never seen his equal. Who does he belong to?"

"Beranger," Emma responded, holding up a hand for everyone to be still.

Beranger moved to his bags and lifted the halter and lead he'd brought all the way with him. He slowly approached the animal. Emma could see the triumph shining in his eyes.

"Be careful, Beranger," she softly called. "He's been free now for two days. He might not remember you."

"What?" Clint asked, keeping his voice low.

Emma put her hand on Clint's to keep him quiet. Now that the horse had arrived, she didn't want Charger to run off again. "He's vicious, and the men are frightened of him," she whispered just loud enough that everyone around her could hear.

Beranger made his way slowly into the street.

The shotgun messenger had returned from the saloon and reboarded the stage. He and the driver watched from the seat.

To Emma, the gelding looked entirely worn out. He didn't resist as Beranger haltered him.

He stood with his head low and his coat matted with sweat. Still, he was gorgeous—scarred, but noble and alive.

Beranger glanced her way.

"Take him to the livery I pointed out. Your belongings will be safe here. I'll see if the hotel has a room."

He nodded and began leading Charger down the middle of the street as people watched.

"Farewell, Miss Brinkman," the stage driver called down to her. "We're ready to pull out. It's been our pleasure to have you aboard."

She waved and smiled, feeling a warm tenderness in her heart for the driver and messenger. The trip was one she wouldn't ever forget.

The stagecoach rolled away.

"Is Mr. North looking to sell that horse?" Larsala asked once the stage had gone. "I have another like him. They would make a beautiful matching pair. He resembles my Diablo almost exactly."

*Diablo? Her horse has the same name as Charger? How strange.*

Emma turned. "No, sorry. He's not for sale."

"Perhaps your young man will change his mind."

Irritation brought heat to Emma's face. She didn't want to let this usurper spoil her homecoming, but she was entirely too direct and bossy. "He's already turned down a good offer. I don't think he'll ever let him go."

"I've not seen another like him until now."

Thank heavens Mavis and Lavinia came to her side.

"We're just about to go in for a cup of tea. Larsala and Santiago, if you'd like to join us, you're welcome. Henry Glass, the town attorney, will be along shortly too. Our table is ready. Adding two more won't be a problem at all."

"No, thank you," Larsala declined graciously. "I must get back to my aunt's home before she sends out the guard."

"Aren't they out already?" Emma glanced across the street at the two men she'd spotted watching their group. She didn't know them, but they looked menacing, with shiny revolvers and black hats with large brims that shaded their eyes. "Those two are with you, aren't they?"

Totally unruffled, Larsala smiled. "Ah, you mean Horeto and Pima. I have become so used to them, I don't even see them any longer. Yes, they are with me. But they have nothing to do with my overprotective aunt and everything to do with my *dear, dear* father-in-law. He sends his men to protect his son's possessions, even after his death."

*Poor Katie. She doesn't stand a chance against a woman like her.* But Emma's chagrin for her sister was tempered by a flash of sympathy. *Larsala is cold and calculating, but from what she's just said, perhaps she has reason to be. She's not free to come and go.*

"I'll bid you good day," Larsala said politely. She crossed the street with Santiago to join her sentinels.

Emma's sympathy for the woman dissipated as she watched Santiago follow her like a puppy dog.

As soon as they were out of hearing, Emma grasped Mavis's arm. "Where's Katie, and what's happened? I don't care for that woman one bit. I'm sure Katie feels the same."

"Nobody knows for sure," Lavinia said gloomily, fingering one of the feathers on her hat. "But I think Katie is going to need us all now more than ever."

Mavis nodded, frowning. "I agree. Things don't look good."

First the letter from Philadelphia, and now this. Watching Santiago and Larsala's retreat made Emma's blood boil as much as it instilled fear.

*Poor, dear Katie. She'd never hurt a fly. She doesn't deserve such a blow. No, she doesn't at all.*

# CHAPTER TWENTY-SIX

Carrying a knapsack, Katie made her way to the swinging bridge, crossed easily, and sat on the bench she'd placed next to Aspen Creek as a memorial to her father. Besides the ranch, this was her favorite spot in Eden. Here, she could be quiet and alone.

She stared as the water splashed merrily along, unaware that her whole world was falling apart. Her mind felt numb. The scenario from the day before in the Spanish Trail Cantina played over and over in her head. Last night she'd expected a visit from Santiago—but he hadn't come.

She gulped in several large breaths.

A half hour ago, on her way to the hotel to join her sisters as they waited for Emma's stagecoach to arrive, she'd spotted Santiago and Larsala together. At least the woman wasn't holding his arm, but Katie had heard their laughter, seen the way he looked in her eyes.

*The same way he used to look at me.*

Katie tossed a stone into the water.

*He didn't come because he doesn't want to hurt me. He doesn't know what to say. Did he stay away so long because of his feelings, or did he know Larsala was returning? Oh, Santiago, I love you so much.*

A rustling sounded above. In the fading light, she could barely make out a baby squirrel as it danced on the branch above her head. The tiny animal was no bigger than her fist, and speckles dotted his back.

She actually laughed.

The critter froze and peered at her intently.

"I mean you no harm, little one," she whispered, feeling her eyes fill. "Are you newly born in this tall ponderosa pine?"

The sound of the rushing water was her only reply.

Searching through her sack for the crust of bread she'd left there yesterday, Katie carefully moved the birthday letter from her father, thinking she should really put the cherished correspondence away in a safe spot and stop carrying it around with her. The missive was more precious than gold.

Finding the crust, Katie tossed the food at the trunk of the tree. "This is for you."

"Do you always speak with animals?"

Startled, Katie surged to her feet.

Warren Wells, oldest son of the man building the new hotel just outside of Eden, rode out of the foliage. He had been on the small footpath that split off from the bridge and cut over the hill to the building site, a quarter mile from town. Since they'd begun work on the structure, the hidden trail had become a well-used route.

"You shouldn't sneak up on unsuspecting people," Katie snapped, embarrassed. She glanced overhead. "You've scared him away."

"Well?" he asked as he rode forward.

Katie didn't know what to say. She'd hardly exchanged more than a handful of words with Warren, other than the ones that had been needed to conduct business. He'd been into her town office twice, and both times with his younger brother, Brody, who seemed much more amiable than he. Warren, twenty-two years old, had lost his young wife last year.

"You've caught me red-handed. Seems I do."

With a chuckle and a lift of one shoulder, he nudged his mount onward. He stopped in the clearing by the bench and dismounted.

"Are you on your way to the mill?" she asked. "Because if you are, Howard and the men are gone by now." Indeed, the place stood quiet after a busy day.

"Yeah." He pulled a piece of paper from his pocket. "I realize that, but I was going to tack this to your door so we'll have what we need first thing in the morning. The note is from Rhett."

*Business. I can deal with that. Anything to keep my mind off Santiago.*

She put out her hand. "The hour's getting late. Give me the order. I'll make sure Howard begins filling it first thing in the morning. That'll save you a few steps, and you can get home to supper."

He drew the paper back. "Sorry, Miss Brinkman. Both Rhett and my father told me to tack the order to the door. They're concerned about finishing the hotel on time. We need that lumber as soon as your men can comply."

Heat flushed her face. That morning, she'd completely forgotten to pass on an order. Rhett had to come into town himself to sort it out. Because of Santiago, her business had suffered.

"Don't get angry," he said. "Nothing personal against you. Just making sure."

She took a calming breath. "I'm not angry, I'm just . . ." She sighed.

Warren studied the river for a few moments before saying, "The investors are holding my father's feet to the fire. He has no leeway, or he wouldn't mind to lose a day here or there."

"I see. Don't worry about your lumber, Mr. Wells. You'll have all you need tomorrow. Go on now with your note."

He doffed his hat, mounted, and rode off in the direction of the mill.

Her throat squeezed closed. *Oh, Santiago. What are you thinking, my love? You have time for Larsala Salazar but not for me. What could that mean?*

She'd not search him out, but wait for him to come to her. That was the only thing she could do. And while she waited, she'd keep her mind on work and not let anything else slip her mind. Today's oversight had been bad enough. She had a reputation to keep.

# CHAPTER TWENTY-SEVEN

After a long, luxurious bath during which she soaped her hair three times, Emma let Lavinia set about making her feel like a princess by styling her hair. While Lavinia combed, wrapped tresses around a hot iron, and pinned them on her head in some new fashion, Emma thought about Beranger. That he was from England. That he'd spent years aboard a ship sailing the high seas. That for the first part of his life he'd been raised in a castle called Ashbury. Those thoughts led to her and Beranger's private moments in the moonlight, and their conversations. She'd never experienced such pleasure before.

Belle had better never find out what she was thinking about the man, or she'd say Emma had fallen in love and lost the bet. But that was out of the question. She'd known Beranger less than a week.

"What in the world are you smiling at, Emma?" Lavinia asked as she put the finishing touches on Emma's hairstyle. She'd taken three tiny fabric birds from her millinery supplies and scattered them around the pile of strawberry gold on Emma's head.

"My reflection," Emma whispered, chewing her bottom lip. She didn't want to hurt Lavinia's feelings, but she thought perhaps her sister was better at making hats than styling coiffures. "I look a little like I have a bird's nest on my head, don't you think?" Except for the first night in Santa Fe, Beranger had not seen her dressed up. And she usually wore her hair plaited down her back. "Maybe even a bird's nest that's barely survived a hurricane. Beranger might laugh. Or worse, think the stagecoach has bounced my brains loose."

Behind her, Lavinia took measure of her newest creation. "Don't be silly. I think you look pretty! Getting your hair curled and on top of your head was not an easy task. The burns on my fingertips attest to it." She glanced at the small fire in the bedroom hearth and lifted a brow.

Emma turned her head this way and that. Perhaps Lavinia was right. "It's different from my normal style, but a change will be nice." She stood, so thankful to be home, and embraced Lavinia. She had dressed before starting Emma's hair. "What time is it?" Emma asked. "Should we gather the others and go downstairs?"

"Yes. I'm sure Rhett has arrived with Mr. North. We've both been looking forward to tonight since we received Belle's telegram. It's been ages since we've had a dinner party. What better reason than your return? Plus the arrival of our very own— handsome—mining expert. With all the hustle and bustle, we haven't had a chance to talk yet, but did you get to know him, Emma? What's he like? Belle telegrammed us about his unique eye color and his origins." She hugged herself, and a dreamy look came over her face. "Did you find out if he's single? He's extremely good-looking."

"Lavinia! What about Rhett? I can't believe my ears."

Lavinia burst into laughter. "You're such a ninny. Not for me. For you! I love Rhett, but you're as single as a lost shoe."

"That's a horrible expression."

"I agree. But the way his gaze kept searching you out, I had to wonder. Let's not be coy. Something must have happened in three days of travel—and if not, why not? That man is a real catch. With his good looks, he won't stay single long."

Emma turned her eyes to heaven, shaking her head. "Lavinia, Lavinia, what's gotten into you?"

"He has eyes for you, Emma. I wondered if you felt the same about him."

A little miffed, Emma crossed to her bed and picked up the rich emerald gown laid across her bedspread. The fabric felt wonderful in her fingertips. "Stop talking like that. You're making me blush. You act like you're some worldly woman. I'm not looking for a relationship or a husband. I'm happy on my own."

Emma stepped into the garment, being careful not to catch the hem, and pulled it up over her pantaloons, corset, and chemise. "Can you help me with this?" she asked, glancing at Lavinia. None of them really understood her or her views on love. But Beranger did. She stopped and stared at Lavinia. "What's wrong?" she asked at Lavinia's expression of consternation.

"What's gotten into you? I've never heard you say that before. What about Tim and Cooper back in Philadelphia? You liked those two just fine. Actually, more than fine, if I remember correctly. You were madly in love with both."

"That was then, and this is now."

She didn't want to share the real reason she didn't want a relationship with Beranger. She'd never want to burst Lavinia's newly discovered bubble of love and happiness. Although she worried a little about Lavinia and Rhett too, especially with the new turn for the worse in Katie's relationship with Santiago. She decided to keep her mouth shut. She knew she shouldn't have gone on the way she had with Belle. Not with her being newly married. That wasn't nice, and she'd regretted her state-ments the second the words had passed her lips.

"I've seen a very profitable store in Santa Fe—actually, the one who is trying out one of your hats. Mrs. Sackett is a businesswoman on her own, and making quite a nice living. And then there is Cricket, the cook who'd heard about us from one of her travelers, and who has worked to make a comfortable position for herself with Wells Fargo. She's doing well in a man's world. That inspires me."

Lavinia's blank expression sent Emma's blood racing. She didn't want to get mad, but she had thought this through many times.

*Doesn't anyone take me seriously?*

"More than love? More than marriage? More than children?" Lavinia asked.

"What?"

"Work and success inspire you more than love? Oh, Emma," she said sadly.

But it wasn't sad. Emma hadn't been home more than a half hour before Katie had returned to the ranch with red eyes and an aching heart. It was easy to see she'd been crying. Mavis and Lavinia had told her the story behind Larsala Zelinga Salazar—that she was Demetrio's love, and that she and Santiago claimed to be just friends, like brother and sister. Why, then, hadn't Santiago sought Katie out? Emma hated to see her happy-go-lucky little sister look so miserable. Katie had tried everything to get out of dinner tonight, saying she wasn't feeling well, that she had no appetite, but Mavis wouldn't let her bow out. As sisters and partners in the mine, they all needed to be present to welcome Mr. North so he'd feel at home in Eden.

Even after all Beranger had told her last night, Emma still felt she didn't know his whole story.

*Why* he'd come to America. *Why* he didn't seem to be in contact with anyone from home. Perhaps, if she had a chance, a private moment tonight, she'd ask him. That's what friends were for.

Lavinia had finished buttoning her dress, so Emma opened her top drawer for the small silk case that held her most precious earrings. She only had two pairs, and she picked the pearls, which were offset by two tiny green stones that matched her emerald dress. As she put the case away, her eyes caught sight of the corner of the envelope she'd placed under her clean and pressed handkerchiefs. She hadn't thought of Mrs. Gamble's letter since she'd been home. Now all the hurtful feelings she'd carried with her to Santa Fe came rushing back. She hadn't told a soul of the correspondence, or that Tim had married and Cooper would say his vows next month. By this time next year, the two could have already started a family.

Brenda's darling smile flashed in Emma's mind's eye. The child singing "Twinkle, twinkle, little star" as the buckboard slowly rolled toward Santa Fe. Looking precious in one of her new dresses as she did her ballerina turn . . .

"Whatever is wrong?" Lavinia asked, taking Emma by her shoulders as she stood behind her. She pressed her cheek to Emma's. "For a moment there, you looked positively wretched. I hope it's not something I said."

Emma put on her most brilliant smile. "Of course not. I was missing Ester and Penny, wishing they could be here too."

"I'm relieved. I thought it was all this talk of Mr. North." She shrugged happily. "With all the sisters we have, we shouldn't let such a dashing fellow get away. If you're not interested in him, maybe he can help Katie past her broken heart."

Emma tipped her head. Katie and Beranger? Her heart dropped like a stone. "We have no idea yet about Santiago. They haven't even talked. Don't you think you might be rushing things a little bit? My goodness, we just met Beranger less than a week ago."

"True. Maybe I'm putting the cart before the horse, but at least he can take her mind off Santiago tonight. I'm not asking them to get engaged."

Disturbed, Emma nodded. She daubed some toilet water behind her ears and a little on each wrist. It felt like a rock and noose were dragging her to the bottom of some lake.

*Beranger and Katie? Are they a match?*

She preceded Lavinia to the door, still thinking about Beranger and Katie. "Let's not talk about that anymore," Emma said. "Tonight, I'm home. Tonight is going to feel like a dream. Tonight is for family, friends . . . and . . ."

Confused, she left the sentence unfinished. If Beranger was only a friend, she'd be happy if he found love with a wonderful woman. No one was more wonderful than Katie.

The two might indeed be a perfect match. So why did Emma feel, in Lavinia's words, so wretched?

# CHAPTER TWENTY-EIGHT

Beranger was on his second whiskey with Clint and Rhett in the library as they waited on the women to descend from upstairs. Lifting his glass, he sipped the expensive liquor. He hadn't tasted any finer in many years.

Once he'd left Charger at the livery, he'd secured a small room in a three-story boarding-house located centrally in town. There he'd also found Jimbo, glum-faced on the porch, after being turned away. Against his better judgment, Beranger had invited him to throw a blanket on the floor for a few days until he could find something else.

Tonight he felt like a new man. The whiskey he'd consumed had warmed his insides consid-erably, bringing out his affable side—more so than he'd normally let show in a group of people he'd just met. Nobody, not even the men, had seemed surprised at the different color of his eyes. Belle or Blake must have alerted them to the oddity.

On the way out to the Five Sisters, he'd been taken by the beauty of the land. The ever-present tightness in his chest eased as he crossed the far-ranging pastures with their brown, blowing grasses that covered gently rolling hills crowned by oaks, aspens, and pine trees. Suddenly gone was the need to find what was around the next bend in the road, to prove to the heavens he wasn't just a byproduct of an urge of his father, the duke. He'd been content just to sit quietly on the back of his loaned horse and take in the view. Even in the waning light, he'd been able to see the loveliness of his surroundings. Eden was properly named.

The spaciousness of the large rooms of the new Five Sisters ranch house was attractive. It had the feel of a profitable operation, but it also possessed a feminine touch as well. He liked the large stone fireplace in the library, the tapestry above of a prairie filled with cattle—so different from the wall hangings in Ashbury Castle. Knights, soldiers, cobblestone streets, and cottages were replaced with cattle and wide-open skies. A quiet simplicity that brought to mind Mozart's Minuet in F Major. The rugged bookcase, with its array of volumes, also tempted him. The shiny black piano in the corner caught his eye. He wondered if Emma played.

*A boy like you has no need of music study. You must learn a trade, make connections. When you reach sixteen, the duke will no longer will have any duty to support you. But if you'd like to stay and listen to Gavin's lesson, I have no objections as long as you remain silent. Gavin will be duke one day. You, on the other hand, if you remain here, will be his servant in one capacity or another. But that shan't be so bad. Better than the streets where you were born.*

But he had played music when his stepmother wasn't around. When *no one* was around. He'd watch Gavin's lessons and attempt to duplicate them later, playing by ear and memory. He had a gift—his uncle had said so when Beranger was caught red-handed one night. But he hadn't played in years.

His stepmother's gaze never rested on him, but always roved between his two eyes. When he was a toddler, he'd believed she just plain despised him. But as he'd grown older he'd realized she was frightened of him—because of his "cursed" eyes. At every chance, she belittled him, made him feel as if he didn't belong. She never let him forget he wasn't really part of the family, that Gavin was the duke's only true son—and heir to the dynasty. And that more heirs would come along soon—even though after Gavin, as far as he knew, she hadn't conceived.

One day, after she'd been particularly vicious, his uncle had explained that the duchess was not only jealous of him, but of Beranger's mother. She knew the duke had loved her until her dying day. And because there was no other outlet, the duchess took out her anger and frustrations on Beranger at every chance. And his father had turned a blind eye.

"That's some horse you have," Clint said, sipping his amber liquid. "I'm surprised with his size he was able to keep up with the stage."

"I am too," Beranger replied. "All I can say is that he's well conditioned from the extra work they put to him, and often. I hope to give him somewhat of an easier life."

Rhett Laughlin, the man he'd met on the ride out to the ranch, was a likable fellow with big dreams and the manpower to make them come true. Like Blake Harding, he seemed trustworthy and honest. He'd started a construction business in Eden just a few months before, and had employed the sheriff's son. He was doing well.

"I haven't seen him yet," Rhett said, "but he sounds intriguing. Lavinia mentioned he'd been abused, said he carries some scars. Sometimes mistreatment can't be trained out of them."

Beranger nodded, knowing that fact well. Didn't he have to conceal his own emotional scars every day? "Understood. That's why I'm not expecting him to be a riding horse, or any other kind of service animal. My first thought was to turn him out and let him live the rest of his life in ease."

Clint wrinkled his brows. Perhaps the sheriff didn't believe him. "You just bought him for no reason?"

Annoyed, Beranger realized the question reminded him all too much of Gavin. His brother undercut everything Beranger said and did. He tossed back the little left in his glass. "That's right."

Sounds of laughter reached his ears. Clint and Rhett turned to the double doors of the library.

The women entered together. Mavis, Emma, Lavinia, and Katie, the youngest, who hadn't been at their arrival. Each had dressed beautifully for supper; they wore matching smiles, and their eyes danced with excitement. It was easy to see they were happy to have Emma home, and heartwarming. And she appeared just as glad to be home as well.

Mavis glanced at Clint.

Lavinia at Rhett.

When Emma glanced at Beranger, his heart tripped over itself and then thumped painfully.

*Could any woman look as beautiful as she does tonight?*

Her silky hair was piled on her head, and curls flitted around her face. Her emerald eyes glittered in the lamplight, offset by earrings on each delicate lobe. An emerald gown enhanced her slimness, showing her curves better than the two dresses she had worn on their journey. If he hadn't already been captivated, he certainly would have been after tonight.

They circled around the men.

Emma reached out. "You look handsome, Mr. North." She laughed and glanced down at her dress. "You clean up well, and I hope I do too."

"Rest assured, my lady," he replied teasingly, "none could say different."

Mavis grinned at Lavinia.

Katie hung back until Mavis drew her in.

"Belle sent a number of telegrams that must have cost a fortune," Mavis said. "She had so much to say about your ancestry, Mr. North. How exciting that you've come to us all the way from jolly old England. We're so happy to have you aboard."

He didn't know how jolly England was.

*Not in my experience. Just the opposite.*

Emma nodded at her sisters. "Mr. North informed us the night we met in Santa Fe that beginning work at a mine before it's named is bad luck."

Beranger shifted his weight, liking the way he felt amid this group. "There's still time for that."

"How long do you think it will take before you'll know if it's workable?" Rhett asked.

"Hard to say. Maybe a week or two. I should have some answers for you by then."

The girls grinned as if they had a wonderful secret. Beranger could see the love shining in their eyes.

"Shall we partake of supper before the food gets cold?" Mavis asked.

Lavinia nudged Katie, who stepped to Beranger's side. "May I show you to the dining room, Mr. North?"

He restrained his impulse to look at Emma.

*Have the women decided this in their rooms? Does Emma really feel nothing for me and instead is encouraging her little sister?*

Emma was going to be a difficult nut to crack, more so than he'd thought. "Thank you, Miss Brinkman. I'd appreciate that very much." They preceded the others out of the library and through an open living room sizable enough to seat twenty guests comfortably. They arrived at a sumptuously decorated dining room fit for the most prosperous cattle ranch in Colorado. A savory scent of roasting beef lingered on the air. Rhett seated Lavinia and Emma across from Beranger, Katie by his side. Katie was a very attractive woman in her own right, but his favor belonged to Emma.

Dinner was served. The mine and the long-awaited meeting that would take place the next day were just a few of the topics of conversation. They spoke of breeding horses and cattle, the guest ranch they intended to open, and of course the women peppered him with questions about England and Brightshire, where he'd been born. Only Emma knew the truth about his illegitimate heritage. She listened intently from across the table, but rarely engaged. He couldn't read her expression at all.

*Is she intentionally giving me a cold shoulder?*

He did his best to entertain and pay attention to

Katie, whose deep, abiding sadness couldn't stay hidden, as hard as she tried to conceal it. Rhett and Lavinia's secret looks were entertaining. And what of the sheriff and Mavis? Those two were somewhat more difficult to figure out; still, he believed something was brewing between them.

Perhaps he'd not taken Emma's vow seriously enough. He could be headed for heartbreak, as Emma had promised anyone foolhardy enough to engage in romance would be.

*Does she think so much of her work that she could close her eyes to love? To marriage and family?*

He considered her attachment to Brenda—surely she longed to be a mother. And yet, if he were honest with himself, she'd never said anything to give him encouragement. He could try all he wanted, but would he be able to change her perception of love?

Usually all Beranger had to do was walk into a room and smile to make women come running. The tables had been turned, and he wasn't quite sure how to turn them back around.

Maybe, he thought, turning toward Katie with his most winning smile, upping the ante would get her attention.

# CHAPTER TWENTY-NINE

Mavis gulped as she faced the crowd of shouting townsfolk, all angrily waving what looked like telegrams over their heads. When she'd realized there was more than a little interest in the new mayor and the upcoming meeting, she'd spoken with Reverend Caskill, and he'd volunteered his church for the meeting so they'd have more space. Usually Donald Dodge, the previous mayor, had had little to say or report. He'd conducted the meetings in the back room of the mercantile, easily fitting in the five council members and a trickle of other attendees. She'd heard his monotone had most people asleep within twenty minutes. She'd also moved the meeting time to midmorning after Clint had suggested that was the time most residents would be available in town.

*But this turnout is astonishing. And why is everyone so worked up?*

She stood next to the table where the other four council members sat. Oscar Hoffman, the butcher; Larry Paxton, owner of the mercantile; the boardinghouse proprietor, Sebastian Evans; and the reverend himself. All wore perplexed frowns. There seemed to be a buzz of hysteria in the air that had erupted after Mr. Moody, the telegraph operator, had arrived and passed out several telegrams. The day Mavis had been dreaming about and looking forward to was exploding like nitroglycerin before her eyes.

She banged the wooden gavel several times in an effort to quiet the room. "Please, everyone! Take a seat and be quiet so we can begin. I can't hear any of you when you all talk at once."

The buzzing continued. A few red-faced people sank to their seats, followed by a few more. Clint stood in the back, engaged in what looked like a serious conversation with Henry Glass. Russell McGrath, the new dentist, sat properly, though he had a tilt of uncertainty on his brows. The Five Sisters ranch hands had shown up for moral support; however, the smiles they'd been brandishing just a moment before were nowhere to be seen.

Mavis glanced at her uncovered left hand, which was holding her agenda, and felt a prick of anxiety.

*Why didn't I wear my gloves? I'd have felt so much more comfortable.*

She banged the gavel again. "Order, please."

The room quieted. She swallowed. Where to begin? Her council gazed at her for leadership. She decided to dive right in.

"Who wants to tell me what's going on? All this pandemonium is frightening."

"Wouldn't frighten a man! You ain't up to the job."

She didn't see who'd shouted the comment, but Clint scowled at the right side of the room.

Rhett and Beranger stood in the back of the room also, as did Santiago and his father, Miguel. Larsala sat primly in the middle of the room, looking around as if she didn't know what all the fuss was about. Mavis's sisters, who'd arrived only moments before, had scrunched into the back pew. Some of the faces Mavis hadn't ever seen—not even on Election Day.

Betty Lou Paxton, Larry Paxton's wife and partner in the mercantile, bolted to her feet. Her face looked like a storm cloud. "I'll tell you what's happened, Mrs. Applebee. Not five minutes ago, Mr. Moody delivered a handful of telegrams. Mine was from our landlady in Ohio. She's sold our building to someone else—*a Mr. Strong*—and it says our rent on the mercantile will double, beginning next month. He can't do that! Is it legal?"

Several people nodded and grumbled that a similar thing had happened to them as well.

"This person can't expect us to be able to pay such an increase, can he?" she went on. "That's outrageous and unconscionable. There's no way we can make such a high payment! No way in heaven. Why on earth would he do this without any notice at all?" She waved a small white paper before her face. "I think I'm going to faint." She put out her hand to Larry, who'd bolted out of his chair at the front table the moment he'd heard the news and rushed to her side, only to snatch the paper from her hand and search the print. "I told you time and again that we should have bought that building, Larry," she said. "Now we're going to lose everything!" Mrs. Paxton crumpled onto the bench.

Shouting erupted again.

Mr. Moody, the drugstore and telegraph owner, stood there white-faced, nodding. His expression was a blank stare. There were still a few telegrams in his hand. "I have ones for you too, Oscar, Sebastian, and Mr. Simon."

*All the major businesses in Eden. I didn't know so many buildings were rented and not owned.* Perhaps because of the timing of the telegrams— timed to arrive during her first meeting—her thoughts immediately flew to the scandalous events of a few months ago. *Is Donald Dodge somehow involved? He was deeply resentful when I won the election by such a large margin. Is this some scheme to gain revenge on the towns- folk who betrayed him? His brother, the doctor, plotted for years to retaliate against our father— and hurt a lot of people in the process. Are the brothers cut from the same cloth?*

"I got one from my landlord as well," the owner of the bathhouse called out, his brows knitted together. "Double! Who can expect a man to double his profit in one month on baths and shaves? It's impossible. I'm ruined!" He grasped the little hair he had on his head with both hands.

Mavis banged the gavel several more times, demanding silence. "Please be quiet. Let's conduct ourselves with self-control, or we won't ever figure this out."

The room quieted down, and she felt a trickle of sweat dribble between her shoulder blades. Clint came forward and stood at her side, but he was clearly waiting for her to make the next move.

*What should I do?*

"Mr. Paxton, does the telegram you received say where you are to send the payment to the new owner?"

The normally olive-skinned man's face had gone white. "Nothing except that payment is expected by the end of the month. We'll probably receive a letter from Mr. Strong telling us where to send payment."

Clint strode down the aisle. "Let me see that," he said, taking a telegram from a blanched-faced woman. He looked the missive over. "Maybe this is some kind of bad joke."

Oscar harrumphed, his face redder than Mavis had ever seen it. She hoped the butcher didn't expire right in the middle of the meeting.

Slowly, Russell McGrath stood in his pew. "Attention, everyone. I'm sorry you received such devastating news today," the dentist said. "I don't know if you're aware, but I came to Eden to invest my money. I heard your town was growing, and I wanted to start anew. I've bought several of the unfinished buildings along the cobblestone streets, with the intention of starting a variety of businesses. I've also given a few"— he glanced around at several of the faces—"of my *new* friends some loans at a very attractive interest rate. Lower than the bank here could offer. And only when they had a demonstrated need." He smiled at Karen Forester, the waitress who worked for Lavinia. "Like a new china hutch and china tea set." His friendly gaze slid over to Nicole Day, Clint's younger half sister who worked for Lavinia part time as well. "Or a new horse. You know, for things that are just out of reach. Things you've been dreaming of but haven't been able to afford. A violin for the young'un, train tickets to visit a relative, perhaps adding on to your home. Nothing big. What I'm saying is, if you need help with these payments, or anything else you've been saving up for, I'm here to assist you. I want to make your dreams happen tomorrow instead of five years from now."

"Those are the loans *I* used to give," Bud Larson, owner of Eden's small bank, shouted angrily. "You're stealing my business!" His glare was troubling.

"At an unheard-of interest rate, Mr. Larson. At a fraction of what you're charging, people are

245

happy to come to me. As a matter of fact, I have one client who came to me to pay you off."

"Why, you—"

Bud lunged for the man. Clint caught his shoulder before he could go anywhere and pulled him back, white-faced and spitting mad. "How come you got so much money, McGrath?" Bud demanded. "Not from drilling teeth."

Cool as a cucumber, Russell lifted a shoulder. "No, not by drilling teeth. I made my money the old-fashioned way: I inherited it."

More voices talking and complaining. The meeting was spiraling out of control.

Mavis's eyes narrowed with suspicion. Yes, it was true, Mr. McGrath had spoken with Henry immediately after he'd come to town about his intentions. He was setting up his dental practice in Eden and wanted to invest in the town as well. He'd bought a few of the unfinished buildings on speculation. Her seeing him everywhere around town made more sense now. He wasn't just being friendly, or investing—he was doing business by grooming his prospective banking customers.

*Does he intend to start a real bank in Eden as well? And how honest would that bank be?*

Meanwhile, who was buying up the occupied properties? Her gaze cut to Larsala Salazar and the innocent look on her face, then Mr. Wells, the businessman building the new hotel with the backing of unknown investors. As much as she hated having the thought, her suspicion also darted for a few seconds to Beranger. He'd known he was already coming to Eden. Belle had said he was extremely wealthy.

*Is he buying up commercial properties, intending to get his hands on all the real estate and then planning to run up the cost for everyone?*

Mavis took a deep breath. Now that she was mayor, she couldn't sit by and let Father's beloved town fall to the unscrupulous.

# CHAPTER THIRTY

In the throng of bumping people, Emma made her way out of the stuffy church, craning her neck as she looked for Santiago. He'd been in the crowd, along the left-hand wall with his father, listening to the impassioned pleas of the townsfolk. The council meeting had dissolved without much more being said. People scratched their heads or looked stone-faced and in shock after learning their livelihoods were at stake. Mavis had called an end to the cacophony so she could meet with Clint and Henry, try to make some sense out of all the telegrams, and see if they could track down the mysterious Mr. Strong who was threatening the peace and tranquility of their growing town.

Eden's population had expanded even more quickly than they'd all realized, Emma thought. Being away a few days made the newcomers stand out all the more. As she made her way toward Main Street, a wagon coming from the direction of Denver rolled past carrying three women who couldn't be anything but saloon girls by the way they were scantily dressed. A buxom woman with a wide smile held the lines of the team, and two small boys sat at her side, grinning happily.

She turned and studied the people.

Santiago had slipped away.

But back to the problem at hand. Somebody with money—and perhaps some influence—had gotten a whiff of how fast the place was growing and wanted to capitalize on the boom. The articles written about the Brinkman sisters had drawn men to town, and continued to do so. A number of those who had arrived first were miners who had had a handful of early successes in the streams and rivers in the area. That news had traveled faster than that of the five single heiresses to places like Leadville and Colorado Springs, snagging the attention of prospectors there who hadn't yet struck it rich. According to Henry, that had caused a further surge in the population. What the sisters had started, the gold and silver exploration had perpetuated.

A head taller than most, Beranger stood out. He was walking twenty feet ahead of Emma. Her heart tripped. For the last half hour, she'd been all too aware of him standing behind her in the crowded church, hat in hand, listening to the conversation along with everyone else. She wondered what he thought of Eden and the Five Sisters Ranch so far. Although she'd waited for a private moment last night, that hadn't arisen. The dining table between them had felt like the great divide. Right now, she longed to hear his voice. She'd grown accustomed to sitting at his right, listening when he spoke, or being a confidante when he had something to whisper.

All night, she'd watched Katie fulfill that role. If Emma was truthful with herself, the sight had hurt. Her little sister had played the good hostess and had kept up appearances, though Emma had seen her broken heart whenever their gazes touched. Katie was clearly pining for Santiago, who normally would have been in attendance.

Off to her right, and striding purposefully toward the church with a red, angry face, were Jean-Luc Boucher and his sister, Amorette. The brother and sister team owned Mademoiselle de Sells, the successful French restaurant in town. Jean-Luc's light brown hair was a mess as usual, and his square jaw was shadowed with stubble. He waved a scrap of paper in his hand while he marched. Amorette ran behind in a pretty sky-blue dress with paisley cuffs and collar, her blonde curls bouncing. They hadn't been at the meeting—they looked to have just received bad news about their rent too. Her heart sank. Eden would no longer feel like Eden if Mademoiselle de Sells were forced to close!

Emma cupped her mouth with one hand. "Beranger, please wait up."

He turned and looked around. "Are you following me, Miss Brinkman?" he said somewhat playfully as he touched the brim of his Stetson. "Haven't you had enough of me after three whole days in the stagecoach together?"

She laughed, her mind atwitter, but thought she saw a twinge of disappointment in his eyes. He was more handsome than ever. Last night, when the men were preparing to depart, he'd addressed her a bit stiffly, and she'd wondered why. He'd saved his smiles for Katie, who'd rallied under his attention, even laughing when he recounted the story of crazy Mr. Tug and the carpetbag.

"Yes, I guess I am following you," she said. "I hope you don't mind."

"Never," he said.

She noticed that, though his eyes were different colors, they both twinkled equally. She would never comment on anything like that, but they were so alluring she couldn't help but smile. He wore the clean pants he'd worn the night before too, which he must have carried with him on the trip, and a different shirt. His easy stance was one she'd gotten to know quite well.

"Thank you again for a lovely evening," he said. "Your ranch is spectacular. I can see why you love Eden so much."

*So formal. No compliments on my pretty dress? Or how nice I look? Where is the Beranger who sat close to me in the moonlight?*

"You're welcome," she said, a little hurt. He seemed preoccupied, not at all interested in what she had to say. "I'm sure we'll share many more evenings like that now that you're here."

Even though they'd just met, she felt close to him, like they shared a secret bond. She'd never had such a good friend.

*But does he feel the same?*

"Isn't this Mr. Strong business troublesome?" she said, searching for a neutral topic. "I can't imagine how this has happened. Until that astounding meeting, all had been right with the world, and now I don't know what to think. I'm relieved *my* shop isn't rented. None of my father's properties are."

"That's fortunate." He glanced toward the livery and scuffed a boot.

*Is he impatient to be on his way?*

She had the sinking feeling that he was putting up with her company and that was all.

"It might be more serious than you think," he continued. "I've seen something like this when I was in Australia."

"Australia?"

"From my time spent aboard ship. A town was eaten away one business at a time by an unscrupulous sheep rancher. Once he had enough power, he bought himself a sheriff. Nobody dared go up against him for fear of going to jail—or worse."

"Clint could never be bought," she countered.

"I agree. But back then, the honest sheriff suffered an unfortunate *accident,* if you will, and was replaced—by one of the sheep rancher's henchmen. Once the law is tainted, no one is safe." He gave her a curious look. "Not even the Brinkmans. I'd not like to see anything similar descend upon Eden." A lopsided smile appeared. "But that's far from happening here—yet. I'm confident Mavis, Clint, and the attorney will figure things out before it's too late. A good rule of law are imperative and should never be tainted with susceptibility to bribes or power. Laws protect law-abiding citizens as well as prosecute lawbreakers, and should be applied without prejudice. That is why Lady Justice wears a blindfold."

Emma stared. She'd never thought about the law that way—or really in any way at all. Beranger, with his knowledge and worldly experience, seemed larger than life. He made her aware of how much there was of the world beyond Eden, or Santa Fe, or even Philadelphia.

He smiled and drew close, lowering his voice. Her pulse sped up.

"By the way, what is Katie's favorite color? I'm sure you must know."

All the good feelings she'd been experiencing flew away on the breeze.

"Katie? Favorite color?"

He nodded. "I'd like to cheer her up. The men explained about Santiago and how sad she's feeling. I thought a pretty ribbon from your shop might do the trick."

"Y-yes, of course," she stuttered. "Blue. Her favorite color is blue."

"Ah, yes, to match her pretty eyes. Thank you. I'll be by later today to pick that up. You carry ribbons, don't you?" He touched the brim of his hat and made as if to continue on his way.

She couldn't breathe. She didn't want him to leave just yet. Not with the way she felt. Beranger was noticeably different here in Eden. Had he only been toying with her during their travels to make the days pass more quickly?

"Since you have nothing to do but relax until Blake and Moses return and take you to the mine, I thought I'd play tour guide and show you the town, the upper meadow, and the hanging bridge. Crossing it takes some nerve."

"I appreciate that, Emma, but Katie has already offered—later today. Maybe we can all go together."

*Katie? Again?*

No, Emma didn't want to be a third wheel.

He held up a hand. "Before you say anything, know that I have no romantic intentions toward your little sister, Emma. We're just friends— exactly like you and me."

"I was not inferring anything about you and Katie." She swallowed, not sure how she felt about that last statement. "It's just that Santiago's silence is repugnant. Katie has been left in limbo to suffer. She won't hold up much longer. An explanation is the least he owes her."

Out here in the sunshine, the difference in his irises was blatant. The colors sparkled, and she knew the instant he realized she was comparing the two.

"I can't believe you ever called them a curse, Beranger. Or ever considered them that way. I'm trying to decide which I prefer, the green or the blue . . ." She couldn't stop a wide smile. "I guess I'll just have to choose both."

His brows shot up as he contemplated her with a small smile. "Emma, I've been hired by you and your sisters in a professional capacity. You made it clear you have no interest in romance. Pleaded your case very eloquently. I totally understand. Did I ever try to change your mind?"

She blinked. His words were said in the nicest way, but she could feel an element of tension woven between them. "No, you didn't."

"Then why are you following me around? As much as I like your attention, it also"—and here he stepped closer, both of his eyes, the green and the blue, smoldering—"feeds my imagination."

"B-because we're friends."

*You told me one of your most intimate secrets.*

"I'm just trying to be hospitable, so you feel at home."

He gently wagged his head back and forth. "But I'm not at home, am I?"

*No, he isn't. Not by a long shot. And what does he really mean by that?*

She forced the question out of her mind. The point was that he'd taken her talk in the moonlight seriously. She was glad of that, because she'd *never* change her mind. Just the sight of poor Katie was enough to convince her that love could only break your heart.

When she focused back on Beranger, he'd taken a step away. "So," he said, his charming smile back. "Will you be joining us today for the town tour?"

"Later today? I'm sorry, I can't. I've a meeting with Mr. Buns, my employee. He's been wonderful for running the Toggery while I've been away. You two go ahead. You'll have fun."

"Done, then," he said, tipping his hat. "You have a nice day too."

The second he left, her smile vanished. She took a deep breath and watched him go, feeling as if she'd lost something precious. Perhaps she'd been misled by his attention on the trip. He *had* promised Blake he'd look after her—perhaps to him, their friendship had been nothing more than business.

# CHAPTER THIRTY-ONE

"Howdy," Maverick greeted Beranger, raking the small pebbles of dirt to the side of the entry to his property. "Your horse is doing fine. I gave him extra feed, being he's had such a tough workout. Interestin' to see if he comes around—gentles down. The marks of his mistreatment tell his story."

At the rail of the paddock, Beranger watched his horse gallop the fence, still sweat-stained from his run from Santa Fe. Beranger hadn't attempted to clean him the previous night. Giving the horse a day to settle and get used to his new surroundings felt more prudent than fighting him.

Beranger struggled to process his conversation with Emma. He'd hoped that the thought of him spending time with Katie would persuade her to open up to him. But she'd been more than convincing about her decision to always reject love during their conversation in the moonlight, and she'd stuck to her guns today. Maybe she'd only ever consider him her friend.

"I should try to rinse him off," Beranger said, still a bit distracted. Glancing around, he spotted a water pump and several buckets just outside the front doors of the barn. Would the horse stand quietly while being washed?

"Want me to do that?"

Maverick was a large man, and he had plenty

of experience with horses. Hell, it was his job. Still, Beranger didn't feel right chancing the livery man getting hurt. Not until he was a little more familiar with the gelding. The kid's words in Santa Fe rang in his head.

*Stay away. Stay far away.*

"I appreciate that, Maverick, but I'll tackle the job later today. Give him more time to get used to his new surroundings—and for me to change into my old traveling clothes." He looked down at the front of his shirt and brushed some dust off one of his sleeves. "I have a feeling I may get the wet end of the deal."

Maverick laughed. "That's probably smart. Whenever I get a new horse, I can't wait to get to know the fella. Settling in sounds like a good idea."

From what Beranger had learned the night before, this was Maverick's livery, and Mavis was his partner. Of all things, there was a stained-glass window in the loft of the barn. Several nice-looking wagons lined one fence with FOR SALE signs propped on their front seats.

Eden had a pleasant feel.

"I said get home and get to your chores, worthless boy!"

The shouted statement from somewhere made Beranger look around. The sun warmed his back as he kept his gaze on Charger. A memory came floating back.

"Please, Your Grace, send the boy away. You've given him enough of your time and treasure," his stepmother pleaded. "How long must I suffer his presence in my life? That was never a condition of our marriage, that I'd be mothering a cursed commoner whose eerie gaze robs me of sleep and keeps me from conceiving another legitimate heir. What if something were to happen to Gavin, God forbid? The dukedom and the duchy would fall to your brother. I believe I've been patient with you long enough. You promised me years ago that he'd only be here for a time, but you've not honored that promise. I want another child, William. Of my own. That is my job as duchess. Please don't rob me of my destiny any longer. As long as your illegitimate son lives under these roofs, that won't happen."

"Why not?" his father bit back. "You're being superstitious. I don't believe in curses or spells. If you don't conceive, do not blame that on him—or his unusual appearance. That is something he can't help!"

"Give me one year, Your Grace. That's all I'm asking. Since you didn't send him to Eton with Gavin, then send him to friends in Canterbury or Northington—anywhere. Frame it so that it won't be a punishment, but an adventure. I'm sure by the time he returns, I'll be pregnant again. You'll see that I'm right—and have been right all these years. I beg of you. Please do this one small indulgence for me."

His father had resisted her demands for years. That day, he softened. Lifting a hand, the duke had run a hand over the side of her hair, and then they embraced. When they parted, the light of triumph shone in her eyes.

"I guess one year won't hurt," his father went on. "And as you say, he'll probably enjoy time away. He is growing up. Already thirteen years old. Maybe he'll find something that catches his eye and remain. I'll write to Sir Stefano Ricci in Bologna. With his position as professor at the university, and also his several sons around Beranger's age, Beranger will be happily settled. More so than here."

She caressed the duke's arm. "A brilliant idea, Your Grace."

His father's capitulation had ripped Beranger's heart in two. He was barely able to attend his father's birthday gathering that evening with a smile on his face. He'd given the duke the present he'd saved to buy, and when it was unwrapped, his father had embraced him and told him he loved him. Later that night, before Beranger lost his nerve, or before his father had time to set the duchess's plan into action, Beranger had stolen away, taking a horse from his father's stable and staying in the shadows as he made his way toward the coast. There, he sold the animal for a few gold coins—and sold away his own freedom for the next four years.

"Pardon me," someone said from behind.

Beranger turned to find the dentist standing close by. In Beranger's woolgathering, he hadn't heard Maverick leave or this man walk up. He held a small paper and a pencil in his hands; he looked to have been taking notes. Beranger waited for him to continue. He didn't seem inclined to shake hands.

"I hear you're new to town, Mr. North."

The fellow stood straight, with his shoulders pulled back. Still, his head only came to the middle of Beranger's chest. His trousers were of the style worn by English working-class men—tradesmen, laborers, and sailors—hemmed up slightly above the man's ankle. But his hands belonged to a gentleman—soft and white, with the fingernails well groomed. He was an enigma, with brown eyes that matched his hair.

*Is he trying to present himself as something he is not?*

"My name is Russell McGrath. If you find yourself in need of dental work of any kind, I encourage you to seek me out. And in case you're like most people I know and have an aversion to dentistry, know that I've recently begun to use nitrous oxide, more commonly known as laughing gas. I guarantee you won't feel a thing. When I'm finished you'll be as happy as if you'd spent an hour in a pub. In these progressive times, keeping your teeth to a ripe old age is possible, with a little help."

The small man's gaze was anchored on Beranger's mouth, as if he were waiting for an invitation to have a look inside.

Beranger figured a man couldn't be shy if he wanted to work on people's teeth. "I'll keep that in mind."

McGrath smiled and nodded.

Maverick, now raking by the water pump, leaned on his tool and withdrew his bandana to wipe his brow. "And now you're giving out loans as well. Isn't that right, McGrath?"

The dentist's face beamed. "Well, yes, Mr. Daves. That's exactly right. If Mr. North was in the meeting today, he probably knows that already. I've made a few small loans, to help out or grant an inconsequential wish. A few dollars here and there. I'm no bank."

McGrath put his hand on the rail of the corral and picked at a tiny chip in the paint, then looked through the breezeway to the interior of the livery as if his razor-sharp gaze could actually see everything inside. "I was wondering if you might be interested in taking out a loan yourself," he went on, turning back to Maverick.

"Now why would I want to do that?" Maverick waved his arm across his property. "Mavis and I keep the place in top shape."

"You may want to give these boards a new coat of paint? That's a quick way to make something a little ragged look new. Or perhaps there's some sort of smithy equipment you've been dreaming about? A new, sharper file, a larger bellows to make a hotter fire? I don't know. I'm not a black-smith. But I'm sure you can think of a few tools you don't have but would like to own. I can make that happen. No waiting."

*This little fella's slick. Comes in pretending that he wants to meet me, with his true intention to sell Maverick a loan. I wonder how many fall for his pitch?*

Beranger crossed his arms and leaned against the fence. It wasn't his place to give Maverick advice, but he wouldn't trust the dentist as far as he could throw him.

Maverick smiled and raised a brow in amusement. "My place looks fine to me, McGrath. I won't need any of your services today, tomorrow, *or ever.*"

McGrath shrugged. "I'm hurt you sound angry. I didn't mean any offense." He chuckled. "I forget Mrs. Applebee is your partner. I'm sure she has ample funds to do all the fixing-up around here to your heart's content."

Maverick's smile stayed plastered to his face, but his eyes narrowed. "That's a fact. But we don't run our business like that. Any expenses come out of the profits, not from her."

*Don't give this little worm any information, Maverick. You're not obligated.*

Beranger didn't really know why he'd taken such a dislike to McGrath. Maybe it was because he'd come in on one pretense as a means to another end. Beranger didn't work that way.

McGrath looked away. "I best be off. You gentlemen have a good day."

He set off down the road and headed straight for the Toggery, where Beranger had seen Emma disappear after their earlier conversation.

"I think I'll mosey on myself, Maverick. I'll be back shortly to wash Charger and see exactly how bad his ground manners actually are. I had an earful of what he's like in Santa Fe before we began our journey, but that's about it."

"If I can do anything, let me know. And welcome to Eden. Excitin' to think about the mine. John Brinkman didn't have the time or interest to do what you and his girls are taking on. Mavis has been speculating for months. I hope they hit it big."

"We're all pretty excited," he responded, liking the smithy.

Beranger couldn't tell if Maverick had feelings for Mavis and might be competition for the sheriff, or not. Clint had actually colored up the night of the dinner when Rhett mentioned Mavis's upcoming birthday. Was he planning to propose? Emma had said she felt they were moving in that direction. Things in Eden were becoming a little complicated. But that would change just as soon as Blake and Moses returned and they set out for the claim.

Out there, the solitude was what he craved, what set his mind straight, and what made him able to breathe deeply. No ghosts of yesteryear pushing him on—and if he hit pay dirt, all the better.

"Things don't happen overnight. Takes planning, digging, and then hours of tough, grueling work. But I like that."

"I can see that you do." Maverick resumed raking. "And now we have this mystery about Mr. Strong. I'm plenty glad we own the land and building as well as the business. I wouldn't want to be in my neighbors' shoes. I love this place and the horses, and I think Mavis does too."

# CHAPTER THIRTY-TWO

*Five o'clock will never arrive! How will I survive one more hour?*

The Toggery was dead, and Emma thought she might die from boredom too. Mr. Buns had happily taken the afternoon off when she'd offered, since he'd covered for her solely in her absence. She hadn't really noticed the slow days before, caught up as she had been in her dreams and ambitions to make her shop into something special. But now, after her adventure to Santa Fe and the journey home, its walls felt like a tomb built to keep her away from the people she loved and a life waiting to be lived. She'd tried distracting herself by straightening the shelves and racks, cataloging the supplies, and adding each column of the accounting books six times. When all else failed, she'd dusted and swept to her heart's content. Compared to Mrs. Sackett's place in Santa Fe, her shop felt a bit ragged around the edges—and lacking in inventory. But once the garments arrived from Santa Fe, things would look up. She'd show the dresses and other items to Elizabeth and her other seamstress so they could draw up similar patterns of their own. Earlier in the day, Dr. McGrath had proved a small distraction—until she informed him she did not need a loan. Once that had been established, he'd smiled and gone on his way.

*I want to be outside in the sunshine.* She checked the watch pinned to her bodice. *One painful hour until closing. How will I survive?*

Emma trudged to the front window and gazed out at the Hole in the Floor saloon, so named because the establishment boasted a urinal at the foot of the bar. *How disgusting!* Even now, men teemed in and out, anxious to drink their problems away. Unfortunately for her and the ladies who might want to visit her business, the Toggery sat between Eden's two saloons. Poor Fred's out her back door, and the Hole in the Floor out her front. She'd not had any problems so far with drunks, except for the noise that sometimes occurred, but that didn't mean trouble wouldn't happen. She'd heard laughter about the long trough at the foot of the bar, and how handy men found the revolting thing once the snows had fallen.

The boardinghouse where Beranger had a room was across the street also, but deeper into the lot. Their earlier conversation troubled her on one hand, and made butterflies hatch in her tummy on the other.

*What a puzzling man. So different from the men around here.*

Perhaps, after they'd parted ways, he'd gone back to the boardinghouse and was on the wide front porch now, sipping a cup of English tea?

She laughed, her fingers dabbling with the neckline of her dress. No, she couldn't imagine Beranger doing that, even if he *was* from England. He was more the whiskey type, but not someone who'd drink to excess. Her mind pictured him walking the cool, stone-paved hallways of his father's castle after a long day in the saddle, wearing snug riding pants, a fitted jacket, and tall black boots that clicked when he stepped. A sword swung from his belt. He'd turn to a massive, ten-foot-tall wooden door and sweep the barrier open with ease. Entering a bedchamber furnished with antique tables carved from the finest wood, velvet-upholstered chairs, and an immense canopy bed covered in costly linens, he'd toe off his boots before a stone fireplace and sink back, locking his fingers behind his head.

An appreciative sigh slipped from her lips.

*I am attracted to Beranger. I can't fool myself any longer. Maybe a little infatuated as well. There is no crime in that. But I'm not in love. No, that will never happen.*

Beranger had been honest with her about his background, and she respected him for that. But he'd never told her *why* he'd come to America. *Why* he'd run away and acted the hooligan, as he'd described himself. Knowing him as well as she did now, she couldn't imagine that type of behavior from him in the least.

Across the street, Santiago rode up to the Hole in the Floor and dismounted. He flicked his reins over the hitching rail and disappeared through the swinging saloon doors.

Emma blinked and grasped the windowsill.

*Why would he go there and not just to his own cantina?*

She had intended to seek him out after the council meeting, but she had been distracted by Beranger. Guilt pushed on her shoulders. Santiago owed Katie an explanation. A conversation at the very least. The more time that passed between his return—conveniently coinciding with the arrival of Mrs. Salazar—the longer Katie suffered in limbo. Tonight, her little sister would have another sleepless night. She was noticeably thinner than she'd been before Emma's trip to Santa Fe. Something had to be done. The truth, no matter how cruel and painful, was better than the unknown. Even if it broke her heart to face the reality that she and Santiago were over, at least then the healing process could begin.

Making her decision, Emma locked up the store and turned the sign. It felt odd to close before five o'clock for no other reason than that she wanted to, but her mind was set.

She marched across the street and into the saloon. Santiago had some explaining to do.

# CHAPTER THIRTY-THREE

Santiago was just raising his whiskey glass to his lips when a surprised murmur from the men rumbled around the room. To his utter shock, Emma Brinkman marched right up to the bar. Determination was etched across her features, and her heels clicked sharply on the wooden planks of the saloon. She wasn't trying to walk softly—she was making a statement. She was clearly about to give Santiago a tongue-lashing. The Brinkmans watched out for their own.

He set his glass down with a thump.

"Mr. Alvarado, I'd like a word with you."

"Certainly, Señorita Brinkman." He glanced around, looking for a quiet spot. He knew very well what this was about. Actually, he was surprised they'd taken this long to confront him. "Where would you like to go? In here?" He swung his open palm to the side. "Or would you like to go outside? Perhaps to your shop, where we can speak in private."

Her face flamed. He hadn't meant to embarrass her. He liked Emma Brinkman—very well. All the Brinkmans, for that matter. And he loved Katie Brinkman, but he was mixed up. Didn't know exactly how he felt. And for that reason, he'd avoided going to see her, although he'd known doing so was cruel.

She swallowed. "That corner will do fine."

He nodded and followed her over. They sat down.

"What's on your mind?"

*Will she even remember the reason I left town in the first place? That my brother Demetrio is still locked up in prison—and will be for many more years?*

"I'm happy to see you've returned safely to Eden, Santiago," she said once she was out of earshot of the rest of the bar patrons.

"Thank you, Emma." He wouldn't jump the gun. He'd let her direct the conversation. "Good to be back."

"You were able to see your brother, Demetrio. I'm sure you were relieved. Katie told me that he's doing as well as can be expected."

He nodded. "Fifteen years is a long sentence."

"Yes. It's unfortunate Demetrio found trouble. Your father has suffered much because of him."

*So true!*

She tried to smile, but her lips wobbled. "We— and I mean me and my whole family—only want the best for you and yours, Santiago. We always have, since we met. The only thing now is that one of *ours* is suffering, and I've come to find out why. Your silence is not helping Katie. To the contrary, the longer you put off seeing her, the longer she has to imagine the worst, and the more the situation disintegrates. If indeed your feelings toward her have changed, which seems obvious to me, the kindest thing to do, the *right* thing to do, would be to tell her immediately."

"Are you finished, Emma?"

"You don't look very sorry, Santiago. Not at all. I could go on all day, if you want."

What should she have expected from him? Larsala Zelinga Salazar, a woman he'd never thought he'd see again in his life, had returned to Eden. He'd tried to keep his distance until he decided how he felt and had a chance to speak with Katie again, but Larsala had sought him out. The very day of Larsala's return, she'd asked him to supper at her aunt's home. Yesterday, she'd sent a note with one of her men asking if Santiago had a moment for an old friend, to show her how Eden had grown since she'd been away. What could he say? No? That wasn't possible. Besides, he hadn't *wanted* to say no. Just the sight of her, the sound of her voice set his blood on fire. He needed time to sort things out. He loved Katie. And until two days ago, he had believed his future was with her.

*Now I'm not so sure.*

"No, I don't want you to," he said, answering her question. "I think you've drawn enough attention to yourself by coming in here."

"I don't care what these men think of me." She glanced around. "I hardly know a face, so

272

why would I mind? I do care about my sister, who believes she's in love with you. Have your feelings changed, Santiago? Do you still love Katie? And if yes, why are you hurting her so?"

Beranger began to doubt Emma's sanity when he witnessed her march across the street and disappear through the saloon door. He'd just finished grooming Charger and was turning the gelding out when a flash of burgundy fabric caught his eye. What could she be thinking? Men in their cups couldn't be trusted. He'd seen more than one fellow go from soft-spoken to beastly in the course of a few short hours. The Brinkman name wouldn't shield her from harm. Altering his course, he ran the distance to the Hole in the Floor. Stopping just outside, he took a deep, calming breath, and then quietly slipped inside. He glanced around.

Spotting Emma only took a moment. There were three full tables and seven men at the bar. She was in the corner, speaking with Santiago Alvarado.

Sensing no danger, he kept his face turned away as he walked to an empty spot at the bar and lifted a foot to the brass boot rail—the one right above the long channel in the floor he'd also heard about. The carved-out trough ran slightly downhill. Needless to say, he'd patronized better-smelling places. He put a dollar coin on the bar.

The bartender approached. "Whiskey?"

Beranger nodded, eyeing the brown bottles against the wall. Back in England, his father had insisted on the best single-malt Scotches only and kept a full supply of those and other expensive spirits. He and Gavin had sampled many of them before Beranger had run away. Then, in America, after Beranger had made his fortune and when whatever town he was in was large enough to carry imports, that's what he drank too.

"You keep anything in the back?" he asked, not seeing any bottles to his liking. "Something imported?"

After having just pulled the cork, the bartender drew back. "My stuff is as good as any."

The man next to Beranger looked over. "Poor Fred's carries a few more choices."

"Much obliged," Beranger answered. He looked back at the bartender. "I'll still take a shot of yours."

The scowl dropped off the bartender's face, and he poured Beranger a healthy amount.

"And one for my friend here," Beranger said, referring to the fellow who'd spoken up. He reeked of whiskey already, and his bloodshot eyes looked painful. "And for the rest of the men at the bar."

Garbled thanks came from up and down the row as the bartender proceeded to fill empty glasses. Men from the tables came forward.

Angling his head so he could see Emma and

Santiago's heated conversation, Beranger watched in fascination. Sipping the rotgut, Beranger almost smiled. He was remembering the last few nights on the road, when she'd gotten hold of a topic and hadn't let go until she was satisfied with his answers. Santiago seemed to be the one getting the once-over now.

"That's *Emma*," the man beside him whispered, having seen the direction of Beranger's gaze. "Miss Brinkman to any of *us*. She's one of them highfalutin gals from Philadelphia that inherited a huge ranch and untold amounts of money." He snorted and tossed back his glass, wiping his mouth with the back of his hand. "We ain't fit for the likes of her. No, siree, we ain't. And she'd be the first to tell us so. She dresses real purty just to get our attention, knowing we can't do a damn thing about it. My mama would call that a tease."

He'd turned his back to the bar and rested his elbows on it, his narrowed gaze anchored on Emma. Beranger sensed the mood in the saloon going sour.

"No, sir, that's not *nice* at all."

# CHAPTER THIRTY-FOUR

"You're not being honest with me, Santiago!" Emma said, trying to control her temper. Losing her self-control in the saloon wouldn't do. "There's a reason you haven't sought Katie out. You can kid yourself all you like, but if your feelings *hadn't* changed, you wouldn't be frightened to speak with her." Although Santiago was Katie's beau, he was closer to Mavis's age. That was one of the reasons she and the sisters had been concerned about Katie's infatuation with him in the first place. *And* the fact that Katie was a total innocent, and he seemed *plenty* experienced. She'd had little practice with men, having spent her last year in Philadelphia studying to be a teacher. Educators at the better schools had to prove they had a teaching certificate as well as a blemish-free background. Velma and Vernon Crowdaire had kept a tight rein on her.

Santiago's face flushed.

"Not being truthful is the last thing I'd do where Katie is concerned. I just haven't figured out how I feel. I'm confused. I haven't seen Larsala for years. Her return has knocked me off my feet."

Emma felt a twinge of guilt. Hadn't *she* been in love with two different men at the same time? Tim and Cooper had had her walking on air. But the difference was that she'd never told either one. Or kept one on the hook while she spent time with the other. She'd never made plans with either.

"That wouldn't be an issue if you truly loved Katie," she threw out, now seeing the difference in their situations well. She had nothing to regret. "I wonder if you *ever* truly did love her!"

Anger flashed in his eyes. "I need time. A few days. Before Larsala came to town, I had many, many long hours on the trail to ponder my life. And even more waiting to see Demetrio. We can't always have what we want."

*How dare he lecture me? I know that better than anyone. Just look at how my own mother's life played out. And how my own father waited years for us to return. If anyone knows heartbreak, it's our family.*

She inched forward and lowered her voice. She didn't want this discussion to get out of control.

"I was led to believe Larsala came back for Demetrio. That *they* were sweethearts and set to marry until she was taken away."

"Who told you that?" His lips barely moved.

"You're not the only one who's lived here for years. For one, Clint knows a lot about your family, and Henry too. What did you think? That your history was locked away tight where no one would remember? Are you after *your brother's* girl?"

"Demetrio has ten years left to serve!"

"That doesn't make what you're doing right."

"He would *want* her to be happy!"

Emma looked at the floor and counted to ten. "I'm sure you're right. Go ahead, court her, marry her. I don't care. Just level with Katie first. Before she catches you and Mrs. Salazar kissing in the moonlight. That would be unforgivable."

His face softened, and Emma actually felt a moment of empathy.

"I'm not saying I don't love Katie."

"Oh no? You just want them both!"

Santiago shifted uncomfortably in his chair. He was dressed nicely, as he usually was, and had a pleasant, spicy aroma. She could see how Katie could fall for his dark good looks and flashing eyes. Santiago was handsome—a fact he knew only too well. When he thought no one was watching, she'd seen him work his charming smile on any unwary young woman. She had no doubt he would drag this out, keeping Katie on the hook for as long as he could.

She couldn't stop her curiosity. "And how does Mrs. Salazar feel about you, I wonder? Did she already know her love was locked up before she came back?"

Santiago's lips flattened out—the first sign she'd actually pricked his anger.

"That is her *private* business."

"You've made her business mine by hurting my

sister and telling me you have feelings for both. Don't you dare try to put this on *me*."

She noticed some of the men had turned and were now watching the discussion play out. She really didn't know many of them. A moment of unease sliced through her. Surely Santiago was their friend? The scowls on their faces attested to that. She slid her gaze surreptitiously to the door. Fifteen feet away. She'd have to pass a host of men when the time came to leave. The sweetly sour scent of urine wafted her way, making her blink. This was Eden. Her home. She was safe here.

Santiago cut his gaze away from Emma and to the door. "Who knows how this will play out? I can't foretell the future, and you can't either."

"Be a man and make up your mind. And then tell Katie. I'm not even sure how she'll respond if you decide you *are* still in love with her. You may have lost her anyway, Santiago. And when that happens, you'll have no one to blame but yourself. I've never seen her so devastated. Speak with her before she gets sick. She's lost all kinds of weight. A strong wind could blow her away."

"I will speak to Katie today. I promise—"

"Why the heck are ya backin' down from some *woman*, Santiago?" a drunkard shouted. He pushed away from the end of the bar and tottered toward them, anger flashing in his eyes.

She recognized him as a miner she'd seen

many times from her shop window, entering the Hole in the Floor around midday each day. She'd never seen him leave. His red bulbous nose was pocked with holes, his eyes narrow-set. Tattered sleeves were rolled to his elbows, exposing large, beefy arms and filthy hands. She'd bet her life his trousers had never been washed; the normally silver rivets in the thick indigo denim of his Levi's jeans were caked with mud.

"And a young whippersnapper at that! She ain't better'n you, no matter how much she looks down her nose. Teach her some respect!"

The tone, although drunk and slurring, was filled with malcontent. Anger radiated up Emma's back when laughter broke out around the room.

*I don't look down my nose at anyone.*

Gazes heated by too much whiskey, and maybe too many broken dreams as well, leered at her. Emma glanced to the door again to see that two men had stepped together in front of it, blocking the way.

*This is Eden. Nothing can happen to me. My family and friends are right outside. My shop is across the street.*

Emma stood, followed by Santiago.

Santiago stepped in front, shielding her, but a scalding fear suddenly raced up and down her spine. There were too many of them. Santiago was badly outnumbered. They wouldn't kill her, but other possibilities raced through her mind.

She glanced around, looking for another way out, an escape if things got rowdy. She'd heard the noise all the way across the street the last time a bar fight broke out, then seen men stumbling out covered in blood—and others carried to the undertaker's.

*These men wouldn't dare harm me, would they? Why are they set against me? I haven't done anything to them.*

Unexpectedly, Beranger appeared at her side. Tall and unafraid, he took her hand. "Back away, men. Don't make trouble for yourselves."

A great relief rushed through her.

"Miss Brinkman and I are walking out of here. Don't make any trouble, and I won't have to hurt you."

She realized Beranger was unarmed, but many of the others were not.

Santiago flanked her other side.

Another man laughed and moved to stand by the bulbous-nosed fellow. "Why's she in here chewing on our friend? First we get women running the livery, the mill, and tannery—then we get a woman mayor! Now they're invading our saloons." He jabbed an unsteady finger toward Emma's face. "This is the last straw. She has the whole town, and all we got is this broken-down seedy saloon."

"Hey, hey, hey," the bartender sputtered. "My bar ain't seedy."

"She's not allowed in here, and she knows that," the man went on. "*No* women is. 'Specially uppity ones like her! Still, in she marches like she owns the place."

"But I'm *not* uppity," Emma said in defense of herself. At least she didn't think she was. "I just had something to discuss with Santiago." Since Beranger had appeared, her fear had abated. "Things may have gotten heated—"

"Keep quiet," he murmured. "We're not out of here yet."

"But this is Eden," she argued softly. "These aren't bad men, or outlaws. They're miners and cowboys."

"Who've all had too much to drink, no luck to count, and more disappointments than you could ever envision."

"You may be right, but I'm *not* uppity." She glanced around. Some of the men who had appeared ready to fight a moment ago hadn't backed off. The ugly animosity of someone feeling sorry for their own plight was growing in their eyes. "I like everyone."

Beranger turned to drill her with a stare. "Would you be saying that if I weren't here at your side?"

She realized he was right. Her bravery was misplaced. Shame filled her.

He took a step away and was pulling her behind him when she heard the click of a gun. She froze, tugging on Beranger's hand.

A fellow not much older than herself, with his hip resting against one of the gambling tables, now had his unsteady revolver pointed their way. "I don't want to harm you, Miss Brinkman, but I'd just like ta hear you say you're sorry. For coming in here and disturbing our day. Can you do that, please?"

"Don't bust up my saloon!" the bartender commanded. "I just got things put back together after last week!" A leather strip tied back his long scraggly hair. He placed his hands on the bar and leaned forward with a sneer. The man had always reminded Emma of a pirate.

The tension filling Beranger was palpable.

Santiago hadn't said a word.

She took a breath. "I would be pleased to—"

# CHAPTER THIRTY-FIVE

"No. She won't apologize. She's done nothing wrong," Beranger gritted through a clenched jaw. An apology from Emma would be exactly the wrong thing at that moment. An apology would give the disgruntled, drunken men the idea that they'd been mistreated. That would be just the excuse they were looking for to start a fight.

"Who're you?" The first man growled, eyeing Beranger as if there was some big conspiracy going on. "Ain't never seen you before today. Have you won the prize of being her husband?"

Before Beranger could answer, the man with the gun stepped away from the table. "Shut up, Jack. We don't want no problems, Miss Brinkman. Not with you or your new dandy husband. Just say you're sorry! Us miners and no-account gents do have some pride. Not much, but some . . ."

"Quit," Santiago stated.

"We're on your side!"

The tension mounted. Beranger knew he needed to get Emma out of there before a brawl broke out. Three more men, looking curious, pushed away from the bar, nodding their agreement with the troublemakers. They inched forward, closing in. Seemed everyone wanted to see a Brinkman eat crow.

Somebody in the back of the room hefted a chair and threw it over the men. The piece of furniture clattered nosily at Emma's feet and broke into several pieces.

She screamed and scrambled back.

When the large red-nosed miner threw a punch at Beranger's face, he easily ducked. He landed his own blow on the man's soft middle. Breath rushed out with a grunt, but two more men stepped up to replace him.

Beranger raised his fists and tightened his muscles, ducking several more punches to his head.

"Leave Miss Brinkman alone!" he heard the bartender bellow amid the sound of breaking glass.

Shouts and profanity erupted. Seemed everyone wanted in on the fight. From the corner of his eye, Beranger saw Santiago standing guard over Emma. They needed to get the situation under control.

"And that goes for her friend and Santiago."

Nobody listened.

Beranger, an expert pugilist, faked left and landed a punch on his aggressor, but didn't see a fist coming in from the left.

"One on one!" someone shouted. "No ganging up. Let Jax take him on, since he won the boxing match last month at the festival—"

"The day *Mayor Applebee* was elected!"

Laughter erupted.

285

"What kind of a name is that, anyway? Yes, Mayor Applebee. No, Mayor Applebee," some-one mocked.

Taken by surprise, Beranger was grasped by his hair. He was violently pulled in and he smacked someone's forehead. Stumbling back, a rushing sound almost overwhelmed him as sights and sounds from long ago came rushing back.

"Keep your fists up, Beranger! Guard your face!" Uncle Harry called from the corner of the three-rope ring. Boys usually weren't allowed to fight, only spar, but Gavin had insisted until the duke's boxing master, and teacher to his brother, relented. Few could stand up to Gavin once an idea took root. And if they did, they ended up in some sort of trouble, brought on by what-ever skewed rendition of events Gavin all too happily reported to their father.

Usually Beranger only watched Gavin's lessons, but this day, Gavin had taken a particularly hard punch to the jaw. He'd been knocked off his feet and humiliated by someone much smaller than himself. So he'd launched a campaign to fight Beranger, his younger brother, who had no formal training except for the few moves their uncle had shown him. Gavin had been taught to fight according to the

Marquess of Queensberry Rules—no blows below the belt, no punches to the back of the head, and when an opponent went down on one knee, fighting must be stopped to allow him to regain his footing. The rules should have been enough to protect Beranger. Nevertheless, in the fight that followed, Beranger took a sneaky knee below the belt, which no one else saw. When Gavin landed a rabbit punch to the back of his head, Gavin's instructor railed at him, but when Beranger fell to one knee, Gavin went in for the kill. Only a sharp command from Uncle Harry stopped him. Once Beranger recovered, Uncle Harry let the fight continue—without the Marquess of Queensberry Rules.

Beranger came away with a split lip and a black eye, but Gavin looked much worse. Satisfaction eased his pain. The duchess was not pleased.

Well, Beranger was no longer a boy. Aboard the *Destiny*, as his body had filled out from long hours of strenuous work, he'd perfected his fighting skills by sparring against the men. Though Beranger was younger than the other sailors, he went on boxing—and winning—until no one would take him on.

The memory of Gavin was like kerosene on

fire. Beranger shook off the stars that danced before his eyes and took up where he'd left off. Two drunkards went down and stayed there.

Soon the bartender was in the middle of things, trying to pull the crowd apart.

The men began backing away.

With the back of his hand, Beranger wiped away a trickle of blood. "Miss Brinkman deserves your respect, not your scorn," he barked. "I'm sure you'll realize that once you sober up." Turning, he strode over to Santiago. Emma had watched wide-eyed from behind him. He took her arm and escorted her out into the bright sunlight.

"Beranger. I'm so sorry." She reached up to touch his face, but he pulled out of her reach. "I didn't think anything like that could happen because of me."

"You didn't think."

She nodded. "I'm so thankful you were there."

"I was only there because I saw you go in."

They crossed the street and headed for her shop.

"Curse it, Emma! What were you thinking going into a room full of drunken men? Surely you know better."

She didn't respond. He didn't care. Anger welled up inside him again. She should have thought through her actions before going blindly into the pub. If he and Santiago hadn't been there, the bartender might not have been able to stop something worse from happening. She took out her key and unlocked the door to the Toggery. He followed her in.

Inside, she relocked the door and left the CLOSED sign in the window before turning to face him. "I needed to speak with Santiago."

She turned on her heel and walked toward the back room.

"About Katie?" he called after her. "Surely you could have waited to find him elsewhere. Those men had a good point. Outside that saloon, they have to abide by the rules of Eden, and for the most part, I'll bet they do. In there, they like to be themselves—without worry."

She returned with a clean, damp cloth that she held out. "Are you taking their side?"

He blotted his face gingerly.

"You're missing the blood," she said, anger in her own voice. "Let me have that."

Conceding because of the ache in his jaw and the headache that was now ringing in his head, he allowed her to take the cloth and gently dab around his face. He noticed that her expression was etched with concern.

After his fight with Gavin, Uncle Harry had done the same, a wide smile stretching his lips.

*"You whipped him soundly, Beranger. He'll not taunt you much anymore. He'll not want to taste any more of what you served to him on a platter. I'm proud of you, my boy, very much so. The duke will be proud as well."*

At the memory, his breath caught. He cut his gaze away from Emma's eyes to look out the window so she wouldn't see his hurt. But the duke had *not* been proud Beranger had pounded his heir and blackened both of his eyes. Possibly even broken his nose. No, he'd been the opposite, and he let Beranger know it. The duke had never been proud of Beranger for anything. He'd been a complication in the duke's life from the very start.

For the first time in years, Beranger wondered about his family. About Brightshire, the small town in Kent, and the people there he loved. Not family, but servants and grounds people. Adults who used to be interested in what he thought and what he had to say.

*Is my father even still alive? There's no reason he shouldn't be.*

Or, by now, had Gavin, the Marquess of Rand, become Duke of Brightshire? So many questions. And not a single answer. And most important of all, what about his uncle, Lord Harry?

Emma's hand stilled. "What, Beranger? You're thinking about something important. The look that came over your eyes just now makes me hurt inside." Gently taking his jaw, she held him still as she pressed the cold rag to his lip. "We need to get some ice at the restaurant before this swells."

"That won't help."

She lowered one hand and placed her other on

his shoulder. They were close. "Please tell me."

"What?"

"Why you left England. Why you'd give all that up."

"I didn't have anything *to* give up, Emma. I was illegitimate. I had no claim on *anything*."

"There's more to your story. You were young. Something must have been a catalyst. Something must have happened. Please share with me."

He'd already told her more than he'd told anyone, including Fran. He'd helped her through the day Brenda had been adopted.

"Beranger?"

"I left to see the world." That sounded stupid even to his own ears.

She stepped back and put her hands on her hips, her brows furrowed. "I don't think so."

*Would telling her really hurt?*

He thought not. "I eavesdropped on a private conversation. My father was getting ready to send me away. To stay with his friend in Italy."

"What do you mean, send you away? For the summer? A season?" Her eyes narrowed. "Not forever."

"My stepmother had said a year, but that was just to get him to say yes. She'd have preferred forever, but he'd never before agreed to send me away at all, so she settled for a year. She was frightened of me."

He leaned against her counter, cradling his arm.

She'd had to stand on tiptoe to see the worst of his face. Retrieving a chair, she motioned for him to sit. "Sit down, please, before you fall off your feet."

He did what she wanted, and she gained a much better view of his cuts and bruises.

"Why was she frightened of you? Didn't you say you left when you were thirteen? You were just a boy. What harm could a boy do?"

"My eyes. She thought me cursed. Thought I was the reason she hadn't conceived again after Gavin. Blamed me for her inability to produce a second heir for the duke."

She stared at him, waiting for more.

This thought, which had always been so crushingly heavy before, felt lighter for having been shared. As much as he hated sounding so weak, especially to Emma, telling her had been the right thing to do.

"I heard her mumbling about certain deaths as well, wondering if I had anything to do with those. She wanted me to go, so she could conceive. Father had, in the past, called her silly. This time he said he would send me to a friend who was a scholar—a professor at the university in Bologna who had children as well. So I'd be happy. That day was Father's birthday. Later that night, I packed a few items and ran off. I told you the story before. I was free at long last, and I never looked back."

Emma stepped away, her complexion white. "Have you written home?"

He shook his head. "Better I didn't. Then they wouldn't have to pretend to want me back."

"Beranger, but your *father*. He must wonder what's happened to you. That was sixteen years ago—a very long time. He might think you dead."

Perhaps he shouldn't have said anything. Now she'd harangue him to death to write, and that was something he wasn't going to do. Not now, not ever.

"Yes, and in sixteen years, my stepmother most likely has had three or four more children. I'm the last thing on their minds."

"That's not for you to decide," she said sternly. "We were kept from my father for eighteen years. Many of those, he was waiting for us to return. He thought his letters were reaching our mother, but the awful couple who were our guardians, the Crowdaires, made sure we never knew he was asking after us. Life is short, Beranger. You should not play God. Please write home, at least to that uncle that you told me about. Surely *his* heart is broken, and he wishes to know your fate."

Before he could stop her, she leaned forward and placed a delicate, soft kiss beside his hurt lip. His heart seemed to constrict.

"The Crowdaires ruined our family, Beranger. I'll never forgive them for that. They were supposed to take care of us, watch over us so that nothing happened when we were too young to do that ourselves. I blame them for our unhappiness." She gave him a hard stare. "But I blame you for yours. You haven't even given your father a chance to prove he never meant to send you away for good. Don't let your pride destroy your family."

# CHAPTER THIRTY-SIX

For Mavis, the six days after the town council meeting sailed by like a leaf on the wind. Several of the business owners were contemplating taking Russell McGrath up on his offer to help them make their rent payments for the next few months, until they could figure out a way to buy their shops or get in touch with the new owner to try to persuade him they couldn't afford such increases. That was *if* they could figure out who Mr. Strong was and locate him. And that was all on speculation that he'd even consider selling. In her mind, why would he? The purchase of all the buildings at the same time smacked of a town takeover.

For some reason, somebody else besides the Brinkmans had a dedicated interest in Eden. But who? She'd spent hours trying to figure the answer out, poring over the few accounting books Mayor Dodge had left behind before he'd left town without a by-your-leave when he lost his bid at reelection. She hadn't thought that much about his departure at the time, but now . . . ? She wished she could find him so they could talk. Henry and Clint were just as concerned as she was. Her sisters were too. Belle and Blake couldn't get home fast enough to suit her. She felt responsible because she was the mayor. She should know what was really taking place behind all the transactions, but she didn't.

And on top of everything else, today was her birthday. She was turning twenty-four years old, and she felt every day of those years. She'd risen at five thirty, as she normally did, implemented her toilette with care, and then donned one of her favorite outfits: a narrow skirt made from beautiful soft violet fabric that bustled just the tiniest bit in the back, making her feel feminine. Her starched white blouse had a ruffled front, but other than that, the garment was simple. She felt pretty—although she was still as nervous as a jittery mouse.

The door to the study opened, and Emma breezed in. She looked surprised to see Mavis and glanced at the clock, which showed quarter to nine. Mavis reached up from her seat behind her desk to accept Emma's hearty hug.

"Happy birthday, Mavis," she said with a large smile. "I expected you to be already gone to the livery. But I'm happy you're not. Gives us some time to talk. That has seemed in short supply of late."

"Maverick is there, so no need for me to rush in."

Emma expelled a large sigh. "I suspect you like his company. The same for me with Mr. Buns. He's opening the Toggery for me today. I like this change in schedule, where I'm not working quite so much. I surely can't complain. Oh, I just spoke with Trevor."

"He's back?"

"Yes. He rode ahead to tell us that Belle, Blake, and Moses will arrive this afternoon with the cattle. They wanted us to hold your birthday celebration until they got home."

"Wonderful," Mavis said. "I was just thinking about them."

Emma nodded. "Have you eaten? Ada has something baking, by the aroma coming from the kitchen." She went to the bookshelves and began searching the titles.

"I've already eaten, thank you. And that's my birthday cake you smell." Mavis got up and followed her. She stood back to see what Emma was looking for. "Have you seen Katie this morning? I looked in her room last night before I turned in, but she wasn't there. I found her, after asking in the bunkhouse, at the cemetery. Darkness had already fallen. I'm worried about her, Emma. Santiago broke her heart. I don't know if she'll ever recover. Anymore, she gives little thought to her appearance and finds reasons to stay out at the ranch instead of going to her office in town. Until this happened, she'd not missed a day."

Emma withdrew a copy of *Ivanhoe: A Romance*. She leafed through the pages.

*Has Emma fallen for the handsome miner from England? What else would inspire her interest in an English, medieval-themed novel by Sir Walter Scott?*

A budding romance between the two wouldn't be hard to believe after they'd spent three days traveling together from Santa Fe. They seem well suited, and Emma, whether she knew it or not, brightened up whenever he was around. She hung on his every word but denied any feelings and proclaimed they were only friends. Mavis suspected there was far more that she wasn't proclaiming.

Emma closed the book and turned, looking Mavis in the eyes. "I've seen all that and more. My heart breaks for Katie, but as bad as I feel, I can't say I'm all that surprised."

Mavis jerked back. "Why would you say such a thing?"

"Love is capricious, my dear sister. And can't be trusted. Don't you know that by now?"

Mavis was just about to question Emma further when Katie came through the already open doors. By her distracted expression and slumped shoulders, she hadn't heard them talking. Relief washed through Mavis. Katie's usually sparkly clean golden hair, which invited everyone's touch, was dull and pulled back at her nape. Loose strands hung around her expressionless face as she approached. She still wore her nightclothes.

Santiago had returned eight days ago. Since then, her eyes had been perpetually red.

She came over to Mavis and gave her a half-hearted hug. "Happy birthday, Mavis."

From behind Katie, Emma snagged Mavis's gaze.

"Good morning, Katie. Thank you for that. Doesn't feel like my birthday with all the troubles in Eden. So much going on has me worried." She was jabbering on, but she was at a loss for real words. Any mention of Santiago, or Katie's heartbreak, would surely have her sister running to her room.

"I know what you mean," Katie replied. "Everyone feels threatened. I was in the mercantile yesterday, and I overheard Betty Lou and Larry talking. They've taken a loan from Russell McGrath. Enough to make up the discrepancy in their rent for *six* months."

Mavis gasped, and her hand flew to her throat. "That's a large amount. I hadn't heard. Larry never said a thing to me. Up until now, various shopkeepers have just been discussing what to do."

"Others might follow Larry's lead." Emma set the book on the desk and paced to the unlit fireplace. "They shouldn't do anything drastic until we know more about Mr. Strong. The whole situation is perplexing."

Katie nodded. "They moved quickly because

they feared if they waited, Mr. McGrath might run out of money doing the same for others. Then he wouldn't have enough to help them. He's not a bank. He must have a limit to what he can lend. And who knows when the proprietors he's loaned money to will be able to pay him back?"

At least with this discussion, some light had come back into Katie's eyes, but she still lacked her normal conviction and passion. Mavis tapped a finger on the desk in front of her. She wished she could take one of the livery's horse whips to that cocky peacock Santiago.

*Dangling two respectable women on his line. How disgusting!*

"There is Eden's bank," Emma said. "Others can go there."

"At a higher interest rate." Mavis felt like the proclaimer of doom. "I spoke with Bud Larson yesterday. He's not inclined to lower his rates just to compete with McGrath. He said the same thing as Katie. The dentist is bound to run out of money eventually. Then the others will be forced to seek help from Bud, and the sly banker will happily loan to them—and make good money in the process."

"That's horrible!" Katie proclaimed. "I'm thankful Father paid off all our businesses so we aren't involved with this."

"What's horrible?" Lavinia entered, dressed for work at the café.

Everyone was going in late today, it seemed.

Lavinia went straight to Mavis and placed a soft kiss on her cheek. "Happy birthday, dear Mavis. I wish you sunshine and roses today and always." She straightened and looked at her other sisters, then picked up where she'd left off. "Besides the obvious, I mean. Mr. Simon is beside himself, frightened he's going to lose the hotel. If that happens, I have no idea what will happen with my café. He hasn't said a thing, but he may have to raise *my* rent to make up the difference. With all the new people in town, I may be able to handle an increase, but then I wouldn't make much profit. And what's the use of working your fingers to the bone for nothing? I might have to close up and concentrate on the Five Sisters Guest Ranch."

Emma's brows fell. "The café is a landmark in town. We can't let that happen. I can't imagine where all the townsfolk would go to gossip."

"You might think about Shawn's Café across the street while the building is still available," Mavis said to Lavinia. "You know the owner. He may give you a sweet deal."

A bright smile appeared on Lavinia's face. Any mention of her intended brought rays of sunshine beaming from her eyes. But Lavinia's glowing happiness made the gloom of Katie's misery look darker by comparison.

"That's true," Lavinia said. "But Rhett has an

interested buyer, and they're already finishing up negotiations."

Mavis nodded. "I've heard. I wonder if the new buyers might be a shill for a certain *Mr. Strong,* trying to get his hands on another business in Eden. I wouldn't doubt that for a second."

"Mr. Strong could be anyone," Emma said. "What if he's our own banker, Bud Larson? Or Mr. Wells and his group of investors?"

*Or Larsala? But I won't bring up that woman's name with Katie present.*

"I think Donald Dodge could be responsible. Maybe he really was working with his brother."

"Has anyone thought about the Crowdaires?" Lavinia asked. "Seems farfetched, but the suspicion has crossed my mind. Henry has never managed to get a lead on where they fled to after stealing the money Father was sending us all those years."

"They stole from us, but they don't hate us," Katie said softly. "They're not Mr. Strong. They're long gone and out of our lives for good. I just hope nobody suspects *us.*"

They all looked at Katie.

"Makes sense," she went on. "We already own or are partners in five of the businesses, as well as own the largest cattle ranch in the region. If we were greedy, maybe we'd want to own the whole of Eden."

Mavis shook her head. "That's unsettling. I hadn't thought of that."

"Five heads are better than one," Emma said, turning to Katie. "How are things at the mill and lumber office? I wondered if some of the new building work has slowed down because of the trouble and mystery with Mr. Strong. I saw Mr. Wells and Warren with a wagonload of lumber yesterday, and it made me wonder."

Katie didn't respond. She was facing the window, but her shoulders pulled back. There was no doubt she'd heard Emma's question. "Katie?" Emma repeated.

Katie slowly turned to her. "I'm not speaking with you, Emma. You're the one who encouraged Santiago to end our relationship. I don't think I can *ever* forgive you for the pain you've caused me. You've *ruined* my life. If not for your cornering him in the saloon, maybe in a few days he'd have come to a different conclusion."

# CHAPTER THIRTY-SEVEN

Emma gasped, and her heart wedged painfully in her throat. "What are you saying?" All she'd wanted to do was save Katie from the agony Santiago was putting her through. And she'd do the same again, if she had to. She'd do anything for her sisters. "I only asked him to be decent, to speak with you. Tell you what he was thinking. I wanted the two of you to talk so you wouldn't be left languishing in limbo, like you had been. I couldn't stand to see the pain in your eyes another day without trying to help. Is that so bad?"

Lavinia hurried forward and took Katie's arm, then turned her around to face the group. "You don't mean that, Katie. You know Emma isn't at fault. She did what any of us would have done. And should have done sooner. She was looking out for you." Lavinia looked from Katie's face to Mavis and then to Emma. She shook her head. "Aren't you glad at least you know? That you aren't waiting for him to ride out to the ranch or come to your office in town? You were in pain. In torture, waiting and waiting. Those few days after he'd returned and then . . ." Her words trailed away.

"And Larsala arrived?" Katie asked, barely above a whisper. "Is that what you want to say,

Lavinia? Don't worry. I won't expire at the sound of her name."

Emma hadn't meant to cause her little sister any pain. Lavinia led Katie to a chair in front of the fireplace and gently sat her down. The room had gone from a festive, happy mood to one of despair. How could they help Katie? Would she ever be the same?

"Yes," Lavinia said. "That's what I was about to say. She came to town looking for Demetrio and found Santiago instead. You can't blame that on any of us. You should be happy she didn't return after the two of you had married."

Katie blinked away some tears. "He's struggling with his feelings. Maybe if you hadn't pushed him, Emma, rushed him for an answer . . . He might have come to a different conclusion."

Maybe she was right. "You'd want someone who loves you so little that he has to search his heart for three days to decide?" Emma couldn't help scoffing. This was exactly what she meant about love. One couldn't trust the sentiment in the least. "I wouldn't. That's lukewarm affection, at best."

Katie burst into tears, burying her face in her hands.

Mavis's look of chastisement told Emma she needn't have been quite so truthful. She went to Katie's chair and squatted beside Lavinia, who was rubbing Katie's back.

Emma inched forward, feeling like a pariah.

"It's, it's j-just," Katie sobbed out, "I never even got a chance to read my birthday letter from Father to Santiago. I'd been waiting for his return. I was so anxious for him to see that we were destined to be together from my very first day. But he was very businesslike. He said what he had to say, and then he was gone. Never gave me a chance to respond or even ask any questions. He was heartless. The man I saw in that moment wasn't the man I fell in love with."

*They never are.*

Emma had forgotten that Katie wanted to share her letter with her beau before she shared it with anyone else, even her sisters. That had annoyed Emma. Putting any man before her sisters didn't seem possible. *She'd* never do that. Would Mavis receive a birthday letter from their father today, at her party? Or had he passed away before he'd had a chance to write them all? Her own birthday was just a little over a month away.

"I'm so sorry," Mavis whispered, stroking her hair. "That *was* heartless. He probably can't understand how you feel. How your heart's been breaking for weeks, how you've been making yourself sick with worry and speculation."

*I'd like to speculate him right in the face. How dare he hurt Katie so?*

"Where is your birthday letter now, Katie?" Lavinia asked. "We'd like to hear you read it. Will you share it with us?"

306

She lifted her head and took the handkerchief Mavis offered, drying her eyes and blowing her nose. "I have it with me, in my robe."

*Poor Katie. How long before she forgives me?*

"I'd really like to hear what Father wrote, Katie. Please read your letter to us."

With a wobbling sigh, Katie took the envelope from her pocket. Two corners were bent, and the envelope a bit wrinkled. When she drew the papers out, they almost looked worn. Emma couldn't imagine how many times she'd taken the correspondence from the envelope to contemplate its words.

My dearest Katie. My baby,

Happy birthday, sweet child. I so wish I could be with you today to celebrate you turning nineteen years old. I had you with me the least amount of time before you girls left the ranch and Eden, but I've held you just as close as the rest of my girls in my heart. I'm certain you've grown into a beauty with eyes filled with love, laughter, and life. You might wonder how I can proclaim that with such certainty. It's because even as a newborn, and then as an infant at three months old, your eyes had the ability to dance. To create such a feeling of happiness. I used to bring your sisters to your crib when they were upset about something, or if they'd fallen down and scraped a knee. One look into your face—or more exactly, into your dancing blue eyes—and it was impossible not to smile back. Soon they'd be giggling, all their hurts or problems forgotten. Your mother and I used to call you our cheerful fairy babe. Those were such good times.

Katie raised her gaze from the letter trembling in her hands and gave them a tentative smile.

"Just like now, Katie," Emma whispered, moved with compassion.

*Or up until that scoundrel broke your heart.*

"Please go on."

Katie nodded.

I'm sorry to say your birth was the only one of the five I missed. As best as we could figure, your arrival was still supposed to be weeks away. I'd gone into Dove Creek on business, at the moment I can't remember what sort—that part of this story isn't important. Your mother, feeling large and housebound, had promised to take Mavis, Belle, Lavinia, and Emma into Eden, which, as you know, at that time was much smaller. Your sisters had been begging for a picnic on the riverbank opposite the lumber mill. There was a patch of grass Mavis liked to pretend was her grand house. I had my reservations, but at Celeste's insistence, I hitched the wagon before I left for Dove Creek.

While playing in the grass, two things happened simultaneously. The wind picked up and began to blow and howl with a force Celeste had never seen before. Frightened, you all began to pack things up. But your mother doubled over in pain. She'd gone into labor, and being you were her fifth and early, things progressed very quickly. She wanted help, but couldn't go herself. The riverbank where they had been picnicking was flat, but the bank back to the wagon took some climbing. Going carefully, she'd been able to manage goingdown, but not to go back up once the labor pains had set in.

Mavis straightened, having pulled a chair over during the telling. She now shared the perch with Lavinia. Emma sat on the arm of Katie's chair. "I think I remember that now, with a little reminder. I see trees swaying and hear the loud rushing sound of the wind. And then Mother cried out in pain. I can't believe she never shared this with us." Mavis's face lit up with excitement.

Emma felt hurt. "Maybe the memory was too painful for her—she might not have wanted to remember the good times after things changed. I'm sure leaving with us couldn't have been easy for her."

"Please keep reading, Katie," Lavinia said. "I'm anxious to hear what happened."

The rain came down in sheets, and the trees whipped violently. Miguel Alvarado happened to be returning from the mill with his two young sons just then. He spotted Celeste on the other side of Aspen Creek. He found your mother in labor, with her four little girls huddled around. He carried her to the cantina. Your sisters followed like baby chicks.

When I returned and heard the news, I ran through the storm to the cantina, but you'd already been born. Being early, and tiny, you were delivered without complications by Miguel—even before Dr. Dodge was located. You looked like a tiny angel, nestled in a napkin-lined tortilla basket. You were being admired by your four older sisters and Miguel's sons, Demetrio and Santiago.

Katie lowered the letter to her lap and sat there in silence.

"Santiago must have been four or five," Lavinia whispered.

Mavis sat there. "Amazing," she finally said. "I don't remember that. Has he ever mentioned your birth, Katie?"

Katie finally looked up and shook her head. "No, he hasn't. But now you see why I believed we were destined to be together. Santiago and me. I was born in the cantina, with him by my side."

Emma found the event astonishing as well. But she was not convinced in the least it meant a union between her little sister and Santiago had been written in the stars. Getting Katie to believe that too would take some doing.

"He wasn't by your side, Katie," she said as gently as she could. "He was at Mother's, and only came over after you were born."

Katie looked up, consternation shadowing her eyes.

"Is there more?" Emma asked, not giving her a chance to begin another argument. The last thing she wanted was to cause her sister more pain. That said, Katie needed to lift her chin and accept the truth. Her romance with Santiago was over—and that fact wasn't ever going to change.

Katie took a deep breath and continued.

You know, sweet girl, that things changed soon after your birth. Now, at the time of this writing, I only remember the wonderful events of your short time with me. Thank you for being the joy-filled infant that brought us so much happiness. Remain that way, my darling Katie. Be happy, keep smiling. As the hours pass, I'm growing weaker. I know my time on earth is almost through. Something I never believed would happen.

Life sometimes takes you by surprise, Katie. I implore you to follow your heart and do what it tells you to do. That is a recipe for happiness, something I want for you and all my daughters.

Happy birthday. I love you with all my heart,

Your father

All of the sisters were crying, wiping at tears with shaky hands.

"He didn't even let me share my letter," Katie whispered.

Katie was speaking of Santiago, of course. Would hearing the circumstances of Katie's birth have made a difference to him? Emma was doubtful.

Emma's gaze strayed over to the copy of *Ivanhoe* she'd placed on the desk. Knights, men-at-arms, destriers . . . An image of Beranger appeared in her mind. So much heartache and pain. Enough for a lifetime. Almost a week had passed since she'd seen him—not since the fight in the saloon. Did he ever think of her, as she did of him? She'd seen him on the street, but he'd never come in to buy that ribbon for Katie.

Well, Belle and Blake would return today. With that, a new chapter would begin: the probing of the mine. But first, a get-together in the café to celebrate Mavis. That would be fun, and Clint had invited Beranger. Tonight would be interesting in more ways than one.

# CHAPTER THIRTY-EIGHT

In the cramped room in the boardinghouse, vacant of Jimbo, his guest, Beranger lowered himself into the rickety chair before the small desk. He withdrew the daguerreotype of his family that normally, for the past sixteen years, had only come out of its burgundy bag on his father's birthday, marking his departure from Ashbury Castle. He stared at the faces, feeling harried and old. His gaze shifted to the blank piece of writing paper he'd gotten from the mercantile only a few minutes before. Emma had encouraged him to write home.

*Am I really contemplating doing just that?*

He allowed himself to think of Ashbury's impressive foyer. It was guarded by several suits of armor, a plethora of swords crossed on the wall, and the imposing coat-of-arms tapestry. As a boy, when no one had been watching, he'd crept up and down the dark-walnut staircase on one side of the entry hall. He'd liked to look at two large portraits of a lord and a lady—they had stolen his breath. Their imposing expression seemed to be telling him to go away. Crystal chandeliers, stained-glass windows, opulent furnishings. To him, the ceiling had seemed as tall as the sky. Dark-beamed triangles held the whole thing up.

At thirteen, when he'd first run away and boarded the *Destiny*, he'd been too busy to even consider being homesick. He spent his time trying to survive, avoiding certain quarrelsome sailors who thought nothing of boxing a lad's ears when they'd had a rummy snootful, and fighting seasickness while he found his sea legs The sea tossed the ship day and night and made the days turn into months—then into years— before his eyes. As difficult as life aboard the ship had been, he'd been freer than at home. He was finally being judged for what he was capable of doing, not who he was. Standing in the crow's nest with the wind flipping his shoulder-length hair about his face, he could choose to believe anything about his past or his future. Anything at all. That he had a loving family that adored him, who were counting the days until his return. That his mother hadn't died, and she was proud of her son. Or that he'd make something out of himself and return to Ashbury Castle rich and powerful, to his brother's dismay.

Then, after four years, he'd walked down the gangplank onto American soil, still a free man. America wasn't for the faint of heart. Being penniless except for the ten-dollar coin the captain had given him, Beranger set about looking for odd jobs, slowly working his way west. He'd pounded red-hot steel for a blacksmith; plowed acres and acres of rich, black soil, learning what true exhaustion felt like; had been a spinning target for a knife-thrower in a traveling sideshow, but only until he was nicked on his ear. A shop owner had hired him as a mercantile clerk, he'd worked cattle, and he'd even been a mop boy when times were hard. Nothing was beneath a man's dignity when he needed to eat, so long as the work wasn't illegal or immoral. All that time, Beranger had never considered writing home. Not even when he thought lovingly about Lord Harry and the kindness his uncle had shown him.

Then he'd learned to prospect with Landry Pike. Pike had been a good fellow, and generous to a fault—as long as you didn't cross him. And Beranger's life had sailed from there on out. Others began to take notice, and to recognize his name. One cold morning, Pike simply didn't awaken. Beranger thought that wasn't such a bad way to go. By then, his good fate had been sealed.

Beranger sighed. Those times felt like a lifetime ago. He picked up a pen and dipped the point into a bottle of ink, but set the writing tool back on the desktop before it touched paper. Nothing came to mind. No words, no sentiments. He stared at the paper, feeling the fool for even contemplating the deed. Still, he remembered the look in Emma's eyes as she'd told him their history, how her guardians had kept John Brinkman's letters from his daughters. How they'd have loved to return to Eden sooner, before he'd passed away. She clearly didn't want him to let his own opportunity pass by.

*Is my father even still alive?*

A knock sounded on his door.

"Yes?"

It was Sebastian Evans, owner of the establishment.

"There's a woman here to see you. Waiting on the front porch."

*Emma?* His pulse picked up. *What could she want?*

He hadn't seen her since the day of the fight in the Hole in the Floor, as he'd purposely stayed away from the places he thought she might go. "Thanks. I'll be right out."

Glancing in the mirror, he saw most of the evidence of that day had faded. His cut lip had been the worst, and that was all but healed. He ran his fingers through his hair, noting that he needed a haircut, then went out to meet her. He was curious about her reason for seeking him out. Had Blake and Belle returned? Was work on the mine about to begin?

Beranger strode out the front door, then abruptly pulled up. The woman waiting for him wasn't Emma, as he'd assumed, but the Hispanic woman who'd been present the day of their arrival on the stagecoach. Mrs. Larsala Salazar. Petite and quite beautiful, she was dressed as elegantly as before, but this time she wore a hat that looked suspiciously like one of Lavinia Brinkman's creations. Had Mrs. Salazar gone into the Toggery and bought the hat from Emma? She'd have to be more brazen than anyone had thought, after what Santiago had done to Katie. The two hulking guards who'd also been there the day of his and Emma's arrival waited across the street, watching from the porch of the Hole in the Floor.

Beranger dipped his chin. "Mrs. Salazar. What can I do for you?"

She tossed a charming smile his way and then glanced over her shoulder toward the livery. "I'm interested in your large black horse, Mr. North. I'd like to buy him."

"I'm sorry, he's not for sale."

A flicker of displeasure crossed her eyes—but she concealed the emotion so quickly he was sure she wasn't even aware he'd seen it.

"I was made aware of the circumstances by which he came to be yours. Quite impressive that he was able to make such a journey—all the way from Santa Fe! A horse like that would be greatly valued in my stable."

"He followed me of his own volition. And for that reason alone, I'll never part with him." He hoped the words were forceful enough to end her pursuit. He'd known women like her. They were spoiled. Liked to get their way. Gave up at nothing.

"I implore you. I'm sure he can be purchased

for the right price. Name your amount. I want him, Mr. North. That alone should be enough to make you capitulate."

*Maybe enough for Santiago, but not enough for me.*

He'd heard her story, how she'd been sent away at fifteen to become wife of a large landowner in Arizona—but he had no allegiance to her, no reason to do her bidding. The loftier tone she'd used the day he'd arrived on the stagecoach again weighted her words.

"Again, I'm sorry to disappoint you, Mrs. Salazar. I've become fond of Charger, and I'm keeping him. End of story."

She frowned. Distaste flickered more clearly in her eyes.

The men across the street straightened up.

Beranger was sure they'd have no compunction taking him on, two to one. That was usually how bullies worked.

"Mr. North, I'm appealing to your sense of fairness. That is a horse that should be seen and enjoyed. At my home in Arizona, he will be a star. I can promise you that."

A wagon packed with lumber approached. Cash Dawson, Clint's son, was at the lines next to Rhett Laughlin. Rhett looked at Beranger questioningly, then furtively pointed to Mrs. Salazar's men. The wagon slowed and then stopped. Cash worked the brake with his boot. Rhett and Cash got out and went about straightening and shifting the already perfectly balanced load. Clint's boy was as tall as Rhett. Beranger appreciated the show of support, felt glad they'd noticed that there could be trouble with the two street fighters. His bruises had just lost their tenderness, and he wasn't in a hurry to get more.

"Charger's not a horse I could sell to just anyone. He can be vicious. For that reason, and the reasons I stated earlier, I choose not to sell him at all. For the time being, he's going out to pasture for a well-earned rest." Charger had become a draw for local gawkers. Maverick had made several KEEP AWAY FROM THE FENCE signs and posted them around his corral. The horse, obstinate as he was, seemed to already be a celebrity in town.

Her eyes flashed indignantly. "Out to pasture! A horse like that needs to be in the ring, or harnessed before a beautiful coach for all to enjoy. I have his double, and I recently lost the gelding I paired him with. I *must* have him, Mr. North. I don't believe you understand how determined I am. I believed he was in fact sired by our stallion. Father and son could be reunited." She glanced over her shoulder at her men.

The two promptly stepped off the saloon porch and started her way.

Beranger smiled, although he'd all but run out of patience with this spoiled woman. Who did she think she was, demanding he sell Charger just because she desired the horse? The men stopped on either side of her and narrowed their gazes at him—as if that would frighten Beranger. They were armed and he wasn't, but he wholly doubted they'd be stupid enough to shoot him down in cold blood in the middle of the day for all to see.

"Mrs. Salazar?" one said, his scraggly black mustache hanging down past the corners of his mouth.

"Mr. North refuses to sell me the black gelding," she said with a pout that belonged on someone much younger. "I can't make him understand how much I love the horse, want the horse."

The other henchman snickered. "Maybe *we* can make him understand, no?"

"No," Beranger stated, unafraid of the likes of them. He'd faced much tougher rivals when he'd been on the ship. And in the gold fields of California. These two were dime-a-dozen thugs. "Thank you for stopping by, Mrs. Salazar. I bid you good day." He turned to go.

"Mr. North!" Reaching into the dark-turquoise bag that had been fastened around her wrist a moment ago, she pulled out a handful of coins— enough to buy ten good horses.

This woman was tenacious. He would give her that. "You have my answer, Mrs. Salazar. I can't be bought. Not like some men." He looked from one of her henchmen to the other. He'd have to watch his back from here on out. He hadn't meant to make enemies the moment he got to town, but it seemed like that was what he'd done. Obviously, she didn't know how wealthy he was or else she'd have tried a different tactic. "Now if you'll excuse me, I'll be on my way. You can stay if you like."

One of the guards stepped into his path.

Rhett and Cash stood by the wagon, watching.

"Horeto, let the man go!" Mrs. Salazar commanded, her chin still high. A small smile played on her lips. "We will speak with him later."

Beranger chuckled at her threat. He stepped around Horeto and headed for the wagon to thank Rhett and Cash for having his back. He thrust out his hand to Rhett and then to Cash; he already liked both very much. He may have made enemies, but he'd also made friends. *Good friends.* He liked being a part of Eden. The camaraderie felt worthy. Like he was a part of something larger than just a growing town. Perhaps his destiny had found him when he hadn't even been looking.

# CHAPTER THIRTY-NINE

The crowd in Lavinia's café had begun to thin, and Mavis couldn't be happier. The birthday party had been a lot of fun, but she was anxious to get to the letter she knew Henry had in his front coat pocket for her. He'd all but said that it was from her father, and with Belle, Lavinia, and Katie all having received one, surely he would have explained if her father had been too weak to complete a letter for her before he'd passed away as well. So much had been revealed about their past lives through her sisters' letters. She hoped to learn more from hers. Just getting a personal message from the father she vaguely remembered was an exciting thought. Clint, her ever-loyal friend, was at her side. He seemed to be able to read her thoughts.

"Would you like me to ask your guests to leave? I can say you're tired." He pushed a strand of hair from her face as he tried to read her eyes. "Because I think you are—tired, that is. These last few days, with Katie's disappointment and the Mr. Strong mystery, have taken their toll. You can't solve this situation on your own, Mavis. I wish you'd realize that."

"But I'm the mayor now."

"So what? That doesn't mean everything falls to you."

She ignored the part about Mr. Strong and the town. She was weary of speaking or even thinking about the situation. The man would present himself in good time, but would that be before or after the rest of the townsfolk had lost their livelihoods? The problem was perplexing.

"No. Don't ask them to leave. Let them wander off on their own when the night is over. They're enjoying catching up with Blake and Belle. Look at them, Clint. They seem so happy. They really seem well suited for each other, and are always touching in some way. I'm happy to just sit here and watch." She laughed, truly delighted at the sight of a deliriously besotted Belle and Blake.

*What would love like that be like?*

"As long as I don't have to make conversation myself, I'm content." The small portion of cake still left on her plate drew her attention. "Ada's chocolate-and-walnut cake was delicious. She outdid herself."

Clint patted his flat stomach. "You're right about that. I'd like to get the recipe."

She laughed and gave him a fond look. "As if you would bake it?"

He shrugged and smiled.

At the table beside them, Belle and Blake were telling Emma and Beranger about their return trip, and hearing in exchange the tale of the encounter with the jumping cacti and how Beranger had helped the poor horses escape their torment with a sword that had belonged to a lunatic who could have killed all the travelers in their sleep. Katie sat close to Rhett, Lavinia, Henry and Elizabeth, and Jeremy Gannon. She was listening and smiling. Elizabeth looked fondly at Henry every few minutes, nodding along with the story and looking pretty indeed for her thirty-six years. She'd arrived in Eden with her young son, Johnny, exactly when Mavis and her sisters had been called to town for the reading of their father's will.

Katie's counterfeit smile almost broke Mavis's heart. Her little sister wasn't her normal self yet. A lot more time would need to pass before the heartbreak was history.

Today the sisters had come up with a name for their mine. Beranger had laughed when Emma had said they were all counting on him to hit it big at "the Lucky Sister."

Earlier the café had been full—more friends, some business owners, and members of the town council. Maverick had left, as well as Mr. Buns, and Mr. Little, the old curmudgeon that ran Belle's tannery. Mr. Wells, the investor who was building the new hotel, along with his sons Warren and Brody, had stopped by. The ranch hands had attended, but left a little while ago to go drinking at Poor Fred's as well as play a few hands of poker. Cash had wanted to go along with the men, but Clint had told him no.

Nicole, Clint's younger half sister, was working

with Karen Forester, serving and cleaning up. For the past two hours, the birthday group had had the café almost all to themselves.

Clint leaned in. "I have something for you, Mavis. Would you like it now . . . or later?"

Startled, she sat back and set her teacup down. Ever since the unscrupulous lumberjacks had knocked Clint out last March, during the terrifying exchange by the Dolores River, something sweet had taken root between them. But she wasn't sure of exactly how he felt. Each time she expected Clint to make a romantic move, to grow their friendship into something else, something more meaningful between them, he stopped just short. Then he'd make a joke and she'd have to laugh along, pretending that a romance between them was tremendously impossible, hysterically funny, and any discussion of one was meaningless chatter.

*Is that what he really thinks?*

"Well?" he prompted her.

He really seemed to be eager to give her . . . whatever it was. Was his gift something important this time? An exciting warmth spread through her body. Perhaps he was going to make his move tonight? Perhaps he'd been waiting for her birthday, so she'd know how special he thought her.

"It's not like you to be speechless, Mavis." He winked.

She liked when he teased her. It made her feel

like she was the center of his world. That seemed to be happening more and more.

*Am I imagining the look in his eyes?*

"I think later, when we can be alone," she whispered softly. "If that's all right with you."

He shrugged, and a cocky half smile lifted his lips. "It's up to you. Just thought I'd bring the subject to your attention."

"Why? To torture me?"

"Can I torture you, Mavis?"

The playful light in his eyes vanished.

*Is he finally being serious?*

She never knew, and that was half the problem. If only he realized how much he *did* torture her in her dreams. Nary a night went by that she didn't hear his voice and laughter, see his eyes, and gaze at his lips. It happened so frequently she'd wondered if he'd cast a love spell over her.

Karen went to the door and turned the sign. The clock chimed nine. The girls still needed to clean up. If her guests didn't clear out soon, Karen and Nicole would be there all night.

"Shall we step outside for some fresh air?" she said. "Maybe our doing so will encourage the others that way as well. Karen and Nicole will thank us later."

He stood and took Mavis's hand, helping her to her feet. Without a word to anyone else, they slipped outside the hotel and sat down on the wooden bench that was used by guests and travelers as they waited for the stage. The cool air of the quiet night wrapped itself around Mavis's soul. At times like this, she loved Eden best.

A few lamps burned along the dark street, pushing back the night. A lantern burned in Clint's office across the way. Voices sounded from the saloon, most likely the ranch hands having a good time.

"Let's go look at the rock cliff," she suggested.

"A little time alone sounds nice."

*Finally.*

"I like the way the granite sparkles in the moonlight."

They stood, and he offered her his elbow. They descended the steps and walked the few feet to the dramatic rock wall that jutted out beside Main Street to rise several hundred feet in the air. Simply beautiful, the enormous formation was a landmark in the town. The moon was in the perfect position to make the cliff face sparkle and shine like the stars.

"It looks like magic," she whispered, hoping Clint would finally kiss her the way she'd been dreaming.

*Is the sight of the sparkling granite the gift he has for me?*

She hoped she wasn't making something out of nothing, as she often did. She knew she should be content with his friendship, but seeing how happy Belle was, and Lavinia now too, made her yearn for more. She'd been married, and Darvid had made her very happy—and yet, the feelings Clint evoked in her were so different, deeper, exciting. Not imagining them together wasn't possible. He'd captured her dreams months ago. She was growing tired of waiting for him to figure things out.

She gazed at the sight before her, keenly aware of his proximity and the way he held her arm close to his warm side. A gentle puff of air stirred her hair, and she thought she detected a barely perceptible clean, spicy scent. It tickled her nose.

*Has Clint purchased some eau de cologne?*

When she felt his finger gently take her chin and turn it toward him she almost swooned, feeling more like a young maiden than a twenty-four-year-old widow.

*Heaven's sakes, Mavis, get ahold of yourself.*

With anticipation swirling within, she closed her eyes and leaned forward.

His chuckle brought her back to reality.

She opened her eyes.

"I don't think we're on the same page here," he said softly. He reached inside his pants pocket. He held out a small gift wrapped in pink-and-white paper and tied with a thin white ribbon. "Happy birthday, Mavis Brinkman Applebee."

*What does that mean? He's passed up the chance to kiss me and used my married name. Perhaps he's trying to gently give me a hint.*

She had been the one to suggest their walk, and that was after speaking about how happy and contented Belle and Blake looked being married. He and Blake were best buddies, but Mavis was sure he saw Blake much less since he'd married.

*Is Clint a lost cause? Is he a confirmed widower for life?*

"Well, aren't you going to open it?" he asked, a tone of disappointment in his words.

With trembling fingers, she took the small rectangular package. She hoped he couldn't see her distress in the moonlight. Forcing a wide smile, she held his offering up to her ear and gave a gentle shake. "No noise."

"Were you expecting a bell?"

She shook her head. "It's light."

His crooked smile was back. "The box is not empty, Mavis, although I know that's what you would expect from me." He gave her hands a nudge. "Go on. What's taking you so long? I'd've had that open lickety-split."

He was right. He would have. She was being silly. The hotel door opened, and she could hear others gathering on the front porch. They'd run out of time for a private kiss! Swiftly, she drew off the bow and unwrapped the tiny box.

A tiny shepherd's staff made out of silver glinted at her. She took the gift out and turned it over to see that it was a pin. She didn't understand the significance of the object.

He cocked his head. "You're the shepherdess of your family, Mavis. Of the Brinkman sisters. I've always admired that about you. And now that you're the new mayor, shepherdess over the town as well. It was made especially for you by a craftsman in Dove Creek."

She just stared.

"Don't you like it?"

"Like it?" she responded, fondling the gift no larger than a dollar coin. "I love it, Clint. Thank you so much for thinking of me. For remembering my birthday." She gazed up into his beloved face, quelling her desire to go up on tiptoe and press her lips to his.

Skepticism crossed his face. "As if I'd forget."

Fumbling to pin the jewelry to the front of her bodice, she cried out when she stuck herself with the sharp point.

Clint chuckled and gently withdrew the staff from her fingers. "Allow a clumsy ol' cowboy to do that for you." Finished, he nudged the pin back and forth until his gift was positioned to his liking. He smiled into her eyes. His gaze dropped to her lips. He moved closer.

"Mavis?" Henry appeared beside them. "Your party's breaking up." He withdrew a snowy white envelope from his pocket, in much better shape than the one Katie had shared earlier that morning. "From your father. Happy birthday."

Henry leaned forward and kissed her cheek just

as Elizabeth joined their group. She looped her arm through Henry's. The couple was enjoying a long courtship, she thought, but at least they seemed to be making progress. Her sisters, and everyone else, were watching from the porch. Blake had driven her and her sisters into town in the buggy. Until Rhett either sold Shawn's Café or married Lavinia, whichever happened first, he would be sleeping in the upstairs apartment of the restaurant he'd renovated when he'd purchased the building back in March.

Beranger North stood apart, looking much the aristocrat as he watched Emma and Nicole in a discussion. The younger girl had just stepped ouside to hand Emma the reticule she'd left behind in the restaurant.

Mavis liked Beranger immensely and easily recognized the romance budding between him and Emma, even as much as her obstinate sister liked to pretend it wasn't happening. It would only be a matter of time before her steely will crumbled and she admitted she was in love.

Henry and Elizabeth bid her and Clint good-night and walked off toward the small rental house Elizabeth had moved into last month on Wild Turkey Road, the same road that led to the new hotel site. So much was changing in Eden, and yet the one thing that dwelled in the deepest regions of her heart was not. She and Clint were still just good friends.

Blake assisted Belle and Katie into the buggy and then looked her way. Rhett did the same for Lavinia.

"I guess we're going," she said softly, leaving the sentence open-ended to see what he would say.

Clint took her hands in his warm, rough ones. "Good night, Mavis. I hope that letter is everything you wish for." He leaned in and brushed her cheek with his own.

Feeling like the ugly stepchild instead of the birthday girl, she nodded. "I'm sure Father's letter will be everything and *more . . .*"

She had to get away before he saw her misery. Turning on her heel, she hurried to the waiting buggy and the family she was the shepherdess over. She blinked away tears as Blake helped her inside and she got comfortable next to Belle. Lavinia, Emma, and Katie were crowded in the back seat. Someone behind put a hand on her shoulder; she turned to find Lavinia smiling into her face.

"Did you enjoy your party? What were you and Clint talking about as you stood so closely in the street? My curious mind would like to know."

"Thank you, yes. A beautiful party. Thank you all. Clint and I were just discussing Mr. Strong and what might be going on with Eden. Something has to be done soon before too many others find themselves in real debt. I don't—"

Belle nudged her shoulder as Blake clucked to the horse and the buggy started off with a bounce. "You need to stop talking business, Mavis. You're much too serious. A man wants to hear you giggle once in a while and see you bat your eyelashes. Not talk numbers, accounts, and what to plant next fall. They want to appear as the leader with all the ideas, and be praised for their manly ways. I think you're scaring Clint off."

Having no idea how much her words hurt, Belle, as if to make her point, pushed playfully into Blake's side, extracting a sound of agreement from him.

A knife sliced through Mavis's heart as she stared off into the darkness.

*I'm a widow who is growing older by the day. Eden is no longer devoid of women like it used to be—and more are arriving every month. Clint could have his pick. Then again, maybe someone else has already caught his eye—someone young, fresh, who wears frilly clothes and giggles at every word he says. I better face the facts.*

She thought of Darvid, and her heart tried to warm, but the heaviness inside made that impossible. Her sisters would all find love, and she'd be their shepherdess. What did she have to complain about?

# CHAPTER FORTY

After the party, Beranger made his way through the quiet streets toward the boardinghouse. Emma had been attentive and nice, smiling at everything he'd said. She'd looked beautiful, with her soft strawberry-blonde hair cascading down her back and a dress that showed her every womanly curve. She'd encouraged him to speak and even rubbed his arm twice, reminding him of the tenderness she'd displayed after the bar fight, when she'd tended to his scrapes and cuts.

Because of her coaxing almost a week ago, he'd come closer to writing a letter home than he'd ever been; he was working on it a little every night. Reflecting now on the dinner at the ranch, he saw her distance a bit differently. Perhaps her confused feelings for him had held her back. Whatever it was, he missed her. Missed sitting thigh to thigh in the Wells Fargo stagecoach. Missed arguing with her in the moonlight over what constituted a rake or a gentleman. A woman like her came along once in a lifetime. He didn't want to mess this up. Glancing at the stars, he rubbed the back of his neck.

*But what does she want? Or feel? Could she really mean to remain single her whole life?*

Maybe he wasn't meant to find happiness. He'd

been alone so long, maybe he didn't know how to settle down.

Someone approached. A man, not tall of stature. In the darkness he couldn't make out who the person was. From the hotel, Beranger had cut between the mercantile and Poor Fred's and was coming up behind the Toggery. Was it Emma's clerk, Mr. Buns? He'd met the man several times, but that didn't ring true. He'd know soon enough.

"Mr. North, what a pleasure to run into you tonight."

It was the dentist, Russell McGrath.

"The town is quiet tonight. I meant to tell you before, if you have any need of intricate work with metal, I do that as well. My dental equipment lends itself to many types of fine detailing." He held a notebook under his arm and several pencils in his palm.

*Strange. He is really going overboard trying to win over the citizens of Eden.*

"Good evening, Mr. McGrath. I'll keep that in mind." The dentist didn't look like he was in any hurry to rush off. "Are you out for a stroll, or . . . ?"

"Oh, this?" he said and laughed. He held up the writing tools. "I'm going over to the field on the west side of town, behind the sheriff's office, to sketch and write poetry. A hobby of mine. I just couldn't let this beautiful evening get away. I like the view from over there."

"I see," Beranger said, although he really didn't.

"Would you like to have a look?" he asked, coming two steps closer.

He opened the tablet to sketches Beranger couldn't see very well in the darkness. Some of landscapes, some of the businesses of Eden—the mercantile, the butcher shop, the hotel, the bathhouse—even some people. He noted one of Emma, looking as pretty as a picture standing on the porch of the Toggery. That surprised him.

*Do others know what the dentist is doing? How many professions does he have?*

There was a sketch of Charger, and the livery, and the last, the Five Sisters Ranch from a view-point he could only have attained by climbing up one of the mountains that surrounded the valley.

Beranger looked the man over in a new light. "You've been busy. What do you do with your sketches? Sell them?"

McGrath let out a burst of laughter. "Oh no. I'm not that good. I just work for my own enjoyment, nothing more. I like to remember what I see."

Beranger glanced around at the already dark sky. "Can you see anything now?"

"I do well in the darkness, always have. Besides, after the full moon a couple days ago, the moon is a good lamp. Tomorrow I'm sure I'll have to clean up my work, but it passes my days, which can get boring without any customers. Getting out and about and running into fine people as yourself is what's really important." He took a tiny step in the direction he'd be going. "I won't hold you up any longer, Mr. North. I wish you a pleasant evening."

*Where does he live?* Beranger wondered as he watched him walk away. *Not in the boardinghouse or hotel. He must be crammed in the back of his dental office. None of my business.*

Sebastian was sitting on the front porch when he arrived.

"How was Miss Emma?" he asked after taking a drink from his coffee cup.

"Don't you mean Mavis? The party tonight was in celebration of her."

Sebastian shrugged. "Don't know. After traveling all the way from Santa Fe with the fair-faced Emma Brinkman, I just thought that maybe—"

"Don't."

Sebastian smiled, his expression submissive—a trait that was beginning to grate on Beranger's nerves.

"So tomorrow," the boardinghouse owner said, "with Blake and Moses back in town, you'll be going out to the claim? Do you have any feel, one way or the other?"

It *was* time to get to work. He was beginning to feel like a loafer. "That's right. Tomorrow we begin. And as for a feel? I'm not a soothsayer or gypsy. I'm a miner who's had a lot of success.

That's why others come to me for advice. Nothing more."

"I didn't mean to offend."

"No offense taken. Now, I'll say goodnight."

Mavis was having no luck falling asleep. She'd changed into her nightclothes, washed up, and was sitting in her bed with her pillows stacked behind her, the unopened letter in her hands. Beside the bed a lamp burned, giving the room a cozy feel. How she wished she felt cozy inside.

A soft knocking at her door drew her from her reverie.

"Yes?"

"It's me, Belle."

Belle? She'd expected Emma, Lavinia, or Katie, but not Belle. Had she snuck away after Blake had fallen asleep?

Belle stuck her head inside. "May I come in? Or are you almost asleep?"

"Of course, come in. I'm far from sleep and would appreciate some company." That was the truth, now more than ever.

In a soft yellow robe, with a matching nightgown fluttering around her ankles, Belle stepped in and quietly closed the door with one hand on the knob and another on the door itself. She hurried to the far side of the bed and climbed up, burrowing in to get comfortable. Mavis was reminded of their second night in Eden, after the meeting with Henry and Blake, when she and Belle had discussed their options over the light of one candle. Belle had been filled with concerns. She hadn't wanted to stay in Eden. She'd wanted to take the payout their father's will provided for if they declined to stay and take over the ranch, go back to Philadelphia, and marry Lesley instead. Oh, how things had changed. Since Belle and Blake had married, she and Mavis hadn't had any more midnight talks. This, however, made up for that.

"Won't Blake miss you?"

She laughed softly. "One night won't hurt. We've been together on the trail for days. I've missed you, but I also wanted to apologize for being insensitive on the ride home. What I said was mean. I didn't intend to hurt you. I'm sorry."

They both knew what she was talking about.

"There's nothing to be sorry for. I *do* come across that way, sometimes. But not always . . ."

"How *are* things with Clint?"

Mavis gave her a quizzical look. "What do you mean? As sheriff?"

"You can't fool me, Mavis. You're in love with him. And you have been since the fracas on the Dolores—maybe even before. Does he know? Have you two talked?"

Shocked, Mavis straightened.

*Am I that transparent? Are others talking about us as well?*

"Mavis?"

"No, we've not talked. I'm not sure how he feels. Sometimes I think he's attracted to me, and then, at other times . . ."

"Oh, he's attracted to you all right. I see plenty of lovesick expressions cross his face when you're not looking. And even Blake has commented to me about how much Clint admires you, talks about you, and how much he's changed since you've arrived."

"Then why doesn't he let me know?" Mavis tried to keep the desperation out of her voice. She wanted to believe Belle, even about what Blake had said, but she was afraid of getting her hopes up too high. She'd thought for certain after the election last month he was going to start calling on her, but he didn't. She couldn't take much more heartache.

"I'm not sure. Maybe *he's* uncertain how *you* feel. Some men, for fear of rejection, won't make the first move."

Mavis had to laugh. "Some men? You sound like you've had a whole host of court-ships."

Belle opened her mouth to object, and Mavis laid a hand on her arm. "But I understand what you're saying. You want me to come out of my shell a little."

"A lot. Maybe touch his hand now and again. Like I said earlier, bat your eyelashes a little, giggle for no reason at all. Do that, and we'll talk again soon."

"Now if I could only get through to Emma," Mavis said, feeling excited and a bit relieved.

"What do you mean?"

"She says she's against love. She gave me a long lecture about how love can't be trusted. If she doesn't open her eyes, she's going to lose the best man right in front of her. She'll be sorry if she lets Beranger get away. I've never seen her as animated as when he's around. She hangs on his every word and can't keep a smile from her face. The air practically crackles when they're together. Don't you think so?"

Belle jerked her gaze away and looked at the dark window.

Mavis frowned. It wasn't like her sister not to share her opinion on matters of love. She was the expert, so to speak. "Belle? Don't you think they'd make the perfect couple?"

Belle nodded but didn't look her way.

"Belle! What do you know that you're not saying?"

"Yes. I think they'd make a beautiful couple. And the fact that he's English is all the more intriguing. And yes, she'll be sorry if she lets him get away."

A moment of silence slipped by.

"And . . . ?" Mavis prompted. "Do you know something I don't?"

Belle turned to look at her. "I do. I was supposed to keep this a secret, but under the circumstances I feel compelled to say something. In Santa Fe, Emma was giving me that same song and dance about love being fickle and how untrustworthy the sentiment was. That she was satisfied to stay a successful businesswoman and live out her life alone. Mavis, she nearly broke my heart. But as she went on, I began to get angry. Blake and I have found such great happiness together, I want the same for *all* my sisters." She paused, reached out, and briefly squeezed Mavis's hand, as if she needed to let her know that she meant that sentiment for Mavis as well. "No matter what I said, she rebuffed me. So . . ."

"So?"

"I told her she hadn't yet met the right fellow, and when she did she would fall harder than the rest of us."

"And?"

"What do you think? She scoffed at that as well. She can be so stubborn sometimes—*all the time.* Anyway, we made a wager. I said she would, and she said she wouldn't."

"You didn't!"

"We did."

"But that will only make her dig her heels in deeper, no matter how she feels. You know very well she's competitive with you. And has been since you were both little girls. I've had to step

343

in while you were arguing over dolls or evening dresses. You both want to be right no matter what." She huffed and looked at her hands, still holding the unopened letter. Perhaps she really was the shepherdess of the bunch. "When are you going to learn better, Belle?"

"Probably never."

"Exactly. Well, she'll relent as her feelings for Beranger grow. One can only hold out against love for so long."

*But what about Clint? Will he ever give in? Does he want to?*

Belle wrapped her arms around her knees and hugged them tight. "I'm not so sure," she mumbled.

Mavis felt her ire growing. "What else? I know there's more. And stop looking like a petulant child. I'm not going to scold you."

"We wagered the first big take of the mine."

Shocked, Mavis bolted up straight. "What! Have you lost your mind? I can't believe my ears. That's the most ridiculous thing I've ever heard."

"I never intended to hold her accountable. I just wanted to teach her a lesson. And for only six months. After that, the bet is off. We thought that only fair."

"Heaven's sakes alive, Belle! What if after two months Mr. North has the mine humming along and he gets the urge to move on? Or what if we strike gold or silver, and his job is done? Or what if he has feelings for her, which I think he already does, and she rebuffs him so stringently he gives up? That's a man a woman shouldn't lose. Especially over a stupid bet. She'd never forgive herself. And you could lose a fortune, but I have to say it would serve you right if you did."

"Like I said, I'd never hold her to the wager."

"That's not the point. Beranger is what we're talking about. You know that."

Silence fell between them.

Belle leaned her head against the headboard and closed her eyes. "I'll make things right somehow. So Emma doesn't end up heartbroken as well as Katie."

*And me.*

"Everything's going to be okay," Belle mumbled. Again, she touched Mavis's hand. "I see the letter from Father is still unopened. Can I stay while you read it? Or would you rather be alone? I'm feeling rather deflated at the moment. I can't go back to Blake feeling like this, or he'll ask me what's wrong. I'll just lie here quietly, if you don't mind."

Mavis smiled. Poor Belle. She always felt so repentant after a row with Emma, but that wouldn't stop future spats from happening. They competed wholeheartedly, but they loved whole-heartedly too.

"Of course you can stay. I don't mind. I've been relishing the moment, thinking that Father wrote a letter just to me. Just thinking about that fills my soul with joy. How I wish we'd learned everything before his horse fell on him and broke his leg. Can you imagine? All of us here, and him alive to be the *shepherd* of us all."

Belle glanced her way with sleepy eyes. "I know. It's very sad. I wish that so much as well, and Mother here too. Our lives could have been so different." She yawned and pulled the crisp white sheet over her. "I'm just going to get comfortable while you read. The trip from Santa Fe was long and arduous."

Smiling, Mavis watched Belle for a moment. She realized she didn't mind being the shepherdess at all. With quivering hands, she opened the envelope.

# CHAPTER FORTY-ONE

My dearest Mavis,

Happy birthday! I've been looking forward to you reading this letter since Dr. Dodge informed me I only have a few days to live. I'm a little weaker today, so I'll tell you now that you meant the world to me. I loved you with each breath I took back then, and every other after that when you'd gone. I hope that through the years, and despite the miles between us, you were able to feel my devotion.

*Dr. Dodge, that evil scoundrel. How dare he do what he did to our family?*

Mavis didn't want to be angry now, not with this wonderful gift she was holding. She vowed to think of that beast no longer. Not now, not ever again.

Being that you're our oldest daughter, I hope you have some recollection of Eden before you left, mostly of me and your dear mother. You were just shy of five the last time I saw you, and I hope you might remember the sound of my voice or some of the places I used to take you as you sat proudly in the front of my saddle.

You were the first child born from your mother's and my new love. She was beautiful and had a smile brighter than the sun, a laugh that sounded like angels, and eyes that could reach deep into my soul. Our marriage didn't start out so smoothly, as her father had just passed, and she was frightened and alone. After the days at the ranch, I was her closest acquaintance. When I asked her to marry me, I could see she didn't really want to, but she felt she had no other choice. It was that very look in her eyes that made me pledge to myself that if she said yes, I'd never let her be sorry for her decision.

Mavis stopped reading and glanced over at Belle, who'd fallen asleep. *But Mother was sorry, Father—she left you and took all of us with her.* With a sigh, Mavis focused on the letter again.

The first few weeks after we wed, we were both tentative and shy. I'd lived with my father alone for so long, having a woman in the house felt strange. Then we became friends, and soon after that, she learned she was carrying you.

A warm, tingling goodness slipped through Mavis, imagining those times for her mother, picturing how living with Clint would feel so soon after they'd first met. Her mother must have been very courageous.

> We grew closer as her time drew near. As much as she complained about losing her girlish figure, I thought she'd never looked more beautiful. We'd sit by candlelight each evening after supper, and she'd read to me from the many books her father had stored in their wagon. I'd watch her face. When she'd come to a beloved part, her expression would either light up or turn melancholy with sadness. I could read, my dear daughter, but I pretended to struggle because I liked hearing her voice and the rendition of her favorite stories.

Mavis paused to wipe a tear. *Why, oh Lord, did this have to happen?* She reached to her nightstand and took a sip from the glass of water she'd put there before climbing into bed.

> I don't mean to frighten you, but your birth was long, and very difficult. I feared for Celeste's life many times. Her labor began in the middle of the night, her tortured moan waking me. Hours passed. A midwife who planned to attend to her just happened to come out to check on her,

to my great relief. My reprieve was short-lived. You didn't come. Celeste labored on another day, and then another. The midwife made teas and rubbed her back and stomach. She burned sweet-smelling bundles of herbs I'd never seen, and even recited prayers. Before your mother was too weak to walk, she had me march her up and down the hill that's out behind the old ranch house still. There's a flat rock beside a pine with a forked trunk a short climb up, where you can go and know that your mother sat there to rest moments before her water broke.

Mavis's small gasp almost awakened Belle. She'd been there already—one day when she'd been overcome with confusion about Clint. About their special friendship that never seemed to go anywhere important. Had she felt something special in the same spot where her mother had rested? It seemed so, but she couldn't be sure. A deep peacefulness had chased away her doubts and fears. Had that been her mother and father?

Finally, after three long, laborious days, you were delivered in our bed into the hands of that capable woman. I was holding your mother's hand and saw the whole thing. Despite your long delivery, you were gorgeous, with a smattering of wet hair smashed to your head. Your hands and feet were very wrinkled, something I learned was normal after more children were born. Your eyes were large and bright, and not a cry did you utter. You were placed in your mother's arms. After that day, you never gave her a bit of trouble—as if making up for the difficulty you gave her coming into the world. You were obedient, and we thought all children were that way until Belle and the others arrived.

His writing became blurred, and one word was unreadable and had been scratched out. The long letter that had begun neat and tidy had become scrawled, and a missing word appeared here and there. The signature line was barely readable.

*Oh, Father, were you so close to death? I'm so sorry I didn't find you sooner. I'm so sorry I believed those horrible people, the Crowdaires. I'll look after my sisters with love, now and forever. I will be the shepherdess with no qualms about my own happiness. I'll remember you and Mother and her long labor. That's the least I can do for you.*

# CHAPTER FORTY-TWO

At the break of dawn the next day, dressed in her ranching clothes, cowboy boots, and wide-brimmed hat, with a thick plait down her back, Emma rode toward the livery, her expectations high. She'd spent extra hours in the store yesterday afternoon, after Blake and Belle had dropped off the purchases she'd made in Santa Fe and arranged the ones she wanted in the store to their most advantageous positions. The place was brighter, fuller. She couldn't wait to see what the reception from the townswomen would be. Then, offering to pay Mr. Buns time and a half, she'd asked if he'd cover for her the next few days. With the naming of the Lucky Sister mine last night, she felt she had to be there with Blake and Beranger while they looked the site over. It felt right, and she'd been cooped up for too long. Penning a quick note to her sisters and leaving it on the breakfast table at the ranch, she'd slipped out undetected. She'd overheard the time and place Blake was to meet Beranger, and she knew she had to leave the ranch before her brother-in-law arose, or he might stop her from going.

With satisfaction at a job well done, she rode

into the livery yard and glanced around. No one was stirring. The sun had barely topped the mountains. Was she the first to arrive?

"Miss Emma?" Maverick came striding out of the barn, a surprised expression on his face. "What're you doin' here so early? Did we have an appointment?" He glanced at Dusty, giving him a quick once-over. "Because if we did, I'm sorry but I've totally forgotten. Or were you out for a very early ride and Dusty threw a shoe?" The blacksmith was clearly befuddled.

She gave a small laugh to chase away her nerves. "No, Maverick, nothing like that. I rode out from the ranch by myself to meet up with Mr. North and Blake. Has anyone arrived yet?" she asked, knowing full well she was the first.

"You didn't ride out *with* Blake?"

*No. He'd tell me to go home.*

"I'm surprising him. I'm very interested in the mine."

Maverick finished wiping his hands on the cloth he held and looped the towel over his belt. "You mean you took it on yourself because you knew everyone would say no."

She laughed. "You needn't be so amazed. I've been saddling my horse for months on my own. And I know the quickest trails." She reached down and patted Dusty's neck. "We had a fine time. Didn't we, Dusty?" She swung her leg over her horse and stepped down, looping Dusty's reins over the fence. "If no one is here yet, I'll just wait."

Maverick shrugged and started back toward the barn. "Coffee's fresh brewed."

"I was hoping you'd say that. Thank you." Wasn't that what all the cowboys did before an early-morning ride? "Moses will be along sometime today with the wagon. He'll meet us out at the mine by nightfall," she called, to show she knew what she was talking about. "To pick up supplies and a few items Beranger and Blake will need while they're mining and camping. Did Blake speak with you?"

"No, but Beranger did. I have everything he requested. They're packed up and ready to be loaded. From my understanding, Blake is only staying a night, and then returning. Will you be returning then as well?"

She nodded. "That's right. From there, Beranger and Moses will take over."

The night before, at Mavis's party, she'd taken the seat next to Beranger—she'd known him the longest, so it seemed only natural. All night, she'd tried not to let Belle see how much she enjoyed his company. Since he'd shared so much about himself, especially in her shop when she'd nursed his cuts, he'd never left her thoughts. A revelation had woken her from her sleep last night. At one o'clock, after an hour of contemplation, she'd come to the conclusion that she'd judged him wrongly. He was anything but a rake. More correctly, he was a champion of young women. Hadn't he taken on a roomful of men for her, without even being asked? But so much more than that, there was the way she felt when he looked into her eyes. Those few glorious hours spent at the café last night, talking and laughing . . . they'd almost, to her, felt like a couple.

*Heavens. Not that. We felt like good friends—nothing more.*

Still, she hadn't missed the way Belle had studied her and Beranger's every move. Each time he passed her something or looked her way, Belle raised a brow in question.

Emma made her way to the stove. Mavis had a small desk next to it, where she did accounts and watched over the business. The sultry scents of the barn, hay, manure, and coffee were nice. She understood why Mavis liked spending time here.

Being careful not to burn herself, she covered the handle of the old speckled coffeepot with a triple-folded hand towel and poured herself some into a clean cup.

*Well, I won't let that silly wager wreck my day. I'm not going to stop being Beranger's friend just because Belle is back in town and watching my every move. She can just think what she wants. I'm fine with that.*

"Morning, Maverick."

*Beranger.*

Maverick returned the greeting.

"Whose horse out front?"

She stepped out of the shadows, her coffee cup in hand. "Mine. Remember I told you about Dusty? That's him."

Beranger's eyes widened. He took in her clothes.

"That's a new look for the Toggery."

She felt a blush. "I'm going with you and Blake out to the Lucky Sister. We talked about the sisters being involved and not leaving everything to the men." She lifted a shoulder.

"And the burden falls to you, even though you were gone for days? Seems strange."

*He didn't have to say it like that. Doesn't he want me along?*

His tone was pleasant, but his words were confusing. She'd thought after last night, and all the laughing and kidding, that he'd be pleased to see her. Had she been wrong?

"I've been interested from the start. You know, to see the things we talked about at dinner that first night."

He gave a small nod, but she wasn't sure if he was pleased with her decision.

"You never mentioned anything last night, that's all."

"I didn't want anyone changing my mind. After the last couple weeks on the move, spending every waking moment at the Toggery has the walls closing in on me. Mr. Buns handled the place before I came to town, and is happy to do so again now when I want time off. I do pay him more for his efforts."

Beranger poured himself a cup. "Whatever you say, Miss Brinkman. You're the boss. And actually, I'm happy to have you along. Cooking is not my strong point. You can help."

"Yes, well . . ."

She didn't dare look at Maverick. He'd be wearing a goofy smile even though he knew that she was indeed, along with the rest of her sisters, the boss. The town's men thought that job lay with Blake. Or maybe he would be smiling at the thought that she could help with the cooking? Lavinia was the sister known for her culinary skills, not her. She watched Beranger take a sip from his cup.

"I ran into the dentist after the party last night. He was on his way to the meadow behind Clint's office to sketch and write."

"Really? I've never heard of such a thing. Night drawing?"

"Do you know him?"

She shook her head. "Just to say hello and such. I went by his shop when he first moved in to welcome him to town. But that's all."

Maverick stepped closer, holding a long piece of wood.

The edges were uneven and looked pretty,

reminding Emma of a flowing horizon instead of a measured line. The beautifully sanded edges and back almost looked soft.

"Thought you'd like to be the first to see," he said, turning the board around to letters burned into the timber.

She sucked in a surprised breath, and a tingle of excitement raced through her. "The Lucky Sister," she read aloud, reverence in her voice. "Father would be so happy today."

Maverick nodded. "You don't want to begin with bad luck, so I did my best to get this finished."

"You worked all night?"

He nodded. "Having women in the mine is considered bad luck too. Have you heard that one, Beranger?"

"Absolutely. I've heard them all. You don't think I'd let Emma anywhere near the inside, do you? But, from what I've been told, there isn't a mine yet, just the bare beginnings of a tunnel."

"What?" Emma retorted. "You never mentioned anything like that to me."

"You never asked. There're a lot of superstitions. I'm not superstitious myself, but mine owners can be. I don't want the blame if the Lucky Sister turns out a dud."

Blake rode into the barn and looked around. "This a private party?"

Maverick held up the sign, and Blake nodded his approval.

Emma laughed, happy to get off the bad-luck topic. She wondered what her brother-in-law must think of her showing up at the last second. Of course, he'd have recognized Dusty as soon as he saw her gelding, and known she was inside. "I wanted to go too. Is that okay?"

Blake narrowed his gaze. "Hmm, what do you think, Beranger? Should we let her come along?"

"She is one of the owners. Don't know how we can say no."

Beranger lifted his coffee cup, and Emma's gaze met Beranger's. Looking away was impossible. There was something there that she'd not seen before. A mixture of invitation, humor, and something else. Something that turned her insides shaky, and then warm and languid, like molasses cooking on a hot stove. Beranger swept his arm out, inviting her to exit the barn and mount her horse. Only then was she able to breathe.

Blake swung Banjo around and followed Emma and Beranger outside into the cool morning air. "Our destiny awaits."

Emma smiled at Blake over her shoulder as she lifted herself unattended into her saddle. Then her gaze strayed to Beranger. "Yes it does, brother-in-law. And I can't wait to see what surprises it holds."

# CHAPTER FORTY-THREE

Beranger enjoyed the ten-mile ride to the mine, appreciating an easy pace and stops to take in the vistas. Golden knee-high grass carpeted the open meadows, which were ringed by towering dark-green pine trees. In the distance, a herd of elk raised their antlered heads before bounding away over the little silver river that wound like a ribbon through the craggy hills. Blake and Emma shared what they knew about the Canyon of the Ancients, some twenty miles farther on than their destination. They discussed the unpleasant shadow cast over the town by Mr. Strong, and what that could mean for Eden if they didn't hunt out who was behind the telegrams. Then Emma changed to the pleasanter subject of Lavinia and Rhett's upcoming wedding, and the plans that had been made.

As the morning warmed and the conversation lulled, Beranger's mind drifted home. As was sometimes the case, he compared what he'd left behind to what he had now. His new home. His new land. America had been good to him. It had taken him in and made a bastard son a significant businessman with a bank account that kept on growing, since he rarely made a withdrawal. He wondered with a twinge of nostalgia if he'd ever see his birthplace again.

He glanced over at Emma. He knew it was high time that he stopped dreaming and began living his life in earnest. Watching her ride by his side made him long for so much more. Love, marriage, family. She was everything he wanted in a woman and partner. If he could only change her mind on her views of love and commitment. He'd finally found what he'd been seeking for so long. But would she fall in love with him or break his heart?

"Have we arrived?" Emma asked, looking around. She placed her hand on the cantle of her saddle, taking in the rugged area. They'd left the road twenty minutes back, and had been covering uneven and rocky ground.

Blake studied the hand-drawn map, filled with misspelled words and more than a few sketchy illustrations of unrecognizable landmarks. His brow furrowed. "Hard to tell. Nothing's marked very well."

Beranger dismounted and listened. "This way." He tromped through some brush, leading his horse, and continued over a rise to find a medium-size stream. "Thought as much."

Emma laughed.

*Seems she likes everything I say and do today.*

He grew hopeful.

"You have a nose for water and minerals," she said. "Better that than whiskey."

"More remote than I expected," Blake said.

"I assume that's an unmarked tributary from the Dolores. It's noted here, but just labeled RIV-HER."

Emma tipped her head. "Father must never have come out. He'd have commissioned a better map if he had. Will we even be able to find the mine?"

Beranger raised an eyebrow in mock offense. "You doubt me, my lady?"

He didn't miss the way Emma's cheeks colored at that. By the grin on Blake's face, he'd recognized the expression as well. Maybe getting her out here, away from all the trouble in town and the distraction of the occurrences on the stage was exactly what they'd needed. Nature had a way of leveling the field.

Ignoring his question, she sidestepped Dusty over to Banjo's side and reached for the map. "May I have a look?"

"Gladly." Blake handed over the crumpled yellowed paper. He dismounted, went to the stream, and watered himself and his horse.

Beranger waited to see what Emma would suggest, even though he had a fairly good idea what direction to go based on the lay of the land and the path of the water.

Still astride Dusty, she turned the paper to the side and then upside down. She raised her chin and scanned the area. Her teeth worried her bottom lip. She swatted at a fly. Finally, she dropped her hands into her lap. "I have no idea."

"Then let's try this way." He led them across the shallow creek and meandered to the base of a small hill. There was an indentation in the hill, but it was overgrown and almost completely concealed. He pulled back some bushes, and there was the forgotten narrow tunnel that went in only a few feet. "Here we are. Now, study the surroundings and see if the map makes a little more sense."

Emma smiled broadly. Clearly, he'd impressed her. "Beranger!"

"Just doing my job . . ." He left off the title "boss," as he'd begun calling her to try to get her thinking in the right direction. The long pause after his sentence and his arched brow had her blushing again.

*Perhaps Emma Brinkman won't be such a hard nut to crack. All we need is a little sunshine and a serenade from the birds and babbling creek.*

Blake pointed. "There's the stump, and granite slab to the right. Beranger, finding this was worth your fee alone." He strode over and enthusiastically shook his hand. Little did they know the real work would soon begin. The gold or silver wouldn't just jump out of the soil into their hands. But he'd allow Blake and Emma another day of fanciful imaginings, and keep to himself the knowledge that there was a load of bloody hard work coming right around the bend.

"I wonder where Moses could be?" Emma paced past the crackling fire and stared off the way they'd come, concerned their tents and sleeping gear had yet to arrive. "He should have been here hours ago." The sun had gone down, but there was still plenty of light. "Are you worried, Blake?"

Squatting by the fire, Blake set the coffeepot into the coals. "Not yet. Something in town may have delayed his start." He gave her a long look and then cut his attention to Beranger as if weighing his next statement. "If he doesn't arrive soon, you and I can ride out a ways and see if he's stuck. That wagon is heavy."

*He doesn't trust leaving me here alone with Beranger.*

"Beranger is a gentleman, Blake. I'm safe alone with him."

At hearing his name spoken, he glanced over. "Absolutely. Emma's just a friend—or perhaps a sister." He gave her a charming smile. "You needn't worry, Blake. We're not suited in the least. As a matter of fact, she intends to introduce me to some of Eden's finest."

Blake blinked several times and stood.

Emma leaned her shoulder against a tree trunk, having forgotten that conversation entirely. She took the cup of coffee and strip of jerky Blake offered. She thanked him, knowing they might have to pass the night with only whatever each had packed into their saddlebags. She was thankful she'd brought along her nightclothes, not left them with Maverick to put on the wagon. Sleeping on the hard ground with nothing but the clothes on her back, no blanket, no pillow, was not a prospect she looked forward to, but she'd not mention that to either of the men. They looked contented even with the delay of their belongings arriving.

Twilight eased in. An owl hooted twice and then soared quietly over their camp.

"I wonder who used to own this place," Emma murmured.

*And if anyone died out here, pursuing their dreams.*

"There's not much history or information. I can't remember when John acquired the claim in the first place. Just that once in a while the subject arose, and then at the reading of the will, I recall. The ranch kept us all plenty busy."

Beranger seemed quiet. Lost in thought. He'd accepted coffee and jerky as well, but had been sitting on a stump fifteen feet away for some time. The shadows disappeared as darkness fell more completely. Climbing to her feet, Emma closed the distance between them. He looked up at her in question.

"Come closer in by the fire." Having spent a good portion of his time at other mines, he must think her silly. "There might be a cougar out here. We should stick together."

"I highly doubt that. Not now, anyway. We'll have frightened them off." He stood. "But if you'll feel better, I'll come closer into camp."

She would feel better. "Thank you."

Once the sun sank over the ridge, the firelight was all the light they'd have until morning. A tiny shiver of fear tickled up Emma's back. Even on the route from Santa Fe, all the stage stops had been equipped with more than a few lanterns, making the remoteness of their locations seem like the least of their problems.

Standing by the campfire, Blake called her over. "I'm sorry about this, Emma. No dinner, and no blankets either." He'd given her the last of the jerky, although she'd tried not to accept. But after the ride, the meager fare did taste good. "We should have ridden back before now, as soon as we suspected Moses might not show," she said.

"Not with the rugged ground, if we didn't have to," Blake said. "Too risky for the horses. Morning will come soon enough."

"I don't mind sleeping out," she said. "And I'm sure Moses will be here first thing in the morning." She chanced a glance at Beranger.

*Would he rather be home at the boardinghouse in his small cot instead of having to sleep on the ground without a blanket? And where is everyone going to sleep?*

Seemed, since the sun had gone down, Beranger had let Blake make all the decisions. The horses had been staked out in a meadow of grass, and the saddles, leather saddlebags, and rifles were all close around camp. As the coffee had percolated, she'd helped the men collect enough firewood to last the night.

*Is there any danger I should be aware of—besides the usual bears, wolves, and outlaws?*

"All right, then. I've been circling this for a while," Blake said. "We have no other choice but to sleep together by the campfire. Emma, I hope that won't be too uncomfortable for you."

"After a flimsy sheet dividing the rooms at the stage stops, I'm ready for anything."

"Good." Golden light from the fire illuminated Blake's face. "Beranger and I'll take turns keeping watch and making sure the fire doesn't burn out. I hope you won't be too frightened. And we don't have a cup of warm milk here, the way you like in unfamiliar places."

Embarrassed, she drew back. She was almost twenty-two years old. The last thing she wanted was for Beranger to think her a child. "Blake, *please*. Does everyone have to keep bringing up that silly old habit I used to have?"

Instantly, she wished she could call back her words. Blake had been sincere, having heard about her habit soon after they'd met.

"Point taken."

They stood around face-to-face. Nobody seemed to know what to do. When cool air rolled off the creek and made Emma shiver, Beranger went to his saddlebags and drew out a heavy shirt. "Put this on. The night is only going to get colder from here on out. You'll be glad around midnight."

"Thank you, but *you'll* need your extra shirt. I brought something too." She withdrew the light jacket she'd brought to wear after the sun had set. She threaded her arms through it.

When she was finished, Beranger held out his bulky woolen shirt once more. "Put this on as well, over the top. Temperatures are dropping."

It was summertime, but the elevation was high.

She did as he asked, then began clearing a patch of ground to sleep on. Blake was doing the same, kicking stones and small sticks away. With nothing else left to do, they may as well have an early night, and an equally early morning.

Beranger brought over his and her saddles at the same time, holding each by the saddle horn. Without speaking, he laid her saddle blanket on the ground and set her saddle where she'd lay her head. Their feet would be toward the fire. Soon there was a matching spot on either side of her pallet.

"Unless someone has some stories they'd like to share," Blake said. "I suggest we make the best of our time and bed down now. I'm sure we'll all be up at the crack of dawn."

# CHAPTER FORTY-FOUR

Keyed up, Beranger took the first watch, telling Blake he was happy to sit up all night. Why not? He'd spent too many nights out alone on claims to be worried about wild animals or outlaws. And Emma Brinkman, the woman who'd stolen his heart, lay only a few feet away, trying to stay warm. He leaned back against a tree trunk and stared at the stars. Some years had passed since he'd done this very thing.

A rustle brought his gaze back to the fire.

Emma appeared at his side. "I couldn't sleep."

"Are you cold?"

"No," she whispered. "You must be, though, without your wool shirt."

He thought he saw her finger the sleeve.

"Thank you again."

"No problem."

"May I sit?"

"I don't mind."

Emma fussed for a few moments, getting comfortable. "What're you thinking about?" she asked. "Are you sleepy?"

"Sleepy, no. I'm used to this. And what am I thinking about?" Blake hadn't moved for the last half hour. Beranger was sure he was asleep. "I'm just thinking about . . . well, how you're wrong about love."

He felt her straighten.

"I mean, I've seen with my own eyes a true, enduring love match before. And when the harmony is right, it's a beautiful thing. When I was a boy, the gamekeeper on my father's estate was a man in his late twenties. His wife was a scullery maid. I'd be out on my rides, and she'd flag me in on her day off, feed me with bowls of stew and biscuits—which are what Americans call cookies. There was such a good feeling in that house, I wanted to live there all the time. When my stepmother was being particularly nasty to me, they'd take me in and let me sleep overnight. Stay as long as I wanted. Those two were an example. As she'd take my bowl away, she'd always say something warm about her husband, like, 'There isn't a green plant in the world that my husband can't grow.' I could see the love on her face as plain as day. And I'd hear him telling someone, 'She's a mum to every child she sees. Loves them all.' I knew that was true, because the care she showed me was love, plain and simple. Do you think she and her husband had an abiding love?"

She fidgeted. "I don't know."

*Well, that wasn't a flat-out no.*

"I've given you and your beliefs, as well as me beginning my search for the right woman, a lot of thought tonight too." He nudged her shoulder and softly chuckled. "What else do I have to do with my time, right? I think you're focusing on all the hurtful relationships you've known. Maybe you should turn that around and concentrate on the happy marriages you've seen. Do you think your father would have traded taking a wife or having you girls to save himself the hurt he experienced in his later life? If I were in his shoes, I'd say no. And another thing." He nudged her again, this time lingering longer against her shoulder. She was so quiet he feared she'd fallen asleep. "I think your beliefs must stem from something you're not even aware of. I don't think you've ever been properly kissed."

She gasped.

"Don't get all huffy. I'm just trying to save my friend a life of solitude. I've been alone a long time. I don't think you know how sad that can be. It will be compounded when the rest of your sisters get married and they all begin having children."

"Beranger, please. I don't really want—"

"Please, hear me out. Have you?"

"What?"

He feigned a sigh. "Aren't you listening to me, Emma? Been properly kissed? Have you ever been properly kissed by someone you had feelings for? I don't mean to get personal, but I think that might be part of your problem." He had the urge to pull her into his arms and kiss her silly, but he knew he had to move slowly. He knew he was right. She *hadn't* been properly kissed, and he aimed to fix that right now. "By your silence, I'll assume I'm correct in my thinking. So I'm going to give you a little kiss, just so you can see how pleasant the experience can be. I'm a bit surprised no one around Eden has tried this yet."

He leaned over and, without taking her in his arms, pressed his lips to hers.

Emma didn't move. Her back wedged a little more firmly against the tree trunk as he leaned over her. Then, the barest amount, he moved his mouth, opening his lips the tiniest bit. The two remained that way a few seconds as he waited for her to get used to the feel of his mouth on hers. A woman like Emma should have had a hundred beaus by now. He drew back.

Her breath jerked out. "Was that a proper kiss?"

"Well, not really. But a start. I didn't want to frighten you. Did I?"

"I'm no child, Beranger."

*What does that mean? Is she giving me the go-ahead?*

"That was more like a peck on the cheek that happened to move over to your lips. Did you enjoy it?"

"Yes, I guess so."

*She guesses so? That tiny kiss fueled his imagination and . . .*

"Would you like to try another?"

"Yes, I . . . uh . . . actually, I would."

Beranger slid his arm behind her back and gently pulled her close. With a slight tug, he had her cradled against his chest. He wasted no time in finding her mouth with his. With as much restraint as he could muster, he caressed her mouth with all the love he held in his heart. She whimpered, and he deepened the kiss. She parted her lips, and he took advantage. He thought he'd die from the beauty of her. Without breaking contact, she crawled up into his lap, and he cradled her in the crook of his arm. She whimpered again, and her head fell back, giving him access to her neck. He complied with her unspoken request by kissing a line all the way down to her shoulder of her open-neck shirt. She pulled him closer, and again he found her lips. The kiss went on and on. He was sure Blake would hear their sounds of pleasure. When he tried to pull back, she wouldn't let him go.

"That," he said against her mouth, "is a proper kiss, Miss Emma Brinkman. The kind lovers share morning, noon, and night—*especially* at night."

"Oh, *Beranger,*" she whispered dreamily, low and seductive against his mouth. "I see what you mean. I think a proper kiss can make *all* the difference."

He was loath to give her up, but to stick with his plan, he knew that was exactly what he had to do. He leaned back against the tree trunk, but she still rested in his arms.

"I'm glad you see my point. Now that you know what to look for, you can go about watching for the perfect gentleman who will generously shower you with proper kisses each and every day. Are there any good prospects in Eden? I've not been here long enough to know, but I'd suggest that young doctor, Jeremy Gannon. He seems like a good fellow. I've had several long conversations with him. The man kindly looked over Charger for me, you know. He's knowledgeable and kind. I think he would be a good start for you."

When her chin dipped, he smiled to himself.

"In case nobody has told you," he said, "kissing is not a sin. Experiment before you tie yourself to anyone. Make sure the man can, well—you know, *arouse* you. Once you tie the knot, it's too late to go back."

She still gazed at something on the ground.

"I'm sorry if I've embarrassed you. The English are open about matters of the heart—and body. Being we're such good friends, Emma, I'd hate to see you get trapped in a loveless marriage."

The sun was about to rise. Beranger knew Blake would be angry when he realized he hadn't woken him to take a shift at watch.

She straightened up and looked him in the eyes. "I may have liked the proper kiss, but that doesn't mean I've changed my mind about trusting love or getting married."

*Poppycock. You don't fancy the thought of marrying anyone else but me, but after your adamant refusal, you're too stubborn to admit the fact, you little fool. I've taken on tougher adversaries than you, Emma Brinkman.*

"I'm sorry to hear that," he said. "A woman like you, with lips like yours, is made for love. But you are the only one who can decide."

A loud rustling of leaves broke the stillness.

Emma gasped and threaded her arms around Beranger's body.

He reached for his rifle

# CHAPTER FORTY-FIVE

Moses strode into camp, jerked to a halt, and gaped. The Lucky Sister sign was tucked under one arm. His dark skin, shiny with perspiration, caught the early-morning rays of the sun, and his rumpled clothes were soiled.

Shocked and embarrassed, Emma shot off Beranger's lap like a bullet out of a Colt, though she instantly missed the warmth and feel of his strong chest. The memory of his "proper kiss," burned onto her lips and into her memory, brought fire to her face. Behind, she heard him climb to his feet.

"Mornin'," Moses gritted out.

Emma was used to Moses's easygoing ways, but he was clearly disturbed. His gaze tracked around, landing on everything except her face. He'd seen her cuddled against Beranger's chest as if they'd spent the night together. And if he thought that, he'd be right. Uncomfortable, she smoothed her messy hair and kept her gaze glued to Blake as her brother-in-law stood.

He immediately picked up on the tension, and his suspicious gaze moved between her and Beranger. "What's going on?" he asked gruffly.

His usually handsome face was lined with fatigue after his night of hard sleep. When no one offered any answers, Moses finally spoke up.

"Had multiple difficulties with the wagon about seven miles back. Tried to jimmy rig the axel myself, just to get this far, but nothin' doing. Tried till the sun went down. Now that I'm here, I can see that wagon wouldn't've made that last climb and descent anyway. John never mentioned anything about gettin' here. That map don't look nothin' like this terrain. Everythin's gonna have ta come in by mule."

Blake scrubbed a hand over the stubble shadowing his jaw. "That was our thought last night as well."

He glared at Beranger. Emma was sure he'd like to demand answers but was forcing himself to hold his tongue.

"Other news too," Moses said. "Clint told me ta pass on seems a lot more townsfolk have thrown in with the dentist. He has a bad feelin'."

"This stinks to high heaven," Blake said angrily.

Finally composed, Emma took a step toward Blake. "What *can* we do?" she asked Moses. "Have they learned something new?"

"Just what I said. Seems McGrath likes havin' more weight around town. People beholden to him. Told Miss Lavinia she should extend the hours she's open 'cause *he* likes ta eat late. Seemed his tone didn't sit too good with her. With so many owing him, he's startin' to believe he has some say in other people's business."

Beranger stepped forward. "I've had a bad feeling about that man myself. With those night sketches he makes. He had one of the Five Sisters Ranch from a hilltop, and another of Emma in front of her store."

"What?" she screeched. "Why would he do that?"

Still looking angry, Blake plucked the coffeepot off the lingering coals and tossed out the dregs. "I don't know, but I believe getting back to town would be best. We'll have to rethink how we're going to go about opening the mine."

His eyes narrowed at Beranger and then Emma.

She stepped forward. "I agree. But first, I need some coffee. I think everyone could use a cup of brew before we head out. Might calm our gnawing stomachs." Without waiting for his answer, Emma snatched the pot from his hands and hurried toward the creek.

# CHAPTER FORTY-SIX

Later that day, back in Eden, refreshed and dressed in clean clothes, Emma set out for Dr. McGrath's at a lively clip. A plan had been hatched between all the sisters—except Katie, who couldn't be found—as well as Blake, Rhett, and Beranger. Blake and Belle were going to wrangle their way into the dentist's office and see what they could find. First, Blake would feign a toothache, a reasonable explanation for their early return from the claim. While Dr. McGrath looked him over, Belle, waiting in the outer office, would snoop around in hope of discovering something significant.

That had *been* the plan. The whole ride back, Emma had endured aggravated expressions from Blake and Moses. Then, at the meeting, it seemed the news about how she had been caught up with Beranger had already gotten around. She felt ashamed and embarrassed. Wanting to get back into everyone's good graces, she decided to take matters into her own hands and see what she could find out. Now was her chance.

Clint, who'd been present for a while at the meeting, shook his head when they'd asked him to intervene. He explained that, as sheriff, he couldn't just barge in and demand to read Dr. McGrath's personal papers. He needed a search warrant from a judge showing a good reason for doing so. He couldn't intrude on the privacy of any citizen. That was right from the Fourth Amendment of the Constitution, as Henry's friend in Denver, Judge Harrison Wesley, had confirmed. And getting a warrant would take some time.

After that explanation, the sheriff abruptly stood up and excused himself.

In Clint's absence, the plotting continued. What he didn't know, he couldn't object to.

But the group agreed they had to be careful. Dr. McGrath had invested in Eden, and had seemingly tried to help others out of the goodness of his heart. He might actually be a model resident. And if so, they wouldn't want to alienate him unnecessarily.

*That's why I can take care of this better than Blake and Belle. One person is less suspicious than two. And if I get caught, I can just say I didn't sleep well last night and got confused, with a pretty smile on my face the whole while. He would be much more liable to forgive me than he would Blake.*

Emma stopped in front of the quiet shop, a sign in the window boasting painless dentistry with nitrous oxide. She inwardly cringed, rethinking her desire to make things right with Blake and the others and assuage their anger. She tried the door of the small dental office, but it was locked.

"May I help you with something, Miss Brinkman?" Russell McGrath had come up behind her so quietly she hadn't heard his approach.

She whipped around, placing her hand against her jaw. "I seem to have developed a toothache. I wondered if you would take a look. I haven't slept or eaten anything since the day before yesterday. It's very painful."

"Oh, you poor thing," he said, his face radiating concern. "You should have come sooner." He withdrew a key and unlocked his door, ushering her inside.

The place was eerily quiet. He opened the curtains of three windows and lit two lamps that helped make the room more appealing. Bare of decorations, there were three straight-back chairs against the wall, and a desk opposite. Two brown folders sat on the upper left-hand corner, just waiting to be snooped through.

He smiled at her expectantly.

The back room, over his shoulder, came into view. The dentist's chair was upholstered in red velvet and had strange trappings all about it, as if it waited like a looming monster. Headrest, armrests, levers, dials, and other unimaginable whatnots made the contraption look like a large wheelchair. A belt around the bottom was the most frightening of all. A drill hung from a nearby stand, and it resembled a small spinning wheel. A cloth-covered table held a handful of sharp silver instruments laid out in a straight line.

Saliva slicked her mouth.

*What was I thinking?*

"Actually, my tooth feels much better suddenly, Doctor. I'll return the moment the ache comes back."

He caught her arm. "No need to be frightened, Miss Brinkman. I assure you, you won't feel a thing. Now come with me and get comfortable. I'll just take a little look."

A second later, she found herself in the back room. McGrath was helping her into the chair. When he reached for the thick leather belt with the silver clasp, she shook her head. "I won't need that."

"You sure? The harness helps you relax. I added the belt myself."

"No, no. I'm positive."

"Suit yourself." Lifting his foot, he pumped a lever at the base of the chair several times, and the chair rose up several inches. Then he twisted a knob, and she rocked back. Feeling very vulnerable, she looked up his nose.

"Isn't my chair amazing? Manufactured by Wilkinson. The best and most modern on the market. Now, relax and open wide. I'm just going to have a small look around."

She swallowed.

"Please, Miss Brinkman. Haven't you ever been to the dentist before? You shouldn't be frightened."

She had. Twice. Both times, her sisters had been at her side. A new doctor in their Philadelphia neighborhood had offered free consultations.

McGrath waited patiently with a dental tool in hand.

Feeling pressured, Emma slowly opened her mouth. She wished she'd told one of her sisters what she planned to do.

Dr. McGrath's hand moved closer. He bent forward, peering into her mouth.

She tensed when the tip of the instrument gently scraped around the back of a bottom tooth. Nothing hurt, and the look on his face was rather pleasing. He seemed fastidiously clean, and had a nice scent of peppermint about him. Because she'd made up the story of an aching tooth, surely he'd find nothing and finish up in a moment. Warmth broke out on her back and chest.

He leaned away, and the instrument withdrew.

She let go a relieved sigh.

He smiled. "I see one little spot of concern." He pointed with the gadget and touched an upper back molar on the side where she'd feigned the pain. "Don't be alarmed, but the decay will grow if I don't drill it out. Takes all of one minute—if that."

He reached for the drill, stepped on something, and a whirring filled the room.

Emma slammed back in the chair as far as she could and shook her head. "No. I'll come back, Dr. McGrath."

"Settle down, Miss Brinkman."

She blinked at his sharp tone.

"I'll administer a small amount of nitrous oxide. You won't feel a thing. You'll come out happy as a lark—and no more toothache."

She clamped the armrests and tried to sit up, but he pushed her back with a hand to her shoulder. He was really quite strong for a man his size. With one hand he held her in the chair; with the other, he fumbled with a cloth bag, a clumsy rubber tube, and a scary-looking mouthpiece.

"Relax, Miss Brinkman. Relax. You have nothing to fear except fear alone." Smiling at his clever words, he brought the jar forward.

"Wait!" Her labored breathing made her sound like a racehorse after the Kentucky Derby. Fear ratcheted up her back. "I have to have my lucky charm."

His hands went still. "What?"

"It's three doors down, at my sister Katie's lumber office. My lucky charm is on her desk. Looks like a four-leaf clover in a small block of clear glass."

He gazed at her suspiciously. "Why would *your* lucky charm be at your *sister's* place of business? That doesn't make any sense."

Emma was trembling like a leaf. "I—I left it there for safekeeping when I went to Santa Fe."

His expression was disbelieving.

"Please, just go get what I ask, and I'll settle down. I promise. I won't put up any more protests and will let you fix my toothache."

*Toothache* seemed like a magic word. His smile reappeared.

"All right, Miss Brinkman. Stay put. I'll be right back." He turned on his heel and was gone.

Emma jumped out of the chair and ran to his desk. Opening the brown folders, all she found were drawings. Some poetry. Nothing of the ranch, like Beranger had said, nothing of her. The top drawer of the desk was locked. She scanned around. Hopefully, Katie wouldn't be there and the office would be locked. She didn't have much time. She ran back into the other room, to a small chest, and opened the drawer. She rummaged around what looked like a random collection of knickknacks, knocking some to the floor. Spotting a key, she grabbed it and stuffed the fallen articles back in. She could never be a detective. With shaky hands, she inserted the key into the desk's front keyhole and turned.

A nice click sounded.

Several folders lay inside. She rifled through the first, finding the sketches of her—and ones of other women. There were writings she didn't take time to read. Below that were the series of articles from the San Francisco newspapers—the intimate profile of the Brinkman girls that had sent shockwaves through Eden and led to the sisters mistakenly accusing their dear friend Lara Marsh of betraying them. But it wasn't the articles that made Emma gasp.

Below them was a page of signatures it looked like McGrath had practiced writing.

Emma blinked in shock.

Russell McGrath was really Harlow Lennington!

# CHAPTER FORTY-SEVEN

"Katie," Beranger said to himself when he saw Emma's youngest sister through the mercantile window as she crossed the street toward the store. Beranger had been killing time by comparing prices of mining supplies with the mercantile's new competition across town. Before that, he'd checked on Charger at the livery. To his surprise, he'd found a beekeeper, who was recovering from an injury, feeding honey to his warhorse over the fence. The gelding was licking the sticky sweetness off his palm as docile as a lamb. That steed kept surprising Beranger. He was responding to kind treatment with gentleness and respect. Perhaps someday, Beranger would even attempt to ride him.

But it was Emma who was on his mind today. After last night at the mine, and this morning's proper kiss, he'd thought she'd finally realize they were meant to be together. She would forget her silly attitude toward love and decide she couldn't live without him. Seek him out and pour out her heart. But she hadn't, and he'd grown more morose with each passing hour.

*I've been wrong. She really does believe that rubbish. Some sentiments can't be changed. Is winning Emma Brinkman's heart an impossible task?*

387

He stepped outside to intercept Emma's sister.

Katie approached, wearing a shy smile. "Mr. North, how nice to run into you."

"All your sisters call me Beranger. You must as well."

She nodded, trying, he was sure, to hide her unhappiness.

Before more than two words could be exchanged, Cash Dawson jogged up to their side. "Strange this, but I was in Rhett's construction office and that dentist came in looking for you, Katie. When you weren't there, he snatched up your four-leaf clover paperweight from your desk, mumbling something about Emma needing the thing in his office. By the time I realized what he was doing, he was gone. Thought I should tell you right away."

Fear slammed into Beranger like a train. Katie hadn't been at the meeting earlier with the family plotting how to catch the dentist in his lies—but Emma had been.

*Has she tried to search the man's desk on her own? She wouldn't do something so irrational, would she?*

Without taking a second to explain, he said his goodbyes and ran off.

Beranger barged into the dentist's office, slamming the front door back against the wall hard enough to rattle the hinges. McGrath spun around from the dentist's chair, his eyes huge with shock. Behind him, Beranger recognized Emma's blue dress.

What he thought had been the sound of a struggle he realized was actually a trill of strange laughter, followed by several giggles.

"Step aside," Beranger commanded, striding forward. He wasn't going to take the man down now, when Emma was so close she could get hurt. He'd tend to McGrath later.

With wide eyes, McGrath dropped the drill. "I—I was just about to fill her cavity, Mr. North. She came to me with a toothache."

Ignoring the little gnat, Beranger scooped Emma into his arms. She gaped at him with a silly grin of astonishment.

"My knight in shining armor has arrived," she sputtered, then giggled into his shoulder. "I knew you'd come for me, my lord. I'm, I'm . . ." She strained her neck over his shoulder, gazing behind as they walked away.

"B-but, my patient . . ." McGrath whimpered.

Emma rubbed her hands up and down Beranger's chest as he carried her toward—where?

*Where should I take her? In her condition, people might get the wrong impression.*

Before he realized what Emma was up to, she'd buried her face in his neck and began spreading tiny kisses everywhere she could reach.

The livery was close. He'd been there some ten minutes ago, and the place had been deserted.

"Beranger. Sweet Beranger," she sighed and then laughed, letting her head fall back and exposing the soft skin of her neck. "I was so scared. Frightened to death . . . Take me away from that horrible place so I can spread kisses all over your face." She giggled hysterically. "That *rhymed*. Did you hear it? Actually, I should have said *charming* face."

He smiled at her silliness, knowing the nitrous oxide wouldn't take long to dissipate. He wasn't sure how she'd feel afterward. Inside the livery, he hefted her higher in his arms and climbed, keeping one arm around her body and one hand on Maverick's ladder.

"Oh," she cried in surprise when he laid her in the hay. An extended round of giggles followed. "What did you have in *mind,* my lord?" she cooed. "More passionate kisses? I'm more than ready." She closed her eyes and pulled him closer. "When I think of you, Beranger, I smolder hotter than any campfire and then melt like butter. You're *everything* to me. When we're apart, I long to hear your voice, see your smile, gaze into your beautiful eyes. I love you. I just can't trust you. I'm sorry, I can't . . ."

With a hand to her cheek, he leaned forward. "Emma," he whispered, gently patting. "Wake up. Take some deep breaths." He pretended her words didn't affect him.

Her smile faded, and she clasped his hand to

her cheek with her own. She turned quiet and introspective. She looked gorgeous stretched out in the hay. Her eyes glittered in invitation. She tried to bring him closer.

"No," he whispered. "You're not in your right mind. I don't take advantage of inebriated women, or ones who've just inhaled laughing gas. You'll feel better soon. Just relax."

Her brow crinkled, and she giggled. "That's what that horrible man kept saying." She moved to her side, facing him, and laughed into his chest.

"Shh, more breaths, Emma. Keep breathing."

She rolled onto her back and slung an arm over her eyes. Her raised arm pulled the bodice of her blue dress tight, enhancing her pretty shape. A beautiful smile stretched her lips.

*If only this were real. If only Emma felt this comfortable with me, anxious for my advances, my caresses.*

She blinked several times from her pillow of hay, then reached up and touched his face with such tenderness he'd swear on his life she was back to herself. "I have a confession, Beranger," she whispered almost seriously.

He held up a hand. "Not now, Emma. You're still under the influence of the nitrous oxide. I don't want to you regret your actions or anything you might say. We'll talk later."

"No, I want to tell you . . ."

Her words trailed off.

*Maybe this is important to her. Maybe I should let her speak.*

"Go ahead, Emma. I'm listening."

"Back in Santa Fe, Belle and I had a small disagreement. We made a wager."

*A wager? What was this about?*

"She was angry at me for pooh-poohing love. She thought I hadn't fallen in love yet because I just hadn't met the right man. That when I did, I'd fall harder than my sisters."

*And, of course, Emma would deny that.*

Hope sprouted inside.

"She was right, Beranger. I've got to admit I was wrong."

She hadn't laughed in the last few moments. Could he hope that this was the real Emma talking? That she was serious and she'd remember what she was saying?

"I know you're looking for the right woman to spend your life with, Beranger. Is there any possibility that woman might be me? I've fallen in love with you. I don't think there's a cure."

# CHAPTER FORTY-EIGHT

I have no idea what Miss Brinkman is saying!"

Beranger watched the weasel Russell McGrath pleading his case. The dentist, along with Clint, all the Brinkman sisters, Blake, and Rhett were crowded into Henry's attorney's office above the mercantile. It was just an hour after Beranger had scooped Emma out of his dentistry chair. Her ashen face troubled him, and she sat slumped in a chair between Katie and Belle. He'd have liked to have given her more time to recuperate, but taking care of such nasty business was best dealt with directly.

The attorney narrowed his eyes. "Emma has no reason to lie, McGrath. If she says she saw the exact newspapers from the *San Francisco Daily Call* that ran the stories on the Brinkman sisters, then she did. As well as a page filled with Harlow Lennington signatures. She has no reason to fabricate that—and she isn't mistaken."

The dentist reached out in supplication. "Hallucinations and fabrications are a known side effect of nitrous oxide, Henry. Surely you know that. You must take everything she says with a grain of salt."

Beranger scowled and crossed his arms over his chest. Although he believed Emma's claims about McGrath, he'd been speculating about the veracity of her confessions of love and desire since she'd so sweetly uttered them while gazing into his eyes. Had the laughing gas worn off by then, leaving her in her right mind? Or had she still been under the influence of the nitrous oxide? It was maddening that there was no way to be sure. He desperately wanted to believe her, but since she'd promptly fallen asleep the second the last question was out of her mouth, he highly doubted it. Since then, she'd kept her gaze far from his. She'd walked quietly by his side on their way to Henry's office, where he'd left her as he went to collect the dentist. Beranger was uncertain, and that was a condition he didn't often find himself in, nor did he like it at all. He shifted his weight from one leg to the other as he leaned against the windowsill.

Emma's washed-out complexion pinked up at McGrath's accusation. As tired as she seemed, she stood and unsteadily grasped the back of Belle's chair.

"You're a liar, Russell McGrath—or should I say Harlow Lennington? Which one is your real name? We'd like to know. You may have over-powered me when you caught me in your desk, but you didn't see that I'd already taken some-thing to back up my claim. I don't know where you quickly hid your things, the newspaper and the page filled with signatures—maybe next door in the other buildings you own, maybe somewhere else. I really don't care." She pulled a small piece of paper out of her pocket. "I'd forgotten about this until now—another side effect of the nitrous oxide."

She opened the paper and held up a portion of the signature page she'd ripped off just before she'd been apprehended. "Sorry, Doctor. Seems the last laugh is on *you!*"

Mavis took the paper, studied the signatures for several moments, and then passed the proof around.

"Why?" Belle asked. "Why did you write the articles? Are you Mr. Strong as well as Harlow Lennington and Russell McGrath?"

The small man heaved a weighty sigh. "Who knows anymore?"

They all gaped at the admission.

"I guess your hearing this now really doesn't matter. A little sooner than I'd like, but I already own most of the larger buildings, as well as a good number of the vacant shops in the cobblestone area, and more than a few townsfolk owe me for small loans. No one can stop me now. I'm rather relieved to have everything out in the open." He sank down into his chair, the object of everyone's scorn.

"Start from the beginning, McGrath," Blake said sternly. "What's your whole story about?"

"And why publish our life stories for anyone to read?" Mavis asked. "We were shocked and dismayed. So much personal information. You hurt us deeply. We know that the information came from our friend Lara Marsh's diary, but why did you publish it? And how did you get her journal? We'd like to understand."

"The question is, why not?" McGrath pushed out his chest with pride. "You see, I've always loved to write. I've dreamed of being a writer all of my life. Instead, my philanthropic uncle, when he was alive, encouraged me toward dental school. I do get pleasure working in people's mouths, but I always circle back to my poetry and prose. That's where my heart lies."

Belle frowned. "Why us?"

"Because that wonderful diary showed up in my office one day. I presume it was forgotten by mistake."

"And you are responsible for mailing the diary back to Lara's house in Philadelphia?" Lavinia asked, astounded.

"Who else?" McGrath stated. "Regardless of what all of you think of me, I'm not a monster. The stories made for fantastic reading. I thought again, why not? I took my time penning out several installments, then sent them to the *San Francisco Daily Call*. I was stunned when the publisher not only bought one, but all three installments. I became fascinated with Eden myself. I began a correspondence with Henry and discovered Eden had begun to grow in leaps and bounds. Delighted, I decided I'd like to live here too."

"Did you live in Philadelphia?" Katie asked.

He shook his head. "No. Southern California."

"Then why San Francisco?" Lavinia asked.

"I'd read somewhere they were looking for human-interest stories, so I had a better chance of being published."

Anger roiled inside Beranger. Back in England, there were plenty of greedy, unscrupulous land-owning aristocrats, dukes, and lords who did just what this little fellow was trying to do. Control others. Be a king among men. Squeeze every last penny they could from law-abiding, hardworking people. Nothing turned his stomach more.

"So you decided to crown yourself king of Eden," Beranger gritted out, unable to keep silent any longer. "You researched and found which buildings were owned and which were rented. Then you went to work."

McGrath beamed. "All that exactly, Mr. North. Ever since I've arrived, I've felt right at home. I couldn't have planned anything better."

"You're sick!" Mavis spat. "What you're doing to our friends and the town is disgraceful."

Beranger, acutely aware of Emma watching him on and off through the proceedings, pushed himself from the wall and took several steps closer to the fellow, making McGrath cringe. "Your pride and relief may be short lived, McGrath. Now that Mr. Strong's identity is known, how much time do you think you have until some bitter shopkeeper who's spent every ounce of effort and every extra penny to scratch out a living here in Eden gets fed up enough to take action?"

McGrath jerked straight in his chair and looked around in fear.

Beranger smiled. "I'd say not much."

"Sheriff," McGrath sputtered. "Tell Mr. North that murder is against the law."

Beranger leaned down into his face. "Your actions offend the laws of decency."

"That's true," Clint said. Everyone else nodded in agreement. "Up until a few years ago," Clint went on, "Eden was a mining town, filled with lawlessness and disorder. There's still plenty of that around, even if the reality looks different. With so many after you, I won't be able to keep you safe."

"I-it's the law. You *have* to keep me safe."

Clint shrugged. "I can try, but I can't promise anything."

The men in the room exchanged looks.

McGrath's face blanched. "But it was all a silly game that got out of control. I didn't mean any harm, Sheriff, Mr. Glass, sisters. I promise you." His beseeching eyes ended back on Clint. "Please, Sheriff, you have to believe me. Something must be done. I'm too young to die."

"What do you mean, you didn't mean any harm?" Henry questioned.

"One of my wealthy friends and I were having supper one night. I was expounding on what a boon my articles had been to Eden. Bragged that I'd contacted an attorney here, who'd said the town was quickly growing. New businesses were sprouting up. Property and land prices were rising. That's when my friend wondered if I could actually buy the whole town. I'd generated the outside interest in the first place. I said I could, and he doubted my veracity. We made a wager."

Emma slunk down in her chair and glanced Beranger's way.

*Does she remember telling me the truth about her wager with Belle?*

"Please, I'm not a bad man; I just like to have fun. Don't you see that now?"

"There may be a way for you to fix things, McGrath, if you're so inclined," Beranger said. "And then, after time passes, you may even become something of a hero."

The man looked at him with wide eyes. "Please explain, Mr. North. I'm not interested in being a target."

"Hire Henry to draw up as many contracts as needed. Offer the buildings you recently purchased to be sold at a reasonable price to the owners of the businesses in those buildings. Their mortgage payment will be that of their pre-McGrath rent. They will go from being tenants to the actual owners over time."

McGrath's face turned red. "Sell off my beautiful properties? But why would I do that?"

# CHAPTER FORTY-NINE

Emma found taking her eyes off Beranger difficult to do. He was so commanding. Imagining he was descended from nobility was easy. She loved his eyes, as well as his smile and profile. His presence seemed to fill the room. He took everything in stride but seemed to have an answer—*the right answer*—ready at any moment. How had he become so wise?

Beranger smiled at McGrath. "Why would you want to make things right with the people you meant to gouge?" he asked, rephrasing McGrath's question. His smile vanished. "Goodwill, perhaps—or to keep your *life*. You admitted in the council meeting that you inherited a great deal of money. You don't need those businesses. They're only sport to you."

McGrath scrambled in his chair, his face losing all color.

"If you make good and reverse what you've done, Mr. McGrath, people might not scorn you as they will when they find out you're Mr. Strong," Katie spoke up. "Actually, the exact opposite might happen. Because of your articles in the *San Francisco Daily Call*, the lumber mill has tripled our monthly gross income. And I don't see that growth ending anytime soon. I'm not sad to see my business grow."

Rhett nodded. "And because of your articles, I picked up and moved to Eden, met Lavinia, and am soon to be married." He lifted Lavinia's hand and kissed the back. "I've started my own construction company too, and Lavinia had to hire another waitress in her café. Lots of businesses, not only ours, have prospered. People will be grateful to you, but only if you stop trying to scalp more earnings for yourself and make this situation right." He narrowed his gaze. "You don't have an accomplice by the name of Daniel Yorkton, do you, McGrath? We've recently made a deal for my restaurant, Shawn's Café."

McGrath shook his head.

Clint rubbed his hands together. "Who knows? If you play your cards right, you might end up a pillar of the community instead of a scorned shyster."

"I can have the new contracts done by tomorrow," Henry said. "All I need is the go-ahead from you, McGrath, and I'll get to work."

"For a fee?" McGrath asked.

"Of course for a fee. I don't work for free."

Blake stood and stretched. "The ranch has never been so productive or sold more beef than over the last few months."

Belle smiled and nodded.

"I too have to agree," Mavis said. "According to Maverick, the livery is doing better than ever before. More citizens mean more horses, buggies,

401

and wagons. The work is hard, but we're grateful for it."

"Ditto for my attorney work."

Emma felt mulish. She was the only one who hadn't spoken up, but she was the one who'd almost had her tooth drilled out. Still, she needed to add her two cents. "I agree too, Dr. McGrath. Your articles brought men, which in turn, brought women looking for husbands. Because of that, I enlarged the Toggery."

Nobody could make the man do the right thing. That decision would have to be his and his alone. As much as McGrath would be hated for being underhanded and shrewd, he hadn't broken any laws.

His face finally lit up. "Why, thank you, Miss Brinkman. Can I consider we're still friends, then? All has been forgiven?"

She narrowed her eyes. "Do I really have some decay that needs attention, or did you just want to drill on my tooth?"

His mouth snapped shut. "Come to mention that, er . . . no, Miss Brinkman. I'm sorry, you do not. I promise to mend my ways." He quickly held up a finger. "I appreciate everything you've presented here. A lot to think about. I like living in Eden and don't wish to leave. Henry, please do as Mr. North suggested and draw up those contracts. If we go back to the old payments, which will apply to principal instead of plain rent, I think a lot of goodwill can be created."

As Henry contemplated the dentist, a look of wise calculation passed over his face. "I'll bet that's the first good and honest idea you've ever had, McGrath. You best walk a straight line from here on out. We'll be watching. Foolhardy bets have a way of going astray, more often than not, and hurt more than they win."

Feeling foolish, Emma was dimly cognizant of at least two pairs of eyes on her. Unable to stop herself, she raised her gaze to Beranger's. He was observing her closely. He didn't smile but he didn't scowl either. His gaze reached deep into her soul. She didn't have to look to know the other pair of eyes belonged to her sister Belle.

Mavis shifted in her chair. "There is one bright spot in this whole affair. I'm thankful Mr. Strong didn't turn out to be Vernon and Velma Crowdaire, resurfacing to interfere in our new lives. *That* would have been too much to endure."

The sisters nodded. Hot anger ran through Emma.

"If I never hear their names again, I will consider it a blessing from above," Lavinia said, smoothing the fabric of her dress in her lap.

Rhett reached over and enveloped her hand in both his own as the rest of the Brinkman sisters chimed in to agree.

# CHAPTER FIFTY

The meeting in Henry's office broke up, and everyone went their separate ways. Emma was frantic to know what Beranger thought after she'd poured out her heart to him in the loft, but he hadn't said a word. He'd looked at her in disbelief at the time. And then, each time their gazes touched during the meeting, he'd glanced away.

*He's been hurt so many times in his life, I don't want to give him any more pain.*

As she was about to descend the steps, Mavis caught her arm. Beranger and Clint had already disappeared into the sheriff's office. Belle, Lavinia, and Katie stood by.

"We'd like to speak with you, Emma."

Everyone looked so serious. She glanced around. Henry had gone into his living quarters. "Here?"

Belle nodded. "Sure. We have chairs, and we're all alone. Katie, do you have that telegram for Emma?"

*Telegram? What is this about?*

Katie withdrew a telegram from her pocket and handed the paper over. "This came this morning. From the nuns in Santa Fe. I tried to find you, but now I know you were busy at the dentist's office." She scrunched her face. "I do have to give McGrath credit for fixing Jackie's smile.

The false tooth isn't flawless, but that child is smiling much more readily."

Emma scanned the short note. "Brenda is doing well," she said excitedly, thankful the nuns had thought to get in touch with her. "They checked on her progress, and she has adapted nicely. She asked about us, and about me." Emma raised her face and gave each sister a tender look. How blessed to be a part of this family.

Satisfied, she folded the telegram. Her sisters were still gazing at her. "Was there something else?"

They all nodded at once.

"I told them about our wager, Emma," Belle said. "I hope you don't mind, but each one of us, at a different time, voiced concerns about you."

Humbled, Emma listened.

"Love is a *good* thing, Emma," Katie said softly. "Yes, Santiago has broken my heart, but I'm not blaming love. Like Father said in my letter, we have to follow our hearts, do what they tell us to do." She looked at her sisters. "Just because I'm hurting now, I'd not want you to use that as an excuse to miss your chance with Beranger. He's a wonderful man. And he has eyes only for you. He's tried everything to get you to notice him, even making you a little jealous because of me at supper."

"*He* did that?" A niggle of dread squeezed her heart. In her nitrous oxide–induced hysteria, had she said something to him about love? She wasn't sure, but she felt she had.

Katie nodded.

Belle took her hand. "Emma, I never wanted to make that silly wager, but you were adamant. I never, in this lifetime or the next, had any intention of seeing it through. I'd never do that. I love you. We all do. The Toggery can't give you the happiness a husband can. And in particular, if we're right about the way he looks at you—that *Beranger* can. You'd be a fool to pass him up."

Touched deeply by everyone's concern, her face heated. She was proud of Katie for speaking her mind. She was getting stronger. They all looked beautiful, and she hated that she might be the reason all those smiles would disappear, but she just wasn't ready yet. As much as she'd loved being in Beranger's arms, she was wary.

*What if one day he just rode out of town?*

*"Love is worth the risk."*

*Why did that saying keep torturing her? From all she knew, love was definitely not.*

"I'm very honored that you all love me so much you'd come and speak to me like this. I am. I'm sure, after all the lectures I've given of late, you were frightened I'd bite your heads off." She reached out and hugged each one. "I'm listening with an open heart. I'll take your words and try to see things your way."

"And?" Mavis asked.

"I'm just saying that I am listening. I only got this far earlier today."

"What?" Katie asked. "Why?"

Emma shrugged. "The heart is a mysterious thing. I could never even try to explain. I'm not that smart."

Lavinia clapped her hands together. "How exciting. Now Rhett and I may not be the only ones with a wedding coming up."

Startled, Emma put up a hand. "That's crazy. Don't move so fast. I count on being courted, if you're right about the way Beranger feels—and I can't be sure about that until we talk. So please, give us a little time before you start asking me for all the juicy details. I'm just not yet ready to take the plunge."

By their expressions, she could tell that wasn't what they'd hoped to hear.

"I think we have another wedding to plan, though. Isn't that right, Lavinia? Belle and Blake are home, so there's nothing to stop us."

Belle nudged Emma toward the door. "You just leave Lavinia's wedding to us. Get going on talking with Beranger. If you don't want to be pestered, we have to see you're striding toward a good outcome."

Feeling better than she had in weeks, Emma laughed.

Henry came out of his private rooms and stopped in his tracks. "What on earth are you all cooking up? There are signs of plotting on each and every face."

They shrugged and looked at each other, innocence all around.

# CHAPTER FIFTY-ONE

On a Sunday morning a little over three weeks later, Emma awoke refreshed and excited. Today was Rhett and Lavinia's wedding day. Throwing off her blanket, she padded to the ranch window and looked out on the sunrise. *Beautiful.* She'd never tire of the sight. The afternoon weather would be gorgeous. They'd spent days preparing the meadow above town. Rhett and Cash had built a gazebo overlooking Eden, where Reverend Caskill would marry them. Without wagon access, they'd all had to help carry up tables, chairs, a punch bowl, and a few decorations. A dance floor had been constructed, as well as a small bar.

Emma pulled the window up and leaned out, taking in a large gulp of fresh air. She wondered momentarily at the happiness she felt. This was due to more than the long-awaited wedding. This was some mysterious thing residing deep inside.

*Beranger.*

She breathed his name reverently. She and Beranger had been keeping company. Not in the way her sisters had hoped, but spending time as friends. The best of friends. Since he spent hours at the livery to see Charger, he visited the Toggery every day—sometimes more than once.

They talked and laughed and solved the problems of the world. McGrath, true to his word, had done exactly as they had suggested. That problem was cleared up, and Rhett sold his café, but the mine had once again been put on hold in order to plan her sister's wedding. At first, she'd been concerned, not wanting to lose her best friend if he decided to move on, since work on the project had been postponed for the time being. But he hadn't. He'd begun working Charger, saddling him, and breaking him to ride.

What she and Beranger possessed was better than romantic love. And she hoped he felt the same. He never brought up the loft, or what words might have been exchanged, but she felt something had transpired.

Someone knocked on her door. Just as she turned to answer, a flash of white outside caught her eye, far off by the river's edge.

She gasped with delight. Beranger and Charger were racing the wind.

"Come in," she called excitedly. "Come in and see!"

Lavinia ran to the window.

"Look," Emma pointed. "Beranger and Charger. I can't believe he rode him out to the ranch."

Lavinia leaned on the windowsill, her eyes huge.

Emma couldn't stop a round of laughter as she watched their progress. "They look magical together." She snatched up a scarf and leaned out the window, flagging it back and forth.

Beranger held up his arm.

"Get back in here before you fall," Lavinia screeched, grasping her arm and pulling her inside.

Remembering this was a special day for Lavinia, she turned and smiled into her sister's face. "Excited or butterflies? Which are you feeling?"

Lavinia glowed from within. Her eyes glistened, and the smile she wore spoke about all the love she held for Rhett. Contentment at what her sister had found filled Emma's soul.

Lavinia hugged herself with gusto. "I am both. I can't wait to be Mrs. Rhetten Laughlin."

"You don't have to wait long. Only a few hours now." She let her smile fade away. "I'm going to miss these early-morning visits, Lavinia. Some of our best talks happen before anyone else is up. Promise you won't forget me just because you have a handsome husband doting on your every whim."

Lavinia blushed deeply. "I'll still come to visit, because we'll be living right here. The house is really filling up."

"And soon there'll be the pitter-patter of tiny feet, right?"

Lavinia ducked her head. "Belle has to be first." She giggled. "I can't imagine."

"You better."

"I did have a reason for coming in this morning, Emma," Lavinia said, her smile fading away. "Katie cried all night. She'll be worn out at the wedding this afternoon if she doesn't get some rest. I'm going to try to get her to take a nap mid-morning. I hope you'll help me accomplish that."

*Santiago.*

"Did they leave?"

Lavinia nodded. "He says he's only making sure Larsala gets back to Arizona safely, but I don't know. She has those two tough guards to look after her already. He says she's misunderstood, and that we would like her if given a chance."

"Why is she going now? Did he say?"

"Just that her father-in-law has called her home. He still holds the purse strings, so to speak. Those tough-looking men follow her around to make sure she isn't kidnapped and held for ransom. She and Santiago may have more planned for once they get to Arizona. We'll have to wait and see."

"I'm just thankful they're gone. This hasn't been easy for Katie. I'll help the best I can. Now, put that smile back on your face. This is *your* wedding day. No worries for you."

They looked at each other for a long moment. Emma couldn't stop herself. She reached out, engulfing Lavinia in a warm hug. They were so much alike in some ways, but different too. What she saw of her sister's feelings for Rhett seemed exactly how she herself felt for Beranger.

*Have I fallen in love? Yes,* she thought, *it's true.*

The simple thought of Beranger made her giddy beyond the moon and stars. Friendship couldn't do that. She decided to tell him at the wedding, as she danced in his arms. Then maybe when the lanterns went on and the twilight had fallen, he'd lead her into the trees and they'd kiss as they had the morning at the Lucky Sister. Her pulse picked up just thinking about the possibility.

"What?" Lavinia asked, searching Emma's face.

"I'm just excited for you. By this time tomorrow, you'll be a married woman."

She nodded. "And a bedded one as well."

"Lavinia!"

Laughing, her sister pranced out the door.

Emma turned back to the window with her scarf, waving madly.

Emma! In the window. Beranger hadn't planned to ride this way, but somehow the Five Sisters Ranch was where he ended up. The night had dragged on. He hadn't been able to sleep at all. He'd tossed and turned until he thought he'd go mad, confused at what might be causing his unrest. He'd grown used to thoughts of Emma beleaguering him every night, but this was different. Something else entirely, and it didn't bode well.

*A premonition?*

He concentrated on the cadence of Charger's stride, not wanting to be left on the ground if the horse spooked at something unfamiliar. His stride was long and fast and, for his size, light-footed. Over the past three weeks, the gelding had gradually allowed Beranger to saddle and bridle him. Carrying him was still new.

The cool morning mist off the river invigorated them both. The crystal-blue water splashed down the rocks as they raced by. Following the river, he lost sight of the house and barns. Today was a good day to get lost in his thoughts.

Emma was a puzzle. As much as he tried to figure her out, he couldn't. She talked a fair game, but what it came down to was that she was frightened. Frightened to make a commitment. Scared he'd up and leave her someday. He'd thought he'd be able to break through her outlandish fears, but nothing he did seemed to make a difference. She seemed content to be friends. He couldn't live wanting her all the time, but leaving felt impossible. He was in the worst kind of bind. There had to be a way to get through to her without coming right out and proclaiming his love. Once he did that, he worried she'd pull back and he'd lose her for good. Was an ultimatum the only way to show her he was serious about wanting to spend his life with her?

A bit discouraged, he pulled Charger down to a

trot, turned him toward a shallow section of the river, and splashed across. It took little more than a touch of his heel to encourage the big gelding to lurch up the bank on the other side and take off through the trees.

# CHAPTER FIFTY-TWO

The upper meadow hummed with excitement as the majority of Eden's inhabitants gathered for the wedding. Emma and her sisters waited behind a blanket they'd hung as a barrier on the edge of the clearing, which Rhett had nailed up between several trees for privacy. The weather was as beautiful as Emma had predicted. She'd seen Beranger at times throughout the morning, lifting and carrying supplies, but they hadn't exchanged more than a few words. When late morning arrived, the girls retreated to the hotel to bathe, dress, reminisce, and talk. They made sure Lavinia was treated like a princess for a day.

Everything was ready, but they were waiting on the reverend, who had forgotten his Bible. He'd hurried away, telling everyone they'd begin as soon as he returned.

Emma peeked out from behind the blanket, spotting the saloon girls she'd seen arriving in town the other day. She was astounded to discover that the little boy who had been with them was actually a little girl. Jimbo was there as well, having shaved and gotten a haircut, and looking very respectful. Not wanting to leave Eden completely unattended, Clint had asked the ranch hands to take shifts staying in town just to keep an eye out while everyone else was up at the wedding.

"There's the groom, Lavinia—*but you can't look*. He's gorgeous, as usual! You're going to faint when you see him. There's Blake too, and Clint and Cash. I've never seen the men more handsome. Cash is certainly handsome, just like his father."

She snapped her mouth closed when she realized what she was doing. Only a month ago, she would have been describing Santiago for Katie, and they'd all be tittering and laughing, thinking of another wedding to come. She chanced a quick glance at her youngest sister. She'd been delivered by two of the ranch hands just in time to dress and partake in their sisterly exchange in the hotel. The two swapped a tiny smile, Katie silently forgiving Emma of any unintentional slip in judgment.

"I was delighted when Rhett asked Jeremy to be a groomsman." Mavis stood behind Lavinia with the bride's delicate, long veil draped across her arms. "The doctor fits right in with the others."

Emma nodded. "He *was* the reason you and Rhett got together so quickly, after all." Emma couldn't hold in her laughter. "Or should I say his delayed arrival in Eden was. You and Rhett were destined to meet, and in such an intimate way—*alone* in your hotel room. Lavinia, I've always thought there was more to that story you weren't divulging. That something may have happened besides his helping with your eye. Would you like to share that with us now?"

Lavinia turned beet red. "Well . . ."

The four stepped closer, their eyes glittering with excitement.

"Something else *may* have transpired," Lavinia teased, twisting a sprig of grass in her fingers.

"I knew it!" Emma breathed. "I'm amazed you've kept the secret to yourself all this time."

Lavinia sweetly smiled. "It's a private treasured memory for Rhett and me."

"Pray tell!" Belle demanded.

"Only if you promise never, and I mean *never,* to breathe a word of it—"

"We promise!"

"As you know, you were all at the church when I fumbled my way downstairs to fetch the stranger who'd just gotten off the stage. He was the man I believed to be the new doctor, so I asked him up to my room to assist with whatever I had lodged in my eye. Being a good sport, Rhett tried. After I was feeling a wee bit better from the warm oil, I asked if he could please assist me as I dressed. I could barely see, and . . ."

"What?" they all chorused together.

"That bad boy Rhett," Katie scolded.

Lavinia laughed and shook her head. "No, you have it wrong. He tried his best to tell me no. He resisted several times, but I insisted. He feared that if he told me he wasn't a doctor, I might be so upset I wouldn't go to the wedding at all. His kind heart wouldn't let him."

*"Riiiight,"* Emma said with a good dose of cynicism. She'd had a feeling about that meeting between Lavinia and her handsome savior since the very first day, but she hadn't expected *this*. How romantic. She hid her smile.

*What other secrets are my sisters keeping?*

"And?"

"When he agreed, I climbed off the bed and dropped my robe. All I had on was my pretty pink corset, silk pantaloons, and stockings. Rhett, the gentleman that he is, graciously helped me into my gown and did up my buttons," Lavinia finished, and then burst into laughter.

Katie's eyes snapped open, round as twin moons. Emma fanned her face with her hand, her mouth moving without saying a word. Mavis's gaping mouth would catch a fly if she didn't watch out, and Belle, with twinkling eyes, embraced Lavinia, laughing too. Soon they all were.

"What a story," Mavis said. "I should try the like the next time I'm alone with Clint."

Her sisters gaped at her.

"I'm kidding, of course. But . . . maybe not so much. How I wish Lara were back from her visit home. She's the only one missing."

Katie nodded. "I miss her too. It's too bad her mother took ill right before she was set to return to Eden. Nothing else would keep her from being with us today. Now Jeremy and Cash have to walk together."

Lavinia giggled. "They're both fine with that. Jeremy will make an exceptional teacher until Eden can hire Mr. Lake's replacement. With his medical education, Eden couldn't have done any better."

"He is a very nice man," Katie agreed softly, contemplating her fingernails.

Emma secretly exchanged a brief look with everyone *except* Katie, then glanced out from behind the draped blanket once more.

"Is Beranger out there, Emma?" Katie asked. "You've conveniently left *him* out of the discussion."

He was. And he looked devastatingly handsome. All day long, any thought of him brought a round of butterflies and jitters. How she longed to be in his arms now, and to be able to proclaim what she'd so recently realized was in her heart. The dancing couldn't start soon enough for her.

"Emma?"

"Yes. And he looks as dashing as the rest."

*Better!*

Sounds of violin floated in the air.

"Won't be long now," Belle breathed.

Lavinia had chosen a simple, white wedding gown with a beautifully fitted satin bodice that made her waist look impossibly tiny. A touch of lace finished off sleeves that reached halfway between her elbows and wrist. The style was a perfect match for the sweet wedding hat she'd spent weeks on. Created in the same flat fashion as her other renditions, the headpiece was decorated with small colorful flowers and a delicate white netting that would flow all the way to the meadow floor. She was a vision.

"For you, sweet Lavinia. Something old," Mavis said, handing her a very tattered-looking hankie. "As you know, this was Mother's."

Lavinia took the treasure in her fingers and held it to her cheek. "She's here with us today. I can feel her presence as I look into each of your faces. Father too."

Belle smiled, looking as beautiful as always, if a little wistful. "And from me, something new." She carefully fastened a tiny pearl pin to Lavinia's bodice. "I didn't want it to clash with the pendant Rhett gave you." After pinning the jewelry to Lavinia's dress, she touched the pretty locket that hung from a chain around her neck. "So sweet."

From her wrist, Emma unclasped the delicate crystal-and-gold bracelet she'd been given by Mrs. Gamble in Philadelphia. She had sent it to Colorado after the woman learned Emma would not be returning to her post. The piece of jewelry was Emma's most prized possession, as all her sisters knew very well. "Something borrowed," she said softly as she fastened the slight chain on

Lavinia's wrist. "And a wedding gift as well," she whispered into Lavinia's ear, for her alone.

How wrong Emma had been about Tim and Cooper. How grateful she was that she hadn't ended up married to either. If she had, she'd have missed Beranger, and nothing was more important than him.

Lavinia grasped Emma's hands. "I can't."

Emma smiled. "You have no choice. I've already given it to you. I love you."

Katie stepped forward. "Something blue." Going up on tiptoe, she carefully wedged a small blue-bird feather in between the flowers on Lavinia's hat. "Rhetten Laughlin is a very lucky man."

They embraced.

From the other side of the blanket, they heard a sound that resembled a disturbance of some kind. Alarmed, Emma turned and looked out.

"What is it?" Lavinia asked. "Can you see anything?"

"No. Not yet. People are looking toward the path. I can't imagine who might cause such a stir. The only one we're waiting on is Reverend Caskill. Wait, there's a man on a horse. A stranger," she whispered fervently. "He's looking around in surprise, and there are more horsemen behind him."

Mavis pulled back the blanket so they all could see.

"Look at those saddles. They aren't from around here," Belle said. "Not even from Colorado."

"Who could they be?" A note of panic laced Katie's voice. "The man in the lead has an air about him."

Suddenly, recognition struck Emma. The man resembled Beranger. Older, but absolutely related. Urgently, she scanned the crowd for Beranger. There he was, striding purposefully toward the newcomers! That was when she saw the English crest on the saddle blankets under the English saddles. Stars danced before her eyes.

Katie and Belle reacted, catching her elbows as she wavered on her feet.

"Don't pass out," Mavis scolded.

The man dismounted, and he and Beranger embraced, holding each other for several long seconds. Unable to stop herself, Emma pulled away from her sisters. She ran to Beranger's side, feeling small and insignificant.

*Why didn't I proclaim my love before? Maybe we could have been married by now.*

Maybe that would stop him from doing what she feared in her heart. But she'd been deathly afraid. Frightened if she gave her heart away, he might go away and never return—taking her love with him. And now, right before her eyes, she saw that transpiring. He would go back to England, and she would be brokenhearted for the rest of her life. Why else would these men have come?

Why else ride in here, proclaiming their English nobility with their saddles and crested blankets? For some reason, they'd come to retrieve the duke's son. They wanted Beranger back, and she had no power to stop them.

"What's happening, Beranger?" she gasped, feeling like her heart was going to explode in her chest.

He took her hands. "My father has passed away, Emma. I'll explain everything in a moment. But first, Rhett, I apologize for the disruption to your wedding day. I'll take the men down to Eden and talk there."

*What? Beranger is leaving!*

She grasped his hands tighter, not wanting to let him go.

"Can't you stay a moment longer and witness the wedding?" Rhett asked. "Then you'll have all night to do as you like. It won't take long."

Rhett glanced at Emma, who felt tiny and befuddled next to Beranger's side. She was praying he'd say yes.

"Absolutely," Beranger responded with a smile. "We'll do just that. Emma, this is my uncle, Lord Harry Northcott of Newchurch. He's been searching for me for some time here in America." He grinned at the man, then again threw an arm over his shoulders and squeezed. The deep affection they had for each other was not difficult to see. "Seems the unusual hues of my eyes left an easy trail to follow."

"Not quite *easy,* Beranger," the man said with a hint of exasperation. "But I was fairly relieved when in Santa Fe several people knew you. You have an enemy there named Letherson. Thinking we meant you harm, he was only too happy to point us in the right direction. But that was only after I cleaned him out in a winning hand of poker." Harry beamed triumphantly. "When will the Americans learn we English can't be bested? We've been on your trail for a year, always arriving just a few days after you'd left somewhere. But now, thank the Good Lord, we have found you. Our search is over, and I couldn't be happier."

He beamed at Emma.

"Y-your uncle?"

Reverend Caskill was back, his questioning gaze taking in the scene. "Shall we get started?" he asked, not asking for any explanations about the new arrivals.

Fear dried Emma's mouth to sand. If Beranger's uncle had come all this way to find him, the reason was important. He wouldn't leave empty-handed. But how could she fight a man from a dukedom on the other side of the ocean? The answer was easy. She couldn't.

# CHAPTER FIFTY-THREE

Beranger observed the wedding from the back of the crowd, Uncle Harry by his side. The knowledge that his uncle had tracked him down touched something deep inside. There were no chairs for the guests, just a few around the wooden dance floor for the ladies when they tired. The congregation made a winding path five feet wide that led from the blanketed waiting room to the gazebo.

The music began again. Katie appeared first, a small bouquet trembling in her hand. She looked pretty in a soft yellow dress, a delicate bloom behind one ear.

For Beranger, concentrating on the ceremony was nearly impossible. His father was gone, passed away.

*But why has Uncle Harry hunted me down? Only to tell me in person? That was a lot of effort. Is there other news?*

As soon as Rhett and Lavinia said their vows, he would find out.

Emma emerged from the blanket barrier next and slowly walked forward to the soft strains of the violin. Her light emerald dress matched her eyes, and she looked as much the angel as she had on the starry last night of their journey. Her gaze caught his. She tried to smile, but all he saw was her fear.

*Will she miss me if I leave Eden?*

He thought she would, but she'd never been able to get past her anxiety around desertion and distrust. Now their chance might be gone.

Mavis and Belle proceeded past. Next came the bride, shining with happiness as she leaned on Henry's arm. She momentarily caught his eye, as all the sisters had, and he felt an acute pang of regret.

*But why?* He wasn't sure. *Perhaps another premonition?*

If he didn't want to leave Eden, no one could make him. To his way of thinking, Gavin's becoming the duke was not an important enough reason for him to make the arduous voyage across the Atlantic.

Henry handed the bride off.

Rhett and Lavinia stood before the town, face-to-face, holding hands.

After the reverend gave a short sermon, he went straight to the vows. Rhett's strong reply could be heard all the way at the back. Lavinia's could not. Rhett slipped a ring on her finger, and before Beranger could pull himself out of his musings, the bride and groom kissed. Like that, they became husband and wife.

They turned to the crowd, beaming with happiness. Beranger's gaze scanned down the row of women to land on Emma. She was struggling to smile, but her expression didn't look normal. As soon as the reverend introduced them as Mr. and Mrs. Rhetten Laughlin, a round of clapping and cheering went up. Before the wedding party could process to the back of the crowd, the well-wishers pushed in. The wedding ceremony was over that quickly.

He turned to Uncle Harry. "You're a sight for sore eyes, Uncle. I'm astonished. How did you find me?"

"I've been paying a private investigator for years, Beranger, looking for clues about your disappearance. I felt sure you'd run away and hadn't been taken from us against your will. We did learn about a horse wearing a saddle pad bearing the duke's coat of arms in Hastings, but that clue didn't turn up until a full year after you'd gone missing. Ships come and go every day. I was looking for a needle in a haystack. Then, five years ago, a lucky break. The *Destiny* arrived. The vessel had a new captain, but there were still a few crewmen who remembered a sure-footed lad named Beranger North. It was your different-colored eyes that made you stand out. You'd served four years of indenture and then set out in America, all alone."

Beranger gripped his uncle's arm. "My God, Uncle Harry. You've dedicated your life to finding me. I don't know what to say."

Harry's eyes warmed, even amid the chattering

people who'd already availed themselves of the punch bowl. Others held brimming mugs of beer. "I love you, my boy. I've always wished you were my son instead of William's."

Emma appeared at his side.

Harry tipped his head. "It's time for a proper introduction. Who is this enchanting creature?"

"Uncle Harry, it is my great honor to introduce you to my dear friend Emma Brinkman. She and her sisters own the famed Five Sisters Ranch here in Eden. In my eyes, she's royalty. Emma, may I present again Lord Harry Northcott of Newchurch, also known as my dear uncle Harry. He is younger brother to my father, His Grace, William Northcott, Duke of Brightshire. There is also my uncle Charles, but I won't go into that now. I'm fairly certain your mind is spinning with all the lords and such."

Emma's face darkened with discomfiture. He hadn't meant to embarrass her—it was simply the way introductions were made in England. And his uncle *had* just spent who knew how long locating his wayward nephew; he deserved the respect given. As did Emma.

"I'm pleased to make your acquaintance, my lord," she whispered unsteadily.

*Well done, Emma.*

Harry smiled and put his hand on Emma's shoulder. "Harry is fine, my dear. No need for such formalities here."

Emma tentatively touched Beranger's arm. "What's going on, Beranger? Do you know?" Her brow was furrowed with worry.

He wanted nothing more than to soothe her fears away.

Beranger shook his head. "We're going to the café, where it's quiet, to discuss just that. I'd like to know as much as you what brings Lord Harry to Colorado. Would you like to join us?"

She nodded. "Lavinia won't mind. With so many people congratulating her, she won't even know I've gone."

"Fine, then."

Emma took the proffered elbow, like so many other times on their way from Santa Fe to Eden, but this time the stakes were higher than ever before.

Beranger wondered where he'd be a month from now.

"So you see, Beranger, there *was* a secret marriage between your father and your mother. All we can suppose from what we've learned is that your grandfather refused to acknowledge William had fallen in love with a commoner. It's easy to magine. He must have threatened him with all kinds of retaliations and somehow made him forsake your mother for a suitable match, a daughter of the aristocracy. Now here is where some facts come to light. Unbeknownst to your grandfather, a marriage between the two had already taken place far from Brightshire, conducted by an elderly priest in a small country church. Your father and mother never revealed his title. The hidden facts weren't discovered until last year, after a fire almost destroyed everything in the church. The new rector recognized your father's name while going through the damaged records, and because of the date on the documents, we realized it predated his marriage to your stepmother. It was then I redoubled my efforts to find you."

Bemusement crossed Beranger's face. "But that would make my father's second marriage, to my stepmother, invalid. Gavin would then be the illegitimate son."

Lord Harry's gaze tracked slowly between Emma and Beranger. "That is correct."

"My God." Beranger's reverent whisper curled around them. "What a mess. How has Gavin taken the news? I'd think it would kill him."

"He never learned the truth. I regret telling you that your brother, His Grace, Gavin Northcott, Duke of Brightshire and Marquess of Rand, came to a bad end in a hunting accident only a few days before these facts were revealed. You are now the Duke of Brightshire. The family needs you to return to England and claim your dukedom."

Emma sat back in stunned silence.

*Beranger is a duke. A duke with a dukedom,*

*whatever that was. A duke being called home to claim his title.*

Her worst nightmare had transpired. She'd lost her heart to love only to have it ripped into shreds.

"And what of my stepmother and my father? Were they ever legally married?"

"They were. When you were just an infant, the duke and duchess 'renewed' their vows. At that point, the duchess never knew that the words she spoke were truly her first vows of marriage to the duke. Your father had the good sense to fix that matter soon after your mother passed and he brought you into the castle. Their marriage was legal, but it didn't take place as a legitimate union when she, or anyone else, thought."

"So Father knew all along I was the true heir."

"It will be no news to you when I say he was a weak man, Beranger. I'm sorry."

Beranger held up a hand as if to silence an imaginary supplication from his father. "And if I don't want to go?"

Emma's breath caught. *Have I heard him correctly? Would he relinquish his title and stay in Eden?*

Harry hefted a deep sigh. "Of course, you could abdicate. There are others who would take your place."

"So my stepmother did conceive again once I was out of the house. She gave Father more heirs. When I left, the curse she had worried about for so long was gone. How many younger half brothers do I have?"

"None. You have a fifteen-year-old half sister. Her name is Lady Audrey Victoria Elisabeth Northcott. If you abdicate, she becomes duchess. Barring any bad luck, she'd hold the title to a ripe old age and pass the dukedom to her children. If anything happens to her before she has an heir, my older brother Charles will inherit. But I couldn't in good conscience allow Lady Audrey or Lord Charles to take what rightfully belongs to you." He smiled apologetically at Emma. "We English like to make everything as complicated as possible."

*Oh, I understand that all right. Beranger will not pass up his chance. Nor should he. With his wisdom and kindness, he was born to be a duke. The people need him.*

Beranger sat in silence, rubbing his chin. "But how does Lady Audrey fit in? Succession follows the male line; it should go to Uncle Charles right away, if I decline."

"True, my boy. For a woman to inherit a duchy is rare, but an intent was written into the letters patent long, long ago. Why it's there, I don't know. It's been gone over with a fine-toothed comb. Very few knew about it because there has always been a male heir up to now. If you stay in America and abdicate, she will take the title."

The café was empty except for the three of

them. The two men who had arrived with Lord Harry sat outside in the evening air, listening to the music from above. "What is Lady Audrey like? Is she a mature fifteen?"

Lord Harry rolled his eyes to heaven. "What do you think? She's been coddled by your step-mother since the day of her *noble* birth." He held up a hand. "I'm not being fair. She's a lovely young woman—if you don't cross her."

Beranger swiveled in his chair and gazed toward the window. The view of the San Juan Mountains wasn't actually visible from where he sat, but Emma believed he was imagining the sight.

*What is he thinking? What will he do? Rise to the challenge and return to England and the title he was born to hold?*

*I don't want to know, not today. Lavinia is celebrating her wedding day. A day of joy and happiness. I should be smiling and dancing up in the meadow with my sisters and everyone else. There will be time enough for crying when Beranger rides out of my life.*

Beranger turned back to them. "Let's return to the party before we're missed. I have a thirst, but more important, for days I've been anticipating dancing with my best friend." He looked at her and winked.

"I think that sounds like a capital idea," Lord Harry said. He stood and stretched. "That ride from Santa Fe was long and hot. I'm ready for a beer and something to eat. There will be time enough later to plan our return."

Beranger's gaze snagged hers, filled with a thousand wonderful memories. How she'd miss him when he was gone. How would she survive?

# CHAPTER FIFTY-FOUR

The moment they returned to the meadow, everybody's inquisitive gazes turned their way. Lord Harry and his men took themselves to the small bar, and Beranger held out his hand to Emma. The shadows had all but disappeared, and someone had lighted the lanterns dotting the meadow. The place looked enchanting. Rhett and Lavinia waltzed in the middle of the dance floor, looking perfect together. How thankful Emma was that her sister had found true love, as had Belle, and most likely Mavis. She still worried about Katie, but it would take her longer than just a few days to walk the road to a new romance. She was thankful her youngest sister had the mill to keep her hands busy.

*What will I do to keep from sinking into an abyss of sorrow when Beranger leaves? If only I'd listened to my sisters and told him how I feel. If only I'd tried.*

She slipped into Beranger's arms, and they joined the wedding party and the others floating to the music.

"So," Beranger said, gazing into her face.

"Indeed," she replied, her urge to cry strong.

He danced expertly, just as she'd expected, and she felt cherished in his arms. And why shouldn't

436

she? He was saying goodbye. He would soon leave Eden to board a steamship to England. Maybe even tomorrow. She wondered how long they had before he rode away. She couldn't think about that now. Could be tomorrow—*or tonight*. She needed to memorize the way he made her feel. As the evening darkened, she laid her head on his chest and listened to the beat of his heart.

"I always knew you'd someday go away," she whispered, more to the night air than to him. "That's why I didn't allow myself to fall in love with you. I felt this day coming. And now it's arrived."

He tightened his hold.

The song finished. Feeling melancholy, she stayed in his arms. She'd stay as long as he let her. A new song began, but for the first few moments of it they were the only two on the dance floor. This turn of events felt right, him being a duke. Had she known it all along?

How her world would pale when he was gone.

Other couples joined them, and soon they were surrounded, shielded by the crowd. He pulled far enough away to study her face. A strange light lit his eyes. Before she realized what he was about to do, he found her lips. It was the first time their lips had touched since the "proper kiss" at the Lucky Sister. Awash with feelings and desire, she never wanted it to end. Oh, how she *loved* him. With every breath she took, with every fiber of her soul. But if she told him now, he'd think she did so because of the news of his title that had arrived today. He'd think her a fraud.

After several long moments of holding her close, he drew away. "You don't think I'd consider going without you, do you?" Merriment sparkled in his eyes. "We travel well together, Miss Brinkman. We've proven that on the stage."

She tipped her head, trying to make sense of what he'd said. "What?"

"I *love* you, Emma," he said softly, accenting the word with all the passion in the world. "I have for some time. I can't live one moment without you by my side. Will you come away with me, marry me, be my wife to have and to hold forever and ever? Be at my right hand always?"

The breath evaporated from her lungs as the meaning of his words sunk in. Her heart had been so constricted, so tight with the pain of losing him. Now, suddenly, it was swelling with joy. The sudden explosion of lightness and laughter within her brought its own sweet pain. Tears filled her eyes. Love *could* last, after all. Love had found a way.

"Beranger!" His smile lifted her soul as they swayed to the music. "Beranger! Do you mean it?"

"I wouldn't ask if I didn't. But you must think this through very carefully. Study every aspect. Once I'm duke, there's no going back. My residence will be in England, at Ashbury Castle. Not here in Eden. We would be able to visit now and then, but the trip is long and hard. I'm sure it wouldn't happen as often as you'd like. The ocean crossing takes about two weeks, give or take. In hurricane season, we may encounter storms you've not seen the like of. And living as a peer has its challenges. My stepmother is still alive. She won't like me usurping the title from her daughter, Lady Audrey. She has always enjoyed making my life miserable. And I can only believe she'll do the same to you."

"That's the reason I'd want to go. To protect you from her claws!"

He threw back his head and laughed. "Does this mean what I think it does?" he asked.

She nodded.

"You'd be leaving your sisters, your ranch, and your business. *Everything* you love."

"Not more than I love you, Beranger—*my rake*. I'm sorry I didn't tell you sooner, it was just, well, I'm—"

He silenced her distressed clarification with another kiss—long, warm, promising. "I know all that, sweetheart," he finally whispered next to her ear as he gathered her closer in his arms. "And besides, you *did* tell me you loved me, the day in the loft. Between a few giggles, but I cherished each word."

Awe filled her breast. "I thought I might have,

but wasn't sure." She went up on tiptoe and kissed him again, relishing the fact that she could now do that anytime she wanted. "I'm so happy, my love. I love you so very, very much. I think I may float away. Beranger, my love and my life— my *husband*." The music was ending. He tipped her head, knowing she'd never tire of his beloved face before her now. "But how will we go about telling everyone?"

With a wide smile he said, "Do you think Lavinia and Rhett will mind if we announce it here? Right now?"

She shook her head. "I don't think so, but I'd like to ask." She hurried away to find Lavinia.

"The only thing that would make this moment better for me is to know you're as happy as I am, Emma," Lavinia whispered into Emma's ear after she'd sprung the news. Her face glowed with excitement, and she squeezed Emma's hand. "But England, Emma? That's so very far away. I will miss you with all my heart. Everyone will."

"I know. I know. And I, you. And the others. But I can't let Beranger go. I love him. We are two halves of a whole. We have to be together."

Lavinia gave her another warm hug. "So you finally understand?"

"I do. Before I went to Santa Fe, I was so confused. So unhappy and heartbroken. I never told anyone, but I'd received a letter from Mrs.

Gamble. Tim has married, and Cooper is engaged. I was devastated."

Lavinia's face lit with empathy. "I see. But aren't you glad now that happened? Tim or Cooper weren't your destiny. That handsome, wonderful Englishman is. And you better get back there before he gets impatient and comes to carry you off."

Emma hurried back to Beranger at the gazebo, feeling as if she were dreaming. Their presence alone on the pretty platform surrounded by lanterns and under a multitude of stars had people curious. Silence fell when Beranger opened his mouth.

"Emma and I have a surprise we'd like to share."

Emma could have heard a feather drop. Lavinia and the rest of her sisters stood in a group next to Lord Harry, beaming as if they'd lost their collective minds. She had to giggle.

"But before we do, I'd like to ask Reverend Caskill to please come forward."

Shock registered, followed by Emma's heart spreading wing and taking flight. Everything that followed happened so quickly.

The preacher passed his cup of punch to someone to hold and hurried forward.

Emma looked at Beranger. He gave a playful shrug.

Beranger whispered into the man's ear. When Caskill cocked a brow of censure, Beranger quickly explained the necessity of speed. He handed him a small scrap of paper he'd gotten somewhere. The reverend's face softened.

Beranger picked up Emma's hands.

"Ladies and gentlemen," Caskill called out in a loud voice, "seems we have another wedding to witness. You all have already heard my sermon on love and forgiveness, so I won't take up your dancing time with another. This young couple just wants a quick exchange of vows."

He turned to Beranger and Emma. "Please join hands." He shook his head. "I see you've already done that." A ripple of laughter slid through the crowd.

Beranger stared into Emma's eyes. He didn't know what his future held, but as long as she was with him, he knew they could accomplish anything.

Caskill blinked comically at the paper several times, then wiped his brow. "Sorry. Someone must have spiked my punch. As I was saying"—he raised the scrap of paper close to his eyes—"do you, Your Grace, Beranger William Harry Northcott, Duke of Brightshire, take Emma Fortitude Brinkman, daughter of John and Celeste Brinkman and sister to Mavis Applebee, Belle Harding, Lavinia Laughlin, and Katie Brinkman . . ." Guffaws rang out from the bar area, and the preacher lowed the paper. "To be your lawfully wedded wife? To have and to hold, from this day forward, through better and worse, for richer, for poorer, through sickness and in health, forsaking all others as long as you both shall live? Do you promise to love her, honor her, cherish her, and cleave unto her until death do you part?"

The most important words of his life. "I do," he proclaimed boldly, with all the love in the world.

"Do you, Emma Fortitude Brinkman, take His Grace Beranger William Harry Northcott, Duke of Brightshire, to be your lawfully wedded husband?"

Now that everyone was over the first shock of his formal name, they giggled and smiled when Caskill said it again. Best of all, he spotted all of Emma's sisters crying, holding each other, and bouncing up and down with excitement.

*They approve.*

"To have and to hold . . ."

The words floated off, and all he could see was Emma's eyes brimming with love.

"I do," she said, holding his gaze.

"By the power vested in me by the great state of Colorado, I now pronounce you husband—er—duke and duchess." He gave them both a stern look. "And tomorrow, you will get your marriage license from our new mayor the moment she's awake."

The crowd, which had clearly been drinking, laughed merrily. Cheers went around.

Beranger pulled Emma into his arms for safety as the multitude rushed forward to pay their regards. He heard her happy laughter and felt her warmth against his chest. Nothing in his life had ever felt so right.

# CHAPTER FIFTY-FIVE

Ten days later, packed and ready to depart, Emma and Beranger sat in the ranch house waiting for Lord Harry and the others to join them in the living room. Instead of going by stage, they planned to travel to a train station north of Eden and Dove Creek. Beranger planned to ship Charger to England, as well as Emma's horse, Dusty. Trevor would drive the buckboard with Emma's trunks, luggage, and whatever worldly possessions she was bringing along. From there, they would travel to the East Coast and book passage on a steamship bound for Great Britain.

As much as she loved Beranger and looked forward to the trip and her new life, Emma had been a teary mess since the night of the wedding. How could she live without her sisters? Her wedding ceremony directly after Lavinia's was one to remember, and since then it had been marital bliss in Beranger's arms, but still . . .

*Eden and my sisters.*

Beranger leaned toward her on the sofa. "Don't be sad, my love. Our lives will be filled with love each and every day. I promise you that. You won't have time to be lonely."

"I don't doubt that, Beranger. It's just . . ."

The night before, they'd had a goodbye celebration in the café—with the whole town. Beranger was now a celebrity. When he'd lived among them, he'd been kind and fair to all, hardworking and smart.

"Life changes are difficult."

"You of all people know that," she responded. "I'm sorry Fran declined your offer to go to England as well. I would have liked to have met her."

"She's too old to change, she said. Wants to be buried next to her husband. I do understand that. She won't lack for anything until that time."

Hearing footsteps, she turned to see Lavinia. Rhett had gone into town to work, conscious of the timeline he had to keep on the hotel. Lavinia took Emma's hands and pulled her to the large front window to speak in private.

"Now *you're* the one who's bowing out on our morning chats, Emma," she said, a pretty smile on her lips. "But I forgive you." They embraced. "This isn't goodbye, it's farewell until later. I'm so happy for you and Beranger. When I think about all you're going to experience, I think sometimes my heart might burst with love and pride."

Emma was still clinging to her hands. "Please don't. Rhett would never forgive me."

"You're right about that. His love for me seems to grow stronger by the day. I'm very happy. And very, very lucky." A poignant moment stretched between them. "You're a duchess now, Emma.

Imagine that. Mother and Father would be so proud—*so* proud! It's difficult to even wrap my mind around all that's happened." Lavinia giggled, and a devilish glint came into her eyes. "Imagine, we were wedded and bedded on the very same night."

"Lavinia!" Heat rushed to Emma's face, and she cut a quick glance at her magnificent husband. He was watching them with a smile. He couldn't hear their whispered conversation—or could he? By that devilish look in his eyes, she wasn't sure. She *was* sure she loved him more than anything she could describe. The moon, the stars, the galaxy. There weren't enough words in her vocabulary to express what she felt. "You surprise me at every turn. I'm still shocked about the secret you shared moments before saying 'I do.' You in nothing but your corset—oh my!"

They laughed, and Beranger arched an eyebrow. "Things sound pretty interesting over there. I wonder if I might join you?"

"No!" they said in unison.

Lavinia's eyes twinkled. "What if we've both conceived? Oh, Emma, I can't wait to have ten children of my own."

"Ten! Oh my. I'll do well with two moppets of my own."

"What's this?" Lord Harry asked, descending the stairs, looking regal. Mavis and Katie were by his side. His brown hair was still as thick as

Beranger's but had a salting of gray around his temples. He had the deep blue Northcott eyes—one of which Beranger had. Her heart warmed. She loved her husband's eyes and couldn't imagine him without them. Lord Harry had won over the entire house, including the help and the ranch hands in the bunkhouse. He said he wanted to return someday and make a camping trip into the San Juan Mountains. "Only two heirs for the Duke of Brightshire? That will hardly put a dent in the rooms at Ashbury Castle. You may want to rethink that."

"Stop teasing my wife," Beranger said with a smile. He stood and went to her side. "Two children or ten, I'm still the luckiest man in the world."

Emma didn't miss Mavis's tense lips or Katie's scrunched brow. What was wrong with Clint? He needed a good swift kick in the pants. If she weren't leaving in the next half hour, she'd make sure he got one.

*What's he so frightened of? He was a sheriff, wasn't he? Lawmen are supposed to be brave.*

She chanced a glance at Katie. No help there. Santiago had done a fine and thorough job of breaking her heart. Time was the only thing that would help her baby sister now. Emma stood back, taking stock: two sisters happy, two sisters sad. Not the best time to be leaving.

Henry, Blake, and Belle came through the front door.

"All set?" Beranger asked.

Trevor, driving the wagon, would be the only person from the ranch accompanying the group to the train station. They'd all said their goodbyes last night. The two men who had accompanied Lord Harry were already outside, ready to get back to their home.

Blake nodded, but Belle hurried to her sisters' sides.

"I'm trusting you, Beranger, to keep Emma safe," Blake said. "Fate has a strange way of working out. Last year, when John's daughters showed up for the reading of his will, I never expected such a drastic turn of events."

His stern expression moved Emma's heart. He might be her sister's husband, but he watched out for them all.

"You have my word, Blake," Beranger said. "Emma is, and will remain, my main concern. Her happiness and welfare mean everything. Now and always." He strode forward and gripped his new brother-in-law's hand. "And I'm sorry about the Lucky Sister. But our quick departure is prudent."

Blake laughed. "We all understand. That mine has sat forgotten for a long time. A few more months, or even years, won't make a difference. We'll wait for your first visit back. How's that?"

The girls locked hands in a circle, just like they used to when they were young. So much emotion welled up in Emma, she couldn't speak. They'd be leaving in moments. Who knew what fate would dish out? Perhaps she'd never see any of their beloved faces again.

Everyone's eyes brimmed. Katie's tears were the first to fall. One moment later, the other four sisters followed suit.

"I'll only be a letter away," Emma gasped, wiping away the dampness from her cheeks. "And I'll visit *every* year."

"Promise?" Lavinia said. "And bring your children?"

"Of course. Beranger assured me."

Mavis studied her face. "Don't be frightened on the ship, Emma. And don't overextend yourself trying to do and learn too much at first. When your mind gets worked up, you have even more difficulty falling asleep. Just relax and have fun. Don't get homesick, because you're where you're supposed to be. Bob and weave with trials and tribulations, and all will be well."

Emma pressed her cheek against Mavis's. Being the oldest, Mavis had had to step in as their mother long ago. No one could ever take her place. "I won't be frightened, Mavis. I'll be brave. And I'll enjoy myself. You needn't worry so about me."

Belle lifted a brow. "No more wagers," she said in a stern voice, but her eyes twinkled with love. "You would have had plenty of time to plan your *own* wedding if you hadn't been so stubborn, betting against your own happiness."

"That'll be the least of my problems, I'm sure." Emma laughed. "But yes, no wagering anymore at all."

Belle sucked in several huge, jerky breaths. "I'm going to miss you so much, sister of mine."

"Don't you dare forget about us, Emma." Katie was staring at her with the most perplexing expression. "You may be a duchess now, but you're still *our* sister first, and an irreplaceable part of this family. Your life will never be the same once you walk out that door. Please, for us, and for Mother and Father, remember your roots and follow your heart. You belong to Eden, and Eden belongs to you. We'll be waiting."

# ACKNOWLEDGMENTS

Heartfelt gratitude goes out to many special people for their help with *Heart of Mine*, book three of my Colorado Hearts series.

First to Megan Mulder, my editor, and Montlake Publishing for believing in this story of five sisters forging new lives on the Colorado frontier. To the Montlake staff, for your love and support throughout the years.

To Caitlin Alexander, my developmental editor. Your fine eye and creative ideas always make my work shine. Thank you so much!

To Saralee Etter, my first-round reader and editor, thank you! Especially now, for keeping an eye on the Victorian aspects of this story. You're a jewel.

To Tim and Justin Popovich, knowledgeable blacksmith docents of the Pioneer Living History Museum in Phoenix, Arizona, for your detailed information on mining and how to find the perfect spot to begin, as well as your input on working with steam and fire.

As always, love and gratitude to my husband, Michael, for taking up all the slack when I need to work, for reading and critiquing, and for tweaking my "man-speak." And lots of love to my beautiful family, with the new addition of Hudson Bryce! Grandsons are very fun!

To my awesome readers, thank you from the bottom of my heart! Without you, I wouldn't be able to do what I love!

And to our *Awesome God* for making my life so wonderful!

# ABOUT THE AUTHOR

Caroline Fyffe was born in Waco, Texas, the first of many towns she would call home during her father's career with the US Air Force. A horse aficionado from an early age, she earned a bachelor of arts in communications from California State University, Chico, before launching what would become a twenty-year career as an equine photographer. She began writing fiction to pass the time during long days in the show arena, channeling her love of horses and the Old West into a series of Western historicals. Her debut novel, *Where the Wind Blows*, won the Romance Writers of America's prestigious Golden Heart Award as well as the Wisconsin RWA's Write Touch Readers' Award. She and her husband have two grown sons and live in the Pacific Northwest.

**Center Point Large Print**
600 Brooks Road / PO Box 1
Thorndike, ME 04986-0001 USA

(207) 568-3717

US & Canada:
1 800 929-9108
www.centerpointlargeprint.com